SURRENDER

Heather Graham

SURRENDER

A TOPAZ BOOK

TOPAZ
Published by the Penguin Group
Penguin Putnam Inc., 375 Hudson Street,
New York, New York 10014, U.S.A.

REGISTERED TRADEMARK—MARCA REGISTRADA

ISBN 1-56865-628-9

Printed in the United States of America

For Karen David,
a beautiful heroine inside and out.

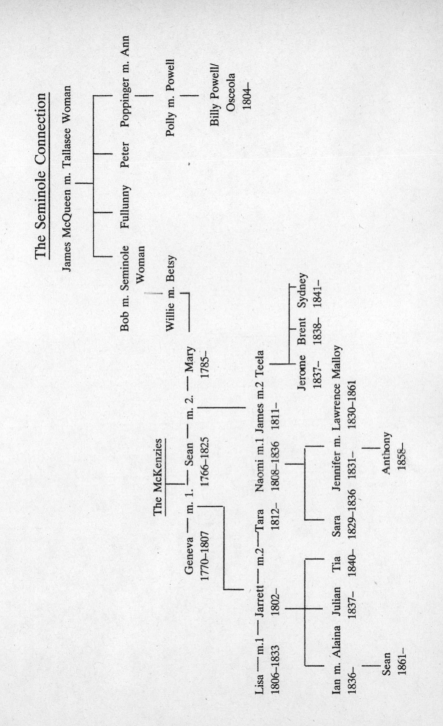

The Seminole Connection

James McQueen m. Tallasee Woman

- Bob m. Seminole Woman
- Fullunny
- Peter
- Poppinger m. Ann
- Polly m. Powell
  - Billy Powell/ Osceola 1804–

The McKenzies

Willie m. Betsy

Geneva — m. 1. — Sean — m. 2. — Mary
1770–1807   1766–1825   1785–

Naomi m.1 James m.2 Teela
1808–1836   1811–

- Jerome 1837–
- Brent 1838–
- Sydney 1841–

Jennifer m. Lawrence Malloy
1831–   1830–1861

Anthony 1858–

Geneva — m. 1. Jarrett m.2—Tara
1802–   1812–

Sara
1829–1836

Lisa — m.1 — Jarrett
1806–1833   1802–

Julian 1837–

Tia 1840–

Ian m. Alaina
1836–

Sean 1861–

Chapter 1

May, 1862
Biscayne Bay, Florida

The night seemed black as an eternal void. The sea was deceptively calm, disturbingly dark beneath a sky scattered with a strange cloud cover. The moon offered occasional fragments of light before the clouds cast the world into a shadow realm that shrouded all but the sound of the water that lapped against the small boat and the rhythmic slap of the oars against the water.

The sound stopped. Impetus alone kept the small boat moving toward the shoreline.

"Why have you stopped rowing?" Risa Magee asked anxiously. She was more than a bit afraid, but she was equally determined that the war would not destroy more lives than necessary.

Finn sighed. "Risa, I would do anything for you, but this is insanity; I can go no farther."

"Finn! You cannot drop me into the middle of the bay," Risa said firmly.

"This is an area frequently traveled by cutthroats, thieves, and murderers—not to mention enemy Rebels! St. Augustine might be occupied by the Union, but this is a Confederate peninsula," Finn reminded her.

"Finn, don't be difficult. You have only to set me down on the isle—"

"Which could be far too late," Finn protested nervously. "I've not been in these waters in a very long time myself, but I've been told that the blockade runners come here often enough, and that sane people should stay away. This is a place of savage monstrosities!"

"Come, now! The Rebels have not bred a strain of

lizard-people to rise from the swamps to do their fighting for them!" Risa assured him with exasperation.

Asking Finn to help her had been a mistake. But who else might have been persuaded to bring her here? Finn was a young, sandy-haired, freckle-faced salvage sailor who had been living in Florida at the outbreak of war; a Yankee diver from outside Boston. An opportunist who had not taken sides in the war, he was still a decent sort of opportunist, and had spent much of his free time assisting with surgery in St. Augustine—and plying Risa with his attentions. She had been flattered, but she certainly hadn't taken the young man seriously. Especially when she had allowed her life to become such a tangle of strange relationships.

When she had determined to find Ian McKenzie in his Everglades lair, Finn had seemed her only answer; a man who could be bribed to bring her down the coast without insisting on knowing her purpose for such reckless subterfuge. And who would not report to her father—General Magee—or simply tell her she couldn't go.

"Risa, if anyone knew that I brought you here—"

"Oh!" Risa cried with frustration. "I've told you, Major McKenzie himself is in these parts, and that's why I'm here."

"If your father were ever to know . . ." Finn said, his voice trailing away miserably. "He'd have me court-martialed."

"Finn, my father cannot have you court-martialed," she informed him. "You are not in the military."

"He'd have me shot!"

"Finn!"

If her father were ever to know, she thought guiltily, there would be hell to pay. Maybe not for Finn, because her father would know that she had coerced the poor young fellow. However, her father would definitely lock her up somewhere very safe, and see that the key was thrown away. But the esteemed General Magee, recently promoted, was now far away, fighting with General Grant.

"My father will never know. You will drop me off, and I will get back to St. Augustine on my own."

"No, this was foolish. We've got to go back to my ship—"

"Finn! If courage is a factor here," she said sternly, trying to appeal to his pride, "we can see why the Rebels are doing so much better than the Yanks!" She spoke firmly, staring at the young man with relentless determination.

Finn's eyes faltered. "Ah, now, that's not fair, Risa, you truly can't begin to imagine the danger we're in."

But she did know the danger. It didn't matter. She was desperate.

Once upon a time, she had been in love with a man named Ian McKenzie; Major Ian McKenzie, USA. She should have been his wife. But circumstances had intervened. Ian was married—to someone else. And oddly enough, she, a Yankee, had no choice now at all except to risk her own life in an attempt to save a Rebel spy, the Mocassin. To save Ian's wife. Even if Risa wasn't certain she would ever forget just how deeply she had once been in love with Ian, she couldn't let anything happen to his wife. In the cruelest of times and circumstances, she and Alaina had become the best of friends. They had both risked their lives for one another before; now finding Alaina was crucial.

There was a price on the Mocassin's head. Dead or alive, preferably dead. Alaina was somewhere near, Risa knew. To prevent Risa from a rattler's strike, Alaina had been bitten herself, and in the fever that had plagued her after, Alaina had tossed and turned—and talked, giving Risa clues to what was happening. Though Risa hadn't been able to keep her from leaving St. Augustine on her spying mission, she had learned just when she would be returning and where. Here, tonight.

Now Risa had to find either Alaina, or Ian. And if she found Ian, she had to let him know that his wife was the spy that he was seeking so that he could find her—come hell or high water—before any other Union man might do so.

And see that Alaina was hanged.

"When the cloud cover lifts, I can see Belamar Isle!" Risa insisted.

"Risa, I'd do anything for you, but we have to go back—" Finn said, and broke off. "Listen!"

She went silent, and she heard what he heard. Oars, slapping water. Near them. Very near them . . .

"We've got to head back!" Finn insisted.

"I—I can't!" Risa told him.

Belamar Isle was right ahead.

"Look, there's an inlet over there! Row hard, and we'll count on the cloud cover to protect us."

Finn suddenly moved, with the speed of lightning and an amazing quiet.

It was a dangerous coastline by nature, and so it was that salvage had been a prosperous business here since the first Spanish ships had sailed to the New World. Dangerous reefs hid beneath the waves to rip at the unwary. In some areas, landfall was smooth beach. In others, mangroves grew out along the shoreline, creating a tangled web of roots, inlets, and coves, uninhabited, surrounded by thick semitropical forests. Snakes, birds, and insects in many varieties plagued the brackish waterways that streamed inland from the bay.

Their rowboat suddenly jarred hard against a root; a flash of moonlight let Risa see Finn's face. So pale that his freckles stood out, he brought a finger to his lips, warning her to silence. She sat quietly, catching a brief glimpse of their surroundings before a billowing dark wave of clouds descended over the moon once again. Finn wasn't such a poor choice for a guide after all; he had brought them into the tongue of a cove. The chirp of insects was suddenly very loud, almost deafening. Something touched her face, and she nearly screamed, but realized it was the brush of a mangrove, hanging right over her head. They were flush against the trees, nearly completely concealed in the night.

Again, she heard oars slapping against the water. Then a few moments' silence.

Risa realized that the other boat was very near. Like them, her passengers were listening.

Finally, the silence was broken.

"Ah, the captain's hearing has become so good he hears the fish swimming at night!" a male voice with a slight Irish lilt complained.

"He knows the sound of fish swimming from that of a small boat being rowed!" a second voice warned.

"But the captain—"

"Would never have given away his own position so thoroughly," the second man said softly.

"Hmmph!"

Again, silence fell on the night. Once more, the din of dozens of insects seemed to rise. From somewhere, Risa heard a *plop!*—and she wondered whether alligators or crocodiles inhabited these coves that rimmed the bay.

"We can't be too careful," the second man said again. "Not with the *Maid of Salem* expected in these waters. The captain thinks that taking her—and her cargo bound for Key West—can give guns to thousands of our infantry boys. And she's heavy-laden with morphine and quinine. What with New Orleans taken now, slow as we may be getting supplies through the state, they're mighty welcome when they reach the battlefields to the north."

"Aye, welcome," the man with the Irish accent said wearily. "Matt?"

"Yes?"

"It's not good, is it?"

"War is never good, Michael."

"Whatever we Rebs capture, they have more. More and more. They have more men, and more guns."

"Ah, but we have more men like the captain. We've old Stonewall Jackson, Stuart, and Lee. Lee was one thing the damned Yankees wanted they didn't get! Our troops have beaten the tar out of greater numbers time and again."

"And sustained losses as well."

"Stop being so worried, Michael, it won't serve us well."

"Aye, now that's a fact. But there's nothing in this cove hereabouts. Let's turn her around."

Risa exhaled on a shaky breath as she heard the enemy boat moving away.

They waited.

The night, on the water, was actually cool. Risa shivered—and felt a trickle of sweat slip down her spine at the same time. She was a fool. How could anyone find a man—or a woman—in endless acres of sea and swamp?

The bay seemed enormous, the swamp eternal. The wait agonizing.

"I'm moving her out. I'm heading back to my schooner," Finn said determinedly.

"Finn—"

Risa broke off, suddenly aware of sound very near them again. A movement, a knocking . . . something not quite right. Something . . .

A second enemy rowboat! she thought with alarm. Oh, God, the second boat had been in the cove, not certain that they were there. Whoever manned the boat had waited in an uncanny silence, hidden even from their countrymen, just waiting for Risa and Finn to give themselves away . . .

"Row!" she cried suddenly to Finn, "Row!"

"Oh, Lord Almighty!" Finn cried as their little craft was suddenly struck hard. Risa was knocked to the damp flooring of their rowboat.

"Who goes there?" came a harsh demand. A match was struck, and lantern light suddenly flooded Risa's eyes; she couldn't see. "Speak quickly, now, and beware! We feed all Yankees to the sharks!"

Risa brought her hand before her eyes, trying to ward off the blinding light, her heart hammering in a fury. She didn't need to reply; Finn was already stuttering out an explanation. "I'm not a Yank; I'm a salvage diver—" he began.

"Salvage diving—in the middle of a dark and cloudy night?" came a second, deeper voice, one touched by just a hint of wry amusement.

And suddenly, a booted foot came down center in the small boat, bringing with it the towering figure of a man. He carried a naval cutlass, and it gleamed long, wicked, and sharp in the glitter of the lamplight.

The little boat rocked wildly with the new weight; the man didn't seem to notice, but balanced effortlessly.

Risa reminded herself that she was the only child of a military man, and such an upbringing had not been without its rewards. She carried a small Smith & Wesson repeating revolver in her skirt pocket, and she knew how to use it. She drew it out quickly, hands amazingly steady.

"Well, sir, you should be just and fairly warned—*we* feed all Rebs to the sharks!" she cried with a bravado that startled even her.

Yet it was to no avail, for he was as quick as lightning. Before she could take aim, her pistol was slammed out of her hands by the swift blur of his cutlass. His steel struck her weapon from her hand without so much as grazing her flesh, and the gun went flying into the night. It was caught just briefly in a flicker of lamplight as it arced—then it landed with a plop in the sea, and sank.

Risa saw again the glitter of the enemy's cutlass.

"Captain!" the man with him called out in warning. "There's another boat coming in; lots of Yanks out—"

They suddenly heard the sound of gunfire, and Risa realized that the little boat stalking them before was engaged in battle with another small vessel.

"Indeed, the time has come . . . we'll secure these prisoners and engage as well," the captain commanded.

"Secure them—or feed them to the sharks?" his companion said lightly.

There were more Yanks in the waters, Risa thought, trying to reason quickly and rationally. And she wondered if just maybe, Ian McKenzie might be in these waters now, and if salvation might be a lot closer than she had imagined.

She tried to shield her eyes again from the light, and look beyond it to their captor. All she could see was the wicked length of the sword—and the dark silhouette of the man.

Better chance the sharks in one piece, she determined. Here, in this little dinghy, with the wicked blade-wielding captain, she was doomed. In the water, God help her, she might stand a chance . . .

She rose. The boat rocked precariously.

"Now, what in God's name—" the deep voice of the captain began. Then he realized her intent. "Wait, you fool!" came the man's irate command.

Wait? Never.

She leapt.

He reached for her, just missing her arm, and catching a wisp of the fabric of her skirt instead.

He couldn't stop her from diving, but he had arrested her momentum, Risa realized in horror.

She made it into the water, but then felt a sharp pain as she cracked her head against the boat.

The lamplight faded. Darkness overwhelmed her as she sank into the sea.

Risa awoke, hearing the crackle of a fire. She opened her eyes very slowly. She could remember hitting her head, but the pain had faded away. For a moment her vision was blurred; the world was fuzzy. Then it began to fall in place.

She lay on a handsome sofa, encompassed in a warm blanket, her head on a soft pillow. She was in a pleasant room, with the fire crackling against the salt sea coolness of the night. The fire was all that gave light to the room, so it was cast into pleasantly soft crimson shadows. Despite the deeply muted light, she could see shapes and forms, handsomely polished pine floors, area rugs scattered about. She was in a home, she realized. Several wing-backed chairs faced the fire. Family portraits lined the coral rock mantel. The crackling fire, leaping in beautiful shades from blue to gold, captured her vision for several long moments.

Then she saw him.

Her heart seemed to stop, then slam against her chest. She couldn't believe her good fortune.

Ian!

Oh, God, Ian!

She had fallen into the sea, plummeted toward death, but miraculously, *he* had found her, and she had been rescued.

He stood in this parlor, leaning against the far end of the mantle.

His back was to her; his dark head bowed. He'd been out in the water as well, obviously, and recently. She must not have been out too long. He'd stripped down to his breeches, which were still damp, clinging to his lean hips and muscled thighs. His feet were bare, his broad shoulders caught the glow of firelight and gleamed and rippled with bronze power.

She sat up slowly, a heady sensation of relief flooding through her. She discovered that her skirts had been cut and ripped away, certainly in his efforts to save her life. She was left with nothing but pantalets, bare feet, corset, and ragged chemise, but she couldn't feel distressed at her lack of apparel—not when she was alive. She was a realist. Ian and his men had ripped up her clothing to save her life, and she was simply grateful.

"Ian!" she cried out, leaping up before he could swing around. She threw herself against him, so very relieved, arms wrapped around him, cheek against his bronze back. She hadn't forgotten that he was married; she was simply grateful to greet an old friend and ally.

"Oh, Ian, oh, thank God, I thought I was dead, in serious trouble at the very least with those wretched Rebs—they're trying to take a supply boat, bound for Key West, I can tell you all about it, I heard them talking! I think they engaged with a few scouting parties in small boats already. But that's not why I'm here, you have to . . . you have to catch the Mocassin! Oh, God, I never thought that I'd make it here, but I had to find you. I *had* to find you . . ." She paused for breath, shaking. She was becoming incoherent. He turned around, but she didn't see his face or his hand on the top of her head, stroking her hair as he drew her close to his chest. Bittersweet pain filled her. She could find comfort with him, yes. She could be soothed. Because they were friends now. But he was Alaina's husband, even if he had loved her first. They had never made love; she had been too proper. Yet the dreams had been there.

For a moment she allowed herself to feel the gentleness of his fingers in her hair. She luxuriated in the feel of her face against his chest, breathing the decidedly masculine scent of him, clean salt, sea air, a hint of brandy and . . .

"You heard about Reb plans to attack a Yankee ship?"

She nodded. "Yes, but you have to go after Alaina. Ian, I'm so sorry, but she is the Mocassin. It's a long story, but she was sick, and ranting, and I pieced together what she was saying. I tried to follow her . . . but anyway, she went to the islands for supplies, and is making landfall somewhere near here. And I'm so afraid that she'll be caught by someone who doesn't care that she's a woman, and that . . . some people have become so vicious with this war, I'm afraid she'll be hanged. Ian, you must find her and capture her; you must somehow dissuade her from her course . . ."

He had gone very tense, and she was sorry, so sorry. Risa knew he had suspected his wife of espionage, but he had surely prayed that she was not the elusive Mocassin—the spy wanted dead or alive, condemned by military justice, no quarter to be given.

Risa swallowed hard. "You have to go. You have to find her. Yourself. It's imperative. But we must stop what is happening as well. Send one of your men out to warn the Union navy that a despicable, cutlass-wielding Reb captain is out to seize the *Maid of Salem,* and steal her cargo of weapons and medicine. Dear God, this is horrible. I know that the war effort must be sustained, that the Reb captain has to be found and engaged in battle and fed to the sharks, but Alaina has to be found as well!"

His fingers were moving in her hair again; he was holding her close, very close. It felt good. She wished that she could forget time and the war.

Forget that he had married.

And that his wife had become one of her best friends.

"Oh, Ian."

"Shh . . . sh . . . it's all right. I will go for Alaina. I will find her."

She nodded against his chest. His fingers brushed her cheek, and she felt ridiculously like a cat, so glad just to be stroked.

She had to pull away.

But she was still shaking, so relieved. It was good to be soothed, touched. No . . .

"Don't, Ian," she whispered.

But there was no substance to her voice.

They were just friends. He comforted her. Another few moments wouldn't matter.

His flesh was as warm as the fire that cloaked it in

crimson, and that warmth seemed to radiate into her, nearly stilling her shivers. His arms had all the strength she seemed to lack. His knuckles moved gently over her cheek, her bare shoulders; his hand stroked her, holding her, warming her.

"No," she repeated, but still, with no conviction.

"So," he murmured, "a wretched Reb is out to take the *Maid of Salem*—and you know all about it," he murmured.

"I heard them talking!" she whispered. "Just before your men came—before the bastard stepped aboard my boat! His men were out in a second dinghy, searching, and I heard them talking."

"Mmm . . ."

She closed her eyes. She had to break away. But she was tired. The war had made everything so hard. She was a determined woman, independent, capable. But tonight, she felt so very weary. And he felt . . . strong.

Warm. Muscle rippled beneath her cheek, her hands. His bare chest seemed electric.

She felt a tender stroke upon her face, lifting her chin. She didn't open her eyes. She didn't want to see. For a moment, just a moment, she wanted the past, the dream.

She felt his mouth. It had been so long. His lips, on hers, demanding, tender, overwhelming her. His tongue parting her lips with an erotic force and thrust, sweeping the fullness of her mouth, seducing . . .

His hands . . .

Moving over her ribs, her hips, her breasts, a blaze of fire despite the fabric of her chemise and bone of her corset. As heady as wine, as seductive as flame, irresistible, so ungodly intimate . . .

He'd married Alaina.

And she couldn't do this.

She tried to shake her head, but his fingers had threaded into her hair, and her lips were fully captured by the passionate assault of his kiss, the thrust of his tongue. His left arm was around her, supporting her, arching her back as his lips at last left hers, falling against her throat. Lower. Against the rise of her breasts.

"Ian, no—"

"What else did you hear?"

"What?"

She was fighting the unbidden rise of an illicit passion, and he was still seeking information.

"Did you hear—"

"No," she said, adding firmly, "stop. This isn't right, Ian, stop." She pressed her hands firmly against him, opening her eyes, ready to face him.

"No—"

She broke off, suddenly dead silent and completely shocked. She was captured within arms that seemed to have the power of steel. Whose arms, she had no idea.

She'd been hearing him speak, his voice deep, low, and husky, yet a whisper in the firelit shadows. She'd stared at his back, seen the way that he stood, the breadth of his shoulders, the rippling bronze of his back.

It wasn't Ian.

This man's eyes were blue, like Ian's. His height and build were nearly identical . . . but his face . . .

His features were different; his cheekbones were higher, slightly broader. And he was very bronze. Though his dark hair carried a hint of red that wasn't just the firelight, she realized, it was very thick and straight. His nose was straight, his forehead high and smooth, his mouth well sculptured, very full, sensual. Damp from their kiss, curved in a curious, mocking smile as he stared down at her. His features, she realized, betrayed Indian blood, strikingly combined with classical European lines.

"Oh, my God!" she breathed at last in sheer dismay. She fought to free her arms, straining desperately against him. "Let me go! This instant! You're not Ian, oh, God, you're so much like him—"

"Stop it, calm down!" he commanded, drawing her harder to his frame as she fought wildly to free herself.

"Calm down?! I will *not* calm down. Let me go, let me go. My God, who are you? Oh! You have to be related to Ian, and if so—oh, God! Then you're a Rebel, the enemy . . ."

She kicked at him, trying to aim high in an effort to truly immobilize him, catching a kneecap instead. He grunted, and swept her up off her feet, striding back to the sofa where she found herself slammed down as he crawled atop her. She tried to pound his chest, strike out against his face. He neatly caught her wrists, forcing them down to the arm of the sofa just above her head. She was left with nothing to do but gasp for breath and stare up at him, stunned and horrified. He was built so very much like Ian, it was uncanny. But he was different as well. He carried Seminole blood. She'd known, of course, that Ian had kin here, Rebel kin.

"Let go of me. I thought you were Ian!" she gasped, struggling to dislodge him. But his hold upon her was as fierce as his temper. He didn't budge.

"Yes, you thought I was Ian. Sorry. I'm afraid that I'm the despicably wretched Rebel captain with the intent to take the *Maid of Salem*—my men will have to do without me now. Obviously, I'm related to Ian. I'm his cousin—Miss Magee. There is a startling resemblance among many of our generation."

Miss Magee. She felt so incredibly stupid. He knew who she was. But she had never imagined that Ian and his kin could be so very much like him that she could mistake a cousin for him! "Which cousin?" she demanded through clenched teeth.

"Jerome McKenzie, Miss Magee," he said, a sardonic tone to his voice. "I'm trying to imagine the situation had you stumbled upon Ian's brother Julian. The two of them are so much alike, you might have bedded with him for an hour before discovering your mistake."

"Oh!" she gasped, so infuriated that she suddenly had the strength of Atlas. She freed a wrist with a wild wrench and brought her hand crashing against his bronze cheek. He recaptured her wrist so tightly that she let out a soft cry, her heart beating a staccato rhythm of pure panic as he leaned low over her.

"So tell me, were you really trying to save Alaina— or were you perhaps trying to make sure that my cousin was aware that his wife was an enemy agent?"

He stared at her, dark blue eyes hard and mocking, and she felt a chill sweep through her, adding to her fury. What in God's name did she care what he thought? Throughout everything, she had behaved with incredible maturity and restraint. After his marriage, she had shared nothing more intimate with Ian than compassion for the war's victims. Yet here she was, caught in this one moment's weakness . . .

"You bastard!" she hissed, shaking. "I don't give a damn what you think, but don't you see? If other Yankees catch Alaina, they'll hang her! I came here to save her life, and someone must do something quickly. If you can find your cousin out here, find him. And if not, let me go, and I'll damned well do it myself!"

"Oh, really? How incredibly arrogant, Miss Magee. I'm afraid that you couldn't find my cousin in the swamps if I handed you a bloodhound and a detailed map."

"I came this far! And you, sir, are an arrogant oaf, so you can just let me up—and I'll be on my way!"

"Oh, no, Miss Magee. I don't think so. I'll find my cousin and Alaina. But you won't be going anywhere."

"What? You can't possibly stop me—"

"Oh, but I can."

Risa froze, a renewed sense of alarm and deepening dismay arising in her. "You can't mean to keep me prisoner—"

"I'm afraid that I can and I do. You are a grave risk to national security, Miss Magee. Besides, just what do you think you're going to do? Survive the swamps?"

"Do you know, Mr. McKenzie—"

"Captain McKenzie, if you please. Confederate States Navy."

"Well, my father is a general—United States of America—and he'll hunt you down and annihilate you on the seas—"

"Will he?"

"Indeed, I swear it! And I have been raised around military men all of my life, McKenzie. I can survive damned well, no matter what the circumstances. And I will get away from you, and I will tell the Union Navy—"

"Oh, really? I don't think so. Not now, you won't."

He smiled pleasantly and leaned close. She was painfully aware then of her ragged state of undress, and of his build, so like Ian's. Long, hard, honed as tight as a drum. A *savage* drum. An Indian, and a Rebel.

"You *will* let me go now!" she whispered desperately.

He shook his head. Dark hair fell over one sharp blue eye. He assessed her in a sweeping gaze. She felt the pressure of his body.

"Miss Magee, your pardon, but we are at war, and you are very definitely the enemy."

"*You* are the enemy!"

"Perhaps, the way you see it—but now you are a prisoner of the Confederate States of America."

"I will not be a prisoner of the Confederacy! I will be damned before I will be a prisoner of the Confederacy. I will escape!"

He smiled grimly. He leaned even closer. "Miss Magee, you will be *my* prisoner. And I promise you, I'll be damned before I let you escape!"

Chapter 2

In all her life, Risa couldn't remember being so acutely uncomfortable. Bedraggled, half-naked, and pinioned. It was all the worse to realize that he assumed she wouldn't be at all adverse to this position if only he were Ian. It would be ridiculous to try to explain to him that things would have gone no further *had* he been Ian, and it was also infuriating to have to tell herself that she owed this wretched creature no explanations whatsoever. He meant to keep her a prisoner! And it was all the more deplorable because she felt as if she were on fire, disturbingly aware of his every brush against her flesh. More than anything, she needed to escape her current position beneath his overpowering weight and strength.

"Really?" she lashed out with all the contempt she could draw into her voice. "*You're* going to keep me prisoner? Will you spend the rest of the evening as a human shackle?"

He arched a brow, a slow smile creeping into his features. "Think of me as Ian. It will not be half so bad."

"Let me up! Where is your Southern honor, sir?"

"Consider this Southern hospitality, if not honor."

"Let me up—"

She broke off, because, to her amazement, he was rising, and something in his features alerted her to the fact that he had suddenly, and totally, dismissed her. He was a cat who had tired of playing with a mouse. She didn't even have time to spring up defensively on her own. He reached a hand down to her, drawing her up. "If you'll be good enough to escort yourself to the guest room, you'll find clothing in the wardrobe, and a more comfortable place in which to be held. There will be a guard at your door, and on the porch, should you be so inclined as to try to escape through the windows. For your own safety, I warn you that this is indeed a dangerous land for those unfamiliar with it. Should you wish to survive this war, you'd be best to accept the hospitality we offer."

"Wait a minute—"

"I can't. If I am to be of any service to Ian or Alaina, I must move now. That was your intent in coming here, right? To save Alaina's life? If so, I suggest you cooperate immediately."

She stared at him furiously, her jaw clamped. She managed to speak. "One question."

"What?" he snapped.

"Where is the guest room?"

He pointed down a hallway. She rotated about and walked, aware that he followed her on a silent tread. She didn't turn around, and yet as she moved down the hallway she was certain she could feel his breath, like a tongue of dragon's fire along her spine. She longed to spin around, unnerved by his nearness, yet she managed not to do so.

"To your left," he said curtly, and she turned.

A single lamp sat atop a warm wood dresser in the room while a fire burned in the hearth beneath a handsome, coral rock mantle. Alaina's home might verge on savage swampland, but it was a very pleasant place nonetheless. The walls were covered with a blue-patterned paper, the four-postered bed boasted a beautiful quilt. A wardrobe, trunk, the dresser, a screen, and washstand completed the amenities. In the center of the room, she turned back to discover that Jerome remained in the doorway, his eyes now darkly enigmatic.

"May I suggest," he said very softly, "that if I find Ian and Alaina, you remember that they are married?"

She had never longed so to strike anyone before in all her life. She folded her hands before her, summoning what dignity she could in her tattered state.

"You may suggest, sir, whatever you damn well choose, since I've no power over your suggestions," she replied. "Yet what an intriguing comment you make. It makes one wonder if *you* remember they are married when you are with Alaina."

He smiled, unruffled by her attack. "Alaina is like a sister to me."

"How charming; how very sweet."

He shrugged, turning around, about to close the door on her. She remained in the center of the room, the previous hours a blur shooting before her eyes as she tried to assimilate how the night had gone so very wrong, and then—with a tremendous sense of guilt—she remembered Finn.

"Wait!" she cried out, just as the door was about to close. She flew for it and all but threw herself back into his arms as he heeded her cry and opened the door again before she could reach it. With a gasp of dismay she steadied herself, backing into the room again.

"Yes?" he inquired, amused.

"What happened to Finn?"

"Finn?"

"My friend. The young man with me in the boat."

"Ah! Finn!" he murmured, shaking his head sorrowfully. "Well, he should hang, you know."

"Hang!" she exclaimed incredulously. "Don't be ridiculous. Why should he hang? For what great sin?"

"We are at war, and though neither you nor my misguided cousin seem to realize it, this is a *Southern* state. Your friend Finn is a Yank spy out of St. Augustine, isn't he?"

"No! Don't be absurd. He's not even military. He's not a spy, honest to God—"

"That's rather hard to believe."

"Why is it so hard to believe? I'm telling you the truth. Damn you! You're Southern, and I made this ridiculous trip at the risk of my own life to save that of a Southern spy! Now you're threatening an innocent young man—"

"He's innocent by your say-so."

"Yes!"

He was silent, watching her. Goading her, she thought, and yes! She was tempted to strike out with all her strength. Prudence kept her from doing so. She forced herself to remain dead still. How did a reasonable man like Ian have a cousin so despicably irritating?

He crossed his arms over his chest. "Well, I admit, I

do see all this as something of a dilemma. I don't *want* to hang the young man. And I don't want to keep you prisoner. I have no choice. I can't possibly let you go with the information you overheard. On the other hand, I have to look for Ian and Alaina. But I can't let you cause bloodshed among us. So there might be room for negotiation here."

"Negotiation! I can't begin to see—"

"Ah, well, then, think about it, Miss Magee. I've been told you are a woman of some intelligence, though one might doubt it from your actions tonight. You—"

"How dare you!" she grated out furiously, shaking.

"May I finish?"

"Only if you intend to assure me I don't need to worry about an innocent man's life."

"Your belated concern is quite laudable."

Oh! She wanted to hit the man! Yet her guilt over all but forgetting Finn—despite the circumstances—kept her silent.

She wondered if Jerome McKenzie read her thoughts as he appraised her with his steady, dark blue gaze. "You want to keep your friend alive. We'll make a bargain. You stay here meek as a lamb and don't dare give either my men—or my family—the least bit of trouble. And when I come back for you, you swear that you'll not try throwing yourself into my cousin's arms again and begging for his help against me. Do you understand?"

Risa felt the blood drain from her face. She looked down. "You couldn't possibly murder a man simply because I chose not to cooperate!" she murmured.

"How on earth could you know what I would or wouldn't do?" he asked her flatly. "This is war, Miss Magee. And a difficult war it is here, on this isle. Not only is your friend's life at stake, but if you cry to Ian that you are in distress, you could easily bring us to blows. And though he is the one enemy I fear in battle, I am equally the one enemy he hopes never to face. If you want to assure yourself that his blood is not spilt here and that Alaina survives the war as well, heed what I've said."

He turned again, finished.

"Wait!" she called one more time.

"What now?"

"Finn—is alive?"

"He is."

"You swear it?"

He watched her with a wry expression. "Yes, I swear it."

"How can I trust you?"

"You just asked me to swear. I've given you my word."

"Your word! You pretended to be another man—"

"No, Miss Magee, I pretended nothing. You wanted me to be another man. Don't ever doubt my word; I don't give it lightly. Now, what about you?"

"What do you mean?"

"I've given you my word, now you must do the same. Swear that you'll give me no more trouble."

"But—I can't. I don't see how—"

"I'm sure your friend Finn would be greatly distressed to know that you hesitated so with his life in the balance."

"Damn you!" She didn't want to swear anything to him. "Have it as you wish!" She hoped that would be good enough.

It wasn't.

He arched a brow. "I'm sorry?"

"So am I. Damned sorry."

"Miss Magee, I want your word, please."

"Fine! I swear!"

He studied her, nodding slightly. "Fine. Bear in mind that I don't give my word lightly, nor do I accept yours lightly in return. If I'm to be of any good to either my cousin or Alaina, I must get moving quickly."

"I cannot just wait here, a prisoner in this room—"

"Then, don't just wait. Pray. Pray that I find Ian and Alaina. Because these are dangerous games you and Alaina have chosen to play."

With that, the door closed, and she was left alone.

Jerome McKenzie paused very briefly in the doorway. He set his hands out before him, and gritted his teeth as he saw them shaking. Damn the war.

Damn his own part in it.

And damn Alaina for being such a determined little fool, and Ian for being the enemy. And damn the elegant and foolhardy auburn-haired wench in Belamar's guest room. He'd almost killed her; he'd been very afraid at first that in his attempt to stop her from her reckless dive into the sea he had cracked her skull. But she'd been alive, and before he'd even had the opportunity to speak to her, she'd mistaken him for Ian and spilled out all that she'd heard about his plans to take the *Maid of Salem.*

So he now knew Risa. The woman whom Ian had intended to marry before fate had stepped in. Leave it to Ian, he thought wryly. She was beautiful, passionate— and reckless as all hell. She was still in love with his cousin, so it seemed, but now she had become his prisoner—and a threat to them all. His softhearted parents were due back from their home just north of here to tend to Alaina's property—a task they had taken on while the rest of the family fought out the war on their different sides. If Risa Magee threw herself on his mother's mercy, or looked to his sister or family for help, there could be real trouble between them all.

It was a dangerously explosive situation.

It didn't matter, he told himself grimly. He did have to move fast. Ian and Alaina must be found. And Alaina must be kept alive.

He moved away from the door and hesitated another fraction of a second. He didn't have the manpower he needed to guard his reckless prisoner properly. His threats were mainly a bluff—he had no intention of hanging the disarming Finn, but Risa Magee was a serious danger since he was certain she would risk life and limb again in service to the Union if need be, and if threats would help make her more reasonable, he would gladly use them.

He couldn't risk her escaping him. Perhaps there was a painless measure he could take to make sure she didn't.

Grimly, he started from the house, then shouted out his orders to the few men he had with him on the islet.

*　　*　　*

The first hour he was gone, she paced.

She was too restless to sit still and too nervous to attempt escape.

She began to feel more and more uncomfortable as the fire dried the last of the salty dampness from her clothing. On impulse she tore into the wardrobe. Alaina was petite; Risa was tall, but anything had to be better than the tatters she was wearing. Yet she quickly ascertained that this wardrobe held clothing belonging to someone else. She found pantalets and a chemise that would fit her well enough, along with an array of dresses that were equally as long.

The washstand offered a full pitcher of fresh water. She doused her face, then stripped away her salt-stiffened, shredded garments. Once bare, she washed quickly and thoroughly with the cold water, down to the length of her hair. She dried herself and donned the new garments she had chosen, heedless of to whom they might belong. Perhaps Ian's wretched Rebel cousin kept a mistress. Good. She hoped the woman would be furious that her clothing had been taken, and that she would make his life miserable.

Yet perhaps this Jerome McKenzie had a wife of his own.

Did a man with a wife act as he had tonight?

She felt her cheeks begin to burn. She didn't want to remember what had happened. She had to set her mind to her predicament. Just exactly what had she sworn? He had demanded her word, yet what had she promised . . .

Not to give him anymore trouble.

Well, he wasn't here. She could, however, *cause* him trouble. She walked to the windows, drawing back the draperies to look out on the night.

The moon had risen high, casting the sky into a strange, but very beautiful, indigo color. She wondered if she might crawl out the window and find some means of escape. She really couldn't stay here, and surely, he couldn't really expect her not to try to escape. Yet as she weighed her chances, someone paced by—a guard with a rifle resting on his shoulder.

Surely, they wouldn't shoot her. Nor would they hang Finn. Would they?

She turned around and walked tentatively toward the door to the hall.

As she did so, there came a tapping on it. She froze. "Yes?" she said cautiously.

"May I come in?"

A female voice had spoken. Alaina's?

She hurried to the door, throwing it open. She was met by a woman near her own height, slender, exotically beautiful. Her hair was raven dark, her eyes a golden hazel. Her features were finely formed. She moved into the room with a subtle scent of perfume and pure grace. She had Indian blood, Risa realized quickly, which was what gave her such rare and unusual beauty. Unnerved, Risa moved back slightly, aware that anyone here could be her enemy.

"How do you do, Miss Magee, I'm Jennifer."

Risa didn't move or reply.

"Ian's cousin. Jerome's half sister," Jennifer explained.

Jennifer. Risa knew the name. Always a good friend to Alaina. Her husband had been killed at Manassas at the beginning of the war. The loss had devastated her.

"Jennifer, of course . . . it's a pleasure," Risa murmured.

Jennifer smiled. "Jerome said that you'll be leaving with him as soon as he gets back. I thought you might be sleeping so I hesitated coming here, but I wanted to make sure that you had found fresh clothing—he said you'd had a boating accident, I'm so sorry. It was wonderfully gallant of you to come here on Alaina's behalf, what a dear, good friend! No wonder Ian loved you so. And Alaina, too. Well, she was frightfully jealous of you at first, but then she wrote more and more frequently about how good you were to her. Oh, God, I'm babbling, but then war does that to people. Anyway, I've prepared a dinner tray for you. Since you're still awake, I'll have it brought in."

"Thank you, and please, stay, talk with me," Risa said. A boating accident indeed!

"Let me get your tray—"

"No, no, please, don't bother. I can come to the kitchen or the dining room—"

"Don't be silly, it's no trouble whatsoever." Jennifer turned, heading out of the room. Risa started after her, only to discover that one of Jerome McKenzie's stalwart young seamen stepped between them when she would have followed. He was a handsome chap with wheat-blond hair and a chin full of whiskers—newly grown, she thought.

"Excuse me," she told him.

"I'm afraid not, ma'am."

His voice was truly sorrowful but firm. Risa stepped back into the room, frustrated.

A moment later Jennifer was back with a tray. The aroma arising from it was tantalizing. Jennifer set it on the foot of the bed with a flourish. "Fresh snapper, pan-seared with citrus wedges," she offered. "Bread beneath the warmer, tomato salad, and Key lime pie made from Belamar's very special little lime trees. And, oh, Jerome left you the white wine, insisting it was best with this fish."

"Can't you join me—" Risa began, but broke off, hearing a sudden, shrill cry.

"Oh, dear, I'm afraid not!" Jennifer said with a laugh. "That was Anthony. My son. Do enjoy your dinner."

Jennifer offered her a warm smile, as if Risa were truly a guest here, and disappeared out the door.

The door was left open. Risa hurried toward it.

She faced the same young seaman. The door closed.

She stared at it, swearing beneath her breath. So much for helping friends! She kicked the door, turned, and leaned against it, then tempted to take the dinner tray and throw it across the room.

But she realized suddenly that she was famished. She sat on the bed, stared at the tray, then tasted the fish. It was delicious. She ate half of it before her thirst brought her fingers curling around the wineglass.

She hesitated. Jerome's hospitality. She'd like to drown the man in the wine. She took a sip, then another. The wine was good. Really excellent. The Reb had a definite taste for fine wine. Well, he was a McKenzie— even if he was from the more *savage* side of the family tree.

She finished eating, telling herself that it was important that she do so; she'd need strength to escape her current situation.

When she finished, she set the tray on the dresser and started pacing again. What she had overheard tonight was important. She had done what she could for Alaina; now she must reach her own countrymen. There had to be a way to stop the attack on the *Maid of Salem.*

She continued to pace, worry about what to do plaguing her relentlessly.

Then, quite suddenly, she realized she was dizzy. She moved quickly back to the bed, thinking she was just barely going to make it. The world was fading, going dark.

As she collapsed on the mattress, she thought irritably that she couldn't possibly escape if she was going to be so dizzy she couldn't stand.

Exactly. She couldn't possibly escape.

She had been drugged. It had to have been the wine.

From somewhere in the distance, she thought she heard the door opening. She struggled to open her eyes.

"Ah . . . she's sleeping," said a soft, feminine voice.

"Indeed," a voice replied. Deep, husky, low. Jerome McKenzie. He was back.

Risa fought to awaken. She needed to know what had happened. And still, she couldn't force her eyelids to open. She couldn't speak, couldn't find the strength to move.

"She'll be leaving with me as soon as she awakens."

"Poor dear. She'll be unhappy on a Rebel ship."

"She understands the situation."

"Must you leave so soon?"

The door closed. Risa could hear no more. She struggled to awaken again, but the effort was futile. She drifted.

Noise again. Voices. Coming from somewhere down the hallway. She willed her eyes to open, and this time they obeyed. She tried to sit up. Her head felt like lead.

"She seems to be doing very well."

She wasn't doing well at all, she thought, but then she realized they weren't talking about her.

Jennifer was speaking, and then the older woman with

the soft, gentle tones spoke again. Then Risa heard a
low masculine voice, and her heart began to thunder.

Ian was here. The voice was *really* Ian's. He was here!

She didn't hear Alaina's voice, but then she heard the
older woman speaking again in her soft, richly ac-
cented voice.

"Boys, she's going to be fine, the wound is clean, her
pulse is strong. Ian, you can see for yourself. Her breathing is deep and steady. She received a surface wound,
no more."

Relief flooded through Risa as she realized from the
conversation that they discussed Alaina. Jerome had
found both Ian and Alaina, and they were all back here.
And others were here as well. His Yankee family members. He couldn't possibly keep her prisoner now!

She tried very hard to rise, but the room was spinning.

The voices came again, this time right outside her
doorway. She heard the deep tenor of Jerome McKenzie's voice as he spoke to whomever stood guard.

"Miss Magee is sleeping?" he inquired.

"Like a lamb, Captain."

"Take the supply boat back to the *Lady Varina,* then,
sailor, and I'll be along before the crack of dawn. What
of the *Maid of Salem*?"

"She's headed this way, for a fact. The men caught
up with her escort ship, Captain, as you commanded.
They grounded her on the shoal, and her captain was a
smart enough fellow. He surrendered her quickly—and
assured the men that the prey we seek is on the way."

"Losses? Injuries?"

"One Yank killed in the first firing; Jimmy Meyers
took a ball in the leg, but it went clean through. He'll
be right as rain soon as he sobers up tomorrow."

"The Yanks?"

"Beached, sir, with water and supplies. O'Hara reckoned as how you'd want to be sending notice they could
be picked up by their countrymen *after* we've gotten our
hands on the *Maid of Salem*."

There was silence then. Risa struggled to sit, blinking
furiously, shaking her head. Every movement seemed to
be a tremendous effort, and she wondered what in God's
name the wretch had given her. She had to make it up

and down the hall—and she had to either disappear, or find Ian.

She managed to stand. It was an enormous feat. She staggered to the door and opened it, and felt a rush of delirious excitement to see that she had indeed been left unguarded. She set a steadying hand upon the wall, and moved at a snail's pace along the hallway, blinking furiously all the while as great waves of darkness threatened to overwhelm her again and again. Suddenly, she froze.

A rush of inexplicable tears stung her eyes as she heard Ian's voice. Pausing in the shadows while looking into the parlor, dimly lit by a dying fire, she could see that Ian stood with Jerome by the coral rock mantel.

It was easy enough even now to see how she had mistaken Jerome for Ian from the back; the men were of an identical height, broad-shouldered, well-muscled, but lean, lithe, and supple. They were men who had been at war now for two years, hardened by the battles they faced. Yet there was a reddish cast to Jerome McKenzie's hair, and when he turned, his Indian heritage was quite visible in the strong rise of his cheekbones. Caught in firelight, his was a hauntingly striking face.

"There is no way that I can express my gratitude," Ian was telling Jerome.

Jerome shrugged, and grinned rather awkwardly. "Sometimes blood is thicker than war."

Ian nodded, smiling. "Indeed, sometimes blood is thicker than anything. It's a pity we can't end it here."

"We both know that we can't," Jerome said softly.

"Right," Ian agreed. "Aunt Teela said that Risa was sleeping. I won't disturb her; you'll tell her thank you, from the bottom of my heart?"

"I'm sure Risa knows how grateful you are."

"She's sailing with you?"

"So we agreed. I'll have her to neutral ground just as soon as I'm able."

"But Risa, after this . . . sailing on an enemy ship?"

"She understands my position here," Jerome said with a subtly wry note.

"Ah, Risa would," Ian said.

No! Risa wouldn't! she thought.

Yet there was a note of sadness about Ian's voice. He

loved his wife, that Risa knew. Yet once upon a time, he had loved her as well. They had spun dreams of a perfect future together. But that had been the past, so long ago now.

Ian offered Jerome his hand; Jerome took it in a firm shake. "I'll say good-bye, then, first," Ian told Jerome. "I've got to let my own men know I'm alive and well. Your folks and Jennifer are tending to Alaina for the few hours I'll be gone." He hesitated. "Take care of Risa," he added softly. "This must be so painful for her, she's such a Unionist, but I'm sure she did agree to sail with you; she wouldn't allow us to kill one another in this wretched war over her own situation."

Risa inhaled, hesitating, as she watched the cousins. She damned them both. Yet she must have made some sound that at last alerted them to her presence as she lurked in the hallway, for they broke apart and turned to her. Jerome instantly came to her, drawing her to his side, a supporting arm far too firmly around her.

"Miss Magee, you've awakened."

"Amazing, isn't it?" she murmured, staring at him. He was tense, eyes were narrowed in warning, the breadth of his body blocked her from seeing Ian.

"Damned amazing," Jerome agreed, his voice lowering out of Ian's earshot. "Don't you dare seek help from my battle-weary cousin. You gave your word. Behave, Miss Magee, or I'll hang you by the toes myself, I swear!"

"Don't threaten me!"

"I'll more than threaten!"

"You drugged me!"

"It was necessary; I apologize. But apparently, I didn't drug you well enough. I mean it, behave, I warn you."

She couldn't reply; by then Ian had reached them.

"Risa, I'm so glad you're awake," he said. His blue eyes were so intense. His hair was roughly tousled; his cheeks were shadowed. He'd been through hell. He drew her from Jerome, cradling her against his chest with the deep affection of a good friend. "Thank you, thank you so much."

"Alaina is all right, that's all that matters," she said.

"But now you're set to sail with this Rebel scoundrel

cousin of mine, and all on our behalf. I thank you again."

She felt his lips against her forehead, then she found herself drawn back. Jerome's arm was firmly around her waist.

"We had best both be going," Jerome said to Ian.

Ian's eyes had a haunted look as he sadly stared at Risa.

He touched her cheek. "You're certain that . . ."

She could cry for help right then and there. Ian would be honor-bound to demand she be given over to him. She knew Jerome's plans; he couldn't let her go. Someone could die. Blood could be spilled, here, now in this room.

"I will be fine, Ian," she said, nearly strangling on the words.

He squeezed her shoulder. She closed her eyes, not able to stop herself from thinking about what might have been. When she opened her eyes, he was gone.

"Where . . ." she murmured.

Jerome was watching her. "Neither of us knows where the other goes once we leave; we don't ask. Belamar is sacred; neutral ground for we McKenzies. It's time for us to be going as well."

"Wait!" she cried, startled as he propelled her toward the door. "I haven't seen Alaina, I haven't the strength, I—"

"You had plenty of strength to slip down the hall and try to enlist my cousin's aid against me!" he accused her.

"I was merely—"

"Trying to escape. When you had given your word. Don't you remember? You were to behave, I was to keep your friend alive."

Her eyes narrowed. "I was—I was not trying to escape. Not really. I was just walking in the hallway. Yet I warn you, if you've harmed Finn—"

"Miss Magee, you are a bald-faced liar, you were most definitely trying to escape. Yet you may thank God that I never meant to risk human life on the virtue of your word."

"Oh, how dare you say such a thing—"

"I often dare to speak the truth."

"The truth as you see it!" she cried. "I can't come with you. I'm dizzy. I—"

"You will walk; you must come with me."

"I haven't the strength; I'll slow you down, I'm in a wretched state—"

"Oh, do quit whining, Miss Magee!" he said, suddenly stopping then with exasperation, cobalt eyes searing into hers. Then, despite her startled gasp of protest, he swept her up in his arms, and carried her out into the red-tinged darkness of the coming dawn.

Chapter 3

A small boat brought them from Belamar to the deep water of the bay. Risa fleetingly considered a second dive into the water—even if she didn't escape, she could cause so much trouble that Jerome McKenzie might wish that she did.

Yet with that thought she turned to look at him, rowing behind her, and she discovered that he was watching her. He smiled grimly. He set a booted foot firmly upon the middle seat where she sat, firmly pinning her in place with his weight upon the skirt of her dress.

"No more swimming. Time is of the essence," he said flatly.

"Where is Finn?" she demanded.

"I'll tell you soon enough."

"You swear that he is alive and well?"

He arched a brow, and for a moment ceased to row, leaning toward her. "I keep my word, Miss Magee. He is alive and well. You are the one who can't be trusted. Here we are. The *Lady Varina*. She was once the *Mercy*. She's been renamed."

The ship that emerged in the burgeoning light of day looked like a ghost vessel at first, appearing from a gray shrouded morning mist against the crimson rise of morning. She was well named for a lady such as Varina—wife of President Davis of the Confederacy. She was beautiful, riding the water with sleek grace. She was compact, small as schooners went, yet long and elegant. As they came closer, Risa saw that she was fitted with five guns on her starboard side, and no doubt five guns port side as well.

She tried to tell herself that most decently sized Union Navy ships could blast this Rebel easily from the seas with superior firepower, but though she had grown up around military men, she'd understood the value of speed.

As they reached the starboard side, a ladder was swiftly lowered. The small boat teetered precariously as Risa rose, a moment's panic making her want to risk the sea again rather than sail away with this captain and crew.

But Jerome was right behind her, balancing the small boat. He took her hands, placing them on the rope ladder, and she had little choice but to climb. The sandy-haired fellow who had guarded her room at Belamar was first to greet her, helping her aboard. She quickly tried to assess the crew. There were perhaps fifteen men visible, though she assumed there were more about, preparing to set sail. The fellows surrounding her wore no uniforms, but worked in various stages of dress—and undress. They seemed to be of all ages, mostly young men, but a few graybeards among them. Many were barefoot and clad in nothing but breeches. Some wore shirts against the morning chill. They all stared at her with silent regard, awaiting Jerome's arrival on deck.

He leapt aboard with the perfect agility of a cat, and stood beside her. "Gentlemen! We've a guest aboard for a spell. And though she deplores all our flag stands for, we'll convince her that Southern hospitality is not a myth while she remains with us. In short, gentlemen, at all costs, we must convince her to stay—she has a penchant for swimming. Thank you for your attention—Hamlin, we sail!"

A tall, slim man with silver-tinged dark hair saluted and smiled. He nodded respectfully to Risa, then stepped forward, calling out orders as he did so.

Risa felt a hand on her shoulder. "Come, I'll escort you to your quarters."

Despite her situation, she had to admire the ship. She was led past the men who now hurried about in a spree of preparation. He propelled her forward along the main deck and then down a small flight of three steps. He pushed a door open there, and she found herself thrust into the captain's cabin. She paused, blinking to adjust to the dim light. Though morning was coming quickly, a handsomely globed lamp remained lit upon a large oak desk, illuminating the cabin. To her left, a large bunk was fitted into the wall. Wooden paneling rimmed the bunk, and around that, the bed was surrounded with shelving that housed an astonishing array of books and a number of crystal decanters. Curiously, to the left of the bunk, was a small door, and before it, caught in the corner shadows, was a large, leather-upholstered wing-backed chair. Across the cabin was more shelving, wardrobe space, and again, what appeared to be a closet. Center, to the far rear of the room, with leather uphol-stered seating before, were windows, covered now with masculine, deep cobalt drapes. It was a striking cabin, tastefully appointed in every way; the woodwork itself was exquisite. This appeared to be the master's cabin of a rich merchant vessel rather than the captain's quarters of a military warship.

"Well?" he inquired politely.

She turned to face him. There was a certain arrogance about him that he wore well. He was now clad in form-hugging breeches, boots, an open white shirt, and a deep gray frock coat. He definitely appeared to be the captain of his ship—and his own destiny.

She certainly didn't intend to compliment him.

"Are you sure you and your ragtag crew are Confed-erate Navy?"

He laughed lightly, a husky sound that seemed to slip irritatingly beneath her skin.

"In the Confederacy, Miss Magee, we make do with what we have. Remember, the Union states entered this war with eighty-odd years of preparation as a country. We began with no government, no treasury, no army—no navy. Forgive our lack of uniformity."

She was startled by his lighthearted response; she wished to have irritated him. "Is this to be my prison, then? If so, I admit to seeing no escape other than through the door, so you may feel free to leave me, and captain your ship."

"Yes, this is to be your prison," he told her. He said nothing more, though his cobalt eyes were now touched with a deep anger. He turned about and left. The door closed behind him, and she was startled to realize that she hadn't actually been ready for him to leave—she had longed to provoke a fight. She wasn't exactly sure why, except that she was afraid. She wasn't sure what she was afraid of, nor could she admit she was afraid—she was a general's daughter.

Left alone, she stood still for several moments. Then she felt a sudden sharp sway, and found herself thrown across the cabin. She landed neatly on the bunk, and remained there. She had spent a fair amount of time aboard ship in the last several months, coming south from Washington to St. Augustine, then from St. Augustine to Biscayne Bay. Yet she was suddenly praying that she wouldn't find herself seasick—it would just be too humiliating under the circumstances.

She lay still, feeling the ship pick up speed as they headed across the waves. She closed her eyes, thinking she would adjust to the sway.

She adjusted. The sway felt good. She kept her eyes closed just a few minutes too long. She dozed off.

She awoke, aware again of the movement beneath her. It was comforting and lulling still. Then she remembered she was a prisoner aboard an enemy ship.

She sat up quickly. The movement made her dizzy, more aware than ever of the continual sway of the ship. But after a moment, she was accustomed to the movement, and she rose carefully.

She wondered at the time. Light filtered in through the drapes, so she knew that she must have slept for several hours. She rubbed her neck, then looked curiously around the room. She stared at the desk, and couldn't help but wonder what correspondence might lie within it. She was a prisoner now, but she wouldn't remain so. And when she escaped . . .

She hurried to the large captain's chair behind the massive oak desk. She sat down, then wrenched open the top drawer to find haphazard stacks of letters. Surely, they contained some useful information! With a pleased cry, she started sifting through them.

To her dismay, they all seemed to be personal. The first was from Ian's sister, Tia, who described her longing to be of some use to someone, and her determination to work with her brother, Julian, at his makeshift field

hospitals along the St. Johns. A second letter was from
Jerome McKenzie's own sister, Sydney, who was living
in Charleston. A third letter was from his brother, Brent,
who had recently been called to Richmond to deal with
a distressing medical problem.

As she glanced at the letters, she reminded herself
that she had been seeking military plans—and that reading the private mail of others was in extremely bad taste.
Yet she discovered herself reading Brent's letter because
she couldn't quite manage not to do so.

". . . God knows, disease kills more men than bullets
can ever manage. I know that my Union counterparts
suffer as we do, trying to keep our boys well enough
from dysentery and fevers to stay out on the fields. To
make matters far worse, you cannot begin to imagine
the newest campaign I am set upon. The surgeon general
has now determined that our boys are suffering from the
most embarrassing of maladies—those caught from their
contact with members of the fair gender. Yes, indeed,
can you imagine, Jerome? The side who wins might well
be the side who first reasons a way to cure the sexual
diseases being transmitted at a cruel rate. Again, I remind you, we must have supplies. I can say with confidence that we have the majority of the best military
minds. The war on land is fought by brilliant generals
and the great heart of a strong people, but as we are
both well aware, the Union leaders are not stupid, and
they know that they can slowly force us to our knees by
starving us out and letting our torn and mangled men
left to live or die with no medicine or anesthesia. I remain based at Richmond if you are able to write. God
go with you, brother."

She set the letter down, startled to realize that she
was shaking. A sudden sense of unease filled her, and
she looked up with a startled gasp.

Jerome had returned.

He had done so silently, or else she had been so involved in the letter that she hadn't heard the door open.
He leaned against the paneling, as if he had been there
for some time, watching her. He had been working, she
thought, sailing the ship, because he had stripped down
to just breeches. A pulse ticked at his bronze throat.

Somehow, in the lamplight, bare-chested, his narrowed eyes very blue against his bronze coloring, his straight dark hair falling free to brush his shoulders, he appeared very much the native son.

She felt the blood rushing to her cheeks as she pushed back from the desk, rising with alarm. She backed away as he grimly approached, yet there was not too far she could go despite the grandeur of the cabin. Angry heat seemed to roll from him in waves. He stared at her, eyes flicking over her with such contempt that she cried out, certain he meant her physical harm.

But he didn't touch her; he slammed the drawer shut and turned, propping a hip on the desk, crossing his arms over his chest.

"Anything interesting?"

"Obviously, not. You'd know what you keep in your desk."

"You had best be glad that I don't keep military correspondences with my personal papers, Miss Magee. You don't wish to remain a prisoner, and I don't like having you aboard. Surely, you must realize you've been spared greater punishment only as a concession to my family. Your defiance, your *rudeness,* can easily wipe out that goodwill."

"You—you can't expect your prisoners to be polite, McKenzie," she told him smartly.

His hand lashed out; he caught her wrist, drawing her close to him. She felt a wild tangle of fear grip her heart.

"Then, you cannot expect your captors to be merciful, Miss Magee," he warned.

He released her. She retreated against the paneled wall, staring at him warily. He watched her still, and she was deeply distressed to discover words tumbling unbidden from her lips. "I'll not seek further information from your desk. I—I swear it."

He rose. "You could swear from here to Kingdom Come, Miss Magee, and I could not trust you. You will not read any more of my papers, because I will have them removed. I came to warn you that we may shortly engage in gunfire. You're not to leave the cabin—unless the ship is sinking," he ordered curtly, starting out once again.

"Which may well happen!" she called after him, feeling oddly hurt and ready to strike out in return.

He came back to her, taking her hands, his grip so strong she couldn't begin to fight. His eyes impaled her own. "The ship will not sink. I built her. She is powerful, light, and faster than anything else currently sailing. When I cannot take my prey with surprise and speed, I escape heavier guns. It is a very simple method of warfare. I suggest, however, that you retire to the bunk and remain there, as I can't promise there won't be rough seas ahead."

He released her again, starting out. She raced after him, startling herself as she slammed a fist against his back. He turned, a brow arching incredulously.

"You expect me just to stay here while you seek to blow my countrymen out of the water—"

"Miss Magee, I fight with all the respect due human life I can manage. I don't seek to kill sailors. My aim is to confiscate supplies. Get in the damned bunk, or I'll have you tied into it."

She stepped back, gasping and furious. "Don't you threaten me so, you half-breed savage parading as a military officer! How dare you—"

She broke off, a scream of alarm rising in her throat. He moved with uncanny speed, sweeping her off her feet. Before she knew it, she was down on the bunk, and he had straddled her. Despite her flailings, he lashed her right wrist to a spiral in the mock headboard with rope he procured from a shelf above it.

"Don't do this!" she whispered. "Please don't do this!"

He looked down at her, dark gaze impassive. He finished tying the knot that bound her in place. "I'm sorry to say, you asked for it."

He rose quickly and left her. The business of battle was at hand. She longed to scream with pure frustration—and growing alarm. But no one would come. It was evident that Jerome McKenzie's men were totally loyal to their captain.

Seconds later, she did cry out as the first gun was fired. It was the *Lady Varina* doing the firing. The ship shuddered with the force of each heavy cannon shot.

She shrieked again as the whole of the ship seemed to shake with a fury. She heard shouting, cries, more gunfire. The ship pitched and swayed as the balls from returned cannon fire fell into the nearby waters.

Caught upon the bunk, Risa closed her eyes in fear.

The firing seemed to go on and on. With each blast the ship shuddered and rocked anew.

Oh, God, if she could only rise! She was so frightened. Terrified that a ball would rip into the cabin. That the walls would splinter, that the cabin would burst into flames, and she would be trapped like a rat dropped in a dungeon . . .

Shouts again. She worked feverishly at the ties binding her in place.

She didn't realize when the firing and swaying had stopped. She was still clawing away when the door to the cabin opened. She lay still, watching warily as the young, blond, bearded fellow who had guarded her room at Belamar approached her.

He was barefoot and in breeches. His chest was grimed with sweat and soot from gunpowder.

He was carrying a knife.

She inhaled to scream.

He must have seen the fear in her eyes, because he quickly assured her. "It's all right—it's just that if I know the captain, no one can simply untie that knot."

His knife slit the rope securing her wrist. She sat up, rubbing the sore flesh there. "Thank you, thank you so much. Thank God someone on this ship has some common courtesy. Thank God you are kind and reasonable, despite the fact that your captain is a lunatic. Thank God—"

"Miss Magee—"

"You've got to help me off this ship, do you realize that? He is a madman, leaving me tied so when the ship could have gone down."

"Miss Magee—" the young man began, distressed, but she was far too aggravated to notice.

"The wretched bastard! Yet what else could be expected of a half-breed, a Rebel—a savage cutthroat?"

"Miss Magee—"

"It's all right, Michael," she heard from the door, and

she froze, staring at the young man who now looked at her with an unhappy grimace. She looked beyond him. Jerome McKenzie stood there, slick with sweat and blackened from gunfire and battle. A nasty red gash cut across his chest. His eyes were brilliantly blue against his grimed face, and they focused on her with sheer fury. "Next time, remind me—she needs a muzzle as well as a solid knot!"

Michael muttered an uncomfortable, "Aye, Captain!" and made a hasty exit.

Risa stared at Jerome, rising cautiously. "Michael is a good, kind fellow, Miss Magee, but I assure you, without my command, he'd never have cut that tie."

"I could have died here!" Risa informed him.

"The man posted near your door was to release you at the slightest hint of danger."

"So . . ." she murmured, sinking back to the bunk. "The *Maid of Salem* is taken?"

"Aye."

"And her crew?"

"Naturally, we slit the throats of all survivors."

Her eyes widened, then she realized he mocked her. "And her crew, McKenzie?" she repeated.

"She lost three men in the fighting; we lost one. Some of my men have boarded her and will relieve her of her supplies, then see that she is painted, renamed, and reoutfitted as a Confederate vessel. Her crew will be deposited on a small beachhead frequently passed by Union ships heading to Key West."

"So you are a success in all things," she murmured.

"I am able to take unwary ships by surprise, yes. It is a modest talent," he said.

Wincing, he came on into the cabin, taking a seat at the desk and reaching into the bottom drawer for a bottle of rum. He uncorked it, and took a long swallow, wincing again when he was done. Gritting his teeth, he leaned back and poured a stream of the alcohol over the gash on his chest.

The rum cleaned away some of the grime. Risa found herself on her feet, clenching her hands together before her as she saw that the gash was long and thick. "That needs to be stitched."

He arched a brow. "You're concerned?"

"I'm merely stating that your wound needs stitches."

"Ah. And you'd like to give them to me?"

"Indeed, I might well relish the task of piercing you with a needle time and again," she said sweetly.

He leaned back, grinning. "Honesty. How refreshing. I do applaud that in a woman."

She caught her breath at how his white smile transformed his face.

"Our ship's surgeon is busy with more serious wounds," he mused.

She hesitated, wondering if she wasn't losing her mind—or if she did relish the task of sticking a needle into his flesh. Maybe it was just that in her many months of working with the injured in St. Augustine, she simply couldn't ignore such a gash on any man.

"If you can call for a needle and sutures, I will happily close that."

His eyes narrowed.

She let out a sigh of exasperation. "I've yet to meet your cousin Julian, but I've worked with those who took over his practice in St. Augustine when he moved inland with the military."

He studied her for a very long time. He was probably assuming she meant to pierce a needle straight into his heart.

No less than he deserved.

But she would refrain, she decided. His men might well do her in to retaliate.

He shrugged. "As you wish. Michael!"

The young bearded fellow opened the door. "Bring us a needle and sutures. Miss Magee has kindly offered to tend to my wound."

Michael's eyes rolled toward her as if he, too, expected the worse.

"Oh, good God, I'm not a fool! I don't intend to attempt to escape by wielding a stitching needle!" she said with impatience.

Michael arched a brow to Jerome who returned an almost imperceptible nod. A moment later Michael returned with the requested medical supplies, a bowl of water and a sponge. Risa approached the desk with a rustle of skirts, thinking then that she had indeed lost her mind. She took the sponge, wet it and wrung it out, then gingerly started to clean the blood and soot from Jerome's wounded flesh. She felt his eyes burning into her, but he didn't move, and he didn't flinch.

"Shall I assist?" Michael asked.

"I think Miss Magee can manage," Jerome said evenly, and again, she felt his eyes.

Michael left. Jerome took a long swig of the rum. She did her best to be gentle as she cleaned the wound, and found herself thinking it was a pity that such supple bronzed flesh had been so brutally torn. She didn't meet his gaze. She touched the needle to the flame in the lamp.

"What are you doing?"

"Some doctors believe it helps stop the spread of disease. I've been told that Julian is among them. He also believes that fresh sponges and bandages help the healing process," she said.

"Fine."

Risa threaded the needle with the sutures.

"Aren't you supposed to warn me that it's going to hurt like hell?" Jerome asked her, his hand catching hers momentarily.

She met his eyes at last. They were strikingly blue, hard as steel.

"It's going to hurt like hell," she told him.

He sniffed, released her hand, and chugged down more of the rum. Biting into her own lip, she began to stitch. She felt the fierce fire of his body warmth and the supple ripple of smooth muscle beneath her fingers. He never moved. When she was nearly done, he let out a growl-like groan of relief, and that was all. She tied off her handiwork, and stepped back. He all but finished off the rum, then decided to offer her some.

She shook her head.

"Go on. It might make your situation look better."

"My situation is rather good right now, isn't it? You said that you would let me go after you took the *Maid of Salem*."

"There has been a change of plans."

"What?" she demanded angrily.

"We must sail for the Bahamas immediately. There's nothing I can do to change that."

"The Bahamas? With me? You're going to force me along—"

"I've really no choice," he said, studying her pointedly. "Have I?"

"I don't know what you mean."

"I think you do."

"I don't. And of course you have a choice! It's your ship, remember? Surely, a great hero such as yourself can—"

"I'm sorry. We're going to the Bahamas. You're to be my guest awhile longer."

"Damn you, no!" she cried. She forgot her recent handiwork and struck out at him, gasping as she caught him in the chest with a powerful blow. His grunt and the massive constriction of his body as he staggered to his feet brought a cry of horror to her lips as she backed away from him. An apology hovered on her lips, but she never managed to voice it. He could still move with the speed of a jaguar. He was nearly atop her, his fingers viced around her own. The veins in his throat pulsed. His eyes glittered a vivid warning. The heat he emanated seemed to engulf her. She wanted to cry out and wrench away. Somehow, she stood her ground, returning his stare.

She heard the grating of his teeth before he spoke.

"You seem to think I'm a savage, Miss Magee. Just keep this up. You're doing a damned fine job of turning me into one!"

"I didn't mean—"

"The hell you didn't!"

But he dropped her wrist, spun away, and headed toward the door. There he paused just briefly, looking back. "Despite your ever-so-kind administrations, I do assure you, it would give me tremendous pleasure to set you ashore. Unfortunately, there is no damned shore here!"

With that, he slammed his way out of the cabin.

Risa couldn't stand. She was shaking too hard. She found herself sitting on the bunk again, more frightened and dismayed than ever. Just how long could she possibly remain his prisoner before . . .

Before what?

She was afraid to ponder the question.

She had turned down the rum before. Now she leapt to her feet, rushed to the desk, and plucked up the bottle. She didn't set it down until she had drained it of the very last drop.

Chapter 4

The surgeon on Jerome's ship was David Stewart. Like most of his crew, David had been handpicked. He had received his medical degree at the same time as Jerome's brother Brent, and so, in visiting Brent at school, Jerome had met David. David had come to the Everglades to study some of the practices of the Seminoles. He'd been especially interested in the fact that the Seminoles, like many other tribes across the continent, chose to strip down to war paint and breechclouts when fighting.

Jerome had long sinced learned from his father that the Indians knew—without organized studies or statistics—that bits and pieces of clothing caught in wounds could cause infection and death when a clean wound might heal well. Jerome had always been impressed with David's ability to study knowledge from any available source. Because of Jerome's naval successes, his superiors allowed him a choice of men. Naturally, it helped as well that he had his own ships to offer in Confederate service, but he also knew that he hadn't a temperament suited for regular military duty. He answered to superior officers within the Confederate navy, but for the most part, he captained his own ship, his decisions were respected by others, and as he always produced results, he was left almost completely alone.

As he bathed deck side, first with salt water and a rinse of fresh, Jerome felt David studying him thoughtfully.

"Good stitches. Damned good stitches. Small and neat. You may even survive this one without a scar."

Jerome shrugged, shaking his hair to lose the excess water. "One fierce, ugly Yank nearly managed to cut my heart out. And though Miss Magee may be a far more lovely enemy, I think she might desire every bit as fiercely to pierce my heart straight through. I think she made the stitches so perfectly small just to be able to stick into me as many times as was humanly possible."

David grinned. "They're still damned good stitches. Maybe she wouldn't mind assisting while she's aboard. Assuming we have another engagement while she remains our . . . guest."

Jerome set down the bucket he'd just emptied over himself, and accepted a towel from Jeremiah Jones, their cabin boy. At sixteen, he was really no younger than many a young fellow who had managed to slip his way into the war, though the minimum age for fighting men, both sides, was supposedly eighteen. The crew kept him out of the hand-to-hand fighting, and he had only been allowed aboard last year because he'd been orphaned by a skirmish in north Florida.

"Has our guest been offered dinner?" Jerome asked Jeremiah.

"Brought her Evan's best seafood stew just thirty minutes ago, sir."

"And she didn't attempt to throw it back at you?"

"She didn't even rise, Captain, just thanked me as I set it on the desk."

"You've removed all my papers?" Jerome asked.

"Indeed, Captain, the minute you came from the cabin, I did."

"Go have your own dinner, then, seaman," Jerome told him.

"Aye, aye, sir!" Jeremiah said, saluting, and disappearing toward the ladder for the lower deck.

"So you're not going to sail north with her and let her free somewhere near St. Augustine?" David asked.

Industriously drying his hair, Jerome asked, "How can I possibly do that now? For one, my brother's letter did have a reference on the back to the dates coming up in the next week when the supply of British bandages and Enfield rifles we purchased are supposed to be arriving at Nassau."

"Yes, but do you think she read that information? From what you said, she seemed to believe that she had found nothing but personal correspondences in your desk," David pointed out.

"It doesn't matter if she did or didn't read the information that Brent sent. If that one pathetically frightened Yank was right, there's going to be an enemy ship slipping into Nassau harbor to take our runner *Montmarte* the minute she loads on her supplies. We've no choice but to sail straight there, dock by morning, reach the captain of the *Montmarte,* and make plans."

"Ah, well. You're the only one out of your cabin," David said lightly.

"There's nothing else I can do."

"You could leave the lady in Nassau," David suggested.

Jerome paused, hands on his hips, looking at David. David was right. He could leave Risa Magee in Nassau. Wash his hands of her. No, he couldn't. He had taken her aboard his ship, and it was his responsibility to see her back to safety—at the right time, of course. She was a sharp thorn in his side, and yet he was loath now to let her out of his sight. She was a general's daughter. She'd managed to make her way south in pursuit of Alaina, and it was quite probable she could get other—damning—information to other parties. He had to keep her, for the time being at least.

David suddenly sighed softly. "It seems we've been at war a long time, eh, Captain? I know that I, for one, shall be dreaming of the lady asleep in your bunk. What eyes, eh, Captain? Not just blue, but crystal. And the length of her hair is sun-touched sable. She is perfection—"

"No one is pure perfection, David," Jerome said irritably.

David shrugged. "Well, as I said, it's been a long war! Perhaps I've been aboard ship too long. She appears damned perfect to me. Aye, indeed, I could easily lust over the lass. She has such pride and passion. And determination. Not to mention curves. Taper thin waist, beautiful breasts, and the curve of her hips. And her translucent flesh—"

"With any luck you'll be free to roam the whorehouses of Nassau tomorrow night," Jerome interrupted. "And if you'll excuse me for the moment, I think I'd prefer my own company."

He brushed past David, heading toward the aft. He called out an order to keep the course steady through the night, and found himself a seat on the decking. The sea wind was cold against his wet flesh. He was glad that it was so. There were fires within him that needed cooling.

He'd always considered himself a reasonable man. Fate had made him so. His father was only half Seminole; his mother had been born pure white aristocracy. They had chosen their home in the wilds of the southern peninsula because they had realized they loved one another in a world where James McKenzie, Jerome's father, would always be torn by the injustices done his Seminole mother's people. Jerome knew that to many whites, an ounce of Indian blood made a man a savage, just as an ounce of African blood made a man black. There was reverse prejudice, as James had realized when he had first fallen in love with Jerome's mother, Teela— he had discounted her ability to see through eyes that never judged a man for his birth, but rather how he chose to live his life. Jerome was well aware himself that good people came in all colors and creeds, and that malice, jealousy, and cruelty were not traits particular to one people in themselves. He was a confident man, at peace with his existence within his own heart. He could even be arrogant at times regarding his own innate abilities. But he was able to maintain his equilibrium by expecting very little from the outside world. He fought mostly for medicine, because two of his closest kin were doctors, and through them he saw the tremendous suffering of individuals, flesh and blood men who were caught in the conflict of warring giants. The agonized screams of the wounded under a surgeon's knife when no anesthesia could be had were enough reason to risk the blockade.

He was also good at it, he thought dryly. And though he abhorred the death and injury brought on by battle, he knew that he enjoyed the strategy of besting enemy ships. Nor was he opposed to the parties and dinners thrown in his honor when he broke through the Union line and came into ports such as Charleston, Savannah, and Jacksonville. It was gratifying to turn over desperately needed goods to doctors and orderlies—and it was damned pleasant to receive thanks from the various women of the communities he entered—both the flirtatious young debutants of the Southern aristocracy and the more decadent damsels, who seemed to offer themselves to him. All women, chaste and not so chaste, were easily swayed by a pair of silk stockings. Just as it seemed that many young ladies—as well as their doting fathers and manipulating mamas—were willing to overlook any small flaw in his lineage due to the romantic daring of his wartime calling. It was amazing how perspective could change with time and place and circumstance.

Still, he was weary of the war—and aware, as he had been from the very start—that they must win soon, or else perish. The North was a giant, bearing down on them. Irish and German immigrants stepped off ships from abroad—and into the Union army. Thousands of Union soldiers died. Thousands were replaced. Thousands of Southern soldiers died. They were replaced with old men and children. They fought a desperate war, and Abraham Lincoln, at the helm of the North, was no fool—no matter how the Southerners and cartoonists chose to mock him. Now the North had taken New Orleans. As a seafaring man, Jerome was well aware that the Yanks would move up the Mississippi and do their best to break the Confederacy in half. It only made sense.

He leaned back against the hull, feeling the breeze.

And now . . .

Now he had a woman aboard. A beautiful woman who was seducing his crew. Eyes like crystal, hair like a sweep of dark fire. He knew what she felt like, what she tasted like, and he knew that she was as perfect as David had suggested.

And that she was still in love with his cousin Ian.

Well, this was war, and that was her misfortune.

Just as it was now his misfortune that he should lie here in a strange blaze of agony . . .

Wanting her.

* * *

When she first awoke, Risa could hear the water lapping against the ship and feel a gentle, swaying motion. It was morning. Sunlight streaked through gaps in the draperies.

She had slept remarkably well. Thank God for rum.

She rose, feeling energetic and redetermined to take on the Southern navy.

She washed in the fresh water young Jeremiah Jones had brought for her last night. There were a few small advantages to being imprisoned upon a blockade runner—he'd also managed to bring her a good toothbrush and French tooth powder. Teeth scrubbed, hair brushed, face thoroughly washed with clear cold water, she felt ready to battle whatever demons she must.

She walked to the leather upholstered window seat at the rear of the cabin, drawing the draperies all the way back. They were at anchor, she realized. She could see an island port in the distance, and other ships at anchor nearby. There was a spyglass on the captain's desk, and she quickly acquired it to peruse her surroundings again.

They weren't far from shore. Small boats from the *Lady Varina* had already headed into port, she was certain, since the sun was well up in the sky. She figured they were probably not flying their flag—for she saw no flags on the other ships anchored nearby. Identities were kept quiet here, she reasoned. What deals were made, were made in secret. What battles were fought, were fought on the open seas.

Yet, as she looked through the glass, she felt her heart begin to pound, for on the deck of one of the ships— not a half a mile away—she was certain she saw seamen moving about in *Union naval uniforms*!

Her breath quickened. She rose, set the spyglass down, and determined that she must move hastily. This might be her only chance. If she had been left unguarded . . .

Her palms were moist. She dried them on her skirt and tried the door to the cabin. It opened. She stepped out carefully.

There were seamen about the deck. They carried their rifles, but they seemed at ease. One of them, an older man—the slim, graying fellow to whom Jerome McKenzie had given the order to sail last night—nodded her way.

"Good morning!" she called politely.

He nodded again. She saw Jeremiah Jones then, sitting on a keg, polishing a rifle. "Hello, Jeremiah."

"Miss Magee."

"It's a beautiful morning. Is it all right if I walk the deck?"

Jeremiah looked to the older man. He shrugged in return. Apparently, it was generally assumed that she could cause little trouble aboard ship. It seemed they'd been given no direct orders regarding her—and that they'd paid little heed to their captain's warning that she had a penchant for swimming.

"I'm sure it would be fine, Miss Magee," Jeremiah said. He offered her such an innocent and earnest smile, she felt a moment's guilt.

"Thanks, Jeremiah."

She walked casually around the deck.

The ship carrying the Union soldier was off the aft of the ship. Risa made her way there, aware that the remaining skeletal crew of the *Lady Varina* paused in their work and conversations to observe her. She smiled to them; they nodded in return. When she reached the aft, she leaned against the railing, as if she enjoyed the breeze. The men who had watched her warily as she passed grew weary of their surveillance after a while and returned to their tasks.

Risa waited.

She heard the hum of conversations as the men talked and worked.

She looked down to the water. The *Lady Varina* was not a large ship, and yet the surface of the sea seemed very far away. She reminded herself that she needed to slip over the railing quietly, without making a splash.

She pondered the distance to the Union ship, and the weight of her skirts. She wasn't laden down with petticoats today. And she was a strong swimmer. Her father had thought that only fools refused to learn to swim when bodies of water were so abundant. Swimming, to

an army man, might mean survival. So Risa swam, and
well. She could do it.

She casually glanced back. The aft of the ship was
deserted except for two fellows who were mending a
canvas sail. Their heads were lowered over their stitches.

She hastily scooted up to the railing, swung her legs
around, and looked down to the water once again. Then
she slipped in with what grace she could manage, attempting to fall with her body straight and slim so that
she wouldn't make a splash audible to the men above.

The water was neither too cold nor too warm, rather
it was cool and pleasant. Her dive had taken her straight
downward, perhaps ten to twenty feet into the water.
She swam hard, trying to put some distance between
herself and the ship before she surfaced.

Her head broke from the water, and she inhaled on a
deep gasp. Air filled her lungs. It was delicious.

The ship with the Union soldier aboard seemed farther away than it had from the deck. Her clothing, even
minus petticoats, was heavy. She needed to move, and
quickly.

She was exhausted, nearly spent, by the time she
neared the ship. She paused, breathing deeply, treading
water. She opened her mouth to cry out to whomever
might be aboard, but before she could do so, she was
gripped firmly by the ankles and jerked beneath the water's surface.

She inhaled salt water. Her lungs and nose burned.

She was jettisoned back up, where she coughed and
choked, desperately gasping to breathe. She wondered
what form of monster had so nearly killed her, and she
struggled to free herself from the arms holding her. She
twisted to realize that her Rebel captor had come upon
her, even there, in the very midst of freedom.

"Let me go this instant! I'll scream—"

"If you do, you're an idiot," he told her flatly, his eyes
reflecting the sun's glitter on the water.

"That's a Union ship—"

"That's a nest of deserters, Miss Magee."

"I don't believe you. And I will scream!" She opened
her mouth to do so. He swirled her around, clamping a

hand over her mouth, and plunging them both beneath the water.

She struggled to free herself, incredulous and irritated by the strength he displayed in the water. Beneath the surface, arms engaged in keeping her prisoner, he still managed to jettison them some distance from the Union ship with the sheer power of his muscled legs before they surfaced.

She wanted to strike out at him—she could not. She gasped for air, clinging to him to stay afloat. "It's a Union ship!" she insisted. "And I will scream and bring every last man jack of them—"

She broke off, hearing a peal of laughter float over the water. She held dead still, watching as a half-clad soldier appeared from a deck cabin, a black-haired woman—just as brazenly half naked—on his arm.

"Hey, Tully!" he called to the man who had apparently been keeping some kind of watch on deck. "Now, tell me, boy, isn't this much better than sweating in a hellhole gun port on the Mississippi somewhere? Leave the rich boys and the abolitionist bitches to their bloody war! This is the life for me! Palm trees, rum—and women! Ah, yes, 'tis your turn now lad with good Mary Terese. She's a might worn-out, but you're a young 'un, quick as a flash in a pan, eh? Pity we have to share, but when the crew is back from gaming and whoring on the mainland, we'll find more women. Aye, boy, that we will!"

Risa stared in horror, rudely awakened to the fact that the world was not so simple as blue and gray.

She was roughly jerked around.

"Still want to scream?" Jerome asked politely.

"Oh, let me go!" she lashed back, and breaking free, she started swimming toward the *Lady Varina*. She was actually sorry she had been so determined to escape him. She was exhausted. Her clothing seemed to weigh hundreds of pounds.

One of the small boats was down, coming toward her through the water. She paused, trying to tread water as she waited. Her skirts swirled around her legs, heavier than ever. She took a deep breath, starting to sink.

She felt swift movement around her legs; she realized

that she was freed from the cumbersome skirt, that she could kick and propel herself upward. She surfaced, aware that Jerome McKenzie had once again made tatters of her clothing in order to save her life. As she emerged above the water line, raggedly inhaling, strong arms reached out for her and she was dragged on board a small boat.

"Miss Magee, you will be the life of us yet!"

It was Michael who pulled her up. She didn't answer him; she couldn't. She laid back, feeling the sun warm her face as she gasped for air time and time again.

She was aware when Jerome McKenzie eased himself over the side into the small boat. "Back to the ladder, Michael, if you will," he said.

"Aye, sir."

She was still struggling for breath as Jerome McKenzie propelled her up the ladder, strong hands upon the damp bands of satin and lace that lined her pantalets in rows. She moved as quickly as possible to avoid his touch, her cheeks on fire.

He came deck side right behind her, silent and swift as a cat. The crew of the *Lady Varina* had stopped at their tasks, and all eyes were on the two of them.

"Gentlemen, to your work," he commanded lightly, just an edge of steel underlying his voice. "And you, Miss Magee, to the captain's cabin."

She spun about, irritated that she should feel so humiliated standing there, dripping. Half clad once again, she was anxious to reach the master's cabin.

She couldn't hear him, but she knew he followed her. She tried to close the door quickly behind her; he caught it with the palm of his hand and entered in her wake. He closed the door and strode by her, wrenching open a drawer in his desk to produce a bottle of brandy and a glass. He poured out a portion of the liquor, and thrust it toward her.

"No, thank you—"

"Take it. You're soaked. Shivering."

She angrily grabbed the glass and swallowed the brandy, then slammed the glass down. They circled one another slowly and warily around the desk. She felt the brandy burn through her, consumed far too quickly on an empty stomach.

He refilled the glass. She assumed it was for her and was about to protest, but . . . it wasn't for her. He tossed down the amber liquor himself. Barefoot and shirtless, dark hair dripping on his shoulders, he carried an air of authority.

"You know, you may leave now," she informed him. "I am safely returned," she said, finding a certain sense of security by remaining on her side of the desk.

He ignored her comment. "You know, Miss Magee, I may be a Rebel, but I don't lie, and I warned you that you were encountering a ship full of deserters."

She stiffened, standing very straight, seeking dignity—which was just a bit difficult when her clothing was shredded once again.

He had poured more brandy—for her or him, she didn't know. She snatched up the glass, swallowed the contents whole, and set the glass back down. "McKenzie," she said coolly, "may I remind you, I was nearly at the ship before you stated that she was manned by deserters."

He ignored the glass then. Staring at her, he took a long swig of the brandy right out of the bottle.

"Miss Magee, may I remind *you,* you were still quite willing to cry out, even once I had come upon you. And deserters or good loyal Yanks—they would have happily shot me in the water. Nice thanks after my gallant rescue."

She did her best to stare at him with cool dispassion. "Perhaps you shouldn't have been so determined on the rescue."

He extended the bottle. She accepted it, and swigged brandy from it just as he had done. He took it back, swallowed deeply, slammed it firmly down on the desk.

"Perhaps," he told her, "I shouldn't have bothered with an attempt at rescue. I should have left you to the wolves. Except that I am responsible for your welfare."

"You're responsible for my welfare! Now, that, sir, is quite amusing."

"Is it?" He took steps around the desk, facing her then just to the side of it. Too close. Far too close.

Her head was spinning.

"Amusing?" he inquired. "I don't see it as so. Not if I'm to hang for whatever ill befalls you."

She shivered suddenly, despite the deceptive warmth of the liquor burning through her. The room was tilting. She wondered if they had set sail again.

"Cold?" he inquired politely, yet she imagined he damned well thought she should be freezing, that she definitely deserved to suffer for her folly.

"Cold, yes. I am soaked. Perhaps, if you would be so good as to leave a prisoner at peace, I could change."

"Oh, could you? Change—into what?" he inquired flatly, crossing his arms over his chest.

Into what, indeed? It wasn't as if she had packed for this trip. Even the tatters she now wore were borrowed.

"Well, surely—"

"Surely, yes, we should find something for you! You know, Miss Magee, there is a war on. We are plagued by endless shortages, and here you are, plunging time after time into the sea, ruining perfectly good clothing. Now, if you can't learn to take care of your things, I'm afraid you're simply going to have to go without in the future."

"Oh, really?"

"My funds are limited. Money is dear to the Rebels, and all goes to pay for the war effort. New clothing for you can hardly be considered a necessity to the war department."

"You may rest assured, McKenzie, that I would not accept so much as a half-cent from you—or your war department."

"Then, what shall you do?"

He said the words with an amused certainty that she would have to throw herself upon his mercy. Her blood seemed to simmer in her veins. In a moment of sheer lunacy and anger, she decided to call his bluff.

She said as lightly as she could manage, "The weather is pleasant enough. If I'm to go about naked, I shall go naked. It will be interesting to see, however, what disciplinary problem it creates among your men. I'm quite certain, though, that being *your* men, their minds are as pure as the driven snow. Of course, they are surely superior to any Yank deserters. I'd gladly cost the Confederacy any victory, but I'd be damned before I'd cost you a red penny!" And so saying, she shed the torn skirt and peeled the soaked bodice over her head.

Lunacy—and too much brandy.

Her fingers were shaking by the time she came to the tiny buttons on the pantalets. Her anger was fading beneath his cobalt scrutiny, yet she had gone this far. She was now literally half naked. No lady, from either North or South, would be so rashly indecent, and yet, as he kept reminding her, this was war.

And she was gratified to see that the glitter of mocking arrogance was leaving his eyes. He stared at her as if she had taken total leave of her senses.

Which she had.

She slipped from the pantalets, and started toward the door, straight, dignified, smooth.

"Excuse me. I think I'll step outside into the sun and breeze to dry," she told him, starting past him.

Yet as she did so, her bravado was turning to panic. What had she done? What on earth would her father say? What of all those officers, politicians, and distinguished men and women she had met as her father's hostess in Washington? She was General Magee's daughter, admired near and far for her intelligence and composure.

And she was about to walk naked before a crew of sailors. She had already stripped in front of the enemy. She suddenly wanted to crawl beneath the floorboards of the captain's cabin—and die. Was it possible to die from humiliation? If so, she would do so now. Should she continue this decadent charade? What choice did she have?

He would stop her. Surely, he would stop her. She had seen the look in his eyes change as she had shed her clothing.

But he didn't stop her. His tone was composed and cool as he said, "My men will be quite thrilled, Miss Magee. We're in a foreign port where almost anything is for sale, and they have the run of the island tonight. You'll surely whet their imaginations. Although, I must say, I'm quite certain that what they can afford on their seamen's pay won't compare to the view they're about to enjoy."

She set her hand on the door. Were they both bluffing?

"Go to hell, McKenzie," she said, her back to him.

"Want a blanket?" he offered dryly at long last.

She replied with what dignity she could. "Yes, actually."

She heard him pull the blanket from the bunk. A moment later it was draped over her shoulders. She pulled it tightly around her, painfully aware that he stood just inches away.

"You are trouble, you know, Miss Magee, pure trouble," he informed her softly.

She kept her back to him. "I believe that the enemy is supposed to cause trouble, Captain," she said, and turned around at last. "And I am your enemy."

He nodded, but there was a strange smile curved into his lips.

"You find my words amusing?"

"I find everything about you to be . . . stimulating, shall we say." He laughed lightly. "At the moment I am gratified. You've just addressed me by something other than 'McKenzie' for the first time. Who knows? We may be heading for a better relationship."

"A better relationship? We have *no* relationship."

"Ah, but we do. This is war. You became involved, and you were caught. That means you're now a prisoner of war, and this ship is your jail. I own the ship, so I am your jailer. Therein lies your relationship, Miss Magee. You'd do well to respect it. Now, if you'll excuse me . . ."

She nearly jumped as he set his hands on her shoulders. Yet all he did was move her out of the way of the cabin's door. His eyes met hers. "By the way, Miss Magee. I'd have been damned before letting you take one step outside this cabin naked," he assured her. He stepped by her, and exited the cabin. The door closed tightly behind him.

She'd had far too much brandy, and she'd played at war far too dangerously. She leaned against the door. Her knees buckled, and she sank against it.

She closed her eyes, swearing silently against him, then Alaina, then Ian . . .

Then anyone so rude as to bear the McKenzie name.

Chapter 5

The brandy and the swim had all but done her in. She'd slunk back to the bunk and fallen into a deep sleep.

When she awoke, darkness had fallen. The lamp burned on the desk, and since she awoke only half covered by the blanket, she worried about who had come in to light it.

There was clothing at the foot of the bunk. A man's white cotton shirt, and breeches. She realized they had probably come from Jeremiah. Though he was a tall youth, he was slender, and he was surely the best candidate to donate clothing to a slim, wayward captive.

She dressed quickly, tying the rope belt tightly to make sure she didn't lose the breeches, afraid as she donned the clothing that someone would appear. And though there was little she need actually hide from her captor now, memories of brazenly peeling her wet clothing from her body were nothing less than entirely mortifying now. She would never take a sip of brandy again as long as she lived. Yet she wondered if she could blame what had happened on the brandy alone. She'd been in a tempest—with him, with herself.

Still, it was chilling to imagine what might have happened if she had managed to reach the anchored ship with the deserters on board before he had come to stop her. She didn't try to tell herself that they might have held enough remembered loyalty to the Union to help her. She was well aware that she was in far safer hands with her Rebel captors.

There was a tapping on the cabin door. She walked to it and opened it. Jeremiah was there, bearing a tray of food.

"Ah, you're awake and well, Miss Magee," he said pleasantly. "You must be starving. I'd have brought something sooner, but Captain McKenzie said as how you were sleeping, and I didn't want to disturb you."

So no one but Jerome McKenzie had been in the cabin. She wondered why the sense of relief she felt was so disturbing.

"I'm awake, Jeremiah. If these things belong to you," she said, indicating her clothing, "I'm grateful for the loan."

"They do, indeed, belong to me. Yet they somehow appear far more appealing on you," he said, grinning.

"Well, thank you."

He nodded and brushed by her, placing the tray on the desk. "Shrimp with brown rice, Miss Magee. Hope you enjoy it."

"I can't complain about the shipboard food," she said.

"We're lucky. Evan Deiter, ship's cook, worked in Paris. Then he was in one of the finest steak houses in Virginia before opening his own restaurant in Jacksonville."

"How fortunate for those aboard the *Lady Varina* that he's not still tending to his own restaurant."

"Oh, well, he couldn't be doing that. The Yanks burned down his place the first time they occupied Jacksonville."

"Oh," Risa murmured.

"Sometimes, I admit, it makes me feel a mite guilty—eating so well. There's places where our soldiers are making do on hardtack and bitter coffee."

She hesitated, sitting behind the desk, and looking at the boy. He had such a charming, earnest young face, with freckles to complement his straw-blond hair and blue eyes. "You shouldn't feel guilty, Jeremiah. You're too young to be fighting a war."

"Ah, well, boys my age have died aplenty, Miss Magee. I do feel that I'm lucky to be aboard the *Lady Varina*. And serving with Captain McKenzie."

She didn't answer that comment, but tested a shrimp. It was delicious. It was quite obvious that the ship's cook had run a restaurant—the trays were not just filled with appetizing food, they were also beautifully presented. That afternoon, her napkin had been folded into a flower. Tonight, a wedge of fresh melon garnished her plate and the crystal wineglass on the tray was filled with ruby-red burgundy.

She groaned, looking at it.

Jeremiah was instantly concerned. "Is there something wrong? I mean, well, we do get little critters in the rice and stores now and then. Maggots in the beef. That's why the cook is so fond of our bringing in fresh seafood—"

"There are no little critters in the rice, Jeremiah. It's just that . . . is there coffee by any chance?"

"Can you make do without milk? We've got sugar; we can pick up some fresh milk now that we're taking on supplies—"

"Black coffee will be just fine," she assured him.

He smiled, and left the cabin, eager to do her bidding.

He was only gone a few minutes, but in that time, she devoured every bite on the tray. She had been starving. Her head had felt like a mushroom. Food made it all much better.

Jeremiah returned with a mug of steaming coffee just as she ate her last bite. She accepted it gratefully from him. It was delicious. Yet as she sipped it, she found herself suddenly ready to lay her head on the desk and cry. He was adorable. So eager, so loyal to his captain, and yet so determined to be kind to her. And it was true. War was killing boys like him, and war was making enemies of them all.

"Whenever you're done, miss, I'm to see you to Mr. Douglas."

"Mr. Douglas?" she inquired.

"Mr. Hamlin Douglas, Miss Magee. First mate."

"And what will I be doing with Mr. Douglas?"

"He's to see you ashore, Miss Magee."

So she was going ashore! Why? Despite the fact she was growing convinced that Jerome McKenzie was determined that no real harm should come to her, the idea made her very nervous.

"My name is Risa, Jeremiah. My friends use it all the time. I'd like to consider you a friend."

He smiled broadly. "Yes, ma'am. I am your friend."

"Jeremiah, why am I going ashore?"

"Oh, well, because we're here for the night. And the captain has decided that you should have a room at the inn, seeing as how he's growing weary of swimming after you all the time—" He broke off, his cheeks pink. "I'm sorry—"

"It's quite all right, Jeremiah. I'm to have a room so that I can't swim away. That sounds fine. I understand."

"You do? Anyway, whenever you're ready . . ."

She set down her empty coffee cup. "I'm ready."

She rose. She'd never been to the Bahamas. She'd heard that the British, sympathetic to the Southern cause, sometimes used these islands to reoutfit ships for use by the South, and to trade with the Rebels, and even donate supplies. Yet, though they were British possessions, the Bahama Islands were a long way from the motherland.

The islands were a haven for pirates and, she had heard, anything could happen here. Anything at all.

She just had to use whatever happened to her own advantage.

Jerome had many advantages in Nassau.

One was his association with the Royal Inn.

Despite its name, the inn was small, situated in a back street just a short distance from the harbor. It was owned by a man called Jay Eagle—a distant cousin. Jay had left south Florida fifteen years ago, armed with a loan from Jerome's father, James McKenzie. The Royal Inn was an exceptionally snug harbor for Jerome; he could actually sleep at night, well aware that Jay would warn him if any danger threatened. It was a place where he could do business in safety and anonymity.

And it was a fine place to bring a captive. She could rant and rave if she chose, bang on the door, scream her little heart out—and no one would lift a finger to help her escape him. She had two good guards, his own seaman, Jimmy, and Big Tim, a giant who worked for Jay Eagle.

So far, however, it seemed his captive hadn't made a peep. Hamlin Douglas had quietly reported to him that Risa had been brought ashore several hours ago, and so far, she had been the model prisoner.

He could almost forget she was with them.

As he needed to this evening.

Now, comfortably situated at his distant cousin's inn himself, he had the use of a discreet private room off the public dining room and lounge. He met with Julio Garcia, a very rich Mexican.

Julio had little use for any Americans or Englishmen—but he had a great fondness for money, and so he had cast his lot with the blockade runners. He was a smart man, slim, dark, and well manicured. He had fought against General Winfield Scott during the Mexican War, and since that war had been lost to him, he continued to dislike the American government. He took pleasure in dealing with blockade runners, and enjoyed discussing the war. He spoke Spanish, since his English was very poor. His two bodyguards, always with him at a respectful distance, were equally ignorant of the English language.

Thankfully, Jerome's Spanish was excellent. Not only was the south Florida coastline often visited by Spanish traders from Central and South America, but many of the Seminole Indians residing there spoke the language as well—they'd traded with the Spaniards for guns and supplies during their years of war with the United States Army.

Julio was listening to one of Michael O'Hara's impassioned arguments about the South's right to rebel. Michael spoke fluent Spanish, since one of his distant relations had been a survivor of a ship from the great Spanish Armada that had wrecked off the coast of Ireland.

They met today to sign the last papers for their trade—and to exchange information. Julio had news regarding the Union ship ordered to take the Confederate *Montmarte* as soon as she had taken on her cargo at Nassau. The *Montmarte* was nearly ready to sail. She was a larger ship than the *Lady Varina,* and would be carrying far more guns and ammunition bound for Charleston Harbor.

That afternoon, they'd taken on a cargo of Enfield rifles, medicines, and bandages. They'd taken on water and fresh meat as well. In exchange, Julio had taken on a good supply of Southern cotton and sugarcane.

Now they finished their business, but it seemed a slow process. Julio was in a talkative mood.

"Sí!" Julio declared in response to Michael's justification of the war. "As your forefathers rebelled against the tyranny of British taxation without representation, so the Southern states now rebel against their Northern neighbors for trying to chain them to a government that does not work for them."

"You understand completely!" Michael said happily. "We are all different states, with different laws."

"This war, though, it is a tragic thing, *sí*, Captain McKenzie?"

"Damned tragic," Jerome agreed dryly. He'd been quiet during most of the conversation. He'd heard the arguments for and against the war and the South's right to secede a thousand times. Civilians and politicians spoke eloquently in taverns. Honor and glory were words readily bandied about. Jerome had seen true heroism on both sides, but the everyday soldiers who fought the war knew that shimmering words were meaningless to them; war meant marching through muddy terrain, freezing in winter, roasting in summer, dying most frequently of disease, and going hungry most of the time.

Julio leaned forward, addressing Jerome. "You joined the Confederate navy; you gave your talents and your ship over to the power of a new government when many men captain their own ships as blockade runners without accepting the command of superior officers."

Jerome shrugged. "Not all, but some captains are profiteers. I am not."

Julio grinned. "And you own no slaves."

"No. My family has not owned slaves for several generations."

"Yet you join a people who fight for the right to keep slaves."

Jerome leaned forward. "The South is built on an economy that makes use of slave labor. With or without war, change would have come. I personally believe that slavery is a dying institution—I hope that it is. And though I grant you that slavery is a major issue, you are misunderstanding the point. The Southern states seceded because they seek the right to make the decisions regarding the way that they are governed and the laws that are to be enforced themselves."

"Lofty words. Yet you are uncomfortable with this, *sí*?" Julio asked him, amused by his ability to provoke the cool captain. "So you fight, you risk your life—when those all around you are fighting for slavery."

"Only the rich own slaves, and I assure you, the whole of the South is not rich. Most of the fighting men and boys in the field own no slaves," Jerome said. He shook his head impatiently. "Many men who don't believe in the institution of slavery are fighting for the South because they're fighting for their states. I'm fighting for my state. For Florida." He fell silent, but he could have continued. He spoke the truth; his effort was for his state—Florida. He hadn't wanted it to happen, but Florida had jumped to secede from the Union. Her government and her people had been passionate. But though she had quickly joined the Confederacy, there was little that the Confederacy had been able to do for Florida. The fighting was taking place elsewhere. Bitter, bloody, brutal fighting. Virginians died on Virginian soil, and troops were called from farther south to replace them. Florida boys were sent north, and the state was left stripped of her manpower and her defenses. Fernandina Beach now hosted the Union ships that patrolled Florida waters in the hopes of seizing or sinking blockade runners. St. Augustine remained in Union hands, and Jacksonville had been taken—and then abandoned.

No one could guard Florida's hundreds of miles of coastline; no one could hold them, either. But most blockade runners, Confederate States Navy and independent, applied to nearby neutral powers—Nassau, Bermuda, Havana, and Matamoros—for supplies, then raced past the Federal ships to ports such as New Orleans, Savannah, and Mobile.

New Orleans was now lost. And it could take six days to make a round-trip run from Nassau to other ports. Florida was but 180 miles from Nassau. The population did not exist to make a dangerous run profitable for those in it for the money, nor could supplies be moved quickly enough to serve the troops in the field. As the war progressed, the Union grew ever more effective with the blockade. The Union meant to starve the South and deprive her of supplies, thus forcing her into submission. It was a tactic that worked well. Though Florida was close to Nassau and offered hundreds of inlets, once a Confederate runner entered a river and ventured deep within it for safety, one small Union ship could block her in and force her into battle.

Not many people were willing to risk Florida. But Florida was Jerome's home. When asked to do so, he slipped through the night and past Union vessels into other ports. But he served the Confederacy for his state, so that his state might survive the war, and it was as simple as that.

"Ah, you fight for Florida! But rumor has it that had the Union chosen to keep troops in Jacksonville, there might well have been a new state created out of east Florida."

Jerome shrugged, running a finger down his whiskey glass. "The Union troops did pull out of Jacksonville— and there is no new state."

"To Florida, then!" Julio said, lifting his whiskey glass and saluting. "To Florida. Salute!"

"Do you have any new information?" Jerome asked impatiently.

Julio grinned and sighed. "General McClellan remains a fool, overestimating troops. General Lee keeps him at bay. They fight all around Richmond, adjusting troops here and there, the wily Lee always ahead of the Yanks."

"So the action remains around Richmond," Jerome murmured. Brent would be where the action was, fighting to save lives. No matter how weary he grew of it all, Jerome knew he had to keep going himself, to keep doctors like his brother supplied.

"That it does. Each side believes victory will belong to the side to take the other's capital. Mark my words; Lee will advance soon enough. He'll take the fighting off Southern soil, and strip the Yankees of provisions. Now, down to the business at hand," Julio said suddenly. He drew papers from his coat pocket, laying them out on the table. He and Jerome signed for the exchange of goods, then Julio showed him the manifest for the *Montmarte*. "She is a steamer, fresh from the docks of Liverpool, an extraordinary ship. And she carries a very rich prize, gentlemen, no? She was to head straight for Charleston, with her cargo intended for the very heart of the Confederacy—Richmond. My sources tell me that the warship *USN Invincible* is already on its way to accost her when she sets sail with the morning tide—perhaps twenty miles to the northeast, in open waters."

"Her captain has been made aware of this situation?" Jerome asked.

"Captain Menkin has been advised. He will meet with you here, near midnight, so that you may make plans to engage. Your *Lady Varina* is much smaller than either ship, but I've been told that what she lacks in size, she makes up with speed and maneuverability. Menkin was quite grateful to learn that you were in port—he, too, is aware of your reputation."

"If we can just keep the Yanks from knowing we'll be prepared to ambush their ambush!" Michael murmured.

"The Yanks will not know," Julio said, a hard gleam in his eyes, as if he remembered Mexico as he spoke. "The Yanks will not know. Amigo—how about that special rum your cousin says he keeps?"

"How about it?" Jerome said, rising. He could use some of Jay's killer rum himself. He'd slept on the deck last night, loath to bunk with Dr. David Stewart in his taunting mood or with any of his other officers. His muscles were stiff, and he was tired and desperate for a good night's sleep. Especially with the work at hand tomorrow.

"I shall find Jay myself, and see to it that we've the best bottle available," Jerome said. He rose, leaving Michael alone with Garcia and his bodyguards.

McKenzie's crew thought that Risa was sleeping.

They thought that she was worn and subdued—considering how her swim had gone.

And they'd been very kind. They'd arranged for a hip tub to be brought for her, and she'd nervously bathed. No one had disturbed her. Indeed, she might have been a pampered guest. A fire had been lit in her room, she'd been supplied with the sweetest-smelling soap, and the fluffiest towels. War shortages did not exist here.

And despite McKenzie's earlier words to her, he'd apparently parted with the cash to buy her new clothing. She had been brought a box containing a beautiful blue cotton day dress, chemise, and undergarments.

Naturally, she'd determined not to touch the things. She redonned Jeremiah's clothing after her bath.

She'd pretended to drink a fair amount of wine with the dinner Jeremiah had brought to her an hour or so ago.

Then she had crawled into bed, and pretended to sleep.

She had heard a number of them whispering now and again at her door, and the words she'd heard had been surprisingly concerned and caring. She was exhausted, poor creature. It was a sorry thing when war involved women this way. But then again, the war was riddled with female spies, so even if they should be treated gently . . . they must be watched.

It seemed that she had waited forever. But finally, the tavern fell quiet, and she knew she had to try to escape. She dared to rise. Peeking out her door, she saw that she hadn't been left alone. Jeremiah, left to watch her, had dozed in a chair in the upstairs hallway of the inn.

She stepped silently around him.

She walked carefully along the hallway, well aware that McKenzie's men must be near, and that they would be wary of her. She passed one doorway and heard the light, tinkling laughter of a woman followed by a muffled, masculine comment and more laughter. She was in port with sailors, she thought, flushing. Naturally, they had engaged feminine company.

As she hurried down the length of the hall, she could hear a murmur of voices from below. Negotiations? From the stairway she looked down into the public rooms, but though she heard voices, she could see no one. Slipping silently down the stairs, she saw that the main room was empty. However, there was a private room off the main public area, handsomely appointed with a heavy oak table and upholstered chairs. She could see a slim, dark-haired, elegant man facing her way. He was well dressed, and appeared very much the dandy. He wasn't alone. Two men stood at a respectful distance behind him. He was talking to someone. She bit into her lower lip, wondering if he spoke with McKenzie. But as she anxiously moved forward, she saw the back of a blond head.

She felt almost deliriously relieved. Jerome McKenzie was nowhere near. She could seek help from these men—Spaniards?—without having to drown herself.

The dignified, dark-haired man at the table suddenly raised his voice, looking toward the doorway to the main room. Risa was certain he saw her. She decided to wait no longer, but rushed forward and accosted the nearest man, taking his hand, entreating him as he stared up at her in surprise.

"Sir! I need your help. Please. You look like an honorable man, one who would give aid to a woman in deep distress. I'm being kept prisoner by a band of Rebels. I'm desperate to reach my own people. Please, if you could take me from here, I promise you that my father would reward you greatly—"

"Risa!" she heard.

She turned. The blond man was Michael. Her heart thundered. But then he was on his feet, alarmed with her cry for help.

"Please, sir—"

"Ah! There you are!" a deeply masculine voice boomed in interruption.

McKenzie. He was back!

He strode into the private room with a brow arched high for the still-stunned Michael. He came immediately to Risa's side, clamping an arm around her like a steel band. She was drawn back, against his body, swept entirely off the floor.

"No, no, you let me go this instant, do you understand—" she protested.

"If only I could, if only I could!" he muttered. He'd gone daft. He said the words to her softly, speaking with a tone that was almost tender. Then he turned to the handsome dark-haired man and began to speak in a long, steady stream of emotional Spanish. She didn't understand a word.

The other man's brows shot up; he stared at Risa, sweeping his dark eyes over her from head to toe.

"Whatever he said, don't listen!" Risa told the man. "Please, you've got to help me—"

Jerome McKenzie broke in again with another long Spanish discourse. The other man broke into laughter, and once again, his eyes swept Risa, this time with a strange little sizzle in them. He asked Jerome a questions. Jerome laughed, and as the other man studied her now, Risa felt an acute discomfort.

"What are you saying?" she demanded furiously.

He ignored her, deftly lifting her into his arms and spinning about with a speed that made her dizzy and afraid of falling. Instinctively, she slipped her arms around him, realized her folly, and tried to struggle free. Too late. By then, he was out of the private room, across the main public room, and on his way up the stairs.

"Who is that man, and what did you say to him?" she cried angrily.

He looked down at her as he swiftly climbed the stairs. "His name is Garcia, he hates Yankees, and I told him that while you might be quite beautiful, you were a conniving little tart, trying now to stiff me out of the dear sum I had parted with for a night of your services. Naturally, he was interested in making a deal for your time at some later date."

She gasped, staring at him. They reached her room. He shoved the door open with a foot, strode on in, kicked the door closed, and set her down.

She stared at him for one brief moment, feeling an overwhelming sense of fury, frustration, and humiliation.

"Bastard!" she cried, and she slapped him with all her strength. He didn't flinch. He inclined his head toward her, blue eyes crystal in ice-hard anger. Yet despite the cold eyes, it seemed that fire radiated all around him, that sparks all but leapt from his muscled form, catching her in their burn. She stepped back despite her determination to stand her ground.

"This time, Miss Magee, I'll let that pass."

"This time! You've abducted me, you—Rebel!" she

cried, close to tears and suddenly unnerved in a way she didn't quite understand. "*This* time! How dare you! How dare you do this to me! I swear, I'll see you rot in old Capitol, I'll see you hanged, I'll—"

"One more attempt to elude my Southern hospitality, Miss Magee, and so help me God, I will retaliate! Are we understood?"

She felt like a schoolchild being chastised for some silly prank. He was keeping her prisoner!

Still, she kept her distance.

"Are we understood? I don't know—are we? Given a chance, *any chance,* McKenzie, I'll shoot out your kneecaps before I aim for your heart. *Are we* understood?" she demanded.

She heard his teeth grating. He inclined his head politely, but then his eyes touched hers again with their blue ice. "Perfectly," he told her politely. He turned on his heel, and left the room.

She stared at the closed door for a moment, then realized she was shaking badly. She moved quickly to the edge of the bed and sat, her heart pounding a million miles an hour. She had won. At last she had won a battle.

Yet, even as she congratulated herself on her victory, the door was suddenly thrown open.

He was back, a towering silhouette, caught for just the fraction of a second in the doorway.

Then he strode toward her with purpose and determination. She leapt up in alarm. "No—don't come near me, don't—what—"

Her words were worthless. He was instantly, angrily, before her, reaching for her wrist. Even as she struggled and stuttered out further angry protests, she felt something cold against her arm—and then heard a snapping sound.

She stared down in dismay to see that he'd come with handcuffs—and he'd just locked her left wrist into one side of the steel cuffs. She quickly shoved her free hand behind her back, thinking he intended to cuff her wrists together.

"Don't! No, don't—" she began, but broke off in pure

horror as she realized that he did not intend to cuff both her wrists together at all.

He intended far worse.

As she stared at him in deepest dismay, he closed the second vise around his own wrist.

And she was cuffed to him.

Chapter 6

Having been summoned back to Washington to be reassigned to the Army of the Potomac, Lieutenant General Angus Magee reached his home dirty, tired, and heavyhearted.

The Rebs had made it damned hard. A man called Stonewall Jackson was in the Shenandoah Valley, creating so much havoc that Lincoln dared not leave Washington undefended. McDowell's troops were on hold to watch over D.C. McClellan, meanwhile was demanding more troops as he struggled to find a way to attack the Southern troops around Richmond. Angus was to bring troops down to fight under McClellan—a fraction of the number McClellan wanted—demanded!—but if Washington was lost, all was lost.

Not that it mattered where he was assigned these days. Every battle he fought seemed to pit him against an old friend. Someone with whom he had fought in Mexico, or a young man he had taught as a guest lecturer at West Point. After every battle and skirmish, his aides arrived, saluted, and gave him lists of the dead, lists from the North and the South, lists that carried the names of those near and dear to him, no matter on which side of the divide they had fallen.

Coming home was going to be good. Hopefully, his wayward daughter had grown tired of seeing to the injuries and diseases of the troops occupying St. Augustine and had come home. After all, he'd never given her his blessing to leave. If she wasn't home, however, there would be a long, soothing letter from her. She did love him, and he knew it, and he took great comfort in that fact. He was a military man, a proud man, and he served his country honorably. If called upon to lay down his life in this great struggle, he would do so—regretfully. For Risa, his only, cherished child, he would gladly die without the least thought or hesitation.

He dismounted from his horse—a good animal, but one he'd named simply "Horse" because he'd had too many mounts shot out from beneath him to grow attached to the animals anymore. Grayson Bierce, his manservant—a free black with hair graying just as rapidly as his own, and old bones nearly as rheumatoid—came quickly down the steps from the house, pleased to greet him. Grayson's smile was broad, teeth white against his ebony skin. Grayson, like the rest of the family, had been in the military a long time.

"General, sir! I was so pleased to receive your letter, but it's still good to see you're really here, home, and all in one piece!"

"All in one bone-weary piece, that's for certain, Grayson," Angus said. "Now, tell me, is my daughter back from that reckless jaunt she got it into her stubborn head that she had to take?"

"No, sir," Grayson said, looking uncomfortable.

"Is there a letter for me?"

Grayson hesitated, and Angus Magee frowned, his steel-gray brows forming a hard line that had given chills to many a young man in his command.

"What is it, Grayson?"

Grayson let out a long, deep sigh, looking down at the ground as the stable boy came and led Horse away. "Well, now, one of the young fellows—Lieutenant Andy Borden is his name—came up, reassigned from St. Augustine. He was mighty upset, thought you should know Miss Risa convinced some young civilian to take her south."

"South? South from Florida?" Angus said, perplexed.

"Yessir—south down the peninsula. Seems she just kind of disappeared in the middle of the night, anxious to find Major McKenzie's wife for some reason."

Angus felt a strange, strangling pain. He clasped his hand to his chest.

"Now, sir, I'm sure that Miss Risa is just fine. From what I understand, Mrs. McKenzie has herself a fine home on an island down there. No harm could come to

Miss Risa. It's just that we haven't got a letter yet, that's all. You know how long communications can take."

Angus still felt as if his heart were in a vise. His face must have been dead white. Grayson took a hold of his arm, deeply concerned. "General, sir, let me get you into the house."

Reminded of his rank, Angus swallowed hard, and forced the pain to go away. Risa had gone sailing south down the length of the Florida peninsula? What in God's name had happened to his levelheaded, highly intelligent daughter? Why would she risk such a thing?

Angus straightened, taking a deep breath. Fear still gripped him, but he was an officer in the United States Army! He was a crusty old fellow, admired and respected by both sides. He'd sat cool through enemy attacks that would have panicked many a lesser man. He'd never realized before just how vulnerable he was, how easily he could be broken.

Not by the enemy. But by fear for his daughter.

"So she's deep into enemy territory," he said gruffly. "Hell! There's reckless, foolhardy, dangerous fellows down there, trying to break through the Federal blockade. There's always been scavengers—salvage divers, pirates, Indians, all manner of vagabonds!"

"Miss Risa has always had a good head on her shoulders," Grayson said at his side now as they walked into the house. "Sir, sit down, take your boots off, I'll get you a brandy and cigar, sir, and you can plan the good scolding you're going to give her when you get the chance. She's got a mind of her own, you know."

"She's stubborn as a mule!" Angus snorted.

"Right, sir," Grayson agreed.

"If the enemy so much as comes near her, it's the enemy who will suffer."

"Yessir, that's true," Grayson said, quickly pouring brandy from a decanter in the handsome parlor of the general's Washington town house.

Angus accepted the brandy with an absentminded nod of thanks.

"I'm going to tan her hide, Grayson."

"Yessir."

"And if the enemy comes near her, if any man touches

a single hair on her head, I'll kill him. So help me God,
Grayson. I'll kill him."

"Yessir," Grayson said again.

"I'll bring half the armed forces out against him!"

"As you say, sir."

"If she'd only married Ian! I thought that was going
to happen, didn't you, Grayson?" He looked at his ser-
vant and friend with anxious eyes. "I was so sure that
was the way the wind was blowing. But then, there he
ups and marries some little girl from his home state,
and Risa's her best friend and godmother to her old
beau's child!"

"Now, that's the whole point, General. She's with
friends Down South. Probably just as close as a pea in
a pod with some McKenzie relation! Happy as a lark."

"I pray that's so, Grayson," Angus said. He sighed
deeply. He was a military man. Matter of fact. He believed in knowledge, strategy, and statistics.

But damn! If he didn't just have a strange, sick-gut
feeling!

There was a war on.

And even as a little girl, well . . .

Risa just never had learned to surrender.

Morning . . . and she was close to a McKenzie. So
close she could see the texture of his cheeks, and
through the open collar of his white shirt, his chest as
well.

Dark hair grew on his chest in rich sworls. It, too, was
touched with a glimmer of red.

Risa was just as tired by daylight as she had been
during the long night. She had barely moved. Ever since
he had shackled her to himself, she had been in a raw
panic. He'd just been tired. He had doused the lamps,
and laid down, dragging her along with him—suggesting
that she sleep.

Sleep!

With him on the narrow bed, doing her very best to
see that she didn't touch him, that she barely breathed,
that her fingers didn't brush his . . .

Seconds had crawled along like hours. She felt now
that she had spent the entire night wide-awake, staring

at the ceiling, aware of him beside her, eyes closed, seeming to sleep as deeply as a dead man.

Yet now, as she opened her eyes and inched away from him, aware of his peace as he slept, and equally aware of his musculature and supple speed should he awaken, she wasn't quite sure that she had managed to stay awake all night. If she had slept, she hadn't slept much. She remained exhausted.

His eyes were still closed. She watched the steady rise and fall of his chest. She studied his features, noticing their distinctive beauty, yet shivering again at his resemblance to Ian. Ian . . .

Could she really remember Ian? Yes, very tall, very dark, very handsome. Principled. Loyal to the core. Honorable. And here was his cousin. The renegade. Muscled flesh very bronze against his white shirt. Features strong, and intriguing. Hair so deep a color, just touched with fire. Eyes . . .

Blue. Staring at her.

She stared back, swallowing, absurdly guilty at the way she had been studying him, then angry with herself for feeling so guilty. She was the wronged party in this situation.

"Sleep well?" she demanded irritably.

"Did you?"

"Not a wink, you wretched Confederate."

He smiled suddenly, startling her.

A handsome smile . . . even though there was a disturbing light in his eyes as he watched her. He seemed to look at her with a mocking regard that was far more amused than malicious; she realized he had probably been awake some time—aware that she'd been watching him.

She inhaled sharply, anxious to be away from his scrutiny. "Could you possibly let me free? I need to stretch my legs and—"

"Go right ahead."

She frowned. "But—"

He lifted his arm. She saw that he was no longer shackled to her. At sometime during the night—while she hadn't been sleeping a wink—he had freed himself from his half of the steel set of shackles.

She swore, leaping out of the bed, and inadvertently hitting him in the head with the steel dangling from her wrist.

He swore.

He'd deserved it, she determined. She didn't look back. She hurried to the washbowl and dumped water from the pitcher into it, studiously scrubbing her face and her hands.

"Hmm . . . it would appear you did sleep some," he said, and she nearly jumped, for he spoke from directly behind her. She spun around to face him. He handed her a towel. The curious light of amusement remained in his eyes. "Apparently, you slept quite well for several hours, at least—either that or you were far more eager for my company than I dared hope! I had a meeting downstairs late last night that ran into several hours, so we were forced to part company despite my concern regarding your whereabouts."

She took an angry swing at him, hoping that she might catch him in the temple and temporarily disable him— since her wrist was still clad in steel. But he anticipated the movement, and he was very fast. He caught her wrist, twisting her arm so that she was spun around, her back to him. She thought he meant her real harm at last; but she heard the twist of a key, and she realized that he had freed her. She moved away from him, spinning warily again to face him.

"I'm so sorry to leave you," he said politely, "but I do have business to attend to. My men believe you to be far more formidable than any of the armed, masculine enemy they meet—they were far more ready to face the guns of battle than stay behind and keep you under guard. Alas—someone had to do it. Jeremiah will be here to see to your wants and needs. He will not be guarding you alone."

He turned and headed toward the door. He was going off to battle someone somewhere—and leaving her behind, she thought. For how long? Where was he going? Why wasn't he taking her?

He was almost out the door. "Wait!"

He paused at the door.

"Where are you going?"

He arched a brow to her. "Miss Magee, you are for the Union, and I am for the Confederacy. Therefore, you are the enemy. And you seem to acquire quite enough information on your own—without my help. Indeed, I think you'd ride right up to Davis in Richmond and ask him for the South's strategy, but *I* certainly don't intend to tell you more."

"Captain, you are very amusing. I'm not asking for your battle plans, I simply want to know if—"

"Oh, I will be coming back for you!" he assured her.

"When?"

"When the battle is over."

"What if you're killed?"

"My men will see to it that you're returned north."

"What if all your men are killed?"

"Oh, well, then, I've left instructions that you're to be given a long and gruesome death . . . strung up by your ankles, skinned alive, disemboweled, the works."

Stunned, she stared at him blankly.

He sighed deeply, impatiently.

"Arrangements will be made for you to be brought to St. Augustine from here, Miss Magee. What else?" he inquired.

Naturally, she felt like an idiot and didn't reply.

"You needn't be so worried," he told her.

"I'm not worried."

"Good. And I'm not going to die," he said, a half smile curving his lip. He offered her a very proper bow, causing a lock of deep auburn hair to fall over his eye. He pushed it back, and started to leave the room again, but paused, frowning.

"Why are you still in Jeremiah's old breeches? New clothing was provided for you."

"I wouldn't think of taking anything from the Confederacy."

"They weren't from the Confederacy. They were from me. And though there are times when I'm loath to admit it, we McKenzies are quite well off."

"I wouldn't dream of taking anything from you," she snapped.

"Well, then, that's your choice. Good day, Miss Magee."

He dismissed her, and exited the room. She stared after him in nervous frustration.

It was horrible to be dragged along on a Confederate ship.

It was worse to be left behind.

She hurried after him, swinging the door open. She stopped short as the door frame was filled with the body of a man.

He had Indian blood, perhaps Spanish or French, and black. He was at least six foot six, and perhaps three hundred pounds of pure muscle. He smiled at her. "You need something, general's daughter?" he asked, his accent heavy.

"Captain McKenzie—"

"Gone. Jeremiah brings you breakfast, books."

He shooed her back into the room as if she were a child or a puppy. With little choice, she returned to the room and plopped down on the bed.

It was going to be a long day.

At Precisely 11:00 A.M., the battle began.

Last night, Jerome had gone over the route with Captain Menkin of the *Montmarte,* and between them, they'd tried to pinpoint the time and place where the *USN Invincible* would most likely attack. They had concluded that she would try for the *Montmarte* mid to late morning, an hour out of Nassau harbor, due north. Their assumptions were incredibly close.

Jerome had taken the *Lady Varina* a fair distance behind the *Montmarte,* yet with the heavily laden vessel always in his sights. At first sight of the *Invincible* speeding in for the attack, he had increased his own speed, flying across the water.

They'd had little choice but to allow the *Invincible* to get in a few shots, yet they were lucky. Her first volley of cannon fire fell short of the ship, and her second volley overshot the *Montmarte.* Her third volley would have been true, dead-on, but she never got off a third volley of fire. By then, the *Lady Varina* had come about, and her first volley ripped into the mainmast of the *Invincible;* her second, fired while the sailors of the *Invincible* ran about in stunned surprise, tore into the aft of the ship. It was evident that the enemy was sinking, even before the *Montmarte* gave the coup de grâce, firing into the forward section of the ship.

Jerome was deeply pleased. They hadn't suffered so much as a powder burn. And there was no hand-to-hand combat to be met that day; the crew of the *Invincible* surrendered. Her men were taken aboard the *Montmarte,* what could be salvaged of her guns and supplies was taken as well.

The *Invincible* did not live up to her name; she died a slow, sad death, taking several hours to sink, as if she fought death gallantly all the while. Jerome, standing forward in the *Montmarte* with the ramrod straight, sixtyish Captain Menkin, felt a genuine regret as he watched her go down. She had been a beautiful ship.

"A good day's work," Menkin said, pleased.

"Can any of this be called a good day's work?" Jerome mused. The battle had not taken long, the aftermath had stretched into the afternoon. Now the sun was just beginning to fall. The sea and sky were beautiful, yet he could hear the groans of the wounded who lay on the deck, awaiting their turns with the two Rebel surgeons from the *Montmarte* and the *Lady Varina*— one of only two direct casualties aboard the *Invincible* had been her surgeon. He'd been killed instantly when a beam from the mast had cracked his skull.

"Captain," Menkin said with a tone of reproach, "it is a good day's work. The Yanks meant to take *me,* but we have taken them instead. Each of our victories brings us closer to resolution of these hostilities. The more ships we take, the more men killed, the greater the effort the citizenry of our Northern neighbor will put on her government to recognize us as a sovereign country. We do not have the manufacturing capabilities, nor the population, to win this war if we can't pressure the average citizen in the North to be done with the death and mayhem!"

Menkin was right, and Jerome knew it. He shrugged though. Menkin was a captain—not a shipbuilder. He didn't mourn the loss of the beautifully crafted *Invincible.* He could feel little satisfaction that day with their victory. He felt a dull pain in his heart, and little more.

"Aye, Captain, true enough," he said. He turned to Menkin. "If you'll excuse me, Captain, I believe I'll see if I can be of some assistance to our surgeons."

"Ah, yes, you've a brother practicing medicine in South Carolina, eh? Your mother had kin there, is that right?"

"My mother inherited a working plantation house outside of Charleston, but my brother is now working with General Lee's Army of Northern Virginia, sir."

"You've a cousin in medicine as well?"

"In the field along the St. Johns, yes."

Menkin looked to the water. "And, then, you're related to Ian McKenzie as well," Menkin said distastefully.

"Yes, another cousin."

"A traitor."

"Many Southerners have chosen the side of the North, especially those who have been military for some time."

Menkin snorted. "The truth of it is, he's a Floridian, a Southerner, and by God, he shouldn't be making war on his own state! You mark my words—he will rue his disloyalty! If I catch him—"

"Truth, Captain Menkin, is often a matter of perception. Quite frankly, sir, both the President of the U.S. and our own Jefferson Davis were actually born in Kentucky. Lincoln must suffer the agony of the damned each day—since his wife's kin are Southerners as well. And I imagine Jeff Davis himself mourns the deaths of many of his old friends in the government and military when they fall prey to Southern bullets."

"Young man, if you were to meet your cousin in battle—"

"Sir, I pray that I will not meet my cousin in battle. Now, if you'll excuse me . . ."

Menkin said nothing else. He was a tall stiff silhouette in the evening as the sun fell. Jerome left him, glad again that he captained his own ship, and that for the most part, his superiors let him be. Menkin was a strange man, seeing many things clearly. Yet there was something cold about him.

Jerome suddenly wished that he could be so damned

certain that they were entirely right. He had to admit, he didn't believe either side was right.

Neither, it seemed, did God.

He walked across the deck, looking for David Stewart. When the wounded men were patched and tended as best as possible, Dr. Stewart was to return to the *Lady Varina* with Jerome and the few men who had joined him to assist. After the incident with the *Invincible,* however, Jerome had agreed his best course was to follow the *Montmarte* until she neared Charleston harbor, and there engage any Union ship that might try to block her. He wasn't adverse to doing so; it was the only logical course of action.

But he chafed, nevertheless, at the time it would take. He had left Risa Magee in Nassau. And if he followed the *Montmarte,* it was going to take him nearly a week to return for her. It made him very nervous, indeed. The lady had a way with her. Though she was guarded by Big Tim—or Jimmy—Risa was cunning, clever, and determined. Yet he was just as determined to return her to a safe harbor. It was a matter of pride, honor, and principle.

And besting the lady herself, naturally.

He didn't know why he felt such a surging conflict regarding the woman. He didn't blame her for fighting—in her position, he would fight. Maybe he blamed himself. Last night, she had, at first, stayed as far away from him as possible while shackled to him and on the same bed. He had known when exhaustion had overwhelmed her, and he had been somewhat amazed himself that she had actually slept all the time he'd been downstairs planning today's work with Menkin. When he'd returned to her room, she'd stirred, and he'd silently resumed his position at her side.

But she hadn't wakened. She'd turned against him, a slim, trouser-clad leg thrown over his thigh, a hand cast upon his chest. She'd even rested her head against his arm. And it had been as if a brush fire had taken hold in his bloodstream. She'd moved upon occasion, nuzzled more closely against him, sighed—and damned near hugged him. He thought at one time that her eyes had even opened. Yet . . .

The room had been dark. And if she'd been dreaming, she'd surely dreamed about his cousin. How odd. There'd been dozens of times he'd been with a woman in the dark. A quadroon doxie in New Orleans, a rich divorcée in Charleston, a saloon keeper's daughter in Key West. In the dark . . . they were all alike.

As a very young man, scarce out of his teens, he'd fallen in love with the sister of an adventurous young Irishman come to make his living as a salvage diver with his brother-in-law, Lawrence, now dead nearly a year himself. Mary had been two years younger with hair so ebony it gleamed blue like a raven's wing, eyes alight with silver glitter. She'd loved the sea, the wild, lush paradise of the South, and she'd loved making love in the sand. She knew no prejudices, and wanted no other world than him.

But none of his mother's medical wisdoms, no doctor's cures, no love and no magic could save her when she had contracted malaria. She died in his arms; her brother followed behind her in a matter of days. They were both buried on his family's land. He hadn't had a chance to marry her, but he would have done so. She had just told him they were expecting a child when she had gotten sick, but she wouldn't live to bear their child. When she had left him, she had taken with her a piece of his soul and more.

Death, his father had told him, was a part of life. And there was much in life that was far worse than death. He knew that his father's first wife, Jennifer's mother, Naomi, had died young as well, and that his father had lost a child with her. His father's sympathy had been real. But James had taught him that life was to be lived, and he lived it. However, he didn't offer love easily. He was wary by nature of his heritage—yet physical, too. So there had always been women in his life.

But in the dark, one could substitute for another. And he couldn't help but wonder if that wasn't something the general's daughter had felt last night in her dreams, as she slept. One man . . . incredibly like another.

Yet why in God's name should it irk him so much to imagine that she dreamed he was Ian? Other than the fact that, yes, she did feel quite different from any other woman in the dark. Tall, slim, supple, elegantly shaped, and yet so generously *endowed* . . .

"Please, sir, water, morphine . . ."

His thoughts came to a jarring halt as his pants leg was gripped by a sailor on the ground. He saw the water bucket just a few feet away, and brought the sailor a dipperful, lifting his head to help him drink. Jerome looked about the deck. It was strewn with the wounded. Some lay down, some leaned against the railing. David Stewart was busy at a makeshift table set up toward the aft. He was amputating a man's leg. Brawny sailors assisted him. Thank God they had morphine.

The *Montmarte*'s surgeon was at work with a fellow who'd been wounded in the gut. Jerome looked at the young Union navy soldier who strained for a few drops of water.

"Where are you wounded?"

The young man's lips trembled. "Leg. Don't let them cut it off, please, sir. Don't let them cut it off. I know you're a Reb, you must want us all dead . . . I'd rather be dead."

"Son, you wouldn't rather be dead. Life is in the heart, the mind!" he said sternly. He set the dipper back. The boy was young—really young. He had pale blond hair, sky-blue eyes, and a chin that hadn't even thought about growing whiskers yet. He'd probably cheated on his age to get into the service. He was sixteen, at the most.

Jerome ripped open the boy's pants leg. He gingerly tested to ascertain if there had been bone shattered. The bone hadn't been touched. A strip of shrapnel had imbedded into muscle.

Jerome looked around the ship again. David was busy; the *Montmarte*'s doctor was still trying to save the life of a man who bled profusely from his midsection. Jerome hesitated, then looked down at the sailor again. "Think you can keep from screaming for a minute?"

The young man tried to scurry up. The effort nearly made him pass out. "Sir . . . what—"

"I'm not a surgeon, but I've spent some fair time with doctors. Trust me. I'm going to get the bullet out. Then you pay attention to me. You make them keep you up

on deck, and you make sure the wound gets cleaned
with fresh seawater daily. Seawater. Has to be seawater,
has to be fresh, understand?"

The young man nodded—both nervous and earnest.
Jerome reached into the sheath at his waist for his small
knife. He thought the young man's heart would stop
then and there, but then the Yank seemed to decide that
he did want to live whole or die. "Go on, sir. Please."

"Brace yourself," Jerome warned.

The young sailor did. He didn't utter a sound of protest. He passed out as Jerome dug his knife into his calf.

The wound began to bleed more fiercely, and Jerome
felt a sheen of sweat break out on his forehead. Then
the strip of shrapnel slid into his hand—lubricated by
the flow of blood. He quickly put pressure on the flow
of blood, holding one hand on the wound while ripping
his shirt with his free hand to create a bandage as
quickly as possible.

"Captain McKenzie, sir, can I lend a hand?"

Jerome turned. It was one of the *Montmarte*'s officers.
"I could use a bucket of seawater."

"Aye, aye, sir!"

Jerome was relieved to see he'd stopped the bleeding.
The officer returned with the water. He bathed the
wound, carefully making certain that he'd stripped all
traces of fabric away from it. He asked for assistance in
making a poultice of seaweed. The officer became his
willing assistant. Between them, they went on to see
what they could do for the others who waited.

Later, a cup of rum in his hands, Jerome watched
David Stewart stitching up a long jagged wound in a
Yank's arm.

David looked at him, arching a brow.

"All right," David said. "I told you—your feisty little
Yank prisoner does do a better stitching job. I admit.
She's just not with us at the moment."

Jerome shrugged. He drank his rum, wondering why
it bothered him so much that she wasn't near. It was
like an itch with him now. An obsession. He saw her
when he closed his eyes. Saw the gleam of her long
auburn hair, the beautiful flash of her eyes, the perfect,
porcelain beauty of her face. The fluid sensuality of her

damned perfect shape as she walked, gestured, moved . . .

"If you're about done, we need to be getting back to our own ship," he informed David, and walked away.

Damn her. The faster he got her back to Yank territory, the better.

Chapter 7

The first day seemed to take forever.
    The second day was so long it was never-ending.
The third day felt like a year.
The fourth day stretched to a decade.
Risa chafed with tense energy under her guard, a man she came to know as Big Tim. She never learned if he had a last name—or if his surname was Tim and his given name Big!—or exactly where he had come from, or why he was so loyal to Jerome McKenzie. She did learn that he was tireless, and that every time she so much as cracked her door open, he was there, alert.

He was polite, and he was silent. He was also as good as a set of steel bars. There was no way past his great bulk.

Jeremiah brought her books, played cards with her, brought her well-prepared meals, hot bathwater, fragrant soap, fashion magazines, and more. But despite his attempts to amuse her, she was ready to pull her hair out. She began to pace the room endlessly. She prayed for sleep early at night. She drank a lot of wine, hoping that she might sleep through more of the time that passed so slowly.

On the fifth day, her life made another change.

Jeremiah appeared in her room along with Mr. Douglas, Jerome McKenzie's first mate. She hadn't seen Douglas since she'd been here, and she was somewhat surprised to realize that he'd been left behind. He was stern-looking, and courteous, but very firm when he spoke with her.

"Miss Magee, I've received word that I'm to take the sloop *Katie B.* to Bone Isle."

"Mr. Douglas, I'm afraid this means little to me. I've never heard of Bone Isle," she told him.

"It's a very small key, miss, not too far south of Biscayne Bay. We're to meet up with Captain McKenzie and the *Lady Varina* there. I'm sure the captain will see to it that you're then returned to St. Augustine."

"Ah . . . well, sir, why don't you return me first to St. Augustine, and then meet up with your captain at Bone Isle?"

"Miss Magee, the captain will make arrangements—"

"This has gone on long enough, Mr. Douglas, surely you see that, sir. You must return me now."

He arched a brow; she wished she'd kept silent.

"Miss Magee, I must follow orders. I had hoped that you'd be more agreeable—"

"Why? Can you guarantee that I'll be brought back to St. Augustine immediately after we meet with Captain McKenzie?"

"Miss Magee," the graying Douglas said wearily, "this is war. I can't guarantee anything."

She was feeling cooped up and very argumentative. She was tired of losing to Jerome McKenzie, and she was not going to give in easily to any of his men. "You're right, this is war," she told him obstinately. "I can't guarantee anything, either. I'm afraid you'll burn in hell before you find me agreeable, Mr. Douglas."

He looked like an old hound dog, saddled with a burden he hadn't wanted at all.

"Miss Magee, I do apologize. I really hadn't wanted this to be difficult for you, or for us—"

"If I have a chance to escape, sir, I will escape. If I can give an enemy any information about you or Captain McKenzie or your movements, I will. Rest assured."

"You must understand, we do have our orders."

"Oh, yes! Captain McKenzie's orders! Surely, all life hinges on nothing else!"

"Now, Miss Magee . . ." Jeremiah murmured unhappily.

"Miss Magee," Mr. Douglas said patiently, "I must say, at the moment, I'm afraid, *your* life does hinge on his orders. And under the circumstances . . ." He glanced at Jeremiah with a sigh and a shrug.

Jeremiah stepped forward. "Sorry. Honest, I'm really very sorry . . ."

Before she knew what he was about, he reached out for her, drawing her quickly against himself.

He might be a lad, but he was a strong one. And she was totally unprepared. Before she could even struggle against his hold, he set a damp cloth over her face. A sweet smell pervaded her senses. She couldn't fight; she couldn't move. Her eyes closed.

"Do we really have to do this, Mr. Douglas?" she heard Jeremiah asking, as if from some distant place.

"You heard the lady. She knew where we were to rendezvous. Were she to manage an escape, she would tell the Yanks to pluck up the *Lady Varina* and Captain McKenzie, the scourge of the southern seas, at Bone Isle. Now, lad . . ."

She was vaguely aware of their voices, fading now.

Then she heard no more.

She knew they were far across the water when she slowly opened her eyes. The sloop *Katie B.* was very small, and her cabin was tight and confined. Risa saw Jeremiah sitting in a chair across from her narrow bunk, watching her with big, guilty eyes. "I'm sorry," he murmured.

"You're a wretched boy," she assured him.

"I said that I'm sorry."

"You should be."

"This is war—"

"Oh, dammit, don't say that to me again!"

He bit into his lower lip. "Sorry. I will try to make it up to you. Well, you are trouble, you know. You have a knack for hearing everything, and you're such a determined enemy!"

"Like you said—it's a war!" Risa reminded him.

"But I really do apologize—"

"Enough! Just don't do it again."

"If—"

"Oh, I know, I know! Captain McKenzie gives the orders, and you follow them! What if he ordered you to shoot me?"

"He wouldn't," Jeremiah said.

"How can you be so sure?"

"I know the captain."

"What if I were a spy?"

"He'd never order me to shoot you."

"Even if I were a spy?"

"Well, if you were really terrible or evil—or if you were a cold-blooded murderess and killed children right in front of him—"

"He'd order you to shoot me?"

"No—he'd shoot you himself, if it had to be done," Jeremiah said. She felt a chill, but then he smiled. "You're not evil."

"I'm the enemy."

He nodded. "You're the enemy—I'm the enemy. And we're neither of us evil."

"You can be very wise, Jeremiah."

"I learn from—"

"I know, I know," she murmured irritably. "You learn from the great Captain McKenzie!" She groaned softly, trying to sit up. Her head hurt. She lay back down.

"You need something to eat. Then you'll feel better."

She didn't think she'd ever feel better, but he brought her some bitter tea and biscuits, and it helped. "Tomorrow will be much better," he promised her. "You'll see. We bring the *Katie B.* right into shore. There's a little town there—well, not a town. A few people live on the island." He shrugged, a half smile on his face. "All right, so maybe they're not pillars of society. There's some salvage divers and their wives and families. A few half-breeds make their living fishing. But it's beautiful. You can swim down, touch reefs, see magnificent colors . . . and the beaches! If you promise not to cause trouble, I know that I can get you a day on the beach at Bone Isle!"

A day on the beach. Freedom from walls closing in on her.

After her confinement on the Bahamas, she wanted it very much.

She didn't want to sound overly anxious.

"If it's such a paradise, why is it called Bone Isle?"

Jeremiah shrugged. "Oh, well, once, a pirate named Barbery Bill came to hide his treasure there. But he'd

stolen his treasure from a pirate known as Edward
Teach, right out of Nassau. Teach followed him and his
crew to the isle, slaughtered them, and left. Years later,
when Spanish missionaries came back to the isle, all they
found were the bones of the pirates, picked clean by
crabs and seabirds."

"Charming."

"Well, naturally, the bones are all gone now . . .
Wouldn't you be happy with a day on the beach?" he
asked her, anxious to please.

"Maybe. Ask me in the morning."

She closed her eyes. The bland biscuits had soothed
her stomach, and the rocking motion of the ship was
making her sleepy.

Besides, she couldn't escape from the middle of the
ocean.

When she woke again, they were docked, and it was
morning.

Jeremiah brought her more tea and biscuits.

"I've asked Mr. Douglas and Big Tim—"

"Big Tim is still with us?"

"Aye, that he is," Jeremiah said solemnly. "But
they've both agreed that you're due an outing. Mr.
Douglas is a good fellow, though he seems like a stern
sort. He just follows orders; he knows how important
our work is."

"Dangerous," Risa warned him sternly. "The Union
blockade is going to get tighter and tighter, and Captain
McKenzie is going to get blown out of the sea. You're
far too good a young man to share such a fate!"

He grinned, but had the smug look of an adventurer
about him. "Oh, no, Captain McKenzie won't get blown
out of the sea. He's a part of it—why, our ship has barely
ever even been damaged! Ah, Miss Magee! We sailed
right by a few Yanks last night; they never even saw us.
They don't know these waters, the reefs, the shoals—
not the way the captain does. But anyway—if you've a
mind, you can spend the day outside."

"*If* I've a mind!"

She set down her breakfast tray and kissed him on
the cheek. "I've a mind!"

"But you must swear to behave. You cannot try to escape."

She was so desperate to get out that she swore without a second thought, then wondered briefly if it wasn't really all right to lie to the enemy. She was obliged to escape if she could.

Mr. Douglas, apparently, was no part of the outing. Risa didn't see him. She and Jeremiah walked past the few crew members on deck and from the sloop to a small dock, where Big Tim and a smaller Seminole man waited with three horses.

She saw the "town" Jeremiah had described. It was a few wooden houses, roofed with palm fronds. Still, as she had hoped, there were dozens of small boats pulled to the shoreline. Escape from here just might be possible.

But not at the moment.

There were only three horses for four people because she was to ride with Big Tim.

Might as well attempt to escape from a gorilla.

As soon as they reached the beach, the fourth man, the Indian introduced to her as Johnny Lightfoot, departed with the horses. She wasn't going to ride away, that was certain.

But as the day progressed, she decided to leave thoughts of escape for later. They had indeed brought her to an exquisite, pristine beach. The sand was soft and pure white; the sky a crystal-clear blue.

The beach was empty of all other life—except for the birds and sea creatures that freely roamed there.

It was so good just to be in the open air. Jeremiah had packed her a picnic lunch complete with sweet oranges, smoked fish, fresh bread, and a bottle of deliciously mellow Burgundy. Not too sweet, not too dry. She wondered how a wine steward might describe it. "Mellow, pleasant. Perfect for prisoners having picnics; blends away the rough edges."

She stretched out on a blanket on the clean, cool sand, and felt the sun above her. Naturally, any amount of sun or wind burn was entirely unfashionable, she reminded herself, but she didn't care. The sun felt wonderful. She didn't care if her cheeks burned as pink as roses.

She'd been left alone. She knew that Big Tim stood guard at one end of the beach, while Jeremiah did so at the other. It was Jeremiah who came to her just as the sun began to fall. "Miss Magee, I'm sorry, but we must head back."

"Must we?" she inquired softly.

He nodded solemnly.

She rose, stretching. She could still feel the warmth of the sun, and the wine. She smiled, feeling both stubborn—and somewhat light-headed.

"One minute, Jeremiah," she told him. Then she walked toward the water.

"Miss Magee . . . ?" Jeremiah said nervously.

She reached the water and waded into it, soaking the bottom of the legs to the trousers she still insisted on wearing. She turned back to him, in a mood to be contrary, yet thinking somewhat guiltily that he wasn't the one she should be making miserable. But then again, he was one of McKenzie's crew members, and therefore a party to her abduction.

"I think we should stay out awhile longer."

Jeremiah shook his head firmly. "We really shouldn't have come out at all." He walked toward her. "Miss Magee?"

She smiled, and he came even closer, she suddenly bent down and scooped up a handful of water to toss his way. "Miss Magee . . ."

She laughed, turned, and started running.

At that moment thoughts of escape were not at the top of her mind. The water was simply beautiful, the sand was so clean and pure against her bare feet, and it just felt good to run. She heard Jeremiah—huffing and puffing behind her. She turned back to him, laughing, skirting around so that he skidded and plunged full length into the water as she changed direction.

"Jeremiah!" she taunted as he rose. "As a young man, surely you can outrun me!"

"Now, Miss Magee, this isn't a game . . ."

But it was a game. One she would win. Big Tim was down at the southward end of the beach. He was huge; he could probably stop a freight train. But he wasn't fast.

The wine would give her the confidence, or the foolishness, she now needed.

She started running northward, back toward the town—with the multitude of ships in the harbor. She ran hard, and fast.

Of course, the beach was long. And she had to pause, look back. Jeremiah was running after her—then he suddenly stopped. Bent over, hands on her knees as she inhaled deeply, Risa frowned as she watched him. He had just suddenly stopped chasing her. Had she gotten so far away then that he couldn't possibly catch her? Or was he winded, too? Would he catch his breath and start after her anew? He looked quite alarmed, and she felt somewhat guilty again. Poor Jeremiah. There would be hell for him to pay for losing her. And still—just what could Jerome McKenzie do to the lad?

She had an uncomfortable vision of the boy strapped to a mast while Jerome ordered his first mate, Mr. Douglas, to take a cat-o'-nine-tails to him. Only back in pirate days did such awful things happen, she tried to tell herself. And still . . .

They had shot and branded deserters in the Union army. She knew that. No matter how young the soldiers. No matter how sad the occasion. She knew that it had happened; her father had told her. It was war, and no quarter was given.

She had to stop thinking!

She couldn't worry about Jeremiah.

After all, the little scamp had expertly drugged her to assure her silence. And McKenzie wouldn't shoot him. She had the opportunity; she had to run. To escape.

She turned to run and stopped in her tracks.

Someone was in front of her. Against the falling sun, she couldn't see who, but a huge obstacle lay in her path.

Big Tim? She looked back.

No . . . no, Big Tim was far back on the beach, moving slowly, he hadn't yet reached Jeremiah.

She looked forward.

The falling sun shifted. The obstacle was a man on a horse. At first he was nothing more than a powerful silhouette on the horizon.

Then he moved the reins, and the horse started forward through the shallow surf. And she saw that Jerome McKenzie had come back at last.

Why she ran then, she'd never know. It was foolish. She was trapped.

Yet she ran anyway.

She heard a pounding in her ears, and she thought that it was the staccato pulse of her own heart. Then she realized that the horse had eaten the distance between them. She tried running into the deeper water. She dived to swim below the surface, changing her direction. Still, she emerged in the shallows, gasping for breath. She quickly looked around and saw the horse, a healthy gray, racing toward her.

Before she could run or dive, McKenzie came leaping from the horse, catching her by the shoulders, and bringing them both crashing down into the surf.

She eluded his grasp, rising, sputtering for breath, and stared at him across the shimmering, shallow water. His dark hair was wet and slicked back. His eyes reflected the deep blue color of the sea. His white cotton shirt, soaked, clung to his muscled bronze flesh while his dark breeches soddenly hugged his lean hips, buttocks, and long legs. His hands were on his hips, and he looked decidedly irate. And yet still . . . she felt her pulse race. She was startled to realize just how striking a man he was, with an immensely masculine . . . sensual power. She was alarmed by her own reaction to seeing him, the quickening of her heart; even the very anger that flared inside her, the need to do battle against him.

"You know," he grated out, trying very hard, so it seemed, to keep his voice level, "I've warned you."

"You've warned me?" she repeated, astounded, her brows flying up in disbelief. "You've *warned* me—about what?"

"I've warned you not to give anyone any more trouble."

"Oh! Don't give anyone any more trouble—or what? You incredible ass. You'll abduct me—keep me prisoner. You'll make me entirely miserable. What can you do to me that you haven't already done?" she demanded furiously. The wine she'd consumed on the beach was giving her a fine sense of temper and bravado. Actually, she wanted to do so much more than yell at him. She wanted to shake him. Drag him down into the surf. Draw her nails down his copper-tinted flesh. Curl her fingers around his throat . . . pound against the hard wall of his chest.

And she wanted to run away from him again . . . and from the strange, savage anger he awakened within her.

She didn't run away. But she did touch him. Jaw locked, she took a long step toward him and slammed a fist against his chest. Once, then a second time, then a third.

"What more can be done to me, Captain?" she repeated furiously.

He caught her wrist, fingers a vise as he stared at her.

"Oh, Miss Magee, there's so—so!—much more that can be done to a prisoner!" he assured her, his voice deep, resonant.

Pointedly, he dropped her wrist. She backed away.

He stood in the surf, wet clothing plastered to his body, hands on his hips, like a king in his paradise. Perhaps it was his kingdom. He knew the swamp, the waters, the islands. They were in his precious state now, where it seemed he ruled over the azure sea and the sugary sands, as supreme as an ancient golden god.

She'd be damned if he'd intimidate her. "Are you threatening me?" she inquired coolly.

"Damned right," he assured her, teeth grating.

It was the wine—surely. That, or pure insanity. But she was tired of his superiority. And she was tired of being a prisoner.

She decided she'd backed away from him once too often.

Her temper soared. Foolishly.

Yet she couldn't control it.

She burst through the few feet of water separating them like an enraged buffalo, butting into him with all of her strength—and an impetus that slammed him down hard into the surf. A battle fought, and won.

For a brief moment she was victorious . . . and free.

Chapter 8

Brief—indeed, her freedom was brief.

She quickly learned that if Jerome McKenzie was going down, he wasn't going down alone. Even as he fell backward, he reached out, arms encompassing her. She came flying down after him, and a soaring spray of crystal-tinted water flew around them as they plummeted beneath the surface.

She tried to escape from his hold, struggling to rise. He didn't release her, but brought them both halfway up, on their knees in the surf.

"You do not act—not one tiny bit!—like a Southern gentleman. You're why the South should lose the war. You should be shot, hanged—sent to prison to rot—"

"Well, do you know what, Miss Magee?" he interrupted, blue eyes blazing against the hard contours of his bronze face. "You don't act one bit like a lady. You could just be gentle and well behaved—like a normal woman!—and a normal prisoner of war! You—"

"Oh, just let go of me!" she cried furiously, trying again in earnest to wrench away from him.

"Stop, you're caught, you're going to—"

His words were cut off by a loud, rending sound as her cotton shirt, caught on his scabbard, ripped cleanly apart as she tried to rise. She swore, spinning around to assess the damage. But her movement ripped it further. As she came to her feet, a large swatch of the white cotton was torn away on the hilt of his sword.

"Oh . . . hell!" she cried. She was on her feet; he remained on his knees. She looked around desperately, cheeks flushing brilliantly as she expected to see Big Tim and Jeremiah. But both were gone. The pristine beach seemed to stretch out forever, empty of other life except for the horse, which had ambled out of the surf and waited in a cove of trees. They might have been alone on earth.

"Rebel!" she muttered, pushing him angrily in an attempt to make him fall, and make good her escape. Her torn shirt flapped out in the breeze as she ran. But she hadn't knocked him over, and he was a strong, fleet runner. She heard his splashing footfalls overtaking hers as she neared the beach. She looked back to see the grim power with which he ran, and she cried out as his arms swept around her, bringing them both tumbling down again, this time to the whiteness of the wet sand.

He straddled her as she gasped deeply for breath. Her torn shirt lay open, and she knew it; she met his eyes, and his eyes met hers.

It seemed that she could not quite catch her breath. Nor would clever words come to her. She stared at him, lips trembling, limbs shaking. "Rebel!" was the best she could manage.

"Yankee," he returned.

"Rebel!"

"Yankee!"

She fell silent, her breasts rising and falling with each anguished breath.

Then he reached out, and touched her face. His knuckles brushed her cheek. She inhaled sharply, amazed by the streak of fire that seemed to sear through the length of her.

Such warmth . . .

It was the sun, it was the wine. It was something that had to do with the perfect day, the sheer blue of the sky, her brief taste of freedom, the pulse of the waves, breaking against their limbs.

Slowly, he leaned down and kissed her.

Touched her lips with his own.

And the fire burned with a blinding heat.

His mouth molded over hers, hard and persuasive. Parting her lips to the thrust and play of his tongue, passionate, determined. His fingers cupped her cheek, then moved . . . soft and mercurial as they brushed her throat, collarbone, breast . . .

She should not be doing this, she thought. But thought

slipped away from her. The world spun. Sand, sea, and sky. The fire of his passion burned deeply into her, like a brand, and she felt the responding heat within herself. His mouth continued to ply hers . . .

And his hand . . .

Stroked her flesh. A touch not quite so light now. His palm cupped her naked breast, his fingers rubbed and teased her nipple. She writhed, anxious to escape the feeling, anxious to know more of it.

His kiss continued. Like no other. Demanding and seductive. She was vaguely aware of a tug at the rope that tied Jeremiah's too-big pants around her waist. Then she felt the brush of his fingers, slipping beneath the belt line and running over her abdomen, stroking lower into the triangle of soft, curling hair between her thighs. It was time to protest. She couldn't, she was too entranced, as if she were drugged. His touch fascinated, awakened, aroused her. She could hear the surf, an ebb and flow, feeding the fires inside her, like the heat of the sun beating down on them. His lips parted from hers at last; she kept her eyes closed, yet somehow she was aware he looked down at her, waiting for her to look at him. She could not. He groaned softly, and she felt his lips again, this time against her throat. He moved lower and rimmed her breast with that same mercurial touch, sucking upon the nipple then, teasing it with his tongue. Her fingers wound into his hair. She should be ripping at it, pulling him away. Her fingers were rigid, shaking, holding him to her instead. Warmth cascaded all around her with a wild, throbbing sense of excitement. She told herself it did not exist. She warned herself that she'd be sorry. But she wanted this. Once she had been in love, and she had behaved properly, a perfect lady, and so she had failed to experience that love.

She wasn't in love now, she couldn't be, not with the enemy! This was so different, but it was something she had felt from the first time she had seen him, known him, heard his voice. She was sane, she was in her right mind; she'd surely pay for this, yet she could not stop it . . . stop him. She knew that no matter how long he might keep her prisoner against her will, or how he might clamp down on her attempts to escape, he would stop now if she protested.

Protest, yes, she needed to do so. But she *wanted* this.

His touch . . . his hand, oh, God, his fingers. He parted her, slipped into her, touched, rubbed. She trembled violently, taut, writhing, twisting. Some kind of a sound escaped her, and he shifted. She suddenly felt the trousers pulled free from her body, and she lay naked in the sun and sand and surf except for the ragged tatters of the cotton shirt. And still she couldn't open her eyes . . .

She gasped, startled, as he suddenly caught her knees, parting them. Then he came down between her thighs. His lips and hands roamed her freely, cradling her breasts, igniting them anew with the fiery gloss of his tongue. Then lower, kisses covering the flesh of her belly. She kept her eyes tightly closed as he moved down lower. Teasing her flesh, taunting, arousing. She should be horrified, shocked. She was shocked . . . she was . . .

Sound left her then in a strangled cry, and if she could have spoken, she would have protested at last. But his hands had slipped beneath her, rounding her buttocks, and his tongue moved intimately between her thighs, a fiery liquid seduction on tender innocent flesh that was appalling and marvelous, and so incredibly intense she thought she was dying as searing sensations began to sweep over her . . .

Her fingers tore into his hair, her head thrashed against the sand and at last, so belatedly, words of protest left her lips, even as a budding climax began to throb from her core. He teased, he savored, he played; he ignored her pleas, until she was writhing and arching wildly against him in sheer, mindless abandon. Then he rose, tearing away his wet clothing, coming down again to blanket her with his form. She felt the hard protrusion of his erection where she still burned, yet he paused. She opened her eyes at last, meeting his hard gaze.

"Last chance."

"To . . . ?"

"Stop this."

She closed her eyes again.

"Look at me."

She didn't want to. The hunger he had created was

still wrenching her body. The earth was drumming with the warmth of the sun and the flow of the surf.

"Look at me!" he said again, more harshly.

Her eyes flew open.

"Last chance," he repeated.

She sobbed out a response, clinging to him suddenly, unable to believe that she was lying with him, naked in the sand, needing him so badly. Her enemy.

"You're not making love with Ian," he said sternly, against her ear.

She would have protested then. It was like a cold blanket being thrown over her soul. But it was too late. By the time his words came, she was wrapped in his arms again. And a sudden sharp thrust of his pelvis brought him deeply within her.

Her nails dug into his shoulders; a shriek of mindless agony tore from her lips. She felt as if she'd been knifed. Tears she couldn't begin to control stung her eyes. She stared at the sky, raggedly gasping for breath.

He went still; dead still. He rose slightly, and she felt his eyes on her. He touched her cheek, and she knew that he brushed away a tear. "Risa, I'd never have sought this victory had I known . . ."

Known what? she wondered. She was dazed. The world still spun. She still felt cut in two. His fingers were in her hair, his whisper against her ear. "Easy . . . easy . . ."

He was moving. Slowly. Retreating . . . coming into her fully once again. She choked on her sobs . . .

Then . . . miraculously, the pain began to fade. And he was moving faster. Faster. Filling her. And against that sudden onslaught of anguish, liquid pleasure was taking root once again. She was aware of the tension and strength in his arms and chest, the bronze suppleness of his flesh, the texture of his hair. But mostly, she was aware of the center of the fire, burning with greater fever inside her with every second that passed. She clung to his muscled chest, cheek against his flesh, as she felt the ever quickening fury of his motion within her. Deeper, faster, deeper . . . something building, excruciating, wonderful . . .

A thrust . . .

And the sea exploded inside her, the sun burst into fragments, and she soared over the highest peak . . . and stars cascaded down upon her. Sweet, so sweet, it was achingly sweet . . . it was ecstasy. It left her mindless, eclipsed the sun, the sand, and even the rush of the surf, now washing over their naked legs. She was only vaguely aware of him, still within her, shuddering, collapsing, his warmth mingling with hers, filling her once again with the liquid heat of the sun.

A shimmering glow surrounded her as slight shivers swept through her again and again. She slowly drifted downward until finally, she felt the chill of the air and the surf against her flesh.

He withdrew from her, and she trembled as the breeze touched her nakedness. She kept her eyes closed. She didn't want to have to open them.

It seemed that her life flashed through her mind in vivid mockery. In so many difficult times, she'd been resolutely poised, mature, responsible. The general's capable, competent, admirable daughter. Ah, the lovely Miss Risa! Untouchable. Proud, independent. She'd kept her head high when she'd heard about her fiancé's sudden marriage to another. She'd soothed Ian, and assured him she was fine—when her heart and pride had both been shattered. She'd befriended his wife, been godmother to his child. She risked her own neck to warn Alaina time and again of impending doom. She'd patched up wounded soldiers, emptied bed pans, assisted at amputations, and she'd never faltered.

And now, suddenly, it was as if her facade of control had shattered. She'd made love on a beach with a half-breed Rebel who was nearly a stranger. She'd not had a single thought for propriety; she'd known only that she wanted him. That she'd become transfixed by the bronze of his flesh, the blue of his eyes, the texture of his hair, the sound of his voice. And he'd made love to her with all his being.

"You might have said something," he told her after a moment.

She opened her eyes, and looked at him. His features were taut; his eyes were nearly indigo in the dying light.

She sat up, hugging her arms around her knees, suddenly feeling her nakedness.

"Said something? Such as?" she murmured, staring across the horizon. Strange now how she could feel so many things, when for so long all she had felt was . . .

Him.

"Well, I'd assumed . . ." he began huskily.

"You'd assumed that I'd slept with Ian?" she inquired coolly. "How kind. He married a Southern girl when they were caught in a compromising position—but you assumed that I had slept with him."

He rose, his back to her. He was very handsomely built. His waist and hips were narrow, his shoulders broad and well muscled, as were his buttocks, thighs, and calves.

He stepped into his pants, then turned back to her.

"Risa—Miss Magee, that wasn't a criticism of the morals of a Yankee woman. I know that he was very much in love with you, and you him."

She swallowed hard, looking down at the sand, fighting a new wave of tears that sprang to her eyes.

"And if I am harsh, it is because—although I do love my cousin dearly despite his sorry decision to fight for the North—I do not care to be used as a substitute in his stead."

Risa rose to her feet, turning her back on him to don her trousers. "Trust me, sir, you are a substitute for no man," she murmured under her breath.

She tied the trousers, then reached for the torn remnants of Jeremiah's cotton shirt. "I can't go back!" she whispered suddenly.

"I'm sorry, but you will have to go back—"

"My shirt; it's destroyed."

"Then, take mine."

"I—"

"My breasts don't excite anyone," he assured her dryly.

Her back to him, she managed a smile. He was wrong. His chest was damned exciting.

She felt his touch, slipping the ripped garment from her shoulders and helping her into the damp shirt he'd been wearing. She thanked him, and quickly buttoned the shirt, knotting the hem at her waist for a better fit.

She turned around. He was staring at her.

"I'm supposed to be sorry," he told her.

Her cheeks flamed. "I don't expect you to be sorry—"

"I'm not," he said, then added softly, "I can't be." He inclined his head, indicating his horse. She walked to the animal, with him right behind her. He set her up onto the saddle, then leapt up behind her. They rode back toward the shantytown.

The *Lady Varina* sat in the harbor. Jeremiah waited at a small boat to row them out to her. Little was said as they headed for the ship.

Once aboard, Jerome spoke to her again. "Jeremiah will see to your supper, and a bath. Tomorrow we're going to sail up the coast. I have to pass St. Augustine to get to Jacksonville, and go down the St. Johns there. The river flows south, where we'll leave you with a trusted escort to see that you're brought safely back to St. Augustine. It will take us two to three days at most."

"Thank you," Risa told him. Ah, yes, there it was! She had found her poise at last, and her dignity. She had lost something, yet regained her pride.

She turned and headed for his cabin.

Jeremiah was reproachfully silent as he brought her a meal—and the small ship's hip tub and water. When she had bathed, she knew that she couldn't redon the clothing she had been wearing. She'd all but destroyed Jeremiah's trousers, and Jerome's shirt carried a faint scent of him that was a staggering reminder of the events on the beach. She told herself she wasn't sorry—at least she wouldn't die a lonely, dried-up, bitter old maid. And still, she was oddly afraid, because she would never be the same again, either. She would live with him haunting her dreams forever.

She had no choice now but to wear the garments he had purchased for her.

She remained in the captain's cabin that night. Oddly enough, she slept well.

She didn't see much of Jerome the following day; they rode out a squall, and he was busy at the helm. Toward the late afternoon, when the rains had stopped and only the wind remained, she went up on deck. She was aware of him at the wheel; he was aware of her. He made no attempt to speak.

The wind continued to howl that evening. When she got tired of slamming against the cabin walls as the ship heaved, she carefully disrobed and went to bed early. The rocking soothed her.

Around midnight, the wind died.

Soon after, she heard the cabin door again.

He stood there, stripped down to his breeches, bronze flesh slick with rain, silhouetted now in bright moonlight. Crystal rain droplets fell from his dark hair.

He stepped into the cabin, came to the bed, and looked down at her. He pulled back the covers, and she felt the sweep of his eyes over her length.

He shed his trousers.

He came into the bunk, over her. He bluntly parted her thighs with his knees. She shifted, swallowing hard, her hands against his chest. But he threaded his fingers through hers, drawing her hands to the sides of her head.

"Yankee," he accused her softly.

"Rebel," she replied.

"You are the enemy."

"You're mistaken. You are the enemy." Oh, Lord. She could feel the force of his arousal against her flesh . . .

"I should go," he told her gravely.

"You should," she agreed with no conviction.

"But it's the last night you'll be my prisoner. In my power. To do with as I will."

"Rebel arrogance," she whispered.

"Is that what it is?" he inquired huskily. He freed her right hand, slightly shifting his weight. His touch moved over the length of her body. His fingers lightly dusted her mound. Parted and stroked her sex. Slid into her. She instinctively tried to draw her legs together, yet his body was lodged firmly between them. "I meant to be more honorable—like my Yankee cousin," he mused. "I tried, honestly. But I can't stay away; not tonight," he told her. "Tomorrow you'll be free. The general's proud, untouchable daughter once again. So tonight, well, tonight we'll battle one last time—and God alone knows who really surrendered. Tonight is mine."

She trembled, waiting, wanting. She closed her eyes in the darkness, thinking he would never know how *she* would cherish this night in the void of time to come.

"Open your eyes, Yank."

For a moment she could not.

"Risa."

She opened her eyes slowly. His had somewhat darkened, and there was a tautness about him.

"Ah, well!" he murmured softly. "Tonight, my beloved enemy, I just can't give a damn whom you'd like me to be."

Frowning and quickly enraged, she opened her mouth to form an angry protest. But she never spoke, for his mouth closed over hers with hungry demand, and the passion of her argument was lost to that of his desire. Even as he kissed her, he thrust into her, filling her.

There was no pain. He moved slowly, arousing her with subtle fluid movement and ever increasing rhythm. There was nothing but the sheer pleasure of the heights to which he brought her, and the soft caress of the shadows that enwrapped them, hiding all sins. Anger faded, passion burned.

It was easy to surrender the night.

Chapter 9

Julian McKenzie silently washed his hands, fighting the deep sense of failure and dismay that was settling over him.

He had just lost a patient.

It wasn't that he didn't lose patients often enough; it was war, he did. His would-be patients died half the time before he was able to tend them, since he followed the few troops desperately trying to cause havoc along the St. Johns River. Still, this recent loss seemed especially bitter.

The boy just taken from his operating table had been hit in the foot with stray rifle fire. He shouldn't have died. He'd only been nineteen. Hell, he hadn't even had any facial hair. If he had been hit with a musket ball, he might have survived. Musket balls were slow. They stopped upon impact, perhaps fracturing a bone. But this boy had taken a minié ball—fairly new cone-shaped bullets that flattened out on impact, causing bones to shatter. They were fast enough to do incredible damage, but not fast enough to exit the body. A bone in the boy's ankle had been shattered. He hadn't wanted to lose his foot, so he bandaged up his own injury—and hid the fact that he was bleeding and in severe pain. Julian had been awakened before dawn when the boy's commanding officer had discovered the injury, but by then severe infection had set in.

Julian realized that his pain over the boy was compounded by worry about his own family. The Yanks might hold St. Augustine, but news still filtered across the line. He'd heard that his sister-in-law, Alaina, had been acting as a spy and courier. She'd left St. Augustine, and not returned. Then a Yankee friend of hers,

Risa Magee, had disappeared while searching for Alaina. He hadn't met Risa, but word was that her father, a general with the Union army, was getting ready to take the entire Fed navy to task and demand that his daughter be found.

"There was nothing you could have done." The words were softly spoken. His sister, Tia, was at his side, touching his shoulder. He turned to look at her, about to explain that it was more than this tragic death that so disturbed him. He fell silent instead. Tia was worried enough, yet seeing her there, his heart felt somewhat lightened. There had been a time when many of the South's uppercrust society condemned any young woman who aided the troops as a nurse. Young women would see things they shouldn't see; it simply wouldn't be proper. Many "nurses" did nothing but read or write letters. Not Tia. She worked. She had come to him demanding to help with the war effort.

He was very proud of her. She was beautiful and competent. She'd acquired their father's ebony eyes, while he and Ian had skipped back a generation to inherit their grandfather's deep blue color. Her hair was as dark as her lustrous eyes, while her complexion was pure cream. She was of medium height, slim and vivacious. At the start of the war, Tia's interests had extended to parties, balls, and travel. She'd wanted to see Europe and more, Egypt, the pyramids, and the Yangtze River in China.

But war had come. And though their father would have gladly sent Tia far away then, she remained close to home, and for the last months, she had been with him, working in the field. Their parents would never interfere in such a decision; neither Jarrett nor Tara McKenzie had ever bowed to the opinions of society. Naturally, it was difficult now to remember that he and Tia had argued like cats and dogs growing up. She'd become such an amazing asset. She read, wrote, and cheered the men, helped them through disease and fevers, and even worked well in surgery. She soaked up blood, made bandages, bathed the wounded, and managed to ignore the smells of putrifying flesh and waste.

As a doctor, he'd been lucky; when the Rebs had held

St. Augustine, he'd had his sister-in-law to help, and she had been an excellent nurse. Now he had Tia.

She glanced at the dead boy, her eyes misted, but she looked back to Julian quickly. "His folks—and his wife and infant—live in Ocala," she said quietly. "I wrote two last letters for him. He was anxious none of them learn how fond he had become of tobacco, and he made me promise to burn his poker deck. He didn't want his mother to find out he'd gambled, and he asked me to make sure that his wife and baby would always be able to remember him as a moral man."

"Burn his cards, then, and get some rest. You're wearing yourself out. You can't fight each battle with such energy."

She was silent for a minute. "Julian, we have a brother fighting *for* the Yankees. And it's a known fact our father has always been an abolitionist. If our side does win this war, there are those who might need to be reminded that two McKenzies of Tampa helped keep Southern soldiers alive."

"You work just as hard for the stray Yanks—and you have to admit, you don't always sound like an ardent Rebel."

She shrugged. "If Ian is injured in enemy territory, I pray he will receive the best care. And you're right. I hate the war, it's wrong. It started as a bunch of boys— and old men who thought they were boys—all threatening each other for months on end, determined they could beat each other up at a single show of arms, or in a matter of months! War still rages. Men keep dying. Homes are destroyed; children become orphans. And when it's all over, I might just go to medical school— certainly, there's going to be no one left to marry!"

As she stared at him indignantly, Sergeant Digby, Julian's medical aide, ducked into the canvas tent, which was his field hospital. Digby, who had been United States Army out in the Arizona Territory until his state had seceded, was young and thin and quick. He saluted, noted the dead man, and sobered for a minute, but then spoke excitedly.

"He's coming, sir, he's coming!"

"Digby, who's coming?" Julian asked.

"Captain McKenzie, sir, CSS *Lady Varina*. Don't it just beat all, sir? Those Union ships, so many of them out there, and he just waltzes his ship in and out along the river, as you please!"

Julian glanced at Tia. So far their cousin might be waltzing around as he pleased. But the work was harrowing, and each month that passed, running the blockade became more dangerous. Jerome was suited to the work as few men were. He hadn't been United States Navy—as so many Confederate officers had been—but he'd been a diver, and a shipbuilder. He'd learned his techniques in the great northern shipyards, and he'd modified all that he'd learned for the Florida waters. His *Lady Varina* was his own design. She was light—five hundred tons. She carried seven small guns, three large ones. She could maneuver in the shallows—and she was equipped with both steam and sails, allowing her both speed and reliability. Julian was going to be damned glad to see Jerome. He desperately needed supplies.

"Let's go to Jerome!" Tia said excitedly.

Julian nodded, yet glanced toward the boy who had so recently succumbed.

"I'll see to the lad, Dr. McKenzie," Digby said somberly.

Jerome nodded. He and Tia looked from his tent—concealed by a cover of pines—down toward the river.

It was barely dawn. Naturally, Jerome moved with the shadows. He was a phantom, using the cover of darkness.

The *Lady Varina* was indeed at anchor in the river. The docks at the hospital site had been destroyed again and again, first by retreating Rebs, then by the Yanks, then by the Rebs again. Julian didn't want docks near his makeshift hospital—he didn't want to attract enemy fire to his wounded men. But as he stared out at the ship, he saw several small boats rowing toward the embankment. And there was Jerome, standing in the lead boat, perfectly balanced, legs spread and feet planted wide. He smiled, lifting a hand as he saw his cousin. Like Uncle James, his "half-breed" kin, as his neighbors whispered, Jerome had always fascinated Julian. They were just months apart in age, but when they'd visited

McKenzie property in the far south of the state, Jerome was able to take the lead in many things—he had learned to alligator wrestle with the best, and he could let out a war cry that was chilling straight to the heart.

Julian smiled. Coming toward them, Jerome looked somewhat like Washington crossing the Delaware. He was definitely an imposing figure. He wore no uniform, just cotton breeches, boots, a gray cotton shirt, and scabbard and sword at his waist.

"Captain!" he cried as Jerome stepped ashore.

"Doctor!" Jerome called in return.

But Tia was first. She raced forward, throwing herself into Jerome's arms. He picked her up and spun her around, hugging her close to him. He set her down, and he and Julian embraced quickly.

"It's wonderful to see you. And unexpected. The river has been exceptionally dangerous of late," Julian told his cousin. "But thank God that you are here. We've heard frightening things . . . Pray God, you have some information. Have you heard anything about—"

"Yes, but let me get the cargo moving off the ship, and we'll talk. In private," Jerome said.

Thirty minutes later Jerome McKenzie sat with his cousins around Julian's camp desk in the confines of his makeshift tent office. His men finished the unloading of the supplies he had brought. Despite the Confederate military orders regarding the dispersal of goods, Jerome was determined that most of what he acquired was going to stay in his home state. Especially, when it came to medical supplies for Julian.

As soon as Digby went to fetch coffee for them, Jerome gave them the assuring news they craved.

"Alaina is fine."

"Oh, God, how can you know that? Have you seen her—" Tia began anxiously.

"I've seen her."

"And? What happened?" Tia demanded.

"Alaina was spying and smuggling goods through the blockade, yes, definitely. And the Feds were damned determined to get their hands on her—'the Mocassin.' But—"

"Someone warned her. The general's daughter," Julian said.

Jerome arched a brow. "Yes, how did you know?"

"Because it was known in St. Augustine—after she had departed, naturally—that Risa Magee coerced a young man into bringing her south. I can only assume it was because she was determined to find Alaina. It's a miracle that she found Ian."

"She didn't. Not exactly. She found me."

"Oh?" Julian said.

"But you saw Alaina? And she's really all right?" Tia demanded. "And Ian—you saw my brother! How is he? Jerome, please, tell us everything."

Jerome hesitated. He trusted his family implicitly. But sometimes, it was better that they not know everything.

"I found Ian, and he had found Alaina. Alaina is back on Belamar, and Ian was there, briefly, as well."

"Ian's gone back to war," Tia said bitterly.

Jerome didn't reply.

"And the general's daughter?" Julian pressed.

"Well, she is the real reason I'm here now. I need you to get her across the river for me."

"Ah . . ." Julian said, frowning. "Why didn't you leave her at Belamar?"

"Because I couldn't. She knew where I was going. She was dangerous to me and my men."

"You think that she would have betrayed you?"

"I know that she'd betray me. She's an avowed Yank."

"That doesn't necessarily mean anything," Tia murmured. "She risked her life for Alaina, didn't she? What makes you so certain that she would have betrayed your position?"

Jerome sipped his coffee, feeling knots form in his stomach as he stared at his lovely little cousin who was so determined to stand up for a woman she didn't even know. "Because she assured me she would," he said flatly. Would she still do so? he wondered. Yes. Not out of maliciousness; she simply remained as loyal to the Union as ever. No matter what had happened between them. Sweet Jesus, what had happened? he asked himself. No great mystery. He'd wanted her. He'd simply wanted her. And on her part? He didn't know. Had she willingly been seduced by his similarity to Ian? Maybe the war itself had sent her into his arms. The war made everyone realize that life was short, and uncertain. Lovers died like flies, and with them, a woman's hopes and dreams for the future.

But Risa hadn't instigated what had happened.

Neither on the beach, nor in his cabin.

He had done so. But she had responded to him with such a sweet burning passion that he had become the one seduced.

And he was the one haunted now, wanting her still.

Under normal circumstances, he should have requested her hand in marriage. In the prewar world, she would have been ruined. After all, scandal, not even truth, had brought Ian to the altar with Alaina.

But passionate Yanks did not wed passionate Rebs. And he pitied couples already in that position.

No . . . what had happened was best forgotten. No future loomed before them; she remained desperate to escape him, to reach her beloved north. She would be quite appalled by the concept of marriage to a half-breed, Southern blockade runner. And the truth of it was that she had been seduced by the moment, and a longing to touch something that had once been taken away from her. And still . . .

It was damned hard to let her go. Just thinking of her made his fingers tense around his cup, his muscles tighten, and a pulse tick faster at his throat. He might deeply resent the fact that she had probably succumbed because she could pretend he was Ian, but that didn't dampen the fires she had stirred within him. She instantly aroused thoughts of pure lust in his heart—and yet he thought that it was her eyes he'd remember until the day he died. Sometimes they were green, touched by blue, then blue, touched by green. Sea eyes, glittering, beautiful, changing, aquamarine.

He set his cup down firmly. "While she had knowledge of my movements, I didn't dare release her. She is, however, quite anxious to return to Yankee territory."

Julian leaned forward, about to speak, then he paused

because Digby arrived, bringing them coffee and biscuits. Julian thanked him, and he departed.

"Jerome, I must warn you. I've heard that her father is breathing fire. He knows she left St. Augustine, and I've heard he intends to hunt down and destroy any man—Reb or Yank—who has harmed a single hair on her head. What happened to the fellow who brought her south, by the way?"

"Finn?" Jerome arched a brow. "He was left with a few Yankees on a small island. A Federal ship will pass by soon enough, if one hasn't done so already."

"Ah . . . well, I pity him when the general finds him."

"Since I'm at war with the Union as it is, I can hardly fear the lady's father," Jerome said lightly. "And I'm damned sorry, but she had more information than a dozen spies. There was nothing I could do."

"I'm sure she's unharmed. At least—I hope so," Tia murmured.

Jerome smiled dryly. "Ah, Tia, I'm quite sorry to disappoint you. She fought like a wild cat. I had to do something. Naturally, I had her tied to the mainmast, and ordered my first mate to give her twenty lashes with a cat-o'-nine-tails," he said with a sigh.

Tia gasped. "Jerome, dear God—"

"Tia!" Julian groaned. "Tia, he's teasing you."

Jerome laughed. "Yes, I'm teasing. However, I was damned tempted."

"Where is she now?" Julian asked.

"On board. She was sleeping. Now that we've talked, I'll go back to the *Lady Varina* and bring her ashore. The crew and I will have to be ready to sail come the afternoon; we need to make the open sea right around dusk to avoid the Yanks lurking south of Fernandina Beach."

"Well, if she's the reason you've come, I'm grateful to her. I'm desperately low on morphine," Julian told him. "How long do you think we can continue this war with so few ships, men, and supplies?"

Jerome hesitated, shrugging. "Well, we started off with nothing, a brand-new country, new government— and new navy."

"So fools like you gave over your own property," Tia said.

Both men shot her fierce frowns.

Jerome said sternly, "Tia, the South has virtually no manufacturing. Yes, I offered my ship, and yes, we are often in desperate situations. If we can continue to win battles when we haven't equal men or forces—eventually, politics will give us a victory."

"If!" Tia murmured quietly. She rose and walked away.

They both looked after her.

"We lost a patient we shouldn't have lost today," Julian explained.

Jerome stood. "We lose a great deal that shouldn't be lost," he said softly. "Then again, so does our enemy. Shall I have Miss Magee brought to you here?"

Before Julian could answer, Digby entered again excitedly. "Sir!" he cried. "There's a message from your uncle." He turned about, realizing Julian's uncle was Jerome's father. "Your father, sir."

"My father? What's wrong?"

"Not a thing!" Digby said with a broad smile. "It's just that we're to have another visitor today. Mr. McKenzie has brought Miss Alaina just south of here."

"That's wonderful, Digby, thank you," Julian said. Digby left, and he looked at Jerome. "Ian has sent her here?"

"Because there's still a war going on, and I imagine he's trusting you to send Alaina on to St. Augustine—Union held."

"Yes, of course."

"Risa will be glad to see her."

"Risa—Miss Magee," Julian murmured. "Jerome, I'll have my men greet her farther downriver so she won't know exactly where we are. She and Alaina, both here! Risa was the woman Ian was to marry once. She might have been a McKenzie now if . . . well, you know, if things had been different."

"If things had been different," Jerome murmured dryly. "If you'll excuse me, I'll go make arrangements for the lady."

*   *   *

Morning had come, but Risa still slept, and Jeremiah assured Jerome that she had been left undisturbed.

He stood in his cabin door for a long moment, watching her. She slept on her back, the covers to her waist, her hands delicately lain atop the sheet. Her dark hair streamed out all around her like a deep, fiery blanket, very long. It was a beautiful color, like sable. It contrasted so sharply with her eyes, and the marble of her flesh. Tendrils of hair just curled over her naked breasts, and her nipples, dusky rouge, were sensually half-hidden beneath those soft locks. Her lips were slightly parted, and he studied them. She had a beautiful mouth. Her lips were full, shapely. In repose, she was all but angelic. The length of her was beautiful. Her throat was long, her hands were elegant, her breasts were . . .

Tempting. Ripe . . .

And his prisoner no more. She was the Yank general's daughter. He frowned, realizing that he'd deflowered his enemy's child. Southerners claimed to have such a sense of honor! And surely, he did. If not the proper sense of Southern honor, he knew the difference between right and wrong, and taking the innocence of any man's daughter . . .

She could have said no. He'd given her a chance to do so, hadn't he?

His pulse throbbed, his fingers itched, his body burned.

Her eyes opened then, slowly—thick, dark lashes parting to reveal their aquamarine color, so like the sea. She blinked, then saw him, and frowned, realizing it was day.

"We're here?" she inquired.

"Indeed, you're very close to freedom," he told her, coming to the bed, his eyes intently on her. He saw that a vein in her throat pulsed a rapid beat. Her eyes widened, and she shifted, drawing at the covers.

"You're going to be modest now?" he inquired.

"It's day. And we've arrived," she murmured, lashes sweeping her cheeks once again. Cheeks now stained with color. He brushed her face with his knuckles, and she looked at him.

"Daylight," he repeated, studying her eyes. "The surrender by night is gone."

She smiled suddenly, shaking her head, and he thought there was a hint of tears shimmering in her eyes. "I never surrender to Rebs, Captain."

"Mmm . . ." he murmured, watching her still. Then he asked, "So why did you allow it?"

"Why did you?"

"I don't think that I actually allowed anything—"

"Why did you—make love to me?"

"I couldn't help myself."

"Oh? Good answer, sir," she murmured.

"What about your father?" he demanded.

"I hadn't intended on telling him."

"No, of course not. You wouldn't want to admit to surrendering to the enemy."

"I've never surrendered to any Rebel cause," she said.

"But you don't want your father to know."

"My God, no! Not my father, not—"

"Not anyone."

She lowered her lashes once again. "No, not anyone." She paused. "You're a Rebel, running the blockade. My father is a Union general. And as everyone keeps telling me, this is war. Father will certainly try to find a way to hunt you down as it is. You are the enemy."

"Risa, I'm not afraid of your father."

"You should be."

"Perhaps your father should be afraid of me."

"Thankfully, he fights on land, you fight on sea. But I'm sure he's furious, he'll have all his friends after you—"

"Then, I pity them, because many of them will die. I am good at what I do, and I'm sorry for any loss of life, but when ships clash at sea, there is bloodshed and death."

"That, sir, is my point. You're the enemy."

He nodded, wondering why he was feeling such a brutal knotting sensation again. Every word she was saying was true. Naturally, she wouldn't want any relationship between them known.

"You said you're going to release me," she reminded him quietly.

"Yes," he told her, stroking her hair from her forehead. "But I remain curious. I am the enemy. Point well established. So why did you allow what happened?"

"You—gave me no choice."

"I think I did. Were you playing at what might have been?"

"I don't know what you mean," she said warily.

"Yes, you do. You were in love with Ian. You were in my arms before we even met, thinking that I was Ian. If only I *had* been Ian . . . it would be so different now, of course. You'd be seeking marriage instead of escape."

He was angry, no more than she. Frustrated, desperate, hungry . . . tormented.

"Ian is married," she snapped, eyes narrowing. "But he has the good sense to realize that you Rebels are trying to destroy what can be a great country. He isn't the enemy."

"Ian the valiant! Well, my good cousin has made his choices, as have I. It's established that I am the wretched enemy. So be it. Therefore, I require—no, demand— surrender, before I allow you to escape."

"I don't know what you mean—"

"I think you do," he said flatly. "Surrender," he repeated very softly. "Let there be no question as to your absolute willingness." He leaned toward her, eyes locked with hers. He felt his own pulse, pounding in his ears, against his temples, his throat.

She stared at him, shaking her head. "It isn't surrender, never!" she protested, but her eyes glistened, and she cried out suddenly, throwing her arms around him, and trembling as he clasped her to him in return. He drew the covers down, laying himself over her. He captured her lips in a hungry kiss, thinking how desperate he was, and that so little time had passed since they had been together last. She returned his passion, her lips locked to his, tongue searching into his mouth . . .

How in God's name was he ever going to let her go?

He knew that he wanted what he could not take. And he still had to have her. His lips trailed from hers. He tasted her breast with his tongue, suckling, caressing, teasing just slightly with his teeth, drawing upon the nipple again. Her breathing was ragged, her pulse raced. She tugged at his hair, grazed his shoulder with her teeth, soothed the hurt with her tongue. He rose, covered her length with his kisses, his tongue delving into her navel, creating liquid swirls of heat upon her abdomen. Time was his enemy. He suddenly, firmly, drew her legs apart, and settled between them, stroking, kissing, teasing her thighs, between them. She cried out, tore into his hair, raked his back, pleaded, whimpered, and undulated against him. He ignored her protests until she trembled with a wild, shattering climax. He rose above her then at last, while she was still trembling. He pulled himself free from his trousers, and sank into her, feeling himself sheathed within her, and shaking with the violence of his own pleasure. He made love then with forceful passion, wanting all of her, drowning in her heat and beauty once again. His hands slid beneath her buttocks as climax at last threatened to burst and spill, and his thrusts became harder, fiercer. Her fingers dug into his shoulders, she arched against him, crying out. He inhaled the sweet feminine fragrance of her flesh, coupled with the musk of their lovemaking. He felt her breathing, felt the pounding of her heart. Everything inside him seemed to explode in reckless desperation. He shuddered into her. Again. Again. Clasping her to him, he moved until he could move no more. And still, she clung to him in turn. Then a sudden sob escaped her, and she slammed her fists against his shoulders and gasped, "You are the enemy, you are the enemy, *my* enemy!"

Despite her outburst, he held her gently for a long time, trembling with the aftermath of his climax. For these last few moments, she was still his.

Then at last he rose from her, turned his back, thrusting his shirttails into his trousers and readjusting them. He stood very still, then said, "As you wish, Miss Magee. I'm still the enemy. And you don't surrender to Rebs."

He didn't look back, but spoke to her over his shoulder.

"Jeremiah will see you to shore. You're free." He walked out of the cabin.

And out of her life.

Chapter 10

Risa lay in the cabin for a long time after, dismayed by the anguish that embraced her so fiercely.

She had wanted her freedom from Jerome McKenzie's Rebel hands. She was a Unionist—a passionate one. And yet . . .

When he left, she knew he did not intend to see her again. Ever. She would never forget the cool contempt in his voice when he mocked her. *And you never surrender!*

Yet something of him would never leave her. She'd known him so briefly yet so well. She could conjure his face with her eyes open or closed, she could feel him, see him, breathe him, in her memory, and from the moment he left, she was afraid that the memories would haunt her into eternity.

But, as they both said time and time again, it was war. She wasn't in love, couldn't be in love, and yet she was entangled in a spell of emotion she knew she must deny, must forget, no matter how he had touched her, and left that touch emblazoned deep within her soul.

It was over, best forgotten.

She remained undisturbed in the captain's cabin for some time, shivering, her heart heavy, though she knew she should be celebrating her nearness to freedom. As the day waned, Jeremiah brought her fresh water, and told her he'd bring her ashore before dusk.

As she had expected, she didn't see Jerome again.

He'd imprisoned her, and he was her enemy. She had to remember that.

When Jeremiah escorted her from the ship, she was touched to see that many of the crew members of the *Lady Varina* had assembled to salute her as she left their deck. In her honor, Michael O'Hara and Matt Conor played a poignantly beautiful rendition of "Loralee" on fife and drum. She thanked all the men for their courtesy to her, but she was shaking beneath her facade.

On shore, she was greeted by eight Southern horsemen, and she was startled to find that she knew one of them. He was Grant Jennar, a fine old gentleman with a head full of beautiful silver hair, a full silver beard, and a twirling silver mustache. He was a slim man, ramrod straight, a retired U.S. cavalry officer of the finest sort. He had left her father's company at least four years ago after serving as his aide. She hadn't heard that he'd joined the army of the Confederate states.

"Miss Magee!" Greeting her, he dismounted from his horse.

Risa forgot protocol, and hurried to him, offering him a warm hug. "Sir! How wonderful to see you! I'm so glad—"

"Ah, Risa, now, don't be quite so glad, miss!" he said, warm brown eyes sorrowful as he held her shoulders gently. "I am on the other side; however, I will see to it that you are safely returned to St. Augustine."

"But are you—"

"A captain, my dear, of a newly formed militia unit. A Florida unit." He sighed. "An old enough captain, I pray, that they'll not try moving me and my men northward! Indeed, I mustn't go on, you're a clever young lady and you'll repeat my every word to your father— who is creating quite a stir regarding this incident, I must say—especially for such an old warhorse as himself!"

"I'll see my father soon, I imagine," Risa said politely.

"For now, come with me to our officers' field quarters for a meal. As soon as darkness falls, we'll begin your exchange."

"Exchange?"

"Indeed, my dear, it all worked out quite nicely. We lost a drummer boy to the Yanks last week. Poor lad. I think he was quite terrified. He'd been taught by some fool that Yanks ate drummer boys for supper. Anyway, you'll both be back where you belong come the dawn. We've a horse for you. If you'll mount up, we'll try to maintain some form of Southern hospitality—even if you're not quite a willing guest."

He winked. Another of his men had dismounted, and waited by a sorrel gelding to assist her up. Risa nodded, and accepted the Rebel's assistance. This fellow, though hard and lean and handsome, was aging as well, she thought, and she mused that it was true—the Southern men who were in their prime years were all being sent north to meet the large Union armies bearing down on the South. On the fringes of the war, only old men and boys were being left behind to put up a defense.

She rode alongside Captain Grant Jennar through trails of pines. Eventually, they came to a copse with a number of canvas tents. They dismounted in front of one of the larger tents, and as she did so, Risa nearly fell from the horse—she was so startled by the appearance of a man who emerged from the tent.

It did not occur to her immediately that he was so like Ian, he might have been his twin. She was initially startled instead by his resemblance to *Jerome.*

Naturally, he was a McKenzie, and had to be Julian, Ian's brother.

She tried to recover her surprise quickly—without making too much of a fool of herself or falling face downward into the dirt. He didn't hesitate in his long-legged stride toward her, extending a hand as he did so. "Miss Magee, I'm so pleased to meet you, though I am quite sorry for the circumstances. I'm—"

"You're Julian McKenzie," she said, taking his hand.

He smiled, and shrugged. His handshake was warm and firm. "Yes, well, I've been told that Ian and I do resemble one another."

"The name itself seems to cause a resemblance."

"Do you think so? Well—"

"We're not *all* alike!" a feminine voice declared, and Risa saw a woman near her own height approaching from behind Julian. "I'm Tia McKenzie, Miss Magee."

Tia was different in appearance from her male kin. Her eyes were darker than coal, her skin fair as pure cream, and when she smiled, she possessed very feminine dimples. Her hair was dark as night. Like all McKenzies, so it seemed, she was an extremely attractive individual.

Risa was also struck by the McKenzies' curiosity about

her. They all apparently assumed she'd slept with Ian—
at some time or another. How very, very strange the
truth of the matter was!

"Miss McKenzie, how do you do?" she murmured.

"Call me Tia, please. We become very informal here,
working in the woods."

"Risa!"

She was quite surprised to hear her name called by a
familiar voice. She turned, stunned, as Alaina McKenzie
came flying out of the tent, throwing her arms around
her and hugging her tightly. She pulled back from
Alaina, studying her petite, golden-blond friend, shaking
her head, then pulling her back into a fierce hug again.

"I was so worried about you—" Risa began.

"Oh, well, thank God you were, you might well have
saved my life!" Alaina said, then she fell silent, remembering the soldiers around them, and the fact that Risa
probably didn't want it known that she had risked her
life to save a Rebel spy from the Yankees. "We've supper for you. The folks here have managed to hang on
to a few Florida beef cows, and there's some time before
we go back."

"We?" Risa said.

"Alaina has retired!" Tia whispered softly.

"Thank God for that!" Risa stated dryly.

"Well, I'm not suicidal, and if I didn't change my
ways, Ian would surely throttle me if the Yank army
didn't. I'm going back to St. Augustine with you."

"I'm—delighted," Risa said. "But—how did you get
here?"

Alaina laughed softly. "Ian asked his uncle, James, to
bring me to a beach south of here with letters for Julian,
Tia, and their family. Captain Jennar met me on the
beach and escorted me here."

"Ian had James bring you?"

"There's been no talk of peace yet, has there?" Alaina
asked with a slight edge to her voice. Her beautiful
golden eyes were glazed, as if she might have just been
crying. And Risa understood. Ian had finally forced his
wife to desist her activities as a spy—yet he had gone
on back to war himself. It seemed the way with men.
But Alaina was expecting another baby, and so she

risked the child's life as well as her own on her dangerous missions. And it was obvious, with others around them now, that she didn't want to say more.

"Come on—let's eat," Julian suggested.

The tent was set up as an amazingly fashionable dining room. As they ate, Captain Jennar explained politely that they couldn't let Risa know exactly where they were, and so she'd be blindfolded later, taken along the river, and then exchanged. Other than that, there was little mention of the war except when Grant Jennar asked about her father.

"I have seldom met so fine an officer, and so good a man!" Jennar said with a sigh.

"Sir," said one of his men politely, "we do have some exceptionally fine officers among our own—"

"Oh, naturally, naturally! And sometimes, a fine officer is a good man, and sometimes . . . well, some of them are stubborn pig heads, with no political savvy whatsoever! Diplomacy has always been a better weapon than a sword, but no matter. Angus Magee is a good man, and a smart officer, and I send him my regards, my dear, and look forward to joining him for a meal one day soon, God willing! You will convey my regards to him?"

"With pleasure, sir," she assured him, thinking that he had remained a charming—and an honorable—man himself. Yet still, she was glad when the meal was done at last, and she found herself alone with Alaina, Tia, and Julian, in Julian's medical office tent, sipping bitter coffee with just a wee bit of brandy. They had spirits at the moment, but Julian was very stingy with them, Tia explained, because he never knew when more supplies of drugs or alcohol were arriving.

"Doesn't your cousin, Captain McKenzie, supply you frequently?" Risa could not help but ask.

"Naturally, he tries . . ." Julian said, a half smile curving his lip. "But it's dangerous. Of all the ways to come to Florida, the St. Johns is surely the most difficult. Fernandina Beach crawls with Yankee ships. The action here revolves around the Yanks trying to stop us up. Jerome can't risk direct contact often. He came this time because of you. I don't know when I'll see him again."

Risa looked down into her cup, trying not to feel the warmth that flushed her cheeks.

"Well, it was necessary that he take the risk to bring you in," Alaina said, rising from the camp chair she'd been seated on, and impulsively giving Risa a hug. She knelt upon the rough canvas rug at Risa's feet, meeting her eyes, her own dancing. "Not that I'm not grateful—I am! But whatever possessed you to force Finn—Finn, of all people!—south to try to help me?"

"The thought of you being hanged!" Risa said succinctly.

Alain smiled, yet shivered slightly.

"Well, I didn't hang."

"What did happen?" Risa demanded. The McKenzies looked at one another, and Risa realized that despite all that she had done, they were weighing the wisdom of sharing a family secret with her.

Alaina bowed her blond head slightly. "Ian captured the 'Mocassin' even as I came ashore."

Risa groaned softly. "Yet Jerome found the two of you. But you were injured somehow—"

"I had a friend once," Alaina began. "A man I thought to be a friend, at any rate. War does strange things to people. He seemed to have lost his sanity with it. Anyway, there was a confrontation—"

"Just tell her the truth!" Tia said impatiently. "Risa, they don't intend to make this public knowledge, you know. The man was no friend. He meant to take Alaina and kill Ian. He hated Ian—from before the war. But the man was killed—and he was a Southern officer. Ian *and* Jerome were involved. So you'll understand that we must be discreet."

"Of course," Risa murmured, staring at Alaina, who met her eyes once again. It was one thing for Ian to have killed a Southern officer. It was quite another for Jerome to have been involved.

"But you! I can't believe that you were so wonderful, going with Jerome so willingly—and all to save me!" Alaina said.

Risa hesitated.

"She knew too much," Julian said bluntly.

Alaina stared at her. "Ah . . ."

"Well, it's over, isn't it?" Risa murmured, not wanting Alaina to watch her too closely. She rose, looking at Julian, and to her dismay, she remembered how Jerome had taunted her that first night when she'd thought he was Ian, and she had let him hold her. *She might have bedded him for hours before realizing he wasn't Ian, they were so much alike.* And yet how strange now, she felt nothing, and all because of . . .

Jerome. Time would pass. She would get him out of her mind, soul, flesh, and blood.

"Doctor!" came a call from outside the tent.

"It's time," Tia said tensely.

Risa quickly stood, looking at Tia and Julian. "It's been a pleasure to meet you both—despite the circumstances. I pray the war ends soon, and that we can meet again as friends."

Julian took her hand. "Friends remain, no matter what," he told her earnestly.

"Even if they do have to kill one another now and then," Alaina murmured.

"Ah, but neither blood, nor love, can be dressed in blue or gray!" Tia advised. She smiled at Risa, then hugged her tightly. "You might have been my sister; I'm so glad you are my friend."

"Come on, we've got to go," Alaina murmured.

Risa hugged Tia back. Then, even as she turned, a young soldier came into the tent. "I'm taking you both down the river. If you'll come with me now, please."

Their good-byes then were emotional but quick; Risa and Alaina departed the medical tent with the young soldier. They were joined outside by a cavalry escort—Captain Jennar at the helm. They came to the river, and Jennar bid them good-bye."

A soldier approached her then, a black hood in his hands. "Sorry, Miss Magee, but you are the enemy . . ."

"It's fine; just do it," she said. He slipped the hood over her head, and he led her to a small boat. She was startled to realize that they were blindfolding Alaina as well, but then, Rebel though Alaina might be, she was married to an infamous Yank, and she was going back to live in enemy territory.

It seemed that they were on the water a very long

time. Then she heard someone call out, "Halt! Who goes there? State your business, or get yourself riddled with fire!"

"It's Johnny Reb with your womenfolk, Yank!" their escort called back. Risa could see nothing. She sat very quietly in the boat, listening, while the exchange went on. She was aware of the night sounds of the insects, of the water lapping against the boat, of the men around her, near and far.

She was aware, too, of the men relaxing their guard. "Mrs. McKenzie and Miss Magee?"

"The same. Have you our boy, Donny Murphy?"

"Right as rain. He'll be coming to you!" the Yank called.

"Ladies," their Rebel escort said, "you can remove your hoods. I'll be leaving you the boat. The Yanks are ahead."

Risa and Alaina removed their hoods. "Thanks, Allen," Alaina said.

Their escort nodded in acknowledgment. "You take care, now, Miz McKenzie. Miss Magee," he said, touching his forehead in a salute to Risa.

"Thank you."

He stood carefully in the boat. "Hey, Yank?"

"Yeah, Reb?" came a return call from across the water.

"Sent you some tobacco with the ladies. Could you spare some extra coffee?"

"Thought you might be asking. It's with the lad. He's keeping it dry."

"Fine. Keep your head low, Yank."

"Yep. You keep down, too, Reb."

Their escort hunkered down and slipped into the river. They heard him swimming away. A minute later a dark head appeared in the water, and the Yank who had been with the young drummer boy just minutes before crawled wet and dripping into their boat.

"Ladies, welcome back!" he said.

"Austin!" Risa said, pleased. She knew the man; he was a young second lieutenant who often rode the streets of St. Augustine, keeping the peace, and offering much more diplomacy than many of the other Northern soldiers occupying the town.

"Lieutenant Sage!" Alaina said, smiling. She shook her head, looking him up and down. "What an interesting way to exchange prisoners. You must get soaked frequently."

"Well, we don't exchange prisoners that often, but your friend there, Johnny Reb and I, meet in the river now and then. We make offers to each other upon occasion—bring threats from the brass, and so forth." He smiled. "Exchange coffee and tobacco. Sure hope he and I both make it through this war. I'd like to sit down to supper with him one day."

"Why, that would be nice," Risa said wistfully.

"Umm . . . Miss Magee, thought you should know, Finn made it back to the city along with a group of Union navy fellows turned off their boats by that Reb Captain McKenzie. So naturally, news of your capture raced north. I heard tell that your father is worried sick and breathing fire, and orders are that you're to head straight home the moment you're found. He says he's going to blast McKenzie from the sea, and he'll find a way to do it from his horse, and that's a fact."

"Oh, poor Finn! Thank God, he's all right! And I'll write Father immediately and tell him I'm safe."

"Finn is fine—but I'm afraid a letter won't satisfy your father."

"But I've work to do in St. Augustine. You know that Mrs. McKenzie and I assist Dr. Percy in his surgery—"

"Dr. Percy, that wily old scoundrel, was caught running coded messages to the Rebs."

"Oh," Risa said, staring hard at Alaina, who flushed and looked away. "What a surprise," Risa murmured dryly.

"Indeed," Austin Sage continued. "I'm afraid his patients will be the men with him in Old Capitol Prison. There's a new doc now. Thayer Cripped. Young fellow, seems able enough."

"Then, I'm sure he'll be looking forward to our assistance," Risa said firmly.

Austin rowed, and took a sideways glance at her. "Perhaps. But I've heard tell your father just isn't the same, Miss Risa. Some say as how he hasn't been as sharp in battle as he used to be. Oh, nothing to endanger the men. He commands with care. But as to his own safety . . ."

Risa inhaled deeply, biting into her lip. She lowered her head, wondering if she hadn't lost her mind. Tears stung her eyes. Her father was everything to her. He'd raised her with love, taught her to think, and been proud of her accomplishments. He hadn't raised her as a son, he'd raised her as a daughter with the same capabilities for learning and reason. She loved him dearly, and naturally, he loved her. How could she have been so thoughtless? She had to go home, see her father, and thank God that, despite the war, they still had each other.

"Forgive me," she murmured. Alaina reached across the boat, squeezing her fingers, and Risa remembered that it hadn't been long since Alaina had lost her own father. She smiled at her friend, then addressed Austin. "I'll make arrangements for the first ship north—"

"There's a ship north tonight, Miss Risa. And you've been booked aboard."

"Thank you." She looked at Alaina. There were tears in her eyes.

"You'll come back!" Alaina said softly.

"I belong in the North."

Alaina shook her head. "We're all linked. Somehow. I can feel it. You will come back, I can feel it, Risa."

Maybe. For now she was going home. Home—to Washington. She'd see Angus, whom she adored, and who loved her in return. She was safe, she'd be among her own people, and she could forget a certain Reb captain. And yet . . .

A terrible sense of emptiness haunted her. She was free, she reminded herself dryly. Free—from her enemy.

Yet she had never felt such a strange imprisoning weight upon her soul in all her life.

Chapter 11

Four weeks later, after a run to Bermuda, the *Lady Varina*, Captain Jerome McKenzie at the helm, defied the Union ships on her tail and made it into port at Charleston. It was one of the hardest runs to make, and despite the fact that he chose dusk to slip past the blockaders, he was seen. The Yanks were swiftly on his tail.

He called out the order to Mr. Douglas to come quickly about and return fire. Against the dying light the cannon fire was brilliant. The first Federal ship on their tail was hit; injured, it listed away. Jerome roared out an order to fire again; guns blazing, he then made for port with all available speed, shouting for a damage report. The element of surprise in his aggressive counterattack had confused the rest of the Feds, and no one else gave chase. The *Lady Varina* had been hit—a blow to her mainmast and upper aft deck. Still, she was soundly built, and had the strength remaining to fly over the water with tremendous speed and head for the safety of the Rebel guns protecting the harbor—and his ship—as they limped the final distance to port.

A crowd had gathered by the time the *Lady Varina* docked; men and women cheered their death-defying deed—and lined up to see what goods they carried.

"We've attracted quite a crowd," Hamlin Douglas warned Jerome, sharp eyes scanning the dock. "Could turn ugly."

"Come, now!" Dr. David Stewart protested. "These are the good Confederate citizens of Charleston!"

"Good citizens—who are besieged by Yankee gunboats. Good citizens lacking provisions—and luxuries.

It's the luxuries they grow surly about," Hamlin said,
sadly shaking his head.

"Well, we must remind them, then, that luxuries must
be sacrificed for morphine," Jerome said flatly. Grasping
one of the mainmast tie ropes, he crawled halfway up
the mast. Using the rope for balance, he cried out to the
crowd, sweeping the people a half bow from his towering
position. "Ladies, gentlemen! The crew of the *Lady Varina* and I do extend our heartfelt gratitude for your en-
couragement, support, and prayers. However, we do sail
as a Confederate states ship—and ladies, I'm afraid we
carry no bonnets or stockings!"

There was a groan from the crowd, and then laughter.
A young woman, beautiful and bold in a low-cut evening
dress, called out in good humor, "Not a single pair of
silk stockings, Captain?"

"Not a single pair, ma'am, yet had I only known that
you were coming to greet the ship, I'd have made certain
that we brought at least one set!"

"Careful, sir!" cried the young woman's father. "We'll
be having an engagement here and now!"

Laughter rose again. "Ladies and gentlemen, again,
thank you one and all!" Jerome called, then made a leap
to the deck. As he landed, he discovered Major Jenson
had come aboard. He was a prematurely graying man
stationed at Charleston since he had lost a leg fighting
with Lee's Army of Northern Virginia.

He greeted Jerome warmly.

"Captain, seems as if you and your crew are going to
have to spend some time in our fair city, seeing as how
your ship will have to sit in for repairs."

"I look forward to it." Jerome smiled. "I've kin in
your fair city. My mother hails from this region. We've
a family home just on the outskirts."

"Yes . . . I've heard of the place. I've met your sister
and brother. However, sir, you are aware, your brother
is with Lee's army, and your sister is living in
Richmond."

"Yes, I've heard."

"But as it happens, my family owns a great deal of
property hereabouts. You and your men are welcome to
our brand of hospitality on the Battery. There, across

the courtyard, is our family hotel, and we do hope you'll abide there. As guests of my family, naturally."

"Sir, I'm not sure that I could accept such generosity for so many—"

"Captain McKenzie, it's well-known that you don't fill your hold with bonnets and silk stockings, and many a Reb is alive because you've given so little thought to your own gain. It will be our honor if you'll accept our invitation." He grinned suddenly. "Besides, we've been used as a hospital often enough already!"

"Well, then. Thank you. But if my ship is to be laid up for any amount of time, I think my men and I will find other accommodations."

"Sir, the railroads can take you straight to Richmond, if you've a mind. But now, edging up toward enemy territory, you might want to have a care."

"How's that?"

Jenson grinned. "Why, sir, you are the talk of the Northern papers."

Jerome frowned. "Why?"

Jenson's grin deepened. "Come along, sir. We'll have supper, and arrange your transportation And I'll show you what they're saying."

Jenson's family was indeed well off. An hour later Jerome and the major, a few fellow officers, and some townsfolk, including the stocking-seeking beauty—a charming flirt—gathered around the cherrywood table in the elegant dining room of a waterfront town house. A snowy cloth covered the table, the china plate was from England, the silver heavy and embossed. The wine was served in the finest hand-cut crystal.

The meal was whitefish, expertly prepared, along with an early summer harvest of vegetables. They did well enough on board ship, thanks to Evan Dieter's culinary expertise, but Jenson's Madeira was excellent, his whiskey even better, and the food was flavorful and fresh. Still, Jerome hadn't discovered just what was being said about him in Northern newspapers, and he didn't find out until the men had retired to the den for brandy and cigars.

"Major Jenson," Jerome said, seated with a cigar and

snifter, "I spend a lot of time at sea, out of communication. May I see these papers you mentioned?"

"Why, Captain, naturally." He winked, and pulled a pile of papers off his desk. "Here's the Washington paper . . . and one from New York . . . and Boston. Harpers is right here."

Jerome accepted the stack, looking over the articles. He was stunned to have received so much attention, then infuriated.

General Angus Magee had been astoundingly vocal after discovering his daughter's disappearance from St. Augustine. He accused the Southern navy men of being barbarians. He called Jerome "a savage pirate, and no true gentleman of any nation." Any righteous father, North or South, should shoot him on sight.

He set the papers down, seeing red.

"Perhaps I shouldn't have shown you," Major Jenson said unhappily. "Most of us find the stories more amusing than anything else."

"Indeed!" thundered Pierce Thompson, the gentleman with the beautiful daughter. "What was his young lady doing floating out in enemy waters? No self-respecting man would allow his daughter to run wild like that."

Jerome tried to smile in return to his ardent defender. "Ah, well—the New York papers mention my father's Seminole blood, which, according to the paper, explains why I am such a barbaric savage," he said dryly.

"Any military man knows you had no choice in the matter," Jenson said matter-of-factly.

Thompson laughed softly. "And, sir, if I may tell you, the story has captivated the ladies. They are not at all appalled as chaste young women should be—they are all eager to be swept away to sea!"

Jerome kept smiling. Teeth clenched.

"Why, not even the young lady's own article did a thing to convince your countrymen you were anything but right and gallant."

"The young lady's own article?"

"Yes, in the *Tribune* . . . there! So sorry—I forgot to give you that one."

Jerome kept his temper and accepted the paper. The reporter had apparently caught up with Risa Magee in

Richmond. It seemed the young reporter had become instantly enamored of Risa—he raved about her beauty, courage, and capabilities as "she sat her horse with fluid grace, eager to be reunited with the general, her father, after her terrifying excursion out to sea with a Southern savage." Naturally, she had been swept away against her will and cruelly imprisoned. She prayed earnestly that God would stand for the Federal forces fighting His battles—and that naturally, God would smite her cruel enemy. She said nothing about being seduced—forcefully or otherwise. Every other paper hinted at ravishment.

He set the paper down, trying to keep his hands from shaking.

"Sir, you've now acquired a reputation that does keep the ladies intrigued!" Trilby Harris, a captain of artillery told him enviously.

"But then again, they do say old Angus is out for blood," Jenson told him, still amused.

"You know 'old' Angus?" Jerome asked him.

Jenson nodded. "Served with him, cavalry, right up until I resigned my commission with the United States Army to come home and serve my own state. He's a fine old gentleman—but he sure does dote on his daughter. Then again, so did every man-jack one of us, sir. Miss Risa is a fine lady. Stunning woman, absolutely stunning. Independent, assured, and uncommonly smart. Why, the men would be spouting off sometimes, and Risa would step in and quietly point out where we were all a group of complete asses! I was halfway in love with her, along with so many other men, except that, before the war, well, we all thought that there was going to be an engagement between her and Ian Mc—" He broke off awkwardly.

"Between her and my cousin?"

"Yes," Jenson said. "But apparently, they were just good friends." He sighed. "If I could only go back! She's a woman to warm a man's dreams! Her eyes, sir . . . pools of purest blue heaven! She's a classic beauty—"

"Indeed," Jerome muttered.

Jenson lifted his glass. "Wish I'd been in your position, sir!"

Jerome didn't have a chance to reply because Jenson's maiden aunt burst through the doors, daring to disturb the men. "Gentlemen! We do hope you are enjoying your cigars, but it's so seldom that we ladies have so many handsome men about. If you'll be kind enough to join us for some dancing, we've found some fellows to oblige us with some music!"

"Ladies, our pleasure!" Trilby cried enthusiastically.

Jerome stood slowly, flexing and unflexing his fingers. He didn't seem to really hear what was being said; he went through all the right motions on instinct and training alone.

It was Matt and Michael from his ship who provided the music, some dance tunes, and a lot of old Irish ballads. Naturally, they played "Dixie," "Loralee," and other haunting songs.

Jerome noted wryly that his "savage" reputation had indeed enhanced his popularity. He was surrounded by the ladies through the evening, and amazingly, even with doting parents nearby, he found himself more than subtly propositioned a number of times. It was, however, the beautiful brunette, Janine, Pierce Thompson's daughter, who lured him most boldly.

The hour was growing late; they danced out onto the porch, overlooking the beauty of the Battery. Sky and sea were blue, deep but different shades.

"It's a long and bitter war, Captain," Janine told him, dancing close, her fingers playing with his hair at his nape, her hazel eyes wide on his. "It makes life far different than I had ever imagined."

"True enough," he agreed.

"I remember when it was all play," she mused. "When I didn't know whether to marry Lawrence Danson, William Rufus, or Sydney Malone. I wasn't sure who would be the richest, the kindest, and the most powerful politically. Now it doesn't matter in the least. William died at Manassas, Lawrence died at Shiloh, and Sydney was just killed at a place called Seven Pines."

"I'm deeply sorry," Jerome told her.

"I'm very lonely," she told him.

At that moment her father arrived on the porch, and managed to cut in most opportunely on their dance.

Though he was heading out first thing in the morning to visit his sister, Sydney, and search the Virginia battlefields for his brother, Brent, he was to stay that night in Major Jenson's fine Battery house. He lay in bed, naked, staring at the ceiling, when she arrived, slipping in by the balcony window. She wore silk and approached him hesitantly at first, then more brazenly, sitting by his side. She was feminine and alluring, and the sheet covering him tented as he instinctively rose to the occasion. But when she bent to him, offering an awkward kiss, he caught her arms and set her back. He desired her because she was there and he had liked her, but there was something wrong. He didn't intend to get into a habit of deflowering decent young ladies. And it was more than that as well. The passion that had driven him to Risa Magee was lacking. He was tempted to make love to Janine just to force himself to feel that passion, yet he did not.

"I know you want me," she whispered, and touched him, stroking the extent of his arousal.

Again, he set her away. "And one day, when the war is over, you'll want the right man," he told her firmly. And he rose then, heedless of his nakedness, seeing her back to the balcony door.

"I may not be so innocent as I appear!" she whispered, and there were tears in her eyes.

"And I may not be quite so jaded as I appear," he told her gently. He kissed her forehead. "Go to bed. Your own bed."

With a sigh and a shiver, her eyes sweeping over the length of him, she at last bid him good night. When she was gone, he remained. The breeze on the dark balcony was cool against his nakedness. He gave himself a shake at last. He'd gone daft. A beautiful woman had thrown herself at him—and he'd sent her away.

He lay back down. Perhaps he hadn't been all that magnanimous. Perhaps he'd simply grown leery of so-called decent women. The only honorable women might be those who charged for their services.

He'd always taken great care with his relationships. Leaving the innocents alone—innocents! Like the general's daughter who had so defamed him in print that his name was now known across the whole of the country-side, North and South.

He lay awake, his temper soaring anew as he remembered the newspaper articles. When he got his hands on her again . . .

If he got his hands on her!

The length of him was afire. Muscles, flesh, and blood—all seemed to ache. He'd had the opportunity to do something about the pent-up tension within him—but he had refrained from the opportunity. Because of Risa. Because of wanting to strangle her. Because of *wanting* her.

It was insanity. After the things she had said . . .

He would get his hands on her again, he determined angrily. And if she meant to write damning articles about him, well, then . . . by God!

He'd sure as hell see to it that he did something for her to write about!

It didn't much matter where in time and place men were wounded—or who they were.

And it didn't much matter what color they wore when bullets ripped into muscle and bone, when sabers tore open flesh and veins.

Injured men, North and South, were much the same. They suffered the same, bled the same, screamed the same—died the same.

That was a lesson Risa learned very soon after arriving in Washington, and being brought to her father.

Despite the anguish and the pain it caused her, Risa was glad to tend to the men. Despite the horrors she faced, she was grateful. She was well aware that many so-called "society" families were adamantly opposed to young ladies working as nurses. It was totally indecent for them to be near the soldiers in any intimate way, seeing men in less than a complete stage of dress. Thank God for her father.

In many ways.

Returning to Washington had been far more over-whelming than she had ever imagined. She'd not stepped foot off the sloop that had brought her down the river before she'd been besieged by reporters. She'd thought she'd been close to truthful and careful and extremely calm when she'd spoken—somehow, her words had all been twisted, and the stories she'd seen after were enough to make her skin crawl. If she were ever to meet with Jerome McKenzie again, he would probably skin her alive on the very spot. In the Northern capital, however, she was a heroine. She was invited to tea at the White House, where she tried again to put a calm perspective upon everything that had happened. But people were eager for high seas adventure that didn't include blood, and so, she was a valiant heroine trying to secure valuable information for the North, and Captain Jerome McKenzie became a savage Rebel with wild Indian blood determined on kidnapping an innocent young woman and having his way with her. Despite the friends she was able to see, she quickly fled Washington. Besides, her father couldn't get to her; he was embroiled in the Peninsula Campaign, and to see him, she had to go to him.

Once Angus had greeted her—dismissed his men and held her with warm, wet tears in his eyes until he all but crushed her bones—they had talked. She had told him that she was fine, that Ian's cousin had done nothing cruel to her, but Angus remained infuriated that any man had had the effrontery to abduct his daughter. He wanted her safely back in Washington, traveling no more. But she had stood her ground, insisting she couldn't keep house throughout the war. And he had sternly painted her a picture of how many possible future in-laws might view her medical service if she insisted on following the army as a nurse. Once she had informed him firmly that she did not care—she couldn't bear the duration of the war if she couldn't do something useful!—he had been entirely supportive.

Not that following the army was easy. Union troops outnumbered Southern, but chasing the Rebs was tedious and difficult. For her ears alone, Angus was sometimes willing to admit that the army had lost many of its best and brightest officers to the Confederacy. The soldiers fell prey to disease far more often than they fell before bullets. Summer complicated their problems. The heat was sometimes terrible; the mosquitoes were often hungrier for blood than either Northern or Southern troops. Malaria, smallpox, dysentery, and other fevers worked havoc on the men. They engaged in a "Peninsula" campaign while McClellan sought with little success to take Richmond.

Some days were nothing but marching and fighting disease. Some days brought minor skirmishes. Some days brought major battles, horrible wounds, and death. To a dying soldier, it didn't much matter. Whether injured by gunfire or laid low by disease, it was terrible to hear the screams of the wounded, the cries of desolation when a man learned he must lose a limb in order to survive. Worse were some of the cases of sexual disease. Nothing was worse than the sight of a soldier dying in the last stages of syphilis. Along with army life came camp followers, and soldiers, scared and lonely and never knowing when death might come, were often eager for entertainment.

Still, following the army kept her close with her father. And working with Doctor Abe Tanner, the old physician and surgeon who served her father's men, kept her busy as could be—too busy to do much brooding. She might have fared better if it weren't for the summer's heat and what it seemed to do to food. All during the remainder of June and into July, she was sick—a fact she kept hidden from her father and the men. She didn't dare let her father know that there were times when the sight of blood completely nauseated her. Or that she did, upon occasion, run from an amputation, unable to stomach the soldier's agony and cries.

Life with the army was not easy. But she had tasted the real metal of war. And she could never go back to quilting again.

They were always on the move. But in June, on a night when the guns were still, the medical corp took over an abandoned house. Late that evening, while she sat in a handsome old winged-back chair reflecting on the war, she was startled to hear her name softly spoken by a familiar voice. When she turned around, she cried out, incredulous to see that Ian McKenzie was standing at the entrance to the room. She rose, rushed to him, and hugged him gladly. He held her close in return, swung her about, and at last set her down.

"Ian! How can you be here? You're safe and sound. I'm so glad to see you. Would you like whiskey? Has my father seen you? What of Alaina? I haven't heard from her. But I haven't tried to write, either, it's been so very busy here!"

"I'd love a whiskey."

She poured him a drink from a decanter on the occasional table by her chair. She handed it to him, and he urged her to return to relax as he sat in a sofa near her. "Sit, now, rest—I know you must be exhausted. I hear you work without stop. Do you know what the soldiers call you?"

She arched a brow. "Nothing evil, I hope?"

He laughed. "General Angel. They say you can dictate orders with the best, but that you've a healing touch unknown to most mortal women—and you look like an angel, with just a hint of a redhead's sweet wickedness."

"Any woman looks good out here, Ian."

"And you look good anywhere, Risa. Except that you're far too thin."

"I'm fine. We're all a bit thinner. Tell me, please, anything you know."

"About the war?" he queried dryly. "Well, let's see, General Pope is hated by the South and North, and yet he thinks that he will eventually halt good old Southern Stonewall Jackson in the Shenandoah Valley while McClellan takes Richmond. The generals fight among themselves like children, and my old mentor, Robert E. Lee, is watching us all and weighing his chances. We outnumber the Rebs by thousands, and yet we wage war knowing that we can lose a thousand men to their hundred and eventually win anyway—it's insanity! What else can I tell you?"

"Alaina?"

He smiled. "I saw her a few weeks ago, and she is fine, but misses you a great deal. She said I must beg you to come back if you are able. All the men have been stripped from Florida, she says, and if the Yanks are to hold St. Augustine, then you should be among them."

She smiled. His hand was in hers, and she idly rubbed the rugged, cavalryman's palm.

"I wouldn't mind going back. I loved St. Augustine. But I'm useful here."

"And not bitter?"

"About what?"

"About Jerome?"

She shrugged dismissively. "Oh, the papers were hungry for scandal rather than more death. It's all in the past—I barely remember it," she lied. "Have you seen my father yet?"

He winced. "Yes."

"What's wrong?"

Ian grinned, blue eyes dancing. "He's quite livid. I guess you haven't seen the story yet. Jerome was interviewed by an English paper and the English paper in turn lambasted Yankees for carelessness—and poor parenting. And you became a notorious spy—deserving of whatever befell you in Southern waters. Naturally, Lincoln and this war have enemies, so the story is again running throughout all the Northern papers. Strange— you've been quoted as replying to it all, and stating that Jerome McKenzie is a Rebel savage, and there's no more to be said."

She stood abruptly, incredulous that others dared speak for her. Snatching up his empty whiskey glass, she threw it across the room where it smashed into the fireplace.

"Risa, hey, come here!" Ian said, gently taking her into his arms to soothe her. "You can't control what people say."

"I shall sue for libel!" she stated.

"I'm sorry I told you, but your father is in quite a state—I thought he was going to run me through for being Jerome's cousin. Come on, sit with me, I've only tonight, then I head back to join my troops again. I came to Washington for new orders, and I was given a few days leave here to visit friends. You are still my friend?"

"Of course." She hesitated a moment. "Of course. The rest of your family is well?"

"Indeed, from what I've heard. We've been blessed, thus far. My brother and sister are fine. My cousin Brent is with Lee's army facing us here, and he is well. And my cousin Sydney is in Richmond, tending the wounded there. It helps, of course, that the majority of my family are involved with medical corps, though canisters and grapeshot are blind when they spew death upon the fields. Only Jerome—" he began, then broke off.

"Jerome defies the blockade—and death—daily."

He shrugged.

"Have you heard from him?" she tried to ask casually.

"I've heard he put into Charleston against great odds and that his ship is undergoing repairs there." He looked at her unhappily. "I believe he is well. I hope so. I'm sorry. He is my cousin, and my parents were quite fiercely determined—having survived the Seminole wars—that we would understand the bonds of family, and love. So I do love him, and therefore, I must be concerned for his welfare."

"Naturally," she murmured.

"You told me you weren't bitter."

"Of course not. However, if he were to be taken to rot in a prison for the remainder of the war, I'm afraid I wouldn't be at all distressed. In fact, if he were fed gruel and water for the next decade, I'd not mind a whit. Perhaps he could be hung up by his toes, and beaten daily with a whip."

Ian laughed. "Ah, well, you're definitely not bitter. I can see that the two of you quickly became fast friends!" He sighed. "Was he really that wretched?"

She hesitated. "I was a prisoner."

"You went with him willingly."

"What should I have done? Had you defend me? Kill him—have him kill you? I—"

"You what?"

"I did know his plans. And I would have taken them to the Union as quickly as possible."

Ian nodded, looking down at their hands. "Ah. But I ask again, was he that wretched? He might have been raised in the swamps along with kin who often claim alligators as family members, but he was raised a gentleman, despite his wild streak."

"He kept me a prisoner, and did not let me go. In time," she said, whispering the last.

"Pardon?"

"Nothing—it is in the past."

"You both did what you did for Alaina and me, and I am so grateful. Come, friend, let's forget the war for a while."

They sat on the sofa together then. She leaned her head on his shoulder. They held hands. She closed her eyes, and thought about how much she cared for Ian. And she thought about what might have been. But even caring about Ian, she knew that she had never known anything like the fire she felt when Jerome touched her with his eyes alone.

She asked him about Alaina again, and he told her that his wife was growing round with their second child, and he said again that he wished Risa could be with her. Risa told him that she'd met his sister and brother, and that they'd been charming. And they talked and talked while the night passed by. In the end they dozed sitting side by side for perhaps an hour. Then General Angus Magee came into the room with the dawn. He cleared his throat with a roll of thunder, and Risa awoke, jumping. Ian had heard Angus enter, and when Risa was steady, they stood together. Angus shook his head. "Daughter, what shall we do with you? The gossips will have all the more to say!"

"Sir, it's entirely my fault—" Ian began.

"Indeed! It is your fault. Damn your family, man!" Angus said, shaking.

"Now, Father," Risa said, approaching him. She slipped an arm around him. "Ian is my friend. And he served as your best horse soldier for years."

Angus gritted his teeth. "Indeed, Ian McKenzie. But you should have known better than to spend the night with Risa! You two have been alone for hours—the soldiers will talk."

"People will always talk," Risa said, somewhat amused.

"Risa, dear Risa! Your reputation is already in shreds!" Angus said, distraught. "What happens, my dear, when you do fall in love and wish to marry?"

"Father, if I discover I have fallen in love with a man who listens to gossips, I will fall right out of love."

Angus shook his head unhappily. "You're young, and rash, and you're not seeing the future clearly. Love isn't planned, child, and we can't turn it on and off. And as to you, young man! What would your poor wife say, Ian McKenzie?"

"Not a word, for she values Risa as her best friend as well. My deepest apologies, sir, for whatever discomfort I have caused you." He saluted. Then he came to Risa and tenderly kissed her cheek. "Keep yourself well." He looked back to Angus. "Guard her carefully, sir. She is one of the greatest assets to our cause!"

"Guard yourself well, Ian McKenzie!" Angus ordered gruffly. Then he left his daughter's side for a moment to briefly embrace Ian. Ian winked to her, and left.

"I shall say no more on the matter, Risa, but you must take greater care," Angus warned her, deeply distressed.

"Ian remains my good friend."

"If only you'd married him! I had thought that you two young people were growing so close!"

"It wasn't to be, Father."

She smiled, smoothing the furrow from his brow. He was wonderful. She was thankful that he was a general, because though he led troops, generals seldom rode in at the front. She knew that he would willingly risk his own life before that of his men, but warfare was a chess game. Castles were more valuable than pawns, and generals were often up on the heights—directing the fire below.

Angus cleared his throat. His eyes, so often blue fire when he commanded his men, were powder soft when he looked at her, gently touching her hair. "It's just that I love you, daughter. The war has changed some things, but you mark my words, decent families will still require chaste wives for their sons! The scandal that has ensued from that wretched cousin of Ian's is disastrous!"

"Father—the scandal made me a heroine, when I didn't deserve applause in the least. They dubbed me 'Lady Liberty.' "

"They all wonder what that rogue did to you as well!"

"Father, I was not forced into anything," she said carefully.

He sighed deeply, then hugged her to him. "Your

mother has been dead a long time, Risa, but there's still so much I remember, there is so much of her alive in my heart! I lost her, but I learned what love was, and it has been a precious memory all these years. I want that for you."

"Oh, Father! I will have it. You must see it this way, then. I will be loved for me, for what I feel and think and do, and not for my reputation!"

He sighed. "There is no arguing with you. You must do me a favor, then. The next time Ian is about, you can be friends in the company of others. Is that a fair request?"

"Indeed, Father."

"Well, to breakfast then, shall we?"

"Yes, for my time with you is equally cherished!" she said, and arm in arm they went off to his command tent.

Chapter 12

Despite the threat of troop movements throughout the South, the railroads brought Jerome quickly and fairly efficiently to Richmond. There, he found that his sister, Sydney, had taken an apartment in the home of an old family friend, and that—despite the refugee situation in the Southern capital—she had use of a guest room for him.

"I can't stay long," he warned her.

"But you must stay a few days!" she told him, hugging him fiercely. He was glad to see her, and find that she was doing so well. Sydney was exotically beautiful with their mother's green eyes, their father's heavy, blue-black hair, and a hint of Seminole blood in her delicately sculpted features.

"I'm not so sure you should be living here alone," he told her gruffly. "I'm surprised Father allows this—"

"Father allows this because I am actually living under the care of old General Payne, one of the few men he admired during the Seminole War. And I'm near Brent this way. And I've promised to come home by Christmas. And as long as I behave—"

"Are you behaving?"

"Am I behaving? I am an angel. I've been taken under the wing of none other than the First Lady herself, Varina Davis. Naturally, I met her first because they heard that I was your sister. Oh! And did you know, Jefferson Davis was quite fond of our errant Yankee cousin, Ian!"

"Davis was secretary of war when Ian was serving in Washington. They were social acquaintances, if not friends."

"Well, I'm behaving, but what about you?" Sydney asked.

"I run the blockade—and you should belong to a bandage-rolling society!"

"Indeed? I think not! My half sister was nearly hanged as a spy, my *female* cousin is working as a nurse, my cousin-in-law has just retired from a dangerous life of espionage, and my *almost* cousin-in-law was—according to the papers!—swept away and ravished by my own brother! And I should roll bandages!"

"Sydney—"

"*Did* you ravish the general's daughter?" Sydney demanded.

"Little sister, mind your manners. Or I'll see to it that our father comes after you!" he warned.

"You wouldn't dare!"

"It's an older brother's responsibility."

"I merely seek the truth," she said primly, then she smiled wickedly at him. "Oh, Jerome! It's really quite grand. They call you a pirate, a cavalier! You're incredibly popular, you know. You'll see—we've a supper to go to tonight."

He groaned. "Sydney, no socials! I came to see you—"

"We've been asked to the White House of the Confederacy," she said. "Do you turn down the President and his lady?"

"No," he said wearily. "We go to supper."

He didn't really mind formal occasions at the White House, which he had attended before. Tall, gaunt Jefferson Davis was not known for a warm, easy nature, but he was a hard worker who meant well, an intelligent man, if not always a reasonable one. His wife, Varina, was tall and buxom, beautiful, and very warm. The doors were most frequently open, and she loved to entertain. She was known to be gentle with servants and slaves, diplomats and generals. What Davis lacked in the social skills, Varina provided for him.

He and Sydney ran late that evening, and had scarcely been greeted in the foyer and offered a sherry before it was time to sit down to the meal—which, as it turned out, was in Jerome's honor for the many supplies he had brought into Charleston. Davis himself, gruff and immaculate in black, lifted his glass to the Southern Pirate of the Caribbean Sea, and Jerome was applauded and congratulated. The women in attendance were charming. One young lady, a relative of Varina's, told him that all military men should be married—since battle threatened their lives, they should see to the business of leaving heirs behind.

A butler brought by a serving tray of summer vegetables, and as he helped himself, Jerome realized that his plate lay unevenly. He moved the plate, and was startled to see a folded note beneath it. Drawing the paper out, he discreetly opened it, and found a message addressed to him.

Captain McKenzie, Southern Pirate, you are a dead man for the abduction of and the cruel dishonor done Risa Magee. Look to your own, for revenge will be sweet.

"Trouble, Captain?" the young lady to his right whispered, eyes aglow.

"No," he lied. "Just a message." But he felt again as if his blood were boiling. The cruel dishonor done Risa Magee!

Dear God, if he could but get his hands on her once again! It was startling to realize how this threat disturbed him. Yet he had to hold onto his temper, respond calmly to all accusations. He could not go completely berserk and *savage* and charge into enemy lines until he had found her.

Later, over port and cigars, he asked one of Davis's aides how the note might have come to be under his plate.

"Sir, I don't know. Our own Jeb Stuart manages to get notes to his father-in-law—who did not leave the Union army!—under his breakfast plate in Washington. It's a dangerous war, sir. I can look into it. Were you threatened?"

"Yes, but I feel that I can deal with threats against myself—supposedly, half the Union navy is out to blast me to Kingdom Come. But this is a dangerous situation.

President and Mrs. Davis do not need traitors so close upon them."

Despite his desire for an early night, it was difficult to leave as Sydney was flirting with a cavalry officer. He chastised her as they left, knew that he sounded like their father, and then realized that he was worried. He had enemies. Enemies who could get notes to him at the White House?

His sister went on to their rented carriage while he bid a cordial good night to their host and hostess. As he started down the steps and out to the street, he frowned, seeing that their carriage was rolling off without him.

A split second later he realized that his fears were being realized—someone was attempting to steal Sydney right before his eyes, in front of the White House of the Confederacy.

"The carriage!" he shouted, aware that the President's home was surrounded by soldiers who would spring to action behind him. He was in formal attire, but his dress sword hung from his scabbard. A handsome black gelding had been left tethered by the street. He sped the few feet to the animal, leapt into the saddle, and raced after the carriage. In a matter of seconds he had caught up with the vehicle. He jumped from his mount to the driver's seat, where he engaged in a struggle with the young, bearded driver for the reins. The driver pulled out a bowie knife, swiping at Jerome with the deadly weapon. Jerome managed to deliver a jarring blow to his opponent's jaw, momentarily stunning him. He didn't want to kill the man; he wanted to know why anyone would behave so recklessly. He slammed the fellow's wrist against the carriage to force him to lose the knife. As he reined in on the runaway horse, the fellow sprang to life again, wrapping his arms around Jerome's throat with such an impetus that the two of them pitched from the carriage to the hard earth below.

Jerome was aware of the impact of their fall and of a cracking sound—someone's bone, he thought. His own? He was momentarily stunned, but aware he remained in danger. He rose quickly from his sprawled position by the man on the ground beside him, expecting to find the

fellow moaning from the pain of a few broken limbs—
but alive.

The fellow was dead.

As he knelt down by the body, a half dozen soldiers,
on foot and horseback, raced to his side in the gaslit
street. "Captain?" one asked anxiously.

"I'm all right. But this man is dead. And not from the
fall." Jerome pointed to the dead man's chest, where
blood spewed over his frock coat. He'd been shot. Looking around with a frown, he demanded sharply, "Who
was shooting?"

"Not my men, sir!" cried the soldier. "We were in
pursuit, but with you and the man entangled . . . with
your sister in the carriage . . ."

Sydney.

He leapt up, racing back to the carriage. Sydney, a bit
shaken but none the worse for wear, was emerging from
the carriage. "Jerome?" she said worriedly.

"I'm all right," he said. Putting an arm around her,
he helped her down, holding her tightly.

The night came alive. Everyone was distressed,
stunned—and baffled. Soldiers were everywhere; Davis
was demanding intelligence reports regarding the incident. That the man had attempted to kidnap Sydney
when so many soldiers were nearby was pure insanity.
That he had been shot and was dead seemed even
more strange.

A man named Lowell Thomas who worked with the
Confederate spy network arrived and spoke with Jerome
and the others, but no matter how many questions were
asked, no one had any answers.

"You've enemies, sir. A man of your abilities acquires
them. You've put lots of men off their ships—and the
North does have a network of sympathizers and spies in
the South, as do we in the North," Thomas told him
respectfully.

Jerome shook his head. "There's a Yank general after
my hide—but I'm sure he isn't the kind of man who
would threaten a young woman in order to have revenge
against me."

"We will look into the matter until it is solved,"
Thomas promised him.

"I want my sister guarded," Jerome said. "I'm going to bring her home on my own ship as soon as I can, but until that time, I want her guarded."

"Yes, Captain, naturally. It will be done."

"She must be watched carefully—"

"Captain," Thomas repeated. "You have my assurances. The President has ordered that your every request be honored."

Satisfied, Jerome at last escorted Sydney home. They rode in a carriage Lowell Thomas arranged for them. Jerome determined to make Sydney understand the situation. "Sydney, you need to go home."

Her beautiful green eyes widened. "But I work well at the hospital. I'm needed. You can't make me—"

"Sydney, you're in danger here. I want you back home with our mother and father."

"No, Jerome, please, you don't realize—"

"There's going to be a guard watching over you until I return. When I come back after seeing Brent, I'm taking you home with me. It's necessary. I'm afraid for you."

"Oh! You're a pirate, kidnapping Yankee women, ravishing them—and so I am to pay the price?"

"Sydney—" he began angrily.

She was instantly contrite. "Jerome, I'm so sorry! But—"

"God knows what might have happened to you tonight!"

She pleaded and argued, but when they reached her rented rooms, her tone changed because, in their absence, a soldier had brought a note from their father.

"Sydney, what is it?" he asked worriedly. "Is something wrong? Mother, Father—Jennifer? What's happened?"

She looked at him, shaking her head. "Nothing is wrong—yet."

"Then, what?"

"I—I'll let you take me home, Jerome."

"Sydney, damn it, tell me—"

"Mother is expecting another baby! We're going to have another sister or brother!" she said incredulously.

He stared at his sister, stunned. His father had told

him once that there were only three McKenzie children because Teela had not had an easy labor with Sydney. He'd been afraid for his wife then. And now . . . so many years later . . .

He felt a severe tightening in his stomach. His father was a powerful man. A warrior, intelligent, wary, scarred, and strong. His mother, however, was a rock. Strong in her gentleness and pure determination. She had fallen in love with his father and no force in heaven or hell would ever change that love. She was a natural nurturer, a healer, steady as the earth, the force, perhaps, behind them all.

"She's too old!" Sydney said.

"Don't let Mother hear you say that," he tried to tell his sister lightly.

"I don't really mean that she's so old . . . but her health! I'm worried, Jerome. Oh, what was Father thinking?" Sydney demanded angrily.

Jerome arched a brow, about to attempt an answer. He shook his head, deciding it wasn't worth the effort. At the very least, his sister had agreed to go home.

Yet that night, he lay awake, and he realized just how very worried he was himself—about so many things.

Three days later, Jerome found Brent working at an old plantation house near the most recent skirmishing. He came straight to his brother's surgery. Brent, in the midst of removing a deeply embedded ball, greeted him with a dry smile.

"Here to help, big brother?"

"If you need me," Jerome agreed, taking a position opposite his brother. He knew Brent, knew his mind. Where another man might not realize that his brother insisted on new sponges for each patient, Jerome could anticipate his brother's wishes.

Surgery lasted throughout the day. It was brutal. They were running short of morphine, and toward the afternoon, Jerome discovered it was his strength that was needed most to hold and steady the men when Brent had no choice left but to remove limbs.

It was late when he at last sat with his brother in the crumbling plantation's study, sipping brandy he had brought from Richmond. He told Brent about the incredibly strange incident that had occurred there, assuring him that Sydney was fine. Like everyone else, Brent was completely baffled.

He told his brother the news about their mother, which worried Brent as well.

"What was Father thinking?" Brent demanded, bringing a smile to Jerome's lips with the echo of Sydney's words.

"The last I remember noticing," he commented dryly, "Mother is equally fond of Father."

"Yes, but they should have been paying much more attention to *when* they were showing their fondness!" Brent said. "But then, it's difficult, I suppose, especially since they are growing older." He shook his head. "I need to get home," he said. "I am worried. Of course, many women do have children later in life. And many do so quite well. Funny, isn't it? To look back. So many men back home were eager for this war. Now home is far away, and we're fighting in Virginia, when Virginia wasn't even anxious for secession to begin with! God, I'm tired. I want to go home. I want to see one of those summer days when the sky is completely blue and no matter how hot the sun is, the breeze comes in off the ocean, and it's beautiful. Or a golden sunset when a heron is caught in silhouette against the darkening sky . . ." he sighed, looking down at his hands. "Perhaps I can get leave close to Mother's confinement."

"I think I'm due a personal favor," Jerome said, remembering how distressed President Davis had been over the bizarre incident with the carriage. "Maybe I can arrange it."

"Well, now you are famous. Or infamous? If you weren't already renowned for your death-defying blockade runs, General Magee's fury would have secured you a place in the heart of the South forever."

"And we're supposed to be the last of the cavaliers!" Jerome murmured dryly.

"Ah, but cavaliers are supposed to run to the adventurous, aren't they?" Brent inquired lightly. "Still, I get the impression that something preceded the carriage incident. What happened?"

Jerome shrugged, and told him about the note he'd found under his plate at the White House.

"You think it came from General Magee?"

"No . . . not from what I've heard about him," Jerome said slowly. "Ian always considered him to be an honorable fellow. He might be mad at me, but . . ."

"Oh, I assure you, Magee is madder than a hornet," Brent advised. "Still, I agree, I don't think that he'd threaten your family. But he is really angry."

"So I've heard. But he is a general—he must understand war! I had to keep Risa with me. She knew too much. A general must understand the common sense of what I did."

Brent arched a brow. "I don't think so."

"Why not?"

"Because I also received correspondence—for you." Brent rose and walked around to his camp desk. Opening a top drawer, he drew a sheet of line paper from it. The writing on it was neat and clear and boldly large.

Dr. Brent McKenzie, Lee's Army of Northern Virginia Medical Corps
Please let your family be advised that with malice toward no other, I intend to hunt down and decimate your brother, the infamous pirate Jerome McKenzie. Be so good as to inform the Devil himself that his days are numbered.

Regards,
General Angus Magee
Army of the Potomac

"Sounds pretty mad to me," Brent advised lightly. "Yet it's different from the anonymous note."

No, this one wasn't like the other note, but Jerome still felt anger burn through him. Magee's reaction to this was incredible. There was a war going on, for God's sake!

"How did you get this letter?" he asked Brent.

"Found it under my coffee cup one morning," Brent said.

"Sweet Jesus!"

"Let's face it—we have Rebs in Federal uniforms,

Yanks in Reb uniforms, and civilians who blow hot and cold with the wind. It was no great feat for General Magee to get this to me. And there are plenty of spies in Richmond. So someone likes to ruin our appetites. A gourmet spy! It's not so incredible. Do you know how close their troops are? The armies are circling one another. I can guarantee you, General Magee is no more than fifty miles from where we sit right now. I've heard that Risa is with him, an angel to the wounded men. The troops adore her, she is all but on a heavenly pedestal."

Jerome stared at his brother for a long moment. Anger seared through him with a fire unlike anything he had ever felt before. Old General Magee and his besotted Yankees weren't just threatening him, they were threatening his family, and all because a bold, beautiful, young woman had cried out to the press that she'd been ravished by a savage.

It hadn't happened like that at all. And now, it seemed his sister was being threatened. Brent had received notes on Jerome's behalf. He'd had enough. By God, he'd simply had enough.

Damn Risa, and damn her well-publicized lies!

"No more than fifty miles you say?" he mused aloud.

Brent arched a brow to him. "Jerome, I don't know what you're thinking, but don't think. The Confederacy needs you. You're my only hope when men are screaming in anguish and pain. You can't get killed—"

"Brent, I'm not a fool."

"You want to ride into Yankee territory—I can see it!"

"I'm a Rebel. And those Yankees are on Southern ground."

"I need you alive."

"The Confederacy needs information. Always. Lee isn't sure right now just what McClellan and Pope are doing. He always plays a dangerous game, pitting lesser numbers, skill, and sheer bravado against the Yanks. If I take a ride into enemy territory, it will be for a reason."

"You're a navy man—waiting for repairs to your ship!" Brent reminded him. "Dammit, Jerome, don't go getting yourself killed over something stupid!"

"I'll be damned if I'll let myself get killed, little

brother," Jerome assured him grimly. "But I promise you this—the Yanks will not threaten me and mine. I need to set up a meeting with one of your cavalry commanders."

"Jerome—"

"And I need a good horse. I understand that fine animals are growing scarcer."

"Major Lance serves Jeb Stuart. He can get you a good horse, but—"

"Good."

Brent rose unhappily, leading the way out of the tent. "Don't you dare die on me. I don't want to inherit the property in the swamp. I want to go home to St. Augustine when this is over, and set up a practice with Julian. Do you understand?"

"I'm not going to die. I promise you."

Major Edward Lance had heard about the tall Reb approaching his tent. Who had not? In a world where each victory was seized upon, the sea captain had become legendary. They said that he was like a phantom, a rich man with Indian blood, raised in the South, imbued with magical qualities. He could ride as one with the swiftest horse. He could move as if invisible, in absolute silence. If McKenzie was hell-bent on discovering the movements of enemy troops, Lance would be damned if he could question motive. Captain McKenzie's ship was in repair. If he happened to be an excellent horseman willing to ride for the cavalry—bless him.

Lance rose, saluting McKenzie, studying the man again. He was at least six feet two inches. Well muscled, his height giving him the appearance of lithe leanness. His features were powerful, cheekbones broad, flesh bronzed, hair reddish-black, queued at his nape, eyes sharp, dark blue, and calculating as he sat.

"I understand you're interested in making a surveillance run into McClellan's army," Lance said. He leaned back. "Suicide mission—Stuart himself was nearly captured, trying to record troop numbers and positions."

"Stuart rides with other men. I'll go alone."

Lance leaned toward him. "If you're caught, you'll be hanged as a spy."

"Yes, I know."

Lance leaned back, weighing the individual before him. Cool as ice.

"You've lived among the Seminole?" Lance asked.

"You harbor a grudge against Indian blood?"

Lance shook his head, smiling. "Nope. Just never met anyone like a Seminole for moving like a wraith in the night." He stood up, throwing a map of the territory across his camp desk. "Here is where we are. Here are the last reports we've had of the Union army movements. Here is what we can garner simply of objectives. McClellan wanted Richmond—but Jackson was in the Valley, and McClellan is a hesitant bastard, always assuming we have more men than we do. Now they've got Pope in the field, but he's one hated son of a gun, rightly so, I know the man. Lee has several objectives himself. Here—obviously, Richmond must be guarded from an assault. Jackson may need help in the Valley—and the powers that be are considering ways to move this carnage onto Yankee territory. Report back to me, no one else. Unless I'm dead. Then you go straight to Stuart or Lee. Understood?"

"Yes, sir."

"I'm giving you the best horse I've got."

"That's all I ask."

"One thing I can't give you, sir, is time. I need your information within ten days. Also, we've received word that your ship can sail in a fortnight. If I don't return you, the naval commanders will hang me from a mainmast. So get back here . . . quickly."

McKenzie smiled, blue eyes a dark ice, features strong and grim. "I don't need a great deal of time, Major. One night will do it," he said. "One night."

Chapter 13

In mid-July Risa and the rest of the medical corps were still treating the injured from the Seven Days battles. Conditions were horrible; the heat was ungodly. Thankfully, they had an ample supply of morphine for the numerous amputations taking place that day, and an ample supply of bandages as well. She had learned that Doc Abe, as the men affectionately called him, cut no limb carelessly from a soldier's body. But when bones were shattered, there was no alternative. Soldiers needed to be treated quickly and efficiently on the battlefield, then sent on to the nearest hospitals.

On this particular day, the sun burned down fiercely. The soldier on the table, a private who was drunk as well as drugged, sang and assured her he'd manage well enough—he wasn't losing his third leg, the one that mattered most. "Hush, now, son! We've a lady attending!" Abe told him.

"Ah, ma'am, sorry, 'tis the drink, of that I'm certain, and yet . . . well, this war will end one day, and so many of us young men will be gone. But some poor lass will take me, since I've at least got that middle leg, eh?"

She couldn't help but smile.

"There's no lady here, Doc. Just an angel."

Doc Abe signaled Risa to be ready with the bandages, then nodded to the two burly assistants who would hold the soldier down while Doc used the bone saw.

"Don't mind me screamin', ma'am. I'm not so much the coward, really," the soldier told her bravely.

Doc Abe started the operation.

The soldier, despite his drink and morphine, screamed.

Risa wasn't quite sure what happened next. One minute she was standing. The next she had passed out cold.

She awoke at a streambed, stretched out on pine needles, with Marny Calverton—a camp follower—by her side, washing her face with cool water. Marny was an intriguing young woman of Creole descent, with pitch-dark eyes and hair, and beautiful skin the color of ivory. She was quiet and dignified, but a woman surviving the war by following the soldiers. Under normal circumstances, Risa would never have been in a position to speak with her at all. Prostitutes and ladies did not mix, in Northern or Southern society.

But Risa wasn't the least offended that Marny had been sent to attend to her—Doc and his orderlies were busy with men who might bleed to death. She could see the makeshift hospital some distance from them, and hear the work still going on. She sat up, still dizzy, confused that she had fallen prey to such light-headedness.

"Go slowly there, Miss Magee," Marny told her softly, still dampening her forehead.

"I'm all right, Marny, thank you. Just embarrassed. That poor young soldier. I failed him miserably!"

"Ah, now, it's all right, Miss Magee. Doc was there, with his men. And General Goth's wife came over, efficient as a mother hen when you went down. You're a fine nurse, Miss Magee. But there are others."

"I should go back now. I'm really much better."

"You should rest, and avoid this kind of heat. Or it will happen again."

"Oh, surely, this was nothing more than a very peculiar incident—"

"If you say so," Marny murmured, her brown eyes touching Risa's. Then she looked down at her hands, folded in her lap.

"I'm sorry, I appreciate your concern, but I can't begin to understand—"

"Can't you? Really?" Marny said, staring at her again with undisguised curiosity.

Risa frowned. "No, I can't. Please—"

"Look, Miss Risa, you're a right decent woman. You're good to everyone—you're not like some of the officers' wives who think they ought to be sitting at the right hand of God the Father!" She paused to cross herself reverently. "I wish nothing but the best for you. I guess things in your life are a little bit complicated, and you're in my prayers. But you don't have to pretend with me."

Risa tried to stand. She tottered a bit, but with Marny's help she made it to her feet. She was better. She inhaled deeply. She was going to be all right.

"Marny, pretend what?"

"Why, you fine ladies just can't be so stu—naive!" Marny said, smiling quickly. "Miss Magee, I'm young, and not all that knowledgeable, but I can see where you're just as blind as a bat. And, of course, your secret is safe with me, though some folk who are just plain unkind do speculate about you sleeping with that married Colonel McKenzie."

"What? What are you talking about? I assure you, I'm not sleeping with Colonel McKenzie, although—"

Marny sighed with the greatest impatience, interrupting her. "I'd bet a year's earnings from these two-bit soldiers that you're going to have a baby, Miss Magee."

She'd been just fine. The world had solidified beneath her feet.

No more. The earth seemed to roar. And she slipped back into the oblivion of darkness.

Angus Magee sat back in his camp chair, exhaling a long breath. Ride, retreat, ride retreat! That's all that they were ever ordered to do! They had the power, they had the guns, they had the men. No matter how many times he tried to tell McClellan and the fools surrounding him to partake of his glory, that General Robert E. Lee often moved by the sheer force of willpower alone, the bastards didn't get it. If they'd just make a stand!

He reached into his desk for a bottle of whiskey and glasses, and looked at his staff before him.

"As you know, gentlemen, Pope has been unable to defeat Stonewall Jackson in the Valley." He distributed the whiskey, then drew out his battle map, displaying it on the desk. "Here, now, Pope is going to begin a movement toward Gordonville. We will leave Lee with his forces—estimates ranging from eighty thousand to one hundred and fifty!—with our forces here, McClellan's, facing him at Richmond. Pope has fifty thousand men in the Valley. We're trying to force the Rebs out into a squeeze, gentlemen, and word will be coming shortly about reinforcements. Are we clear?"

"Yessir," his staff agreed, one by one, the gentlemen all rising, aware that they were dismissed.

"Sir, if we would only move with force—" began Lieutenant Courtenay.

"Hopefully, one day, we will," Angus said wearily.

Courtenay cleared his throat. "Sorry, sir."

"Good night, then, gentlemen."

His officers disbursed. Angus poured himself another whiskey, and walked out of his command tent, into the night.

They were on Southern ground. The abandoned plantation still served as their military hospital, and some of the officers had taken up quarters within it. He hadn't. He had always loved Virginia. It hurt in his heart to destroy so much of the landscape with his own invading army. He'd made his quarters this tent, here, in a small copse of tall pine trees, just a stone's throw from the plantation house. Risa's tent was near, but closer to the ambling little stream that ran along the ridge of the mansion property. She could reach the house easily if necessary. And she was near to the water, which she adored.

He sighed, shaking his head, even as his heart swelled with pride. His daughter was beautiful, adored. And many a man here would gladly die for her. In fact, they were surrounded by thousands of men, and he never need fear for her chastity or safety. She showed no fear of battle zones, nor did she flinch at any injury. She never tired. She raised spirits with the musical sound of her laughter, and she sometimes sat at the campfires with the enlisted men, and sang songs they longed to hear, songs their sweethearts had last sung to them, before they'd marched off to war. If only . . .

His fists clenched at his sides. That son-of-a-bitch Rebel sea captain! He hoped she didn't have to learn the hard way how she might have to pay for her reputation—deserved or not.

He sipped his whiskey, looking down the long slope to her tent. He shook his head. To make matters worse, she just loved to swim in that little stream. The soldiers had their own place farther downstream to bathe and play—no one could abide the horrible heat. Risa bathed with a guard, and she had told him once that the stream helped wash away the scent of blood.

He drained his whiskey. The breeze picked up, and he raised his head, looking around. A little shiver rippled down his spine. Odd, he felt as if he was being watched. He'd had the feeling since his men had arrived for their latest briefing.

He returned to his tent, set his whiskey glass down firmly, then strode out into the night again, his pistol in his hand. He crept into the pines, waited, listening. He searched again, then returned to his tent.

Foolish. The Union was holding this land securely. There couldn't be a Reb for miles and miles around. He removed his boots and stretched out on his bunk.

Tonight he could rest at ease. All was well.

What in God's name was she going to do?

The question assailed her relentlessly, when she talked with others, when she laughed with the soldiers, when she bandaged up their wounds. Why hadn't she thought of this? How had she been so incredibly damned stupid that a camp follower had to be the one to make the obvious observation that she was expecting a child.

By nightfall she was in a fever. She'd risen quickly enough from her faint, and insisted she was fine. She had assured Marny that she was wrong. Naturally, Marny hadn't believed her. Didn't matter. She had to work, had to patch up soldiers, had to do something to keep her mind busy.

But night came, and she felt as if she were burning up with tension. She was desperate for a way to keep moving. Easy enough. She asked Sergeant Wallings, who looked after her meager living quarters, to stand guard at the top of the trail to the stream, and she walked through the small copse of oaks and pines until she came to the water's edge. She shed her shoes and stockings and pantalets and the simple cotton dress she wore for work in the surgery. She had no need for a corset or petticoats in the hospital, so stripped down to her linen shift. She picked up her sliver of soap and plunged into the stream, walking until she reached the depths—which were unfortunately only about four and a half feet. Still, she loved the cool crystal water.

She remembered the baby.

Baby!

She could have screamed aloud. What was her father going to say? What was he going to do? Oh, God, he thought her reputation was bad now! Her father . . .

The baby's father. Jerome.

Jerome might not even think that the child was his, after all, it had been quite some time since they'd met. Maligned by her father in the press, he'd become an even greater Southern hero. Fawned over by Southern womanhood. Other than surely longing to skewer her and her father, he'd probably given her little thought since they'd met.

He was a McKenzie. He might think himself honor-bound to marry her. A Yankee. No, no . . . he'd hate her. Loathe her, despise her. What had happened between them had been absurd, it had been the war, fantasy, a surge of desire when it seemed there might be no real world . . .

It would kill her father. Kill him. And then, there was herself. Lady Liberty. Heroine to the Union. How very amusing.

Oh, God! Worse! What if others—like Marny—assumed that the baby was Ian's? That she had been having an affair with a married man? Jerome himself might believe it. And Alaina! And her father—oh, Lord! Naturally, Ian himself would know that it wasn't true, but . . .

She came to a place in the stream—her place—where a flat boulder sat next to the fallen log of an old pine. Stripping off her wet shift, she secured it on the pine so that she might slip right back into it. Then she proceeded to soap and lather herself, shivering all the while, yet glad of the soap and the cold, because she needed it so badly after her time in surgery. She scrubbed with a vengeance. Washed her hair, rinsed it, washed again.

Her sliver of soap disappeared. She ducked into the water, rinsing back her hair.

She surfaced, eyes closed, hand reaching for the log as she blindly groped for her shift. She couldn't find it. She swore eloquently, rubbing her eyes to free them from the last vestiges of soap. She reached out again, blinking.

She touched flesh. A scream rose in her chest.

She opened her eyes in raw panic. Her scream froze in her throat.

She was seeing things; surely, she was seeing things.

Jerome McKenzie was there. Casually stretched out on the fallen log, leaned upon an elbow as he watched her. Barefoot, bare-chested, breeches wet and hugging his thighs. Dark hair wet and ebony and longer than she had remembered. Eyes catching the moon's reflection off the water, deep blue, menacing, deadly.

She blinked. He couldn't be there. She was surrounded by thousands upon thousands of Yankee troops. She stared at him, aware of the fury in his eyes, of the menace in his very being. A pulse ticked at his throat. He seemed casual, yet ready to pounce at the least provocation. She moved her jaw, trying to speak. A sound emitted from her throat. No panic! She wouldn't betray fear. She gasped, searching for words.

"You fool!" she managed at last. "What on earth are you doing here? You're surrounded by the enemy—you'll be hanged, you idiot!"

"I don't think so. I have to be caught to be hanged," he informed her arrogantly. His voice was rich, deep, damning.

"All I have to do is cry out—"

"You'll never have the chance," he informed her.

She swallowed hard and demanded again, "What are you doing here?"

He smiled, teeth flashing whitely in the moonlight against the bronzed darkness of his face. And despite herself, for the love of God, she felt something stirring within her. She was falling prey to his magnetism once again. She wanted to reach out and touch him. All he wanted to do was reach out and strangle her. He was furious. And he was her enemy. Avowed.

She was carrying his child . . .

He could never know.

"What are you doing here?" she cried again in a rising panic.

He swung around on the fallen tree, legs dangling into the water. She saw that her shift had been cast far aside. His toes brushed her thigh. He was close, far too close. "I have been maligned. One might call it libel. Doesn't matter anymore."

"Captain McKenzie, I never said—"

"There have been incredible lies about me in an awful lot of newspapers, Miss Magee."

"I never—"

"Savage, barbarian, wild Indian, Rebel, ravisher, rapist, etcetera, etcetera."

"You're risking your life over words in a newspaper?" Risa asked contemptuously.

He shook his head, staring at her, and she felt the sheer sensual power of his dark blue eyes. They flicked briefly over her as she stood in the water. Her breasts felt warm. To her dismay, she felt her nipples hardening. The cold of the water, nothing more, she told herself.

Except that she was burning.

"You're a fool. You're supposed to be at sea!" she hissed. "And here you are, risking your life over mere words!"

"No, not the words," he told her, smiling grimly. "I suppose I'm risking my life over the Yankee shrew who apparently found lies far more useful than the truth."

"I never lied to anyone—"

"Then, since I am justly condemned for the ravishment of such sweet innocence, I had best live up to my reputation."

Her cheeks flooded with bloodred color. She couldn't breathe or swallow; she could do nothing but stare. Then she shook her head, trying to back away.

He slipped into the water from the log with the easy grace of a gator. And then he was standing before her. "You are absolutely mad, you've lost your mind! Don't you understand where you are? You musn't—"

"Oh, Miss Magee. Surely, I must!"

He reached for her. She gasped, turning to escape.

She plunged beneath the water, but his hands were on her. Fingers brushing over her back, her bare buttocks, along her thighs. She escaped him, swimming hard.

She paused, rising, inhaling sharply. Her body seemed to burn against the cool air. Where was he?

"Ravished, eh? By a savage 'blooded' Rebel?"

He was directly behind her; his mocking whisper was low and husky against her ear. His breath was hot, touching her naked flesh so that she trembled as a new wave of warmth seared into her.

She stood straight and still, her back to him. "I don't know how you got here, how you slipped past thousands of Yankees and my personal guard. But you've exactly ten seconds, sir, to disappear. Then I shall scream."

"Will you?" he queried. His tone mocked, challenged. She spun around, ready to give him a second warning, but the glittering blue fury in his eyes gave her pause, and she sputtered out another threat. "I am giving you fair warning, Captain!"

He crossed his dripping arms over his bare chest. "Indeed?"

She let out an oath of impatience. In the distance she could see her shift, cast farther along the log. She pretended to ignore him entirely, plunging beneath the water again to swim and retrieve her garment. But when she reached the log, he was there, waiting. She let out a soft, involuntary cry, turning to elude him once again. But this time, his hands slid along her nakedness even as she swam. He let her escape him then, but when she would have kicked cleanly free, his fingers wound around her ankles, jerking her irrevocably to him. She had to grasp his shoulders to surface to breathe. Then she was caught in his arms. Held. Against him. Against the tense, sleekly muscled bareness of his chest. Against the hard rise that protruded from the cotton breeches plastered against his body. She stared into his eyes, telling herself that she needed to scream. No sound came to her lips. Then he was moving, and she had little choice but to cling to him as he walked through the water toward the soft spongy embankment. He fell to his knees with her, then laid her down, pressing her hard to the earth as he blanketed her body with his own.

His eyes met hers, still with the same searing blue fire. She didn't scream. His fingers threaded into her hair, his hand cupped her nape, holding her to his pleasure, and she couldn't have uttered a sound because his mouth was on hers, molded hard and forcefully, pressing her lips apart. His tongue filled her, plunged deeply, erotically, sweeping with hunger, fury, and passion. The weight of his hips wedged determinedly between her legs. She felt the pressure of his sex, freed from his trousers, against her inner thigh. A blaze seemed to ignite within her. She tried at first to writhe free from his kiss, but he was far too determined. She dug her nails into his shoulders. He caught her wrists, dragging her hands high above her head, pinning them there with the vise of his left fist.

His right hand was free. And as he kissed her, he touched her. His knuckles on her cheek, soft, brushing. Along the side of her body, teasing the circumference of her breast, sliding down her ribs, her hip. His fingers trailed upward again, he palmed her breast, rubbing the nipple, then teasing the nub with an intense pressure between his thumb and forefinger. She struggled to free her wrists. He released them. Her hands fell upon his shoulders again, and her fingers kneaded his flesh, her nails dug . . . but lightly. He lifted his mouth from hers, rising, just enough to meet her eyes. Her heart thundered. Her body trembled. He didn't speak. Neither did she. His dark lashes fell over his eyes; a lock of damp hair dusted his forehead. He bent low against her, his lips bringing a fresh brush of fire to the pulse that raced at her throat. She didn't think about the damp earth beneath her, or the warm, sultry Southern night, the balmy touch of the humid air . . . or the fact that thousands of Yankee soldiers slept nearby. She had wanted him before with an instinctive desire that had defied every convention she had learned in her life; it was no different now. His very touch awakened and aroused her, heart, soul, and senses. She thought fleetingly that he couldn't really be there; that she was indulging in some strange, erotic hallucination. Yet his touch was so real. His fingers stroked a bold pattern down her abdomen, into the triangle at her pubis, deeper. Deeper. Probing, seeking . . . finding.

She cried out at last, clinging to him, her face burrowing against his shoulder, teeth raking lightly into his flesh, tongue delicately soothing the light nip. She couldn't bear what he was doing. He had to cease. But he did not. His fingers moved inside her. His mouth moved over her breast, hot and wet, his tongue circled her aureole, the tip playing upon the hardened peak of her nipple.

Then he shifted, and he was full and hard within her with a single forceful thrust that burned deeply into her womb and beyond. His hands were beneath her, lifting her buttocks, pressing her ever closer to his quickening passion. She felt the damp, cushioning grass beneath her back, the night breeze licking against the soaring heat of her body. Sweat glistened their flesh. His movements became harder and wilder, more impassioned. He braced above her, body moving with a merciless, lightning speed, his eyes like cobalt pikes that impaled her as surely as his every thrust within her. She cried out, hands slamming against his chest as the sweet violence of climax seized her. The starry sky suddenly seemed to rend into shattered crystal above her and around her, breaking, falling, blurring her vision, tingling her flesh. She held him tighter as he reached his own surcease, body jerking powerfully into hers. Searing sweetness invaded her. He shuddered, holding close.

Then, abruptly, he lay at her side, bronze shoulders sheened in sweat, chest rising and falling rapidly as he regained normal breathing. The summer's night was suddenly cool; she felt the breeze keenly on her bare flesh.

"You neglected to scream," he said after a moment.

"You didn't give me time. I can, however, do so now," she reminded him softly. She shook her head against the damp earth beneath her, staring up at the sky. "You've no right to your anger. You *did* kidnap me! And you—"

"Abducted and ravished!" he murmured, rolling toward her. She edged away. Propped on an elbow, she watched him warily.

"This is not a private war," she informed him.

"Isn't it? Well, Miss Magee, I think it is. And it's time for you to surrender or pay one hell of a price."

She arched a brow, stunned by the venom in his words. She shook her head then, lashes covering her eyes. She was alarmed by the depths of his anger. What had caused such deep contempt? He had sought her out in fury. She should have called for help; he should be headed for a prison camp this very minute. But she hadn't called for help.

She had capitulated to his seduction with no protest whatsoever. Fool! This was her chance. If he was captured, they might both survive the war! And God knew, his imprisonment could only help the Yankee cause.

She was about to cry out—yet he sensed her thoughts. In two seconds he straddled her, his hand covering her mouth. "Don't even think about it—unless you want me dragging you back to Southern captivity."

She stared up at him, tears stinging her eyes, frustration raging in her heart. She tried to bite his fingers; he adjusted his hold on her mouth.

"If your Yankee defenders threaten my sister again, Miss Magee, I can promise you that you'll spend the remainder of the war enjoying Southern hospitality."

Her eyes widened. He lifted his hand, watching her.

"Your sister! Someone threatened your sister?"

"Yes. Come, now—are you so surprised?"

"Indeed, I am."

"She was nearly kidnapped in Richmond—after I received an anonymous threat under my dinner plate promising that I would die for my treatment of you!"

"Don't you dare make such an accusation! Do you think that I would do such a thing, cause such a thing? You bastard! I didn't send a note, and I know nothing about it. And—"

"Then my brother received a letter. Ah, but this one was signed. It was from your father. He apologized to my family for intending to go straight for my throat."

"Just what were you expecting? I can't help what my father feels and does—"

"You might have taken greater care when describing your barbaric treatment at the hands of a savage Reb."

"I'm telling you that I didn't say—"

"I can read, Miss Magee."

A burst of anger exploded from her. "Can you? I'm not so certain! I have been warned that Southerners can be slow. Then again, sir, maybe your behavior was despicable, and maybe you shouldn't have abducted me, or ravished me, or taken me aboard your ship! Go to hell, Captain! Go straight to hell! None of this was my making. And I'm very busy now with a war effort that wears upon everyone, body and soul—"

"You seem to be weathering it all quite fine," he remarked dryly. "In fact, you look quite well. Exceptionally well, I might say."

"Damn you, Jerome—"

She broke off, swallowing hard. For as harsh as his anger had been, he was suddenly touching her once again. He sat straddled atop her, balancing his weight on his haunches—and touching her, his hand gently cupping the weight of her breast. "You were too thin. I think you've actually gained some weight," he murmured.

"Don't be absurd! I've lost weight—" she began. But then broke off abruptly.

Her breasts were larger. Very round and full. Of course. She should have noticed the changes herself. She could only hope that he didn't really remember.

Or know why she might seem different.

"Don't!" she whispered in a panic to divert him. "Don't! Don't come with your foolish accusations and—and . . ."

But he wasn't listening. He had shifted off her again. His gaze swept the length of her. He leaned low, lips suddenly against her belly.

"McKenzie—"

"What?"

"Stop it. I will not be seduced again."

"I'm not about to seduce," he murmured against her flesh.

"Then—"

He raised his head, and his eyes met hers. Challenging once again. "I've come purely to ravish!" he informed her. Then he caught her knees, one with each hand, drawing them apart. He pulled her hard toward him. She gasped, struggling to rise upon her elbows. She was ready to argue in full measure, knowing . . . anticipating his intent. Yet her words died as she choked out a gasp of unwilling pleasure as a throbbing began instantly within her as he buried his head between her legs . . .

And ravished.

She managed a desperate protest at last, voiced in frantic whispers. Wicked, burning sensations coursed through her as he teased and provoked with lips and tongue, entering, thrusting . . . licking, a light touch, a hard touch. Tears stung her eyes, she lay back, writhed, twisted, all but died in his searing brand of ecstasy. Anguish, need, pure pleasure combined.

Then he ceased and rose above her, and entered her. And it seemed that he moved like the night wind, whipping through her like a storm, sweeping her into his tempest. And when he had finished, she was crying out, because she had never felt such pure, physical pleasure. And even afterward she was seized again and again with ecstatic little climaxes that gripped her, released her, and left her trembling, exhausted . . . staggered.

He did not move so quickly from her. He held her very close, and the night breeze cooled them both, though she refused then to respond to his touch. She groaned softly. "You must . . . go. I will scream; you should be in jail, you're a madman, they'll take you—"

"They'll hang me. But you won't scream."

"Why?" she demanded weakly. She felt as if she would surely burst into tears any moment. "You've come with some ridiculous search for vengeance I do not deserve—"

"If you were to scream, your father might well be the one to come."

She was dead silent. Then she inhaled deeply.

A slight smile played upon his lips. "Actually, you know, you were doing a little screaming. It was charming."

"Oh!" she cried with sudden fury, and she tried to pummel him, lash out at him. She would have gladly taken a few gouges out with her nails. But he was prepared, and he subdued her, straddled atop her again, pinning her arm down while her breasts heaved with exertion and anger.

He arched a brow. "No threats, Miss Magee?"

"You could kill my father. And nothing you could do or say would be worth his death!"

He smiled with a hint of admiration.

"You will pay anyway," she warned him. "You are surrounded by Yankees. *Surrounded.* I need do nothing, and you will be caught!"

"Perhaps. Perhaps not."

"I don't know what you think I've done—"

"You know what you've done. I have been slandered, and my family has been threatened. I will find the truth, and I won't be threatened."

"Indeed! You're the one with the threats."

"Bear in mind, I carry out my every threat. You've a tremendous amount to answer for."

"I've nothing to answer for! You are the one with a great deal to pay for, sir!"

"This war is not over," he told her.

"No, it is not! And I warn you, if you do not get off of me and disappear—"

"Not yet."

"Not yet?"

"One more time."

"One more time?" she repeated blankly, then gasped. "Oh, you are out of your mind, you are despicable. I'll not—"

"That's the whole point of ravishment, isn't it?"

She wasn't certain if she longed to laugh, or rip him to shreds. But his eyes were dead serious; his arms were powerful around her. His tension was as electric as it had been through the night. "Once more," he whispered.

He knew how to make love. With anger, without. From the very beginning, she had been fascinated with him. Surely, she hadn't fallen in love, but . . .

But some unique thread linked them, a golden web. His eyes were like no other's. She loved his features, his face, the hint of Indian blood in his cheekbones, in his deep bronze coloring, in his thick dark hair, just touched by hints of red.

They were bound by anger, she warned herself.

But it didn't matter.

When he touched her, she was fire. When he made love to her, she knew that she could never want another man. And yet it was sheer fury that brought them together.

They were enemies. But she was going to have his child.

And yet . . .

Again, she forgot all else in the rising desire that spiraled through her. And again, the night itself seemed to explode with the sheer ecstasy he created within her, and in his arms, she didn't even realize her fear that half the Union army could come upon them . . .

This time she said nothing as she trembled, drifting downward from their passion. She lay in his arms, silent, aware that he watched her in return. She wondered what he was thinking, but she didn't ask. She knew he wouldn't answer.

She closed her eyes, utterly spent, yet glad of him.

After a while, she opened her eyes.

He was gone.

And she was alone among the pines.

Chapter 14

It was early October when Jerome stood on the bow of the *Lady Varina,* watching the movements of the ship cutting across the Atlantic to his north. Her flag was obscured; she carried several guns.

They had come from Bermuda, where not all of their promised supplies had arrived from England. It had been a long time since Jerome had been engaged at sea.

And he was hungry for action.

His time on land had proved to be far longer than he had imagined. The information he had accrued in the Union camp was helpful, adding credence to what the Confederate generals had already estimated. Summer had moved bloodily onward in the eastern theater, battle following battle, and since word had arrived that repairs on the *Lady Varina* were taking longer than expected, Jerome had determined to remain with his brother, accepting cavalry assignments. He was capable of slipping into places alone where others might not be so able. As a navy man waiting for the return of his ship, he was basically a free agent, able to be of service. He was most frequently required to run information between armies and brigades, and it was gratifying work. He was able to verify Lee's knowledge that McClellan's troops were moving by water to reinforce Pope. He was also well aware of the general's plan to use Clark's Mountain to screen his troops and deliver an attack against Pope's eastern flank and cut the line along which McClellan's forces intended to reinforce him and cut off the line of retreat to Washington.

Jeb Stuart's adjutant general was captured by Pope with a copy of the battle plan, allowing him and his troops time to withdraw. The armies then faced one another across the Rappahanock. Lee probed for a vulnerable point. In one cavalry raid Pope's headquarters near Catlett's Station were captured, and Jerome was with the Rebs, who were able to bring back the information that Federal reinforcements would soon increase Pope's ranks to one hundred and thirty thousand men—to face Lee's fifty-five thousand. Lee decided to split his army—counting on the panic that would arise if he threatened the Federal position and its proximity to Washington.

Bloody engagements followed. Groveton, Bull Run, Chantilly. Lee did not manage a decisive hit against the Federals, but he did accomplish the amazing—with his inferior numbers, he delivered serious losses on the Federals while maintaining the defense of strategic Rebel locations. He not only eliminated the immediate threat of the Federals against Richmond, he sent them back defensively to D.C.

Although Jerome slipped behind enemy lines several times again, he was not able to find Risa. He had told himself that he was not searching for her anymore. She was the enemy, and had been duly warned not to fight him, slander him—or cause others to attack his family. His obsession had been put to rest—or so he told himself. But he could tell himself anything he damned well pleased. Thoughts of her plagued him. She haunted his nights. He might heartily desire to put an end to his obsession with a woman who considered him to be a wretched savage, the worst of all enemies, but desire and determination had little effect on his longing for her.

He had remained with the Army of Northern Virginia as Lee continued his campaign. On September 15th, Jackson took Harpers Ferry, and when Robert E. Lee heard of Jackson's success, he decided to stand his ground in Sharpsburg, Maryland.

In all his life, Jerome had never seen such fierce fighting as occurred in a little place called Sharpsburg, by Antietam Creek. Vast cornfields were mown down by rifle fire.

And men were mown down like corn.

The ground was slick with blood, and in areas the bodies were piled high, several feet deep. An alley became known as Bloody Lane as more and more men were mired in the blood with the dead, and joined their ranks.

Staring out across the endless field of death as a bloodred sun set upon the bloodstained earth, Jerome questioned not only his judgment, but his sanity. The losses in the war were unbearable, North and South. He walked over soldiers who were boys, called upon to die before ever knowing what it was like to really live.

He heard many men weeping. Men who had fought valiantly, brave men, courageous men. And he had to wonder if God hadn't turned against them all.

As long as he lived, he would never forget that mid-September in Maryland. For weeks to come, he would smell blood as he slept, and sweat out nightmares in which he returned to those fields of hell.

It was a pity that a man couldn't simply quit the war. But he couldn't quit it, and he knew that to leave the fight was to turn his back on the men who had died. Only God alone knew who was right anymore. But even as the gunfire ended and the tragic job of seeking to winnow the injured from the dead began, he knew that it was most important he return to his ship. Medical supplies were more desperately needed than ever.

Thankfully, his nightmares had ebbed somewhat now that he was back at sea. His first order of business had been to return to Richmond for Sydney, but he discovered that his younger sister had moved into the hospital—and that she had been taken beneath the wing of the First Lady herself—and wanted to remain just a few more months. She'd received a long letter from their pregnant mother, Teela, who was feeling not just fit, but exceptionally well. She asked that her daughter be home by November, if at all possible, and Sydney happily agreed. Jerome couldn't force Sydney to leave the hospital. She was too badly needed. '

The *Lady Varina* was in exceptionally fine shape as well—she'd been scraped, painted, entirely overhauled. Her damaged sails had been replaced; she was spit and polish new. He had been deeply pleased to see her.

In Charleston, he had been entertained by Jenson and the Thompsons once again. Janine had flirted boldly, and he had enjoyed her company through a night of dinner and dancing. It wasn't hard to enjoy her company. Yet watching her as he sipped brandy late into the night, he found himself making comparisons. And though Janine Thompson was a genuine beauty, he wanted her to have Risa Magee's long throat, and the rich auburn tumble of hair. He wanted to see Risa's eyes . . . the fullness of her breasts, the haunting contours of her body.

Despite her outrageous flirting, Janine didn't arrive naked in his bedroom—though she had hinted that he might visit hers. He considered doing so, yet he didn't.

He left the house of his good friend, visited a tavern he had known in days past, and spent the rest of the evening in the arms of a practiced tavern wench he'd known over the years. If anything, she left him more restless than he had been.

Running the *Lady Varina* out of Charleston Harbor had been Jerome's first test of his repaired ship, but his lady had come through with flying colors. He'd been anxious to pick up supplies and make a Florida run—to his home in the southern peninsula first, and then down the St. Johns. But he was vastly disappointed in the supplies he'd managed to purchase in Bermuda, and there was going to be a scant quantity of the drugs Julian had requested if he couldn't find another source from which to fill his hold.

And so the ship on the horizon greatly intrigued him.

Hamlin Douglas stood at his side, taking the long glass from his hands to observe the ship in turn.

"Well, Hamlin?" he asked his first mate.

"She's a Yank."

"We've got to be certain. If we attack a British ship, we could lose the whole damned war for the Confederacy. I learned in Richmond how terribly important it is now for our European neighbors to recognize the validity of our government."

Hamlin scratched his sharp chin, shaking his silver head. "She's a Yank."

"How do you know?" Jerome demanded.

Hamlin's cool, nearly colorless eyes touched his, and he arched a furry brow. "You think she's a Yank, too, right."

"I do."

"Why?"

Jerome grinned. "Gut instinct."

"I say the same."

"Gentlemen, what a way to wage a war!" David Stewart said as he approached them. He was at leisure to serve as counsel now; he hadn't a single man in sick bay, and he stood with them just forward of the aft, watching the horizon.

"What do you say, Doc? You are an officer aboard this lady," Jerome reminded him.

David grinned. "I say she's a Yank. Get her."

"Mr. Meyers?!" Jerome called to Jimmy, commander of his gun crew.

"I say we take her, Captain! Any French or English ship in these waters would be proudly flying her flag!"

"Bring her hard about, Mr. Douglas!" Jerome commanded. "Mr. Meyers—see to your gunners, sir! Matt! Down to the steam room—full speed upon our prey. Wait for my order, but we hit like lightning—she's got fierce enough guns aboard!"

It took them nearly two hours to catch up with the ship. She was trying to outrun them; she could not. She was riding very heavily in the water, which further encouraged Jerome. She was carrying a lot of cargo.

He leapt up the rigging, watching the activity aboard the ship. He saw the officers convening, discussing the situation. With the glass he could tell that they were arguing heatedly.

"Call for a warning shot, Mr. Douglas!" he ordered his first mate. "Give them a chance to surrender."

"We can't let them fire the first volley, sir—" Hamlin warned.

"And we will not, Mr. Douglas! But give them a chance to surrender. I don't want to sink her. I want her cargo!"

"Aye, aye, Captain!"

A warning shot was fired; it landed perfectly dead ahead of the Yank's aft.

Hamlin called out for the surrender of the ship.

From his vantage point, Jerome could see the enemy preparing to fire.

"Mr. Meyers! Fire at will!" he commanded.

The *Lady Varina* let loose with her guns blazing. Her aim was accurate; her hits were deadly. Fire tore across the deck, splitting the mainmast with a crack like a thunder so loud it might have foretold the doom of the sea itself. Shouts rose from the injured Yank; her crew scurried to put out the fires. Her guns roared in reply; her shot fell short.

"Fire again, Mr. Meyers!" Jerome ordered.

The second volley was all that was needed. The Yank was crippled. She hadn't been flying any colors; now a white flag crept slowly up the one remaining mast.

"Prepare to board her, men!" Jerome ordered.

Shouts of victory rose from his crew, along with the sounds of the grappling hooks that attached them to their prey. Jerome paused by his cabin as the ship was secured, slipping into his jacket to accept the surrender of the Yank. Stepping aboard her, he saw that David was already at work with the Yank's surgeon.

The ship's officers were lined up at the helm as Jerome came aboard. The captain was a stiff man: tall, thin, fiftyish, his bitterness apparent in his eyes. His second officer was younger, and nursing an injured arm. The gunner's mate was a heavy fellow, covered in powder. Jerome saluted them, and was saluted in return.

"We flew no flag; you had no right to attack!" the captain told him.

Jerome arched a brow, smiling slightly. "Well, sir, you are in uniform. You are a United States ship; we are enemies at war. And, gentlemen, you, your crew, and whatever passengers you may carry are now Southern guests—in a manner of speaking."

"We were bound for England, sir, with—"

"I've no doubt you have a hold filled with raw goods, which we will be delighted to put to good use. I'm afraid, gentlemen, that you'll have to be confined to quarters for the time being. Mr. Douglas will be bringing your ship in. You may take the longboats into the shipping lanes, if that's your desire, or we can see to it that you are left near a Yankee port."

"My officers and I will accept the longboats," the captain said stiffly.

"But, sir—" objected his first mate.

"My mind is made up, Lieutenant Waylon."

"Your pardon, sir! But we must consider the welfare of all aboard."

The captain frowned, apparently realizing what it was the first mate was trying to tell him.

He cleared his throat.

"You may confine us to our quarters, Captain. I have surrendered the ship, and we will offer you no more resistance if we are to be treated fairly as prisoners."

"That is my desire. Mr. O'Hara!" he called, bringing Michael to his side. "If you would be so good as to accept the surrender of small arms from these gentlemen and see them to their quarters . . . ?"

"Aye, aye, sir!"

Michael escorted the men away. Jerome strode across the deck, pausing as he saw a very young man down on the flooring, grasping his leg and fighting tears. Jerome stooped down beside him. "Where are you hit, sailor?"

The youth looked up at him, cringing at first. Jerome didn't blink. "Where are you hit, sailor?" he asked again.

The youth swallowed. "My knee. I'm going to lose my leg. Jenny won't love me no more; how can she love a half man?"

"Losing a leg doesn't make a man half himself. What's inside makes him half or whole," Jerome said firmly. "But don't give up as yet." He pulled a knife from the sheath at his calf, causing the boy to blanch. But when he ripped the bloody fabric free from the lad's leg, he breathed again. He tested the bone, aware that the boy whitened even more, biting down hard to keep from crying out. "It isn't shattered. The hit was behind the kneecap. We can probe for the bullet, and if no infection sets in . . ."

The boy grasped his arm. "Doc Deakins just said he'd be cutting, " he said anxiously. "I don't want to be cut, please, Lord, God, Captain Reb, if you can stop him . . ."

Jerome paused a minute, hoping he wasn't playing God. He wasn't a surgeon himself, but he'd spent a lot of time with some of the best, and he knew when limbs could be saved. If infection set in, that could kill the boy.

But infection could set in after an amputation as well. He hesitated, then straightened. "David!"

His own surgeon, bent over another man, rose. David nodded that he was on his way, and gave orders that his current patient not be moved. Then he strode the deck to Jerome. "Take a look. Can we save this limb?"

David bent to the boy. He looked up at Jerome. "Yes, it can be done. There is risk." He shrugged then. "Then again, there's Northern boys who think we're out to kill them in our hospitals. I'd like him willing for me to treat him."

The boy grasped David's arm. "If you can keep my leg, sir, I won't just be a willing patient, I'll be your slave, sir, the remainder of my life!"

David grinned to Jerome.

"Have someone get him aboard the *Lady Varina*," Jerome advised. "Mr. Douglas, see to the ship. Bring me a list of dead and wounded, see to the cargo, and bring me an inventory. I'll be in my cabin."

He departed the captured ship, leaving his officers and men to take her over. In his cabin he drew out his maps, trying to determine the best route to bring his spoils home. He didn't want to sink her if he didn't have to— the Confederacy was far too desperate for ships. After a number of calculations, he decided on Jacksonville— assuming he could make certain that the city wasn't in Union hands. The ship could be reoutfitted in Jacksonville, and turned over to Confederate authorities. He'd also be along the St. Johns, much as he had previously planned. He'd have to postpone his trip to the southern tip of the peninsula, but going home right now was actually a luxury he couldn't afford. He would get there soon, he promised himself.

There was a tap on his cabin door. Expecting his men with reports, he didn't look up. A second later he heard a throat being cleared. He glanced up then. The injured young man who had been brought aboard was facing him—balancing on a broken timber as a crutch.

"Are you trying to bleed to death?" Jerome demanded.

The boy shook his head. "I just . . . well, you fellows are right decent. You're Captain McKenzie. They call you a devil, and a sea dragon, and all kinds of things. But they're wrong, and none of your crew tried to slaughter us or mow us down, or sink us or . . ."

"I'm not a dragon," Jerome said, amused.

The boy was hesitant again. He inhaled. "Well, I've got some information you should have, because my friend, Sully—he wasn't hurt in the action—anyway, he told me that Captain Briggs and Lieutenant Waylon are planning some kind of escape—with the general's daughter."

"The general's daughter?" Jerome inquired sharply, amazed at the knot of tension that tightened around him.

"Miss Magee, sir." He cleared his throat. "All the world just about knows that you kidnapped the lady before, Captain."

"Wha . . . ?" *Risa was on board the ship he'd taken?*

"So naturally, they intend to save her."

"So—why have you come to me?"

"Because those fools will kill her! They'll get drowned—and eaten by sharks. Seems to me, even if—like the newspapers say—you're a savage and you abducted and ravished her, she's better off with you than dying with them."

"I see. Nothing like the lesser of two evils," he murmured. "Thank you, sailor. Now, young sir, back to sick bay. I'll not have your death on my conscience!"

Ian McKenzie was military; he'd been trained military, and he understood the tragedy of war.

But it all grew increasingly bitter. He had a wife, and a child, and he was expecting another child. After tremendous trial and tribulation—not the least being that his wife had served the Confederacy as a spy—his domestic situation was not just happy, but blissful. He loved his wife; she loved him. But months had gone by now without his being able to see her, and he missed her—and his Florida homeland—intensely.

It wasn't possible to point out to his superiors that the Southern generals on the eastern front were walking all over them. Simple statistics should have given them numerous victories, which hadn't occurred. After a bitter summer of fighting, he was back in Washington.

The realization that he was bound to come to blood with his own family had caused him to ask for a transfer to serve once more on the battlefields in Virginia. Lincoln had summoned him back, determining that he was far better utilized doing what he had been doing before—waging small scale war in his home peninsula. What it boiled down to, Ian reckoned, was that he and other Yanks stole supplies from the Rebs—and the Rebs stole them back from them. But with the fighting continuing at such a brutal pace, each side had its objective. To the South, supplies were a lifeline that must be kept open. To the North, the lack of supplies was a way to send the Rebs down to their knees.

Still, he was glad to be preparing for his trip homeward when a messenger came from General Angus A. Magee, requesting his presence. Ian left his Washington town home, glad to see his old commanding officer and friend before setting off.

But he had barely entered Magee's residence before his host came striding into the parlor.

"General—" Ian began, only to have the old fellow catch him squarely in the jaw with a solid punch.

Stunned—and dampening down the instinct to strike back—Ian worked his jaw.

"Sir—"

"Don't you 'sir' me, McKenzie! You were like my own boy, the son I never had! I embraced you to my heart; I assumed you meant to marry Risa, and it would have done my heart good. You married elsewhere, sir, and that is a man's choice, but how dare you do so and then use my daughter so cruelly!"

"General," Ian said, tenderly rubbing his chin. "Sir, I would gladly answer these accusations. But I haven't the least idea what you're talking about! It was my most recent understanding that Risa had set sail to visit friends in England—"

"Indeed! Without so much as sharing her troubled condition with me!"

"Her troubled condition . . ."

"I do have my ways of learning the truth!" Magee exploded, still stiff and straight as a statue, soft blue eyes emitting powdery sparks.

Risa was . . . expecting? Ian wondered. The situation was quite incredible. It wasn't his child, so . . .

"You may hit me again, sir, if it will make you feel any better," Ian offered politely. "But I'm afraid . . ."

He paused. His cousin was no rapist, no debaucher of innocents. No matter what the newspapers had claimed, he knew damned well that Jerome would have never forcefully raped Risa Magee, or any other woman. In fact, women flocked to him.

So . . . what the hell had happened?

Apparently, General Magee's mind was moving in a like direction. "I shall kill him! That half-breed wretched red savage kin of yours! I will personally find him, and tear his heart out!" Magee said, his voice shaking.

"Sir, I know my kin, and under normal circumstances, you yourself are the first to understand how others have chosen to fight for their home states. My cousin returned Risa safely as soon as was strategically possible—"

"His heart! I will skewer it through, roast it, and feed it to the dogs."

"Sir," Ian protested politely, "I cannot believe Jerome is responsible. I've recently heard rumors that he met a young woman in Charleston, and there was talk of an engagement. I understand she's quite the belle, from a prominent Southern family. Risa was angry with him, but she'd have been honest with us. My cousin did nothing brutal or cruel to her. I know that. Perhaps . . ."

"Perhaps what? Are you making insinuations against my daughter?"

"No, sir, you know that I love her—"

"So you do love her!"

Ian inhaled deeply—wanting to cut out Jerome's heart himself at that moment. "Risa is my friend, sir, one of the best I have ever had. But perhaps she has simply fallen in love elsewhere, and neither of us knows anything about it."

"Hmmph!" Magee snorted, narrowing his eyes. Then they misted. "She's left me, Ian. Without a word about her situation. Didn't she trust me? Doesn't she know how I love her?" he demanded, sounding a little lost.

"She wouldn't want to hurt you, or your position, sir." And maybe she was just a little afraid that he would want to cut someone's heart out! Ian thought wryly. "Sir, will you trust me to do my best to find the truth of the situation?"

Magee stared at him a long time. He was furious, and deeply hurt. "Ian, Risa is on her way to London, and I am on my way back to battle. The Lord knows where you will wind up. Yes, I will trust you. But if that wretched half-breed—"

"Actually, Jerome's blood is a little thin. My uncle is the half-breed," Ian corrected, the trace of resentment in his tone eluding Magee in his distraught state.

"If he has harmed her in any way, I will slice him to ribbons!" Magee vowed.

Ian saluted. He didn't want to tell Magee that if it came down to a contest of strength, Jerome would easily tear him to shreds.

But then again, Jerome would never behave so *savagely*.

Chapter 15

The decision to leave America had been difficult, but she felt she'd had no choice. She meant to come back as soon as possible. She couldn't bear hurting her father by leaving, but neither could she hurt him with her situation. She'd actually considered writing Jerome McKenzie about the child, but their last encounter had been such a whirlwind tempest, so swiftly come and gone that she did, at times, doubt her own sanity. It didn't matter. He had made it clear, as perhaps she had herself, that they were enemies. England began to look better and better to her. She had close friends in London with whom she'd gone to school, and she could make arrangements for a discreet delivery somewhere in Scotland perhaps. And when the war was over . . .

What then? How would she explain her babe when she went home? And could she wait for the war to end if it dragged on? Her father loved her, and needed her. She supposed she could claim she had adopted a war orphan. But would her father believe her? Could she live with the charade? The conflict within her was great, because she did so adore her father. But she didn't want him upset now. He needed to concentrate on the business of war—not worry about his daughter!

So she had set sail. England, a season in London with friends. She would take charge of her life, and she would do it on her own.

But God, it seemed, was a trickster.

The moment she had seen the *Lady Varina* on the horizon, she had known that Jerome McKenzie would seize her ship. Captain Briggs had been warned that he was taking on far too much cargo—he had no speed left to him, and no maneuverability. Lieutenant Waylon, who had become somewhat smitten with her, had talked more than he should have. He was sorry to be serving beneath Briggs, whom he considered to be an old war-horse who should have been put out to pasture.

But Waylon had read the newspapers as well, and he knew, when they saw the Rebel ship on the horizon, that it was the demon of the seas himself, Jerome McKenzie, hard on their heels. He had quickly seen to it that she was kept hidden in the captain's cabin, and he assured her he'd do everything in his power to see her safely from the ship.

And, the demon that he was, Jerome had behaved with chivalry, honoring every code of warfare, when he took the ship. The officers were courteously escorted to the captain's cabin to remain under guard. The cabin was inspected once for arms. She kept her head cloaked, her eyes upon some needlework, while pretending to be Lieutenant Waylon's wife as Michael O'Hara inspected the cabin. Small arms were taken, but the officers were invited to dine with officers from the *Lady Varina,* and the capture was respectfully carried out.

But Waylon did not forget his promise.

"The ships are disengaged. The hour after midnight, Miss Magee, we slip out. We release the port side long-boat and take her—there is but one latch remaining upon it, for the men have prepared for your escape. Briggs and I will accompany you, and see to your safety. We are in the shipping lanes. I promise you that we'll be picked up by morning."

"Lieutenant Waylon, I see no need to take such a risk. If you've surrendered, you could sacrifice all by attempting an escape," Risa argued.

"Oh, but, Miss Magee! If Captain McKenzie seized you again, your father would murder us with his own bare hands!"

She actually longed to escape this ship without Jerome managing to discover her. Under the circumstances, she certainly didn't want him finding out about her condition.

"All right, as you suggest, Lieutenant," she agreed.

A half-moon rode high against a clear star-spangled sky. It was a perfect night on the Atlantic. The waves rolled gently.

The Yankee ship and the *Lady Varina* rode parallel across the waves, moving slowly. Michael O'Hara was at the helm of the Yank while Mr. Douglas himself guided the *Lady Varina.*

Cloaked in the darkness, Jerome stood vigil at the bow of the *Lady Varina.* It was late; the sailors had been given a measure of rum for their efforts that day, and now slept in the lazy glory of a solid victory. The surgeons had long since patched up the last of the wounded.

The dead had gone to their watery graves.

Night, and all was quiet.

Except that he had taken a ship of deeply disgruntled enlisted men, and Hal Smith, the lad whose leg had been saved, had been allowed a visit from his friend, Sully. Sully not only knew that there was a plot afoot for the captain, first officer, and a lady passenger to escape, he knew that the attempt would be made that night.

Sure enough. Jerome had stood, still as a great heron, for hours. Then he saw the dark figures moving along the bow to the longboat.

The longboat fell with a minimum of sound.

Jerome stepped to the rim of the bow, caught hold of a guide rope, and swung down the length of it to one of the longboats tied to the ship. He looked across the few feet of water that separated him from his men—Jeremiah Jones, David Stewart, and Jimmy Meyers—in a second boat. "Gentlemen, it's time," he said quietly.

And the longboats shot out into the night.

Within a matter of seconds they had come around the *Lady Varina,* and were in pursuit of the escaping Yanks.

"Dear God! The man *is* the Devil himself!"

Captain Briggs was the one to first shout the alarm. Turning swiftly, Risa felt her heart sink.

"It can't be! It's impossible!" Lieutenant Waylon sputtered.

"You, ahead there, Yanks—halt!" came a thundering command.

"Never, sir!" cried Lieutenant Waylon.

"Waylon, don't be an idiot! The man can cut you down in a wink!" Briggs retorted in disgust.

"No! We can fight!" Waylon insisted.

"I told you, I want no more blood spilled!" Risa protested. "Lieutenant Waylon—"

But to her dismay, Waylon had jumped up. He had managed to keep a small repeating revolver, and he leapt to his feet, firing.

"Sit down, man!" Captain Briggs roared, but too late. Despite his valiant if foolhardy effort, Waylon had unbalanced the longboat. It didn't just rock; it pitched. Waylon went flying into the blue-black of the ocean. Briggs tried to fling himself across the boat to shield Risa, but to no avail. The little boat rocked up on its side, and they were both thrown overboard. Risa felt herself instantly sinking; her clothing—chosen for the night chill in the midst of the Atlantic—was heavy. Her boots were heavy. Her cloak was laden with silver coin for her trip.

She managed to rip off her boots, and kick her way to the surface. She was worried about Captain Briggs and Lieutenant Waylon, but she discovered a more powerful instinct for self-preservation; she meant to save her child. She came to the surface, gasping, and saw the overturned boat perhaps thirty feet away from her. She paused, treading water, seeing Jerome's men dragging Waylon into their small boat.

Jerome was perched alone in the longboat, seated in the middle at the oars, looking down at her. He wore a loose white cotton shirt, dark breeches, and boots, and looked more like a rogue pirate than a military man. He leaned upon the oars, eyes obsidian in the night.

"Swimming again?" he inquired politely.

"Go to hell, McKenzie."

"Not a good place," he mused, watching her tread the water. "We're far out at sea. No place for you to swim to, actually. Water is cold here. Lots of sea creatures. Sharks, jellyfish. Ugh. Quite unpleasant."

She stared at him, ignoring his light tone, seeing through to his eyes. She refused to reach for his boat, but she was tiring, and she knew it.

"Take my hand!" he snapped angrily, reaching out for her. "Now! Do it! I'll be damned if I'll let you drown—the newspapers would crucify me for that!"

She couldn't protest further because she would die.

He caught hold of her arms, lifting her into the boat. It swayed, but didn't pitch. She landed, seated and dripping on the floor. He stared at her, shaking his head in disgust. "This has got to be the most stupid thing you've done yet."

Cold. He was right. The water had been very cold, and her teeth were chattering. "It might have worked—"

"You might have died! Considering you were in the hands of idiots. You could have floated about endlessly until you died of exposure, dehydration—"

"We would have been picked up immediately in the shipping lanes."

"To what end?" he demanded with a shattering bellow. The force of his fury was truly frightening. "You know damned well that no harm would have come to you or anyone in my hands!"

"You might have chosen to keep the officers as prisoners—for exchange!" she reminded him swiftly.

"The men were offered the longboats, Miss Magee. So what about yourself? You were so desperate to get to England?"

"Well, sir, my own country seems to be infested with snakes who can slip in when and where they please!" she retorted. Then a fabulous lie sprang to her lips. "And if you must know, I'm due to be married."

He sat back, a brow arched. And she knew that she had startled him.

"Really?" he inquired. "How intriguing. When did this come about?"

"It's none of your business."

"Indeed? I'm just curious to know if this fellow is aware of what he's getting."

A strange panic seized her. Did he know?

"A wife who will adore him," she said.

"And do so with experience and expertise!"

Anger began a slow burn inside her. "My groom to be, sir, is an English gentleman who loves me, and does not condemn me for a kidnapping that was hardly my fault."

"Ah, yes!"

"You're not rowing, Captain," she commented.

His arms moved automatically at her words. The little

boat seemed to explode across the water with his
impetus.

"So—he will understand."

"Indeed, God knows. Perhaps he will appreciate my
expertise—as I'm sure your fiancée will yours. But then
again, sir, perhaps she has already!"

"My fiancée?" he inquired, ignoring the rest.

"I read about her in the paper . . . Toms . . .
Thompkins . . . oh, something of the like. Your beloved
in Charleston."

"Ah . . . Janine."

"Ah, Janine," she repeated flatly.

The boat banged against the bow of the *Lady Varina*.
To her surprise, he instantly rose, catching a rope that
was thrown down to him, and using it to pull them closer
to the rope ladder cast over the ship's side.

"Miss Magee?" he invited.

She moved quickly to the ladder, trying to climb up
before he could help her.

She felt his hands on her back. She bit into her lower
lip. He gave her rump a shove, and that was all.

A few minutes later she stood dripping on deck. She
had maintained her cloak—and her silver. For that she
had to be glad.

As she was glad to see the men of the *Lady Varina*
lined up on the deck, waiting to greet her. One by one
they doffed their caps. "Miss Magee!" Dr. Stewart said
pleasantly.

"Welcome, miss!" Jeremiah Jones told her shyly.
"The captain's cabin is ready for you."

"We've taken the liberty of bringing your things over
from the Yank vessel," Dr. Stewart told her.

"Thank you, thank you so much," she said, aware that
Jerome had reached the deck, and stood to her left, arms
crossed over his chest. She didn't look at him. If he
wanted to force her to be here, she was damned well
going to make herself at home.

And pray to somehow keep her distance.

"Gentlemen, I am soaked to the bone. If you'll excuse
me, I'll change. Jeremiah, would you be so good to ask
Mr. Dieter for some soup and hot tea? It would be excellent now. And I know that war effort leaves you with

few luxuries, but I'm sure some brandy was taken from my Northern escort, if you'll be so kind as to fetch it. Gentlemen, thank you again for your welcome. You do make being a prisoner in this wretched war tolerable."

She knew the ship, and she knew her way to the captain's cabin. If she didn't squish with every barefoot step she took, she might have made an incredibly dignified exit.

Jerome had ordered his maps and papers moved to David Stewart's quarters, as they were the largest after the master's cabin. Assured by Jeremiah that his guest had bathed, donned clean, dry clothing, and eaten her soup before retiring for the night, he sat in the bunk opposite the surgeon's own.

Drinking. Staring dourly at David Stewart, Jerome downed a good measure of rum.

Marriage. So she'd intended to sail to England, forget the war—and marry! How could she?

And why, in God's name, shouldn't she? They were enemies; they had met passionately, but in lust and anger, not love. She'd named it from the very beginning, and she'd meant what she had said.

Marriage!

He'd be damned if it would happen. Yet it seemed she believed the newspapers that said he intended to marry Janine Thompson. Janine had probably created the story, perhaps planning on making it come true.

"This time, you could have just let her go, you know," David said.

"Would you have left her in the shipping lanes with those idiots?" Jerome demanded.

David shrugged.

Jerome thought for a long moment. "We're going down the St. Johns. I'll arrange escort from Jacksonville to St. Augustine. A far better place to leave her than the shipping lanes."

"As you say, Captain. Are you willing to share that rum?"

Jerome looked at the bottle, grimaced, and sat up to hand it across to David.

"Don't you want to make sure she's sleeping where she's supposed to be?" David suggested.

"No," Jerome lied. Then he sighed. "All right, I shall see to our guest." He rose, surprised to realize he was reeling a bit. He gave himself a mental shake, and slipped out of David's cabin and across the deck. He saluted Matt at the helm, and saw that Jeremiah sat quietly near him.

"Miss Magee?" he inquired.

"I believe she's sleeping, sir."

He nodded and said, "I'll make sure she's settled." He strode toward the captain's cabin. Opening the door, he found the room in almost total darkness. Moving across to the bunk, he forced himself not to dwell on the last time he'd seen her there.

Even in the darkness, he could see that she had the covers pulled to her throat. He reached down to touch her forehead. She felt warm. No—hot.

He swore, going back quickly for David. Jerome lit a lantern, David felt Risa's forehead. She stirred, her eyes opening. They were glazed. She smiled. She might be ill, but her smile remained beautiful. "David . . . hello."

"You're sick, Risa," David told her.

She shook her head. "Just—a fever. I'm all right."

"I'm going to make you a draught with honey and lemon and whiskey, and I want you to drink every sip, and then we'll keep your head cool, all right?"

She shook her head. "You mustn't stay with me. You've injured men, David."

"I'll be in here," Jerome said firmly.

Her eyes touched his. She didn't protest. She was shivering from the fever. Her eyes closed.

David called for Jeremiah, giving him instructions as to how he wanted her toddy made. The lad ran off and returned, Jerome supported Risa, and she drank down the potion he gave her. She lay down again, and he remained at her side, cooling her forehead with damp cloths. After a while she stopped shivering, and she seemed to sleep. Then her rich dark lashes raised just slightly, and she spoke softly.

"Despite the fact that you're a sea devil—a red savage

Rebel—you might make Miss Thompson a good husband, Captain. You do seem to be good at this."

"I don't dare let you get too ill, Miss Magee."

"How noble of you."

He gazed down at her, unable to read any emotion in
the glitter of her beautiful blue, feverish eyes.

"If you decide you still want to go to England, Miss
Magee, let me be your escort next time. I can actually
get you there. But I'm afraid the wedding may have to
wait awhile. You're going to St. Augustine. And may I
suggest that you don't try to leave until I can escort
you safely?"

"You can suggest anything you wish," she told him.
But as her eyes closed, she smiled. Then her smile faded,
and he thought that she slept. Her forehead didn't feel
so hot. He shifted, easing down at the foot of the bunk.

Sometime later, he slept.

She awoke, thinking that she was going through the
violently ill stages of her early pregnancy again and that
it was her head and stomach pitching, and not the ship.

It was, however, the ship.

She tried to rise, but fell back into the bunk. While
she struggled to come to her feet again, the cabin door
burst open, and Jeremiah Jones entered. He wore a canvas raincoat and hood, and dripped in the cabin.

"Miss Magee!"

"Yes, Jeremiah."

"Sit tight—we've encountered a squall!"

"Ah," she murmured. "How bad?"

"Bad," he replied. "But the captain's at the wheel,
and we'll come through!" he promised her.

Jeremiah had told her to sit tight, and she did so. It
seemed that the ship creaked and groaned as she was
thrown mercilessly about on wild, bucking waves. At
times Risa was convinced that they were doomed. The
Lady Varina rocked up and down so high and so violently that it seemed she must roll over, but she did not.

By late afternoon the storm had passed them.

The crew, however, spent the rest of the day rescuing
the men and the most necessary supplies from the Yank
vessel—she was sinking. Hamlin had managed to bring

her through the storm, but the already crippled ship had been no match for it.

When Jeremiah came to see her that night with a supper tray, he told her sorrowfully that they were all worried about a number of the Yank crew—Captain Briggs and Lieutenant Waylon included—who had opted to depart in the longboats after she had been taken from them. "If the storm came upon them in the small boats, well . . ."

That night and the following day, Risa saw no one but Jeremiah. She slept a great deal, getting over the fever that had plagued her. She didn't know if Jerome ever looked in to see if she was well, but she was deeply grateful that her illness had gotten no worse. An examination by his own ship's doctor would have certainly put her in a perilous position.

She needn't have feared. With the Yankee ship lost to the storm and at the bottom of the sea, they made fast time. But the end of the third night, she learned that scouts had been sent in to make certain Jacksonville was in Rebel hands. Then the ship ran at full speed through the night. From her bunk in the captain's cabin, Risa awakened in terror to the sound of cannon fire. They were running past the blockaders into Jacksonville. It seemed that they raced, and that the guns blazed forever. But when the barrage was over, she stood in her white nightgown in the center of the cabin, bracing herself. The cabin door opened, and Jerome was there, splendid as always, a rogue with his long hair, billowing white sleeves, tight breeches, and high boots. A formidable silhouette in the night.

"You need to dress," he told her abruptly. "I've made arrangements for your transport down to St. Augustine."

She nodded, amazed at the disappointment that rose in her throat like bile. He didn't intend to keep her, to come near her again. Well, what had she wanted?

"Thank you," she said coolly.

He strode to her in the darkness of the cabin, just barely keeping his distance. "I should keep you, you know. Hang you from the yardarm. You've maligned me, and endangered my family. My sister was nearly abducted, you know. Shots were fired; she could have been killed."

"You are indignant regarding your sister, yet you thought nothing of kidnapping me."

"You knew my plans; I had no choice."

"And that's why you seized the ship I was on!"

"Now, Miss Magee, I didn't know you were on that ship but I probably saved your fool life. You were sailing on a long journey with total idiots."

"Oh, really? Captain, your arrogance will hang you yet."

"Perhaps, but I doubt it. And despite everything, you are now free."

"Thank you," she said coolly. "I'll be pleased to see St. Augustine again and delighted to see Alaina."

"Good," he said, watching her with enigmatic eyes. "Because you'd best not plan to leave. If you have to get somewhere, tell Alaina. She'll know how to find me."

"That won't be necessary. I'm planning a wedding, remember?"

"The warning remains. Don't leave St. Augustine, Miss Magee. The wedding will simply have to be postponed."

"Ah, but what about your own wedding, Captain?"

"That's not your concern."

"Well, my *life* is not your concern, Captain!"

"Don't attempt to leave."

"You will not win this war!"

"But you *will* learn to surrender."

"Not on your life, Captain."

"We shall see, Miss Magee."

With that, he left her. And she was furious to realize that there were tears in her eyes.

Chapter 16

Coming down the St. Johns was more difficult than it had ever been before. Since the Union forces had seized northeastern Florida, they had made the waters incredibly dangerous. Yankee soldiers had destroyed well over a thousand boats along the St. Johns, determined to keep Rebel forces on the western banks of the river. Their gunboats patrolled the river constantly, and they had done a good job of making it hell for the Rebels fighting them.

To the dismay of the Southern troops, there were many Floridians now swaying toward the Union side—and well-planned attacks were often discovered by the Union forces due to defecting Rebels who secreted information across the river.

Skirmishes along the water tended to be quick, violent hits. As Jerome ran past the Yanks down the river, eager to unload his rich cargo, he was barraged by Union guns a quarter of the way. He fired in return, keeping up his speed. Luckily, the Yanks were poorly supplied, and their guns were heavy and awkward, and couldn't follow. When he reached the camp south of the river from St. Augustine, he was quickly guided into a cove, and warned by old Grant Jennar that the troops were moving upriver to meet a Yankee attack. Jerome and his crew joined with the Reb guerrilla forces, and found that their fellow Rebs had dug into shallow trenches, preparing for the violent fire that was to come.

The day passed, and then the night, as, on both sides, the officers tried to decide the right time and angle from which to attack. The dawn brought sporadic bursts of fire, then a series of raging charges that began and ended quickly. At the end of the fighting, no one had retreated, and no one had moved forward. Jerome saw his cousin Julian and a number of his orderlies arrive to remove the wounded from the field on crude, mule-drawn conveyances. He left his position to help with the wounded, accepting Julian's grim nod as the best greeting they could give one another at the time.

The wounded were secured, and Jerome slipped back into his position. Once again, the troops waited.

They were all certain that the firing was due to commence again when a white flag was raised from the enemy position.

"Reb! Johnny Reb!" came a call from the Union side.

From their own ranks, one of the soldiers at the front of the line answered. "Yeah, Yank?"

"Hold your fire. Got a Colonel McKenzie here, looking for his cousin. You got a Captain McKenzie back there?"

"We got a couple of McKenzies. A doc, a—"

"Sea captain?"

"He's here, right as rain."

"See if he'll meet with the colonel. We can probably give them about two minutes before the bullets start flying again!"

The man at the front turned, cupping his hand around his mouth to shout out. "Captain McKenzie?"

Jerome had heard the exchange, and was already rising, his heart quickening to realize that Ian was in the same battle at last.

He strode quickly down the line and across the field that separated the Rebs from the Yanks. As he walked, he saw Ian coming toward him. His cousin was thinner. They all were. Ian, a colonel now, was still a dominating figure: tall, straight, taking long strides until they faced one another. They stared for a second, meeting one another's eyes, and then they embraced. Jerome pulled back. Smiling ruefully, he told Ian, "Your brother is back there, working a field hospital. He's going to be mad as hell that you asked to see me instead of him."

"I miss my brother. Tell him so," Ian said.

Jerome nodded.

"And Tia. Is she well? Safe? Surviving the war. I worry that she's too reckless, even if she's with Julian."

"Tia is well. She'll be furious, too."

"I'm sorry. But I had to speak with you."

"Oh?" Jerome arched a brow.

"Sirs—best hurry!" a soldier warned from the field.

"Well, I can't be subtle, I don't have much time," Ian said. "I'll speak quickly. Oh, hell, I'll—"

Suddenly, out of the clear blue, Ian socked him in the jaw. Swift as lightning, the blow *might* have been seen by the watching soldiers as an affectionate tap upon the chin.

It was no tap, and Jerome instinctively raised his fist to punch back, then stopped himself, thinking Ian had lost his mind. They couldn't break into a fistfight out here in the middle of the battlefield. They'd both be shot down.

"What the hell are you doing?" Jerome demanded instead. "I should deck you here and now, cousin—"

"Sorry, it's just that I got slugged harder—for you."

"Ian, you've lost your damned mind, and I swear—"

"General Magee called me out, Jerome. It seems he suspects that his daughter is in a family way—and he blamed me! I know damned well I'm not responsible, so I thought I should pass along the news—and the right hook to the jaw. Magee is aging, but he can still manage a mean punch."

"A family way?" Jerome demanded, stunned. "Risa . . ."

"Yes, Risa is expecting. As I said, the child isn't mine. Therefore, I thought you should know. I'm not supposed to be here, with these troops, but I felt that I had to reach you with the information." He was silent a moment, then added quietly, "You've taken enough risks for me!"

"Sirs! The firing is due to start!" a private called urgently from the line.

"We've got to go," Jerome said. "Thank you, Ian."

"The child is yours?"

"Yes."

"Captain McKenzie!" Warned a fellow from the trenches.

But Jerome held fast to his position a moment longer.

"Will you be seeing your wife in St. Augustine?" he asked Ian.

"Yes, I intend to, tonight."

Jerome nodded. "Warn Alaina to expect me in the next few days. Tell her I'll need a discreet clergyman, sympathetic to the Southern cause."

"I thought you might see it that way."

"Tell Alaina not to say anything to Risa."

"Cousin, I'll make certain she doesn't," Ian said, tilting his cavalry hat with a slow grin. "Since I'm not at all sure how Risa is seeing things."

"Not too clearly. She meant to marry some Englishman."

"Colonel McKenzie, you must get down!" a Yankee soldier cried from his position.

Jerome quickly embraced the cousin who had just belted him. "God go with you," he said, a deep tremor in his voice. "Keep your head low."

"You, too," Ian replied.

"Down, sirs! Down!"

They parted, both sprinting toward their battle lines. Jerome fell back into the cradle of his narrow trench just as a barrage of fire began to rain again.

He heard the terrible roar of bullets. He loaded and fired, loaded and fired again. His movements were automatic.

He watched men fall around him. Heard them scream, saw them bleed. He prayed that Ian was alive on the other side.

Toward dusk the firing stopped at last. Neither side had gained ground. Both retreated: the Yanks back to St. Augustine, the Rebs to their inland camps.

A silly, stupid battle, Jerome thought wearily. There was no major theater of war here—just a waste of bullets and medicine, youth and life.

He worked throughout the night, helping Julian and Tia with the wounded. Strange work, because Julian was indignant that his brother had talked to Jerome and not him.

"I don't know the last time I've seen my brother!" Julian complained irritably.

"He is the enemy, and it's difficult to communicate as

the enemy," Tia reminded him, frowning at Jerome. "But what did he want?"

"He wanted us all to know he's still a McKenzie," Jerome said. "He asked for me because I was the one on the battlefield. Medical personnel are seldom at the front of the skirmish. Oh, and he wanted to let me know that I'm about to become a father, and might want to do something about it."

Tia's jaw dropped. Julian arched an amused brow.

"Not a word!" Jerome warned sternly. "Not a word from either of you."

"What are you going to do?" Julian asked politely.

"The right thing, what else?" Jerome inquired bitterly. The right thing! She'd been trying to run off to marry an Englishman, with a Reb's child growing in her womb. God—it was suddenly possible to understand why the Yanks couldn't win the war when the statistics were all in their favor. They hadn't a lick of sense. Not a lick.

"Jerome, how can you?" Tia asked.

"I'll have to slip into St. Augustine for an evening."

"That's madness!" Tia protested. "They just had a purge in the town. The Yank in charge expelled Southern sympathizers. Men and women who wouldn't take the oath of loyalty were forced onto a transport ship."

"Tia, no matter how many have been expelled, there are still Rebs living quietly in that town. I won't be completely surrounded by the enemy."

"You'll wind up imprisoned in the *castillo*!" Tia warned.

Jerome felt a strange chill settle over him. "My father was imprisoned there once with Osceola and other Seminoles who had been betrayed. My father escaped. I'll know the way out."

"*If* you get in to town," Julian argued.

"I'll get in. Nothing could keep me out."

"Not even a half dozen companies of Yanks?" Tia argued.

"Not even a thousand Yanks," he assured her.

Risa hadn't really been away from St. Augustine for very long, yet as she arrived by carriage, she saw there had been changes made.

The Federals had made a commitment to keep the town. Once, when they had feared a Rebel attack, the soldiers had withdrawn into the old fort, the Castillo San Marcos, as the Spaniards had named it, or Ft. Marion, as it was now called. It was a fabulous architectural creation, rising from the Florida marsh like a European castle or fortress. Its walls were thick and imposing, beautiful, built with coquina shell. The fortress was as unusual and charming as the rest of the city with its old Spanish houses and churches. It had a special feel to it; it was the oldest European settlement in the country.

Risa had learned through her escorts, Bartholomew and Mary DeGarmo, that there had recently been a meeting called, and the residents were asked to sign oaths of loyalty to the Union. Those who refused had been expelled. There were feelings of resentment in the city, despite the fact the *Burnside*—the decaying tub of a Federal transport ship—had been met off Jacksonville by Union General Terry, who had countermanded the order. Too many people had lost their homes and possessions already in the expulsion. Risa sympathized with both sides; the Rebels might be furious that their families were treated so callously, but the Yankees resented feeding people who plotted against them.

As Risa looked around, Bartholomew, a large, musclebound Spaniard, gave the guard their traveling passes.

The Union troops had made improvements on the town's defenses. An entrenchment had been dug north of the fort, running from the North River to the Sebastian River, and a wall closed off the interior of the peninsula on which the town sat. Numerous cannons sat on top of Ft. Marion, and fields had been cleared of trees to allow for clean firing. Pickets guarded the San Sebastian bridge at King Street—which was the only way into the town from the west. The troops, she assumed, were still quartered at the southern end of town, but she could see that military tents dotted the outskirts to the north and west as well.

She heard her name called and swung around to see Alaina coming. She had sent a message to her friend from Jacksonville, hoping that Alaina would be able to meet her, and help soothe the loneliness she was feeling.

Seeing Alaina, she cried out gladly, running to her, hugging her, then laughing, for Alaina's pregnancy had come along, and she was round enough to cause them to bump off one another.

The guards quickly cleared her party through, and she introduced Bartholomew and Mary. Alaina brought Risa to her carriage, where she was pleased to see Finn McCullough waiting with another man. She hugged Finn first. She hadn't seen him when she'd come through St. Augustine after her first captivity: he'd gone to Washington to be interviewed by a Union naval commander. "I'm so glad to see you!" she cried. And he smiled, flushing, hugging her back. "Risa, I'm always glad to see you! You're all right? Yes, of course, you look beautiful, and healthy. It's wonderful to have you back here!"

"And this is Dr. Thayer Cripped," Alaina said, introducing her to the man who waited by Finn. Cripped was young, handsome in a thin, aesthetic way, and friendly.

"I understand that you assist in surgery, Miss Magee. It will be nice to have a good Unionist at my side, since Alaina torments me daily with her talk about the states' God-given right to secede."

Risa arched a brow to Alaina. "And I had thought that you meant to behave, embrace motherhood, and be a good and obedient wife to Ian!"

"I am a good wife, but Ian has never expected total obedience!" Alaina murmured dryly. "I am all talk these days."

"Talk will get you expelled from this town!" Risa warned.

"They can't expel me. I am Ian's wife. But come along now. We've new living quarters, and they're quite comfortable."

"I must see the baby first—my godson!" Risa reminded Alaina, and Alaina smiled with great pride, going on and on then about Sean's miraculous development.

Risa rode with Alaina, Finn, and Dr. Cripped to the medical housing facilities. At Alaina's she hugged and kissed her godchild—tremors assailing her as she wondered if her own babe would have the telltale McKenzie eyes and rich, dark hair. Sean was put to bed, and the adults had dinner. When Finn and Thayer left, Alaina helped Risa settle into her temporary home in St. Augustine.

They were quartered in Old Spanish row houses, with Thayer's surgery set up at one end, his residence next to it, Alaina's next to that, and Risa's at the far end. She had a charming parlor with double fireplace that connected to the bedroom behind it, a pleasant room with brocade drapes, a copper hip tub, a "necessary" room, and a large, four-poster bed with a warm white knit cover and a half a dozen pillows.

Servants quarters were in a separate building behind the row houses, and all were surrounded by fruit trees.

With Sean in bed and his nurse in attendance, the DeGarmos and Dr. Thayer Cripped and his household all settled, Alaina sat with Risa in her own little parlor, sipping tea.

"So you were headed to England. I never imagined that you would leave the country!" Alaina told her, curious cat's golden eyes upon her. "You—Lady Liberty! Devoted Daughter. Miss Union."

"It seemed . . . the right thing to do," Risa said lamely.

Alaina leaned forward, frowning. "You were going to marry an Englishman?" she inquired with serious concern.

"Where did you hear that?" Risa asked sharply.

Alaina sat back, lashes lowered, savoring another long sip of tea. "They try to cut off communications here between the townsfolk and the Rebels on the other side of the river, but . . . well, you know, my brother and sister-in-law are close and . . . actually, Ian is still in the area."

"Ian?" Risa said, surprised.

Alaina nodded. "Of course, I'm happy because I get to see him. And I'm also miserable because—oh, Risa! He actually faced Jerome in a skirmish the other day! What if one of them had killed the other? It was a silly, no outcome fight, but men were injured, a few died . . . and all this nonsense about expelling people from St. Augustine was over soldiers killed by Rebs. So on the one hand, I hate it that Ian is in the state, because it's his state, and the people he fights are his people. His own kin, his own blood. But St. Augustine is Union now, so it's not unusual that I open my eyes at night, find him with me, and life worth living."

"I'm glad for you and Ian, and I understand your dilemma," Risa murmured, sipping her tea. "But I'm still curious as to how you heard about my engagement." Very curious—since she had made it up.

"I suppose the news filtered through Jerome to Julian or Tia and on to Ian, I'm not sure. But is it true?"

Risa lowered her head. She and Alaina had been through a great deal together, and they risked much for one another. But she found herself loath to admit that she was expecting Jerome McKenzie's child, and could not do so. It was far too complicated.

"Yes—I suppose I was intending to marry. But I'll have to write and explain that my plans have changed. If my father finds out that the Union ship I was on just happened to be taken by Jerome's Rebel command, he will probably lock me away in a tower somewhere until this is all over. Which is why, of course, I need to make some plan quickly," she murmured.

She looked up to discover that Alaina was staring at her intently. Alaina looked away. "Had you heard about Teela?"

"Teela . . . Ian talked about an 'Aunt Teela.' "

"Yes, his aunt—Jerome's mother. Like my own, I grew up down there, you know. Teela's lovely and giving—and strong. But she's expecting a baby, and we're all very concerned."

"Jerome's *mother* is expecting a child?"

"Yes." Alaina looked at Risa. "Such things do happen."

"I know, but—" Risa murmured. How ironic! "Well, it's getting late. We should probably both get some sleep."

Alaina rose, hugging her again. "You're sure you're comfortable? And there's nothing else I can get for you?"

"I'm perfectly comfortable, and there's nothing I need."

"There's nothing you want to say, you're fine on your own?"

"I'm fine. Go to bed!" Risa told her.

Alaina kissed her cheek then, smiled at her strangely, and left for her own little house.

Risa watched her go, wondering why she hadn't managed to tell Alaina the truth. She'd been too much of a fool regarding McKenzie men.

Chapter 17

It was far easier being in St. Augustine, than following McClellan's army.

McClellan was constantly surrounded by death.

The ills that prevailed in St. Augustine were not so constant, nor thankfully, so severe.

Many of the Union soldiers had scurvy, which could be cured with readily available citrus fruits. As fall cooled the temperatures, there were not nearly so many mosquitoes, and there were far fewer cases of heat exhaustion.

Soldiers steadily arrived on the operating table due to frequent skirmishing on the river. But the numbers of wounded seemed far more manageable, the ability to treat them greater. They were not required to move in the middle of surgery, nor did they fear cannon fire exploding overhead as they operated.

On the night that marked her first full week in St. Augustine, Risa went to bed thoughtful and exhausted. Sometimes it was difficult maintaining a normal routine in the city. The Southerners resented her, while the Unionists were too friendly. She had a habit of being very opinionated, and she was far too quick to become embroiled in the local situation. She'd insisted that day that an officer vacate the confiscated premises of a Southern lady, stating the woman had done him no wrong, nor had she been involved in the war effort, nor had she insulted any of the Union soldiers. In the upshot, the colonel had been called in, the officer ousted. He was angry with Risa, though she politely explained that it wouldn't further their cause if they were to be known as thieves. The aging Southern lady resented Risa for

begging the Yankee to return her property—though that
didn't stop her from moving back into her house.

She should have been in England, Risa reminded
herself.

But what then, and what now?

How long would it be until she could no longer hide
her condition?

She laced a cup of tea with a few drops of brandy,
determined that she was going to sleep well that night,
and then somehow decide what to do with her future.
She thought wryly that if she had gotten into her predicament just a few months earlier, she might have had
Alaina tell the world she'd given birth to twins. But she
knew in her heart that there was no pretense she could
make, no charade she could play. She wanted her baby,
and she wanted to be its mother. But the mere thought
of how viciously the world treated unwed mothers and
illegitimate babies made her fearful. A marriage of con-
venience to a good friend just might be in order. Since
the baby's father was marrying elsewhere, the concept
of informing him was irrelevant.

Her days were still wearing, and that night, ensconced
in her comfortable bed, a fire burning low in the grate
against the slight damp chill of the Florida fall, she
slept deeply.

Only to awake in panic.

A hand clamped over her mouth. She felt the heat of
a human body next to her, but before her heart could
completely fail her, she heard Jerome's whisper, and
breathed in his subtle, masculine scent.

"Don't scream. It's me."

He released her and stood, coming around to her side
of the bed and staring down at her in the flickering red
firelight. He was shirtless, wearing damp breeches, no
shoes. His dark hair curled over his shoulders, auburn
highlights caught by the fire. His features were hard and
set, eyes fierce with a sharp blue glitter.

"I should most certainly be screaming," she said, "and
you're a fool if you think I won't. You've abducted me,
you've ravished me, you've attacked a ship on which I
sailed. Now you're in my bedroom in a Union-held town.
You are the most annoyingly active enemy—"

She broke off with a little gasp because he reached down, pulling her covers away. She sat up, indignant.

"You know, McKenzie, I really will scream! Out of respect to your family, I'd like to keep you from becoming Yankee target practice, but—"

"Get up."

"Get up? You fool! St. Augustine is being held by Union forces. Didn't you know that? You can't order me—no!"

But he had swept her up despite her protest and set her firmly on her feet. His eyes scanned her deliberately.

"Captain McKenzie, get out of my house, and my room. I warn you—" She broke off, a startled cry escaping her, for he ripped her white cotton nightgown over her head, leaving her naked. Furious, she tried to push free from him, tried to grab hold of the fabric he wrenched away.

"Stop it!" she demanded frantically. "Damn you! I won't let you—I will scream!"

But she found herself lifted and set back on the bed. He didn't crawl atop her with unbridled passion, but sat at her side, hands exploring the definite rise of her abdomen and enlarged globes of her breasts.

"Don't!" she whispered, trying to push his hands away. But then his eyes were on hers, blue flames in the firelight, and again, there was no hint of passion about him, just a tightly leashed fury that made her stomach catapult.

"You have a bloody nerve!" she told him, trembling.

His eyes shot to hers. "This is why you were so eager to avoid me aboard ship."

"Captain, you were busy aboard ship, if you'll recall. Seizing, plundering, humiliating your enemies."

"Neither Captain Briggs nor Lieutenant Waylon needed my help to be humiliated. And yet I must be grateful for their lack of seamanship—which allowed me such an easy conquest. Since you were attempting to slip away to England, and marry elsewhere—with my child."

She could not help but go on the defensive then— even if all the arguments she had waged with herself in favor of leaving had been solid. It didn't much matter now that she'd entirely made up the man she claimed

she was going to marry. "You—you've really no right to
be here. You don't know that it's your child—"

"I think that I do."

She swallowed, longing to have his absolute arrogance
and assurance, if only for a moment.

Well, she did have it, she could have it—she was a
general's daughter. She pushed up against the bedding,
ignoring the chill that touched her bare skin. She met
his eyes. "It seemed senseless to bring my condition to
your attention since there was nothing you could do.
Nor do I blame you, or hold you accountable—"

"Ah, you are so noble," he interrupted.

His tone was unnerving, as was the way he looked
at her.

"Look, there's a war on—"

"Yes, there's a war on. And there's blood and death
and dismemberment daily. So I damned well don't appreciate your attempts to rob me of this new life."

"I didn't know what you'd think—"

"You didn't bother to ask me!" he snapped.

"Go to hell! We are enemies. Besides, you're engaged,
and you must take Miss Thompson into consideration—"

"I've taken everything into consideration," he told her
angrily, "including the fact that I can't take a cat-o'-
nines to you—since it could injure the child!"

"Oh, how dare you be so self-righteous—"

"How dare I?" he demanded, his eyes narrowing
sharply. "You knew! You knew this when I found you
in Virginia. And you didn't say a word—"

"You didn't stay very long!" she reminded him.

"Long enough for you to have mentioned the fact that
we were expecting a child."

"To what purpose?" she cried out.

"Get up!" he demanded, rising, and catching her
hands to draw her to her feet before him.

"Why? What are you planning to do?"

"Marry you."

"What?"

"Marriage, my love. That is the purpose."

"Here? Now?" she queried somewhat hysterically.

"No—in the parlor, in two minutes," he countered.

He left her standing, turning to her wardrobe to sort through her clothing. "We don't need anything too fussy—I'm not exactly dressed for the occasion, but coming by river doesn't allow for much in the way of formal attire. Here, this will do."

He spun back around with a white cotton day dress, suitable for an afternoon barbecue. He tossed it toward her, and she reflexively caught it. "No corset tonight or in the future. Brent and Julian both consider it barbaric the way women try to hide their condition, while strangling their poor babes. Dammit, get dressed."

Tears stung her eyes. Despite the fact that he'd scared her to death and his temper was foul, she'd been ridiculously pleased to see him. Yet what had she been expecting? A bent-knee proposal from a man engaged to another woman?

She shook her head. "I can't marry you."

"Can't?"

"You're a Rebel," she reminded him, teeth grating.

"I'm a Rebel?" he repeated.

She narrowed her eyes, frightened of his mood, and the animosity he bore her, yet hurt and determined to hurt him in turn. "You're a Rebel—and worse," she informed him contemptuously. "You've Indian blood in your veins. You do have a savage streak, and you're the most incredibly rude man I've ever met. I simply can't marry you."

He came to her swiftly, catching her arms and dragging her to him so that her head fell back and she met the glittering fury in his eyes. "I should make your backside crimson for that, Miss Magee, and I warn you, the temptation remains. Pay attention, lest you tempt me too far. You're going to marry me. Because you weren't forced into anything—we're both responsible for that babe. I will deal with my previous relationships; they are none of your concern. But you will put that dress on and you will marry me—because my child isn't going to be a bastard, nor will he call any other man father. Now, let's go!" he snapped.

She wrenched free from him. "You bastard!" she cried.

His eyes narrowed. "Whatever I am, you're about to

be my wife. Get dressed," he commanded, and left the room.

Shaking so that she could barely manage, Risa slipped into the white gown. It wasn't a matter of bowing down to the orders he barked out; she was making her own decision.

He was right regarding their child. The world might be different when the war was over, but she was certain that illegitimacy would still bear a terrible stigma. The baby was innocent, and deserved the best she could give.

She took the time to brush her hair, and he came back for her, dressed now with boots on and a smart navy jacket. His features hard and fathomless, his eyes swept the length of her. "You've agreed."

"I've agreed," she said coolly, absurdly ready to burst into tears and absolutely determined that she wouldn't do so. He was so tense and hostile that she nearly reneged. She didn't want to be a despised wife. Not after all that burned between them, the fierce passion and longing that had so seduced her. But passion was a fire that could burn too brightly, and singe all else.

She started toward the bedroom door, then swung back, her hostility as great as his. "I've agreed—for the child. But I'll not tolerate your arrogance, and know that I despise all that you stand for. I'll give you your wedding vows, if that's what you wish, but you stay away from me, Captain McKenzie, do you understand? You keep your distance. Am I clear?"

He arched a brow, strode to her, and allowed his gaze to sweep over her once again in a dry assessment.

"The world is full of women, Miss Magee. Young, beautiful—and welcoming. Rebels, if you will. So live in a glasshouse, if you so choose, but let's get this done. For the sake of the child. However," he said, enunciating sharply, "you should be fairly warned. Should I desire things differently, neither time nor distance will ever deter me from claiming what is rightfully mine."

She felt like ice, and it was all wrong, and she was afraid that she was equally the cause of it, but she couldn't seem to force herself to stop it.

He took her by the elbow, and led her to the parlor. She shouldn't have been surprised to see that not only was the local Anglican reverend in her house, but both Alaina and Ian were there as well. Risa realized that it had been a very long time since she had seen the two of them together.

Alaina looked incredibly guilty and uncomfortable, but her long stare at Risa was accusing as well. Risa should have shared the truth with so close a friend.

Ian seemed impatient, disturbed that an infamous Rebel was testing sanity by being in this town.

Risa didn't hug either of them. She gave them both sharp glares—which they ignored.

"Well, well, under the circumstances, we should get started," the reverend murmured nervously. "The two of you, Risa, Jerome, before the fire here . . . ahem!"

He began the ceremony. Risa was aware of the total incongruity of it all. There was Ian—whom she had intended to marry. And Alaina, her best friend. And next to her . . .

Jerome. Her enemy. And yet he was the man who had so enticed and fascinated her that she had wanted him when wanting was madness. Towering, dark, handsome, an irresistible force. Eyes lowered, she saw his hands, and felt a tremor as she recalled his touch. She thought of his eyes, rivetingly blue against the bronze of his face, made all the more compelling by the richness of his heritage. She heard his voice, clear and strong, as he recited his vows, and she closed her eyes, and thought of the mercy he had shown his enemies when seizing their ship. And she realized then, marrying him, that she was in love with him. The passion they had shared had been overwhelming in its intensity, and the fires had perhaps blinded her from the truth. She hadn't wanted to avoid this marriage because he was the enemy, but because she was afraid. Afraid that she loved him, and he could not love her. Her eyes and throat burned—she'd had no right to allow her own fears to risk her baby's future. And yet . . .

"Risa," she heard his voice, felt his elbow's prod.

"Yes!" she said startled.

Apparently, it was the right word at the time. She was prompted to state her vows, which she did—somewhat haltingly. But it didn't seem to matter. Her hand was in his, and he was sliding a ring on her finger. Oddly enough, it was an excellent fit.

"Champagne?" Alaina queried, trying to sound natural.

"Quickly, quickly," Ian agreed. "For the reverend— and now, to the paperwork."

Alaina had been prepared. While Risa shakily signed her name to the legal license making her a McKenzie, Alaina procured the champagne. She popped the bottle, and as the champagne spewed out, she caught it in glass flutes. As she handed Risa hers, she hugged her and whispered, "It's for the best!"

Risa accepted the champagne from her. She was sure her eyes conveyed a silent accusation: *Traitor!*

Alaina returned a helpless shrug.

Risa found herself engulfed in a warm hug, and Ian looked down at her, smiling. "Well, you've become a McKenzie, Risa. I'll always be a bit jealous."

She smiled. He was a liar who adored his wife and would have done nothing differently. She longed to tell him that she wasn't really a McKenzie. She couldn't really be a McKenzie. They had gone through a formality, and nothing more.

"It's nearly dawn, Jerome," Ian reminded his cousin.

"Yes, I know." Risa heard his drawl from behind her.

"I'll be on my way, then," the reverend said.

"My thanks, sir," Jerome said, taking his hand with his own, which carried a United States gold piece. "For your flock, sir," he said.

"Indeed, indeed, thank you! And you won't forget now, that I was forced into this—the Yanks here can be so brutal to those who fraternize with the Rebs!"

"You were forced, sir," Jerome agreed.

The man nodded nervously, and slipped out. Risa watched as Ian set an arm around his very pregnant wife, leading her toward the door. "You haven't much time," Ian warned Jerome.

"I don't need much time," Jerome replied.

"Good night, then. God keep you both," Ian said.

"God keep us all—to surviving the war!" Jerome agreed passionately, raising his champagne glass to the others as they departed. He set down the glass, turning to Risa. She felt a warm, crimson flush color her face, and instinctively moved backward, groping for the mantel to hold.

He approached her with long strides, reaching for her chin, tilting her head so that her eyes met his. "Don't worry, Mrs. McKenzie, you haven't a thing to fear from me."

"When have you ever seen me afraid, Captain?"

He smiled, a curious, grim smile that somehow mocked her words. "I must admit . . . your behavior runs to the foolhardy rather than the timid. Still, I assure you, you've nothing to fear—if you can remember that 'obey' part in the wedding vows. Stay here, where I know I can find you, Risa."

"I've no plans to leave."

"I'd thought that you should go to Jacksonville, but the city is far too unstable. There is Charleston, of course."

"No," she said quickly. His arched brow caused her to add, "It's far too—Southern."

"That would be the point."

She shook her head, sincere in her words. "I can't make you a Yankee, Jerome, and you can't turn me into a Rebel."

"True enough," he said softly.

"And your fiancée lives in Charleston."

"Married men do not have finacées."

"Your ex-fiancée resides in Charleston."

"So she does."

"I'd not complicate the issue for you."

"How very kind and thoughtful."

She wanted to hit him. She managed to refrain.

"I'll stay here," she told him.

"In a town held by the North," he commented dryly.

"In a Southern state. With Alaina. In Florida."

Her lashes fell. She felt him watching her. He didn't argue. After a moment he said, "I'm naturally aware of the danger involved in transportation these days," he said. "But I want my child born at my family's home. It's not a grand plantation like my uncle's Cimarron, but it is my family's estate. When the time comes closer, you'll receive word from me that I'm taking you home."

"Can that be prudent, sir, under the circumstances?" she demanded. "My father—"

"Your father will have to accept that you are a married woman," he interrupted.

"I've not heard from him yet. He's sure to be worried—"

"Then, write—and tell him that you are well, and that you are married. And that it is no longer your duty to follow your father, but your husband."

"I will always follow my own heart and mind!" she informed him passionately.

"Then, pray, my love, that they lead you in the right direction." He stepped back. "If you find that you need me for any reason, you need only summon me; I'll come as soon as I can. Good night, Risa. Take care of yourself—and our child."

He turned, and opening the door, slipped out into the darkness of the night.

Like a demon wraith, he was gone.

Chapter 18

"So what is the news?"

Sydney looked up from the letter she had been reading, flushing to discover that her patient—prisoner of war Union Colonel Jesse Jon Halston—was awake, watching her.

He was an intelligent, handsome man with rich brown hair and sparkling hazel eyes. He'd been taken at the awful battle of Antietam Creek—half dead at the time—and still considered an incredible prize by the Confederates who had seized him. He was a cavalryman, hailed by the North for his ability to ride as well as any Southerner and actually encircle Rebel positions. He was also a respected man in the South—since he had put a halt to the hanging of five Southern soldiers in the Shenandoah Valley. Certain that the men had been spies who had betrayed their position to Jackson's men, they had nearly been lynched when Jesse Halston had stepped into the situation, calmly reminding his fellow officers that there was no evidence whatsoever against the men—and that God would smite them all if they didn't maintain some code of ethics. However, it wasn't his humanitarianism that made him important as a prisoner. Lincoln had commended Halston for a scouting raid that had given Union troops the position of an ambush, and saved the lives of hundreds of men. It was all a big chess game. Halston, though a colonel, had a reputation that might make him worth two generals in a prisoner exchange.

He had lived, Sydney believed with pride, because her brother Brent had been called in to attend him. Halston had taken five bullets—yet, miraculously, none had shattered his bones. Other Union soldiers had been horrible patients, convinced Brent meant to kill them if he didn't amputate an injured limb, and convinced he wanted to hack them into being lesser men when he had no choice but to cut.

Jesse Halston had opened his sizzling gold eyes against the blood on his face long enough to see Brent. And he'd kept his silence, not accusing Rebel surgeons of any butchery whatsoever. He hadn't screamed once during surgery—despite the fact that his only anesthesia had been the remnants of a bottle of whiskey. In the end, he'd passed out rather than cried out. During his slow, fevered recovery, he'd reached out frequently for someone called Mary—and he'd come to think that Sydney was Mary. Due to his tremendous importance, the matron at the hospital had ordered Sydney to make Halston her priority. Brent was one of the growing number of physicians who heartily believed in fresh air and ventilation as important for healing, so as soon as Halston had been able, she'd become his escort on those mornings when he'd asked to see sunlight. Today, he'd already been out in the courtyard when she'd arrived, eyes closed, dozing in his wheelchair. He could walk now, but hadn't the strength to take himself far. He would always limp, Brent had said, but what a small price for a man to pay for the beating he had taken.

"Gossip, family gossip," she told him.

"I should love to hear it," he told her.

She shrugged. "It's not that fascinating."

"Anything is fascinating when you've been hospitalized long enough. And I imagine, Miss McKenzie, that anything in your life must be fascinating as well."

She smiled, shaking her head. "All right. My cousin-in-law, Alaina, is due to have a baby very soon."

"Yes, Alaina."

She arched a brow. "You know her?"

He smiled, shaking his head yes. "But I've ridden with Ian often enough."

"Oh!" she said, surprised. "Then—"

"Indeed, I recognized my surgeon as a McKenzie relation the moment I opened my eyes. Ian often praised both his brother and cousin's surgical skills, sometimes incurring the wrath of other physicians by advising them what Brent or Julian McKenzie would do under the circumstances. Let's see, naturally, you are a far more lovely version, but still very definitely a McKenzie of Florida, though you've a distinctive exotic look. If I may be so bold as to suggest—"

"Indian blood," Sydney said matter-of-factly. She was quite proud of it.

"It makes you exceptionally beautiful."

"What is this flattery, sir? Careful, you are beginning to sound like a Southern gentleman."

"Men are gentlemen or they are not, North or South," he advised her pleasantly.

"And some are wickedly adept at flattery, and some are not," she informed him saucily. "If you are thinking to somehow charm and escape me—"

"Why on earth would I want to escape you?"

Sydney arched a brow, wondering why this man should so unnerve her and cause her to flush so easily.

The war was full of men. And in nursing, she had certainly seen her share of them—all of them.

"Well, you won't escape, so behave. I'm also about to be an aunt. Again. My older sister, Jennifer, has an adorable little boy. But it seems that my wayward sea captain brother has taken a bride as well—and is to be a father."

"The wayward sea captain—who married General Magee's daughter?"

"That would be the one," Sydney said. "Why?"

"General Magee is still steaming. Please, go on."

"Well, the most important news of all, of course, is that—" She broke off, looking at him. He was interested. Really interested in the domestic side of her life. Of course, he was Ian's friend. And he'd served under Magee.

"What?" Jesse Halston asked, smiling.

She shook her head. "I'm telling you everything. You've told me nothing."

He grinned. "I am the only grandchild of a rich fur merchant, I'm afraid, with wads of money, and an incredible mansion in New York City."

"Humble, too, I see."

He shook his head, still smiling. "The money has been growing by itself since soon after the Lewis and Clark expedition—I can take no credit. And, you see, the money came through my mother, who eloped with my father—a soldier. He fought in the Mexican War. Therefore, my appointment to West Point—where I met your cousin Ian. And my commission now. What more can I tell you?"

Sydney looked at him, hesitated. Then she asked, "Who's Mary?"

He took a while to answer. "My wife. She died of malaria two weeks after I rode to war."

"Oh! I'm sorry."

"Thank you. So go on. Tell me more about your letters."

"What? Oh!" Sydney stared back to the pages on her lap. "My mother is about to have a child."

He smiled. "You sound so disapproving. Do you think she's too old? That it's not quite . . . proper?"

Sydney shook her head. "No. I love my mother. I don't want anything to happen to her. I'm worried. My brother Brent is getting leave. He has fought the entire war without so much as a day's absence, for which I am grateful now, because after his service at Antietam, his superiors have determined he must have some time away. Jerome, my oldest brother, has tremendous freedom of movement—there's not an officer in the war who wouldn't help him because his talents in securing supplies are so miraculous. But he runs a dangerous game, and I worry terribly. He should have been here for us by now."

"The sea captain?"

She nodded.

"Don't worry," Halston told her. "From what I've heard, he'll come."

"You can't possibly know Jerome as well."

"Only by reputation," Jesse Halston assured her. He reached across the few feet separating his wheelchair and her bench. He squeezed her hand. "Don't worry," he assured her. "You'll reach your mother."

"I wish I had your faith."

"All there can really be now is faith," he told her. "Keep believing."

*   *   *

Two days later, when she sat with Jesse Halston once again, Jerome arrived.

The hospital staff was in a fluster. Jerome was a Southern hero, defying guns that kept other men home. By appearance, her brother quite lived up to his reputation. He seemed exceptionally tall and imposing in his sweeping blue military cape, and wore a plumed, cockaded hat. His features were very bronze from the sun at sea, and his eyes were a flaming blue against them. He courteously greeted the nurses, both the gaping matrons and the swooning, sweet young debutantes, and stopped to talk to old friends and new in the wards along the way. Sydney, who knew him so well, saw the pain in his eyes for those who suffered. When he reached her bench in the courtyard at last, he wrapped her in his arms. Jerome had changed. They had all changed. But he had always been the most like their father, confident in all that he was, recklessly brash and charming, yet somewhat untouchable. He retained his devastating smile, and his dark charm, but there was something far more serious about him now. It was visible in his walk, his casual, agile movements, even in the deep tenor of his voice. And still, his arms were warm and his words for her tender as he greeted her with a long hug and a compliment, telling her how wonderful she looked.

"You, too, big brother!" she told him heartily. He did look good. Lean and hard and wary, like a wolf. She drew away to introduce him to her patient. "Captain Jerome McKenzie, Colonel Jesse Halston, USA."

"Captain McKenzie, sir! The scourge of the sea," Jesse Halston greeted him.

Sydney saw Jerome's half smile, a sure sign that he had heard of Jesse as well. He offered his hand to Jesse. "Colonel Halston—the only man to rival our own Jeb Stuart."

"Unless it be your cousin, Ian, sir," Jesse said modestly.

Jerome laughed, taking a seat on the bench. "Well said, sir." He sobered then. "I'm glad to see you alive. It was rumored at Antietam that you had been killed."

"Left for dead, I'm afraid. Alive, thanks to the skills of your brother, Brent. And your sister."

Jesse glanced at Sydney, who flushed. Jerome studied them both carefully, then rose. "Sir, it's a pleasure to meet you. I'm assuming the intent is to exchange you for one of our own fellows, but I pray that you remain our guest for quite some time—creating no havoc on our forces, and staying alive and well yourself."

"Ah, sir! I understand the sentiment. I will pray for your health as well, Captain—yet pray that they take you off the seas!"

Jerome nodded, reaching for Sydney's arm. "It's time to go," he told his sister.

She nodded. "Stay well," she advised Jesse Halston.

"I'll be waiting for your return," he assured her.

Jerome rather firmly led her away.

In the carriage taking them into the center of the city where they would pick up Brent, Jerome watched Sydney from beneath the plume of his hat. "Perhaps you should remain with Mother for the next several months."

"Well, I intend to stay awhile, of course, but they do depend on me at the hospital. And nothing even slightly dangerous has happened since that very strange carriage incident."

"I meant—perhaps you just remain at home."

Sydney arched a brow, then leaned forward, taking his hands. If her brothers and father banded against her, she was doomed. It was suddenly very important that she get back to Richmond.

"Jerome, when the war first started, women were scarcely allowed in the hospitals. Then we were allowed in—if we were suitably ugly! I was able to be of help because of Brent; Alaina and Risa made their way in because of Julian and Risa's father. I have to be of some use in this war!"

Jerome leaned back, blue eyes dark in the shadows of the carriage. "Are we any use—or do we just prolong the carnage?" he asked softly.

"We will win this war," she said, determined to change the conversation.

He leaned toward her, taking her hands in turn. "Sydney, it worries me to see you so close with the enemy."

"The enemy? Oh, you mean Jesse."

"Yes, Jesse."

"He was injured. We treated him."

"I believe you're doing more for him than you imagine."

"Well, we are leaving now, aren't we?"

"And you shouldn't go back," he said softly, then there was bitterness in his voice. "Trust me, it isn't wise to know the enemy too well."

Sydney sat back. "Hmm. I haven't seen you since you became a married man. How is your wife? Other than well along in the family way."

He was her older brother, and she adored him, and she knew that he would never hurt her. But there was something so chilling in his eyes then that she wished she'd never spoken so flippantly.

"Risa is well."

"I'm sorry, Jerome," she murmured. "It's just that—"

He sighed deeply, gently tilting her chin as her head lowered. "Sydney, I don't wish this horrible schism on anyone. I am weary of the war. Sick to death of fearing that I am bound to come along a trail one day and be forced to fire at Ian. I am sorry that I have married a woman whose father longs to kill me. And I am sorry that she remains in my homeland—only because she does so in a Yankee port. I am warning you to guard yourself with Jesse Halston. He seems an exceptionally fine young man. His reputation is shining. But he is a Yankee, through and through, and will bring you heartache."

"You mustn't worry about me so much, and there's nothing at all between Jesse Halston and me. He is my patient, I am his nurse. And we've Mother to worry about, don't we?"

Watching her gravely, he nodded. For the time the subject was closed.

Years ago, Jerome reflected, his mother had called their home the Castle by the Sea. His father had laughingly informed her that Shanty by the Sea might be more like it. Jerome didn't agree with either of them. The long, sprawling house had been built from Dade County pine—exceptional lumber with the capability to defy all structure-gouging little insects. If it was a castle at all, it was rather like a castle out of a German fairy tale, towering suddenly out of a sea of pines, a beautiful, natural beach as one border, the semitropical forest to the north, the family groves to the west, the river to the south. Though beautifully appointed, it was a comfortable home, with a huge working kitchen inside that sprawled into a massive dining room. There was a breezeway in the center of the home, as was customary in the Southern style, and they'd often held parties there that spilled into the big dining room, and into the parlor and library. Upstairs, there were seven large bedrooms and a playroom. Surrounding the main house were numerous small homes for the household servants and grove workers, many of whom were Seminole kin who came to the house as needed, and earned money to acquire what they could not make themselves from the white traders.

He loved his home. Loved the beach, the coconut palms, the sea, and the brackish river. From the time he'd been a small boy, he'd played with putting together pieces of pine, sea grape, mangroves, oak—any wood from which he could form crude, shallow boats. First, they were to play with in puddles. Later, learning a great deal about dugouts from his family in the deep swamp, he had begun building fishing boats, then sailboats, and then his father had suggested that he go away to school. He was loath to do so at first, because any school was so far away from his family. But shipbuilding could best be learned in faraway places, and he had been sent to Boston, Massachusetts, to study with the masters there, and he had spent time in New York City, Norfolk, Charleston, and Pensacola. It was in the shipyards of Virginia that he had first seen his designs realized, while the *Lady Varina* had been built in England to his specifications with capitol he had earned by selling a number of his other vessels. Before the war—when the *Lady Varina* had been called the *Mercy*—he'd spent a great deal of his income as well to dredge a safe mooring for his ship in the cove along the riverside of his home. Yet, aware that the Yanks might expect him to berth there, he ordered Hamlin to leave him, his sister, his brother, and David Stewart in a longboat, and take the *Lady Varina* back out to sea.

They arrived to find the property enveloped in a wall of quiet. Beaching the boats, Jerome was instantly overwhelmed by a sense of unease. As they stepped upon the sand, he heard the sound of guns being cocked, and a number of men, Seminoles mostly, stepped from the shrubbery to greet them. One of them, a tall, slim man with an eagle's profile, smiled—though his eyes remained dark and grave—as he came forward, enveloping the three McKenzies one by one in a tight embrace.

Jerome stepped back first. "Billy Bones, meet David Stewart, a doctor, like Brent. David, Billy is my second cousin or so through my grandmother."

David nodded at the introduction.

"Billy, what's wrong?" Jerome demanded. "Has there been trouble here?" He glanced around, indicating the armed men.

Billy shook his head. "It's a war, and we are wary of soldiers—as you know. So we keep guard. Your father cannot do so now," he said sorrowfully.

"What's wrong with my father?" Sydney queried with a sharp edge.

"Your father is well, Little Eagle," Billy told her, calling her by the Seminole name she'd been given as a child.

"Mother!" Brent breathed, and he turned, starting toward the house.

But Billy caught his arm. "She is alive; your father is with her. He sits with her night and day. Jennifer is here, and not even she can make your father leave your mother. But you need have no fear that you are late, for the doctor Teela learned from in the old war, Joshua Brandeis, is here as well. He always loved your mother. He would die for her."

Staring at Billy, Jerome knew that he was right. Teela had learned her own gift for medicine with Dr. Brandeis during the second Seminole war. She had never studied medicine herself; women had only recently begun to graduate from medical schools. But she'd had an instinct, which she'd passed down to Brent, and Brent had been sent to spend a summer with Brandeis before he'd gone into medical school himself. Brandeis had been in love with his mother for some time, Jerome was always certain. And Teela's regard for him had always been high, though her passion had been for his father. It was true that Brandeis would die for her, but . . .

God, what was happening? She couldn't be dying.

Jerome broke out of his freeze, heading swiftly for the house, with Brent, Sydney, and David at his heels. Again, Jerome felt the strange, dismal chill.

"Mother!" Sydney cried out suddenly.

Jerome raced up the stairs, taking two at a time. He hurried to his parents' room, where he managed to pause, knocking softly before pushing the door open. Brent and Sydney piled against his back, yet they all paused then, once they had entered.

James McKenzie sat at the side of the massive bed where Teela lay, still as death, against white sheets, her auburn hair splayed out in a fan about her pale, delicate features. Head bent deeply, James McKenzie's fingers curled over his wife's where they lay upon the sheets.

She was dead, Jerome thought, and a part of him wanted to die as well.

"Mother!" Sydney cried out with terrible anguish, starting forward. Jerome caught her, holding her. James rose, startled, and saw his children. His striking features were worn and weary. "Children!" he said quietly. Sydney began to sob, and as James stepped forward, Jerome released Sydney to rush to their father. He enveloped her in his arms. "Sydney, precious darling . . ." he murmured. He looked up, and managed a smile. "Boys. Welcome home."

Jerome swallowed hard, well aware that his eyes were filling with tears. He strode forward, meeting his father's eyes, falling to his knees at his mother's side. His head fell upon the bedding, and he felt a burning heat on his cheeks. Tears.

Then, miraculously, he felt fingers brush his hair. "Jerome, my dear, I am quite grateful to be so loved, but please, you'll distress your father and sister even more."

His head shot up. His mother's emerald green eyes were open, though just barely. She'd managed to bring a smile to her lips. He caught her fingers, kissed the back of her hand, held it reverently. "Mother!"

"My God, Mother!"

Sydney was there, down on her knees, and Brent was on the other side of the bed. They all had to have some reassurance, and still, Jerome didn't need to catch his brother's eyes to realize that their mother remained in mortal danger. Brent came around for Sydney. "We mustn't tire her!" he whispered. "We'll stay, one at a time. Father, you must let Sydney take you downstairs, outside, get some air, have a drink. It will help Mother."

James shook his head impatiently. "I cannot leave her. Jennifer has been here, with me, I haven't been alone—"

"Where is Jen?" Brent asked.

And then they heard it. A squalling, mewling sound. And Jennifer appeared in the doorway, her toddling son at her ankles—and a swathed bundle in her arms.

"All of you!" Jennifer cried softly with pleasure. "Well, my dear half siblings, meet our new baby sister."

Baby sister! For a moment, Jerome felt the urge to toss the squealing little bundle right out the window. Oh, God, what the babe had done to Teela . . .

But then his mother, though weak as a kitten, nonetheless tried to tug upon Jerome's fingers. He looked quickly down at her. "I must speak with you," she mouthed. "Alone. Soon."

He nodded, then said thickly, "Jen!"

Going to the doorway, he meant to hug Jennifer. But he paused, and as he did, Jennifer pressed the new baby into his arms. "Mary, in honor of our grandmother," Jennifer said.

"Mary."

He had no choice but to take his new sister. And as he did, a deep sense of shame overwhelmed him. The baby looked up at him with huge blue—trusting—McKenzie eyes. She had a thatch of hair that was already thick and russet. She wagged a little hand before him, and he took it.

He kissed her forehead and handed her on to Sydney. "See what you can do with Father," he told Jennifer, who nodded.

"Please, Father, come downstairs. Jerome will stay

with Teela while you spend a few minutes with Sydney and Brent."

James swallowed hard. He was haggard, his hair was long and disheveled. He leaned over Teela, smoothing back her hair. "I'll be right back, my love."

"I'll be here," she promised.

When the others departed, Jerome sat by his mother's side, taking her hands once again. Her voice was weak, but steady, and her will was strong. "You need to help your father. Such a brave—stubborn!—man. He needs you now."

"Mother—"

"I'm going to try very hard not to die, Jerome. But you're my oldest, and I need you to be the strong one if things do not go well." She smiled, and she was beautiful, and he thought of how she'd been determined and strict at times when they were children, and yet so wise, always refusing to judge others and doing her best to understand the ways of all men. He felt tears brimming to his eyes again.

"Don't cry on me, please, dear. You've given me great happiness, you know."

"I . . . how?" he asked blankly.

"Well, I might have liked to have attended the wedding, but this is war!" she said. "I've heard my first grandchild is due well before the suitable interval after the marriage."

He was amazed to find himself flushing. But then, this was his mother. "Mother—"

"Your father and I barely managed to have a wedding before you were born, dear, so I'm happy that you two have taken care for your child."

He nodded, squeezing her hand.

"She's a lovely, remarkable woman, Jerome."

He frowned. "When—"

"I saw her at Alaina's house—the night she rushed into the swamps to save a friend, remember? The night you abducted the poor girl. And she's written to me."

"Oh?"

"Very nice letters, asking about my health, and apologizing for informing us about the wedding after the event, rather than asking our blessing before it."

"She is a very proper young woman," he said lightly.

Teela smiled. She lifted a hand with great effort, and touched his face. "I know you, son. I know your temper, and your ethics. And if she's expecting your child . . . then there was something between you. Give happiness a chance. You're such a prickly pear, so much like your father! All raw confidence and inner strength—and uncertainty when it comes to matters about which you really care."

"We'll be all right, Mother," he said. "You shouldn't talk so much, you're tiring yourself—"

"You're right. I'll get to the point. If I die, Jerome—"

"Mother, don't—"

"If I die, I want you to raise your little sister for me with your new wife."

He swallowed hard. "I don't—think—"

"You are married, Jerome. You'll have a home and a wife. I pray that Jennifer will find a new life with the war over. Lawrence is dead, and she has one baby on her own as it is. Brent isn't settled, neither is Sydney. And I don't think your father would have the heart to start anew."

"Oh, God, Mother . . ."

"Promise me, Jerome."

"Oh, God, Mother, you can't, you are all our strength—"

"Promise! Promise me, son, please."

His heart was heavy; the pain was unbearable.

"I promise," he told her softly.

She smiled, and closed her eyes.

Chapter 19

For three days Teela wavered on the brink between life and death. She had lost an incredible amount of blood with the baby, and it had taken all Joshua's skill to stop her bleeding. Jerome knew that between Joshua, his brother, and David, Teela had the best possible care. And still, it seemed that her strength ebbed, and their vigil stretched onward.

He was glad that their arrival had given their father new strength. He loved all his children, but Sydney had always had a magic touch with him, and she managed to get him to rest, and she cut his hair, and she would sit with him hour after hour by Teela's bed.

Jerome sometimes sat with his newborn sister, rocking her in her cradle after the wet nurse had finished feeding her, and he would tell himself that he couldn't blame the innocent infant for her own birth. He was aware that his father avoided the baby, and that his mother asked after her little one when she had the strength.

They were grim, dark days, and even the war receded. On the third night, he sat vigil with his mother alone. He sat by her side, dozed, awoke, and looked anxiously at her. She was snow-white and deadly still. He bit deeply into his lower lip, afraid that the time had come. But even as he started to reach out to pull her to him, her eyes opened. Wide, shimmering green. And she smiled.

"Jerome?"

"Mother?"

"I think . . . why, I think I'd love some soup."

In the days that followed, Teela improved rapidly. As soon as she was strong enough, she demanded the baby,

Mary. His mother's delight in his newborn sister filled him with a sense of shame as he remembered how he had first despised the infant, but through his mother's eyes, he began to love his new sibling with the same protective affection he felt for Jen, Brent, and Sydney. Teela insisted he take the baby often. "You're about to become a father, Jerome. Practice!"

"Mother—she, er—diddles. I think that Sydney needs practice. She will actually be a mother one day—"

"If the war leaves any men to marry!" Sydney interjected dryly.

"And I'm afraid it's most unlikely I'll be available when my own child is born," Jerome said.

"But you're here—"

"We were worried about you, because you're—you're—" Brent began, and stuttered.

"If you call me old, I'll have your father drag you out to the woodshed!" Teela teased. "James, your children are calling me old."

"Teela, dear, we are old," James said patiently.

"Oh. Well, then, excuse me!" Teela said, and laughed.

After two weeks, she joined them in the dining room, and it was a great event. The night was highlighted by the arrival of one of Billy's cousins—who had come from Tampa Bay with the news that Alaina, who had gone to Cimarron for her child to be born, had been delivered of a little girl. Mother and child were thriving. Jerome asked Billy's cousin if Alaina had come to Cimarron alone, or if she had been accompanied by Risa. She had not; Risa had remained in St. Augustine.

He wondered if she had remained in St. Augustine because she had said that she would, or if she had chosen to remain because St. Augustine was in Yankee hands.

No matter.

It had been good to come home. Teela had survived when they had so nearly lost her, and the world was a far better place because of it, despite the ravages of war. With his mother—and new sister—doing well, Jerome suddenly found himself growing restless. He was eager to sail again.

He had to return Brent to his command, and Sydney

was determined to serve at the hospital in Richmond again. But once they were returned, he had good reason to sail to north Florida. His mother grew many herbal remedies. Julian was always desperate for medicines.

He himself was growing desperate for north Florida.

He intended to see his wife, and he would damn well do so—and the hell with her ultimatums and dictates.

Time passed slowly for Risa.

Compared to the days when she had ridden with her father and McClellan's army, life was quite easy. Women continued to bear infants, children continued to acquire coughs. The soldiers continued to break arms and legs in rough-housing and drills, and the intermittent skirmishing continued between the opposing sides of the river. The war effort in Florida was quiet. The generals in the interior begged for reinforcements, and the generals and politicians, who knew the war must be won around Richmond, Virginia, told the state to look to her own resources. Once the Confederacy wanted to hold the key coastal positions. Now they left the indefensible coast, and their strategy was to hold bases in the interior.

As the blockade tightened, it became more evident to the visionaries on either side that Florida was going to become more and more important as a breadbasket. But as they approached the winter of 1862/1863, the state was, for the most part, ominously quiet.

With Alaina gone, Risa was lonely. She enjoyed Thayer Cripped, who was a good and interesting man, but since her marriage, he seemed to be afraid of being with her, and they spent little time socializing.

There had been a complete shift in feelings toward her in the city. Before she had been trusted and beloved by the Union officers—she'd been General Magee's daughter. Now she was Captain McKenzie's wife, and the Unionists were wary while the old brigade Southerners were ready to embrace her. One day, in the midst of assisting to remove a ball from a young soldier who had shot his own thigh while cleaning his rifle, she'd gotten so aggravated with his hostile attitude toward her that she'd informed him she was no man's daughter and no man's wife, just herself, a damned good nurse, and if he wanted to walk again, he'd better remember it.

Thayer had stared at her, the soldier had stared at her—and her announcement had appeared in the paper the next day. Life was incredibly aggravating.

Hearing nothing from Jerome, she toyed with the idea of returning to Washington. Winter was setting in, and since heavy snows would have to impede troop movements, it was naturally a time of little activity. But she was afraid if she sailed, he would hear, and come after her, and she would endanger all aboard with her. Yet getting military passes to move by land through the Rebel heartland would be nearly impossible—she couldn't use her husband's influence to head *north*.

Toward the end of November, however, an incident occurred that changed everything.

To her amazement, her father arrived in St. Augustine.

She was folding bandages in the surgery when Lieutenant Austin Sage, accompanied by Finn, looked in on her.

Austin remained her friend, no matter what.

As did Finn—who was frequently with her here, keeping her company, making her laugh. Perhaps it was because he could assure her that he had come through the night without injury other than to his dignity that he could be her friend now.

"Risa!" Finn, with Austin at his side, called to her.

"Yes?"

"You'll never guess . . ." Finn said.

"Yes?"

"Your father!" Austin announced.

"My father, what about him?" She set the bandages she had been rolling down, worried. Troops did continue to clash, and it felt as if her heart had risen to her throat.

"He's here!" Finn announced.

She gripped the table to stand. She swallowed her heart back down, then felt her stomach flip-flop. She wasn't afraid of her father, she'd never been afraid of her father, and she loved him dearly. But though her skirts somewhat hid her condition, she was definitely growing. The baby was big and active, and would be born in another three months or so. And she had married a Rebel. Not just any Rebel. Jerome McKenzie.

"Risa, come on!" Austin urged.

"His ship has docked," Finn added. Having already survived her father's wrath regarding his part in her first excursion south, he now seemed amused—mischievously eager to see her father's reaction to her marriage and her condition. He had been indignant when she had announced her marriage to the Rebel Jerome McKenzie. "I would have married you!" he had told her with a woeful expression that had been very touching.

Austin, who had never seemed to have had an opinion on her clandestine marriage, reached out a hand to her. She braced herself mentally, and took his hand. "Come on!" he encouraged. "Courage under fire! Let's face the general!"

Finn led. They hurried through the streets toward the docks. Finn paused. Austin crashed into him.

"What are you doing—" Austin began.

"Risa!" Finn told Austin. "Should she be running like this? I should have hired a carriage—"

She flushed, since she seldom referred to the baby in her conversations with her friends. "I'm fine. Keep going, gentlemen."

They reached the docks. Angus Magee stood there, surrounded by officers who asked anxious questions. She heard him telling them that no matter what the Rebs tried to say, the horrible battle at Antietam had been an exceptional victory for the North, a victory that proved the Southerners could not move the war into Northern fields. Eventually, the North would prevail. The soldiers were cheering him when he looked across the crowd and saw his daughter's face.

She nearly burst into tears at the look in his eyes. So much pain, so much betrayal, and so much love.

"Father!" she called out to him, and began barging her way through the soldiers and Unionist civilians who surrounded him. For one brief moment she thought that he meant to stand perfectly still, and ignore her—or repulse her. But his arms opened, and she threw herself into them, and he picked her up, hugging her close. "Precious, precious, child!" he murmured to her. "Ah, Risa, oh, God, how I have missed you. How I ever consented for you to leave . . . but then, I had thought you'd

be in England, away from all this death and madness . . .
and *not* married to a Southern rogue!"

"Father!" she murmured, as they were surrounded.

"You're right; we'll talk later."

"Later" took a while in coming. Her father was naturally wined and dined by the Union officers of the city
and the local Unionist population. Risa nervously went
through the social hours with him, smiling while aware
that upright matrons talked about her behind her back.
How could she have married that rake, that Southern
scoundrel? Yet—how could she not? whispered many
gentlewomen in return. After all, she was in a *family*
way.

Oddly enough, in the whispering that she heard, she
was far more to blame than Jerome McKenzie. After all,
he was a *man*. And since he was known for his ethical
treatment of Yankee sailors when he captured their
ships, obviously, she had behaved like a jezebel, seducing him to madness.

A Miss Ivy Pendleton was the worst of the ladies, Risa
decided. She was about Risa's age, thin, and homely.
She professed to have been a loyal Unionist all along,
but she had sung "Dixie" loudly enough when the Rebels had ruled the city.

"Don't you worry," Finn said. He stooped to whisper
in her ear as her father talked with the soldiers who had
just put on an arms display at Ft. Marion. "She's just a
shriveled-up prune, jealous—because there's not a man
alive who would kidnap her."

"And there's definitely going to be a shortage of men
at the end of the war," Austin agreed, whispering as
well, "so all she'll be able to do is say nasty things about
the women who do have husbands."

Risa flashed them both appreciative smiles, but then
sobered quickly because her father was looking at her
curiously.

She had to admit to being somewhat thankful that her
father intended to quarter with the officers—and that he
wouldn't be sharing her little house. But he escorted her
home that evening, and when they were behind closed
doors, he shouted at her at last. "Married! You married

that rogue, that rake, that sea monster—they call him the Devil, a demon—"

"Father, he's a man. Ian's cousin."

"You married him!"

"I thought it was what you would want—under the circumstances."

"I didn't want the circumstances!"

He was red and shaking. He sank down into one of the comfortably upholstered armchairs before the fire. "Risa—you claimed there was no truth to rumors that he—that he—"

"He didn't rape me, Father," she said flatly.

"Oh, God! I raised a proper young woman! You're not even supposed to *know* that word."

"Father, please—"

"So, in other words, you purposely . . . you purposely became intimate with a Rebel scoundrel?"

He had stopped yelling, and she knew that he was hurt. And deeply frustrated. He threw up his hands. "Why? I can't begin to imagine the circumstances."

"Well, Father—"

"No, no, wait! I don't want to hear the circumstances. I still can't help but believe that he forced you. I surely can't believe that you were foolish enough to fall head over heels in love with a man who viciously abducted you—"

"Father, woah! Wait, please. He didn't viciously abduct me. I was in enemy territory. It was my own doing. But I did know his plans, and I am your daughter, sir, Unionist all the way. He had no choice but to take me on the ship."

"And no choice but to . . . oh, God, you're my daughter, Risa! My beloved girl, my pride, my joy. Can't you see how it hurts me to think that any man might have done you ill?"

She knelt down by his feet, taking both of his hands in hers. "You're my father, and I adore you. And I swear to you, sir, no one used me ill. I didn't intend what happened myself, but you see . . . well, I'm not so certain that I can explain. The war is robbing us of so much, and I wondered if there would ever be a time when I . . . when I wanted something so much. I should have thought more, definitely, sir. But I didn't, and here we are. And, I swear to you, no one abused me, he isn't

a monster, merely a Rebel." She tried to smile, to lighten
the moment. "My name *is* McKenzie!"

He cast her a withering glare.

"Father, please, I am expecting a child, and therefore
marriage was the right thing. I'm still your daughter,
who loves and adores you, and who is still a Yankee."

He touched her cheek, his eyes deeply troubled. "And
your husband is still a Rebel." He inhaled deeply, shaking his head. "Daughter, don't you see? I've near to
ripped my own hair out over the foolish mistakes of men
such as McClellan, and any military man can see that
the Southern generals have been outmaneuvering us!
But they can win battle after battle, and they will still
lose the war. And your reckless blockade-runner is sure
to get himself killed!"

A chill swept over her. She hadn't heard from Jerome
since their wedding, and she had been cold on that occasion, a touch-me-not shrew. But no matter what she had
said, she knew that she loved him, and her father's words—
not viciously but truthfully spoken—sent fear spilling
through her. He did risk his life, constantly. The Yanks—
many of whom would gladly put a bullet through his
heart—didn't even need to actually aim at him—his ship
could be blown out of the water. He would never stop,
because the Confederacy was desperate.

"Father, I pray daily that you won't get yourself killed
as well," she said softly. "This is really the wicked job
of women in this war—we pray. Brothers, fathers, husbands, lovers, sons! Oh, Father, I can promise you this—
it's far better to be among the fighting men, or nursing
in the field, then waiting. I'll never forget the times I
have been in Washington when battles end, and the lists
of the dead and missing are read. Mothers lose two,
three, four sons in a single day! Daughters despair to
hear their fathers and brothers have been killed together.
But I can't change you—nor can I change Jerome. All that
I can do is pray, and wait. And do my best to help patch
up men on either side, believing that a Rebel woman
would patch you up if need be. And then all I have is
faith that God will not let this war go on forever."

Angus stared down at her, then stroked her hair. "If
the wretched Rebel McKenzie is your husband, then I

must hope he stays alive. And that the war ends. Forgive me, daughter, my anger and frustration. They come with my love for you."

"Oh, Father, I do love you, too!" she assured him. She crawled up into his lap, as she had done as a child. He grunted. "You're getting a little heavier there, child."

"Want a grandson, or granddaughter?" she queried.

He groaned. "I wanted a Yankee son-in-law!"

"Too late. Grandson, or granddaughter?"

He paused, looking at her. "I want you to deliver safely a healthy baby, and no more. Now, get up, young woman. I'm off to bed. I'm an old, tired man, and you're adding more gray to this head of mine daily."

"Father, I'm sorry to tell you, but you're completely gray already."

"That would be your fault, daughter."

"And that from a general!"

He smiled. She stood, offering him a hand to help him up. He sighed. "I'm going to try to reconcile myself to this, young woman. But it would help if you were to come home!"

She hesitated. "I love St. Augustine, Father. It's a beautiful city."

"Hmmph! Well, this discussion will continue."

He started limping toward her door. Frowning, she followed him. "Father, what have you done to your foot?"

"Nothing," he said too quickly.

"Sit. I want to see it."

"No, no—"

"Now!" she demanded, dragging him back to the chair.

He chastised her as she unlaced his boots. "Now, don't do that—"

"Oh, Father!" she cried in dismay, for when his shoe was removed, she had to peel away his sock. His foot was bleeding. She dabbed at the blood, trying to find the source.

"Picked up a little shrapnel, that's all—"

"That's all, indeed!" Risa said worriedly. "There's still metal caught in your foot, and there's pus beneath the blood. You're headed toward a serious infection, gangrene—"

"I'll not have my foot cut off by a saw-happy surgeon!" he said adamantly.

Risa stood. "Father, a good surgeon can perhaps remove
the offending metal without having to amputate. But—"

"Your Dr. Cripped looked at my foot earlier today—
and his only suggestion was amputation."

"If that is the only answer, sir, you will buck up and
behave like an adult—as you would surely tell your men!
But perhaps . . . perhaps we could find a way to save
your foot. I know surgeons who would attempt it."

"You do?"

"I'm going to clean this for you, then you go to bed,
and I'll speak with Dr. Cripped, and decide what must
be done." She was determined to send for Dr. Julian
McKenzie.

"Don't you go deciding on *my* foot without me!"

"I wouldn't dream of doing so, Father."

When he had left, Risa swept her cloak around her
and hurried to the servants' quarters behind her house,
where she found Bartholomew. "Can you get someone
to cross the river, find Captain McKenzie, and tell him
I must see him?"

"Someone, somehow, yes," he assured her. "Right
away. You go home, now! It's not safe in the streets,
here, anywhere."

"I'm fine, Bartholomew, but thank you." Yet, as she
hurried from the servants' quarters back to her row
house, she paused. She had the uneasy sensation she
was being watched. She shivered, trying to shake off the
uncomfortable feeling.

She returned to her little house. Bartholomew's wife
had been over to fill her hip tub, and leave a kettle of
water heating over the fire. She added the hot water to
that which had grown cold, removed her clothing, and
settled into the hip bath. It felt good to bathe, and as she
rubbed her abdomen, her unborn baby moved in turn. A
tiny little hand or foot jutted out in a funny little arc, and
she found herself smiling with pleasure. An overwhelming
sense of tender, protective love swept through her, and she
realized that she very much wanted her baby—just as she
was very much in love with its father.

She sighed, rising, drying, and slipping into a white cotton gown. The baby's father might be in Charleston right now—making love to his onetime fiancée. After all, things had been blunt and clear between them. She'd told him not to touch her—and he'd told her there were other women to touch.

She bit into her lower lip, wishing she could take back the words, and push time back to the night of their wedding. It was one thing to be alone. All across America, North and South, women were alone. But they were secure in their love, missing husbands who longed to be with them. While she . . .

She curled herself around her pillow. She wasn't immense yet, but the roundness of her stomach was visible. She lay there, torn, grateful for the life growing within her, while fighting a temptation to cry. There was one definite truth regarding Jerome—the scoundrel was always leaving her. And it didn't matter that she'd basically sent him away last time; she was being eaten alive tonight with jealousy.

Still, she must have dozed, because she awakened suddenly, certain that she'd heard something not quite right, yet not at all sure what.

She lay in bed, listening, and there was no more sound. She had imagined, or dreamed, whatever had awakened her.

Yet after a while, she rose. The house was dimly lit by the dying embers in the fireplaces. She cautiously moved from the bedroom to the parlor, walking to the front door to be certain that she had bolted it. She had.

"Risa."

She turned around, startled, frightened, gasping at the spoken sound of her name.

And there he was.

Jerome.

He stood by the mantel, casually leaned against it as he watched her. She stared at him in amazement in return.

At least he wasn't in Charleston.

"Jerome!" she whispered.

And he offered her a wry, half smile in return, and said mockingly, "Yes, my love. It's me."

Chapter 20

"My God!" she breathed. She hadn't known that he was anywhere near—she hadn't heard of any of his exploits, or that a Southern runner might have made it along the river.

"What—what are you doing here?"

He arched a brow. "What am I doing here? You can't be quite so surprised. You summoned me, Mrs. McKenzie."

"I—" she began, but broke off. Summoned him? Naturally, obviously, he had made a run up the river. But she hadn't summoned him—

Oh, God, she understood.

She had sent for Julian. Word had apparently gone across the river that she was trying to find a McKenzie, and Jerome had come.

She was incredibly glad to see him. And he was there. And she wasn't about to tell him the truth of the matter.

He had come across the river alone, apparently. Literally, across the river. His Confederate naval jacket was hanging over a chair, she saw, drying in front of the low-burning flames.

He looked wonderful. Extraordinary. Broad, bronzed shoulders glistening in the reddish light. Handsome features caught in the dancing shadows. Blue eyes sharp as ice fire.

"Well?" he inquired tightly.

She lowered her lashes, looking downward, breathing far too desperately. "I . . ."

"Yes?"

She forced herself to look up. She wasn't a coward. "I—" she broke off. No, she definitely wasn't going to tell him that she hadn't summoned him. She would ask him later if there was any way that Julian could look at her father's foot.

Later.

She lifted her chin, meeting his eyes. "Yes, I'm sorry, I hoped I caused you no difficulty. I was in no distress, I had just hoped that it might be possible to see you."

He lifted a hand. "You're seeing me. I'm here."

She smiled. "I sent for you—and you swam across the river because I did so?" she queried.

"It's the easiest way to get here without causing a disturbance," he told her dryly.

"Ah."

"Well?"

She inhaled deeply, staring at him.

"I didn't mean to cause you hardship—"

"You caused no hardship. What is it that you want?"

Again, she inhaled, hesitating.

"All right," he said impatiently, "so it wasn't exactly a hardship coming, but it is a long and possibly dangerous swim. Perhaps, since I am here, you'll be so good as to tell me why you sent for me."

"I'm—"

"Damn it, Risa!"

"I'm sorry," she told him.

"What?"

"I'm sorry!" she repeated, color flooding her face.

"Sorry?" He frowned, arching a brow, confused.

She shook her head. "I—I—"

"Sorry about what? That you sent for me?"

"No! I'm sorry because—I said horrible things when we parted, and I didn't mean them."

His brow hiked further. "Ah . . . well, exactly what horrible things did you say—and exactly what part didn't you mean? I mean, an apology is nice, but it's strange to be called from the midst of a war just to hear one."

"I said a lot of horrible things—I said that I didn't want you anywhere near me, touching me, because I didn't want to marry you—"

"You made that quite evident."

"No, you don't understand—"

"Personally, I found it strange that you should determine so late that you didn't want to be tainted by 'red, Rebel blood,' but then—"

"Damn you! Don't you understand? I'm trying to explain!"

His dark lashes swept his cheeks. "Go on," he said quietly. "I'm listening."

"I didn't want to marry you because of my circumstances if you were in love with someone else, engaged to marry someone you really wanted to marry. Even for a child."

He continued staring at her, blue eyes crystal hard.

She moistened her lips. "This—this isn't an easy position for me. You know, I was raised to be very independent, and it just seemed that there was too much between us . . . for a relationship that . . . that . . ." her voice trailed.

"Indeed, there is a tremendous amount between us," he agreed, a strange, dark tremor to his voice.

She looked downward again, unable to meet his eyes. "I didn't want our marriage to be hateful, although I know that I certainly helped make it so. I didn't want you to feel forced into anything. Well, I—" She broke off for a moment, breathless again, then she managed to look up at him.

"Yes?"

"You could make this a little easier."

He shook his head firmly. "No, I couldn't. I want to hear what you've got to say."

She groaned softly, staring at the flames, then back to his eyes. "I—I—"

"Quit stuttering."

"Quit being mean!"

"What do you expect from such savage, Rebel blood?"

"A chance!" she said softly. "Damn you, I am trying very hard to apologize. To . . ."

He smiled suddenly, crossing his arms over his chest, and waiting expectantly. "Madam, I am eagerly listening."

"I'm sorry I said those things, and I didn't mean them!"

"You're quite certain?"

She groaned with aggravation. "Indeed, I'm certain. I needed to tell you, and—and—where have you been?"

"What?"

"Where have you been since we parted?"

"Why do you ask?"

"Naturally, I'm curious. I'm asking after your welfare."

"Oh," he murmured politely.

"Well?" she demanded.

"Why are you *really* asking?"

"That is why I'm *really* asking!" she cried, completely aggravated.

But he was smiling again, not taking a step toward her. Yet something in his voice was changing, as well as the fire within his eyes.

"All right," she murmured breathlessly. "Actually, I was asking because I hoped that you hadn't been to Charleston."

He studied her for a long moment. Then he left the mantel, striding to her, taking her arms and pulling her against him. He set his forefinger beneath her chin, causing her to look up at him. His eyes were deep, dark blue, fathomless.

"I have one question for you, Yank," he told her.

"You do?"

"Are you still in love with my cousin, Ian?"

"What?" she murmured, too startled to make a flippant reply.

"Are you still in love with Ian?"

She smiled, slowly shaking her head. "No."

"Ah."

"Ah?"

"Ah, well, then, is that the best you can do?"

"I beg your pardon?"

"As an apology. Let's see, we agree that you were hateful. Quite hateful."

"And I have said that I'm sorry."

He cupped her chin tenderly in his hand, stroking her cheek with the pad of his thumb as his head lowered. "Surely, you can do better than that," he whispered against her lips.

Yes, she could.

And she longed to do so.

She met his kiss with passion, and an urgent hunger. She found his tongue, dueled with it most sensually with her own, exploring his mouth, her arms around him, her fingers tangling into his hair. God, he felt good. His scent was masculine, his arms were strong, his flesh was hot, alive with the underlying play of muscle. They kissed, and kissed . . . feverishly, desperately.

He swept her up into his arms, and she felt the dampness of his breeches against the thin material of her nightgown. He strode with her into the bedroom and laid her down, but when he rose to peel away his damp breeches, she rose as well, glad of the shadows as she stripped the soft white cotton material over her head, letting it fall to the floor. On her knees on the bed, she crawled over to where he stood naked. The length of him was as hard as steel. Muscles rippled with his every movement, and he was lean and wiry and aroused, and completely tempting. She'd never been the aggressor; and she was nervous, awkward, but determined to touch him, to explore, and play, and tantalize. She wanted him to remember her, his wife, throughout the long days of the war to come. She slipped her arms around him, pressing her body to him, stroking down the length of his back with her fingertips. She brushed his cheek with her palm, met his lips in a brief, fiery kiss, then kissed his shoulders, licked his nipples, found the thundering pulse at his throat. All the while, she felt the extent of his arousal, brushing against her. She slipped from the bed, and to the floor, and with just the barest uncertainty, took him into her mouth. The deepest satisfaction swept her as she felt the convulsive force of his shudder, heard the groan that tore from him. Inflicting this fair torture was sheer delight, the sweetest sense of power. Her fingertips roamed over his buttocks, cupped them. She played, explored, experimented. Teasing with the tip of her tongue, taking him deeply. Taunting, provoking . . .

Until a gruff cry tore from him, and she was up and in his arms, and meeting his mouth again in a wild, reckless kiss. His hands were on her, his lips raked her body, burning it with wet fire. Her breasts . . . oh, God, hunger ripped through her as he teased her nipples. All her senses had been heightened, so it seemed. He skimmed her belly, delved between her thighs, licked, teased . . .

Tortured. She trembled. Cried out, arched, writhed, wanted him as never before.

Yet he paused suddenly, and she was still, wondering what was wrong. She realized that he was studying her body. He traced a blue vein in her breast, and ran his finger down the length of her, over the rise of her belly.

"He moved."

"What?"

"He moved. I'm not so sure he wants me touching you."

"Oh!" she cried softly. "But I . . . I mean, I know it's all right, women talk, I've listened all these years—I help deliver babies!"

He smiled at her then, rising to kiss her very tenderly. "I know it's all right. And still, I would be more gentle . . ."

He flipped her about, fingers stroking down her back, kisses now liquid and as searing as a curving sweep of lava down her spine. Then the pressure of his body was behind her, no weight upon her, yet he filled her completely, and she cried out again, so glad just to feel him within her.

He was gentle, yet she felt his strength and power, and the passion that could so ignite her. She had so craved him, even the anticipation of each stroke was sweet. He swept her away, higher and higher, until she thought that she had come to an unbearable precipice; no more, she could bear no more . . . and yet she did, until all exploded, and fire was bursting through her, enwrapping her, sating her, filling her. His arms remained tightly wrapped around her when the last sweet shudders faded. And she was content, happy as she had never imagined. She was his wife; she was in love with him. He was with her, and they were going to have a child. And the rest of the world, North and South, could go hang.

She felt his fingers moving in her hair.

"I wish you would send for me more often," he whispered.

"I seldom know where to send," she murmured, si-
dling back against him. His hand lay against her abdomen, and she felt the gentle seeking of his fingertips
there. "You—weren't in Charleston, were you?"

"I've been a number of places," he told her. "But
Charleston wasn't among them. Most recently, I've been
home. I've been across the river because I had picked
up some herbal remedies we grow in the far south. He's
moving again."

"He might be a she."

"He might, but I doubt it."

"Oh?"

"My father had two boys first."

She turned to look at him. "And men like to have
sons."

He smiled, shaking his head. "Little girls are fine."

"You wouldn't mind a girl?"

"I just met my new baby sister."

Risa halfway sat up, startled. "Your mother—"

"Had her baby, a girl. Mary, for my father's mother."

"You fell in love instantly."

He shook his head again, drawing her back down to
lie against him. "No, I didn't fall right in love. I hated
her."

"I don't believe you!"

"She nearly killed my mother."

"Oh, Jerome, I'm so sorry—"

"My mother is fine, but she went through a rough
time."

"Well, she is older—"

"She had a bad time with Sydney. Age doesn't always
matter. I'm going to be worried about you now, as well."

She rose up again, leaning against his chest to look
down into his eyes, and was startled by the depth of
emotion she found there. She trembled, unnerved.
"Alaina had her baby. A girl. She went to Cimarron—
she had her first child in Washington, and was determined to get to Cimarron for this birth."

"I know. I heard," he said, lacing his fingers behind
his head and studying her still. "Do you recall that I
told you to go to my family home when your time
drew near."

"Yes."

"Well, I don't want you to do so anymore. I want you to stay here. Julian isn't far away, and if you do have any complications—"

"Most women are having their babies with midwives, nurses—friends! It's hard to spare doctors from the war effort these days."

"The action is slow in Florida," he said dryly. "And my cousin Julian is very close, and will come if you send for him. I'll hope to be near myself, but God knows what February will bring." He brushed her cheek with his knuckles. "I need to go. It will be light soon."

She leaned against him, feeling the beating of their hearts. "I wish . . ."

"What?"

"I wish you didn't have to leave."

"Really?" he inquired.

"Yes, really. I wish that I could curl up against your chest, and sleep there."

He offered her a wry half smile. "I can't even sweep you away aboard my ship now. You're far too close to your time."

"Not so close—"

"Too close to take a chance on bringing you aboard a blockade runner," he said. "I have been lucky, thus far. Running past Union guns. But the war grows more desperate daily. I dare not risk your life—or that of our child."

"I don't want you to go."

"Dear God, and I don't want to go."

He slid his fingers through her hair, cupping her skull and pulling her down to meet his lips. His kiss touched a spark within her, all too easily lit, and in moments they were entangled in the bedding, and one another. Oh, God, it was good, a storm, sweeping thunder, sensations that shattered deeply into heart and bone and soul . . . but when their passion was spent, he did not hold her.

He untangled himself from her arms, and rose quickly. Naked, by the bed, he ran his fingers through his hair, then reached for his damp breeches and slid into them. He plucked up her gown, coming back to her. She rose to her knees, and he slipped the gown slowly over her head and shoulders, kissing her lips lightly as it fell around her.

He turned without words then, going out into the parlor for his jacket and boots. She followed him, and when he was completely dressed, she rushed to him, circling her arms around him and pressing her cheek to his chest. "If only I could summon you at any time—and have you so magically appear!" she whispered, tinged by just a shade of guilt as she remembered that she hadn't really summoned him at all—she had wanted to find a way to bring Julian to her father.

She would find Julian by morning's light. For now, she could not let her husband go.

His arms came tenderly around her. "If only I didn't need to be summoned—if you could await me in my bunk each night! But now I'll have tonight in my dreams for many weeks to come," he said. "You apologize very, very well," he teased.

"I was really very sorry."

He smiled, and brushed her lips with a kiss once again. "I *must* go," he told her.

Buckling on his scabbard, he walked to the door. He drew the bolt.

"Wait!"

She raced after him, throwing her arms around him, and kissing him one last time with trembling passion. Distracted, he wrapped his arms around her.

Then suddenly, the unbolted door was thrown open.

Jerome instantly stiffened. He cast her behind him protectively as he drew his sword, defensively striding through the open door to meet the threatened attack.

"Seize him!" came a cry, and blinding light was suddenly cast before their eyes.

"Sweet Jesu!" Jerome grated out. "Be on guard, don't risk your life!" he warned, drawing tall and still as he shielded his eyes against the blinding light. Despite the reflection from the many lanterns now blazing upon them, Risa saw the soldiers lined up before them.

"Drop your weapon, Captain McKenzie!" shouted a soldier.

"Be damned!" Jerome roared. "Take me, gentlemen, if you will! I swear we'll dine together in hell tonight!"

"No!" Risa shrieked as a dozen guns were cocked.

"Ready and aim, men! Captain, drop your weapon!"

Risa realized that someone had known that Jerome had come to her—and her house had been surrounded. But her husband wasn't about to be taken. He'd never give himself up.

"Surrender, Captain!"

"Like hell!" Jerome returned. He moved forward.

Even if they shot him, Risa realized, he was so fast and agile he could bring several men down with him. But he didn't intend to surrender.

"No!" she cried again. "No!" And she rushed out into the fray, casting herself in front of Jerome, and daring both the guns—and his sword arm.

"Hold fire!" a Union officer called.

And as he turned, Jerome lowered his sword. But the steel in his eyes pierced into her mercilessly. She realized then that he believed that she had planned this. That she had sent for him and purposely seduced him—to set him up for capture.

She longed to protest, to cry out. It would do no good.

He would never believe in her innocence.

He smiled at her, a bitter smile that mocked them both. "Bitch!" he said very softly.

Jerome was certain, beyond a doubt, that this affair had been staged.

She had betrayed him. With malice, and intent. It was obvious, and there was no denying it in his heart. She had known he was near; word had spread that he had come down the river. She had sent for him. And he had come.

And then, the Yanks had come for him.

Guns remained aimed upon him. He couldn't win, and he knew it. And though the anger in his heart was blood-red and bitter, he was equally frightened for her. She'd wanted him taken, not killed. "Fool!" he cried angrily to Risa, and despite the dark emotions swirling in him, he caught her forcefully, and set her aside. He moved his sword as he did so, and he instantly heard the guns clicking again.

"Captain, please!" the Yank soldier in charge cried.

Grating his teeth, Jerome set his sword on the ground. Frankly, he didn't know what the hell he'd been doing.

He knew that he didn't want to die, and that his furious actions against a company of so many Yankee soldiers had been pure suicide. And though he surely couldn't tell his wife that he was grateful she had thrown herself in front of him, somewhere deep inside, he knew that he was.

Of course, his temper was sizzling. Scorching.

The situation was mortifying, and he wanted to strike out at her with the ever deepening realization of how easily she had played him for a fool. Betrayed him.

Rage burned its way into his soul.

She had planned this, the cunning little Yankee seductress had planned this! She had set him up, and he, the great sea captain, the scourge of the seven seas, the Devil wraith who had taken out at least a dozen enemy ships, had fallen like any fool.

He was being taken prisoner. Handed over by a woman.

"Jerome!"

Her eyes were on his. Beautiful eyes. Aquamarine. Sea eyes, liquid eyes. Shimmering with theatrical tears, she was coming toward him.

He was not moved.

He stared into her eyes, swept his gaze over the classical beauty of her features, noted the full auburn cloak of her hair, and the marble perfection of her flesh.

He turned his back on her.

"Will someone be so good as to escort General Magee's daughter back into the house?" he demanded coldly. "And then, gentlemen, I surrender. Bring on your shackles, if you will. I think I might welcome a known prison of brick and steel—rather than the invisible snares that take a man unwary."

He looked back at her. She was dead still, staring at him. Her head was high, her eyes were narrowed. It was all the more infuriating to realize how sensual and beautiful she was in her nightgown, before all these men.

"Risa . . ." someone said.

She turned away. He did likewise.

"Risa . . . you should be in the house," he heard a soldier advise with a stutter.

He knew that she paused. And then she walked away.

He stood very still, staring straight ahead, as soldiers rushed forward to take him.

They did have shackles. He must have been considered very dangerous. They slipped the shackles around his wrists—and his ankles, as if they were afraid he would burst free and run. Even then, they seemed nervous, on edge, with his slightest movement. Fools. He could not burst free from steel.

He could only allow himself to be taken, with what dignity he could manage. He wasn't going to give them any further trouble at this moment. He couldn't win here—and he meant to live.

He stood in the night, trying not to shake with his fury, mocking himself. He was a fine Rebel soldier. Tall, broad, powerful—and completely powerless.

He walked forward, into captivity.

Damning her a thousand times over as he did so . . .

Chapter 21

Jerome was held for a week in a cell at Fort Marion. But an alert, older officer recalled the time after the capture of the Seminole Chief Osceola, when a number of captives had escaped through the bars of the fortress and into the darkness of the night.

One of the captives had been Jerome McKenzie's father, and the Yanks did not want to see history repeating itself.

And Fort Marion was not good for another reason.

Since August, a man sometimes called "Dixie" had been in the field. He was John Jackson Dickison—his middle name in honor of his father's good friend, Andrew Jackson. He had formed one cavalry unit previously which had been changed to artillery, so he'd resigned and formed a new unit, which had been mustered into service on August 21st, 1862. They called him the Gray Fox, or the War Eagle, and he was a force. He could move his men almost a hundred miles in a single day, forage well off the land, and hit and run against Yank companies with lightning speed. With Dixie guiding forces already renowned for beating back twice their number—and since the Rebs were bitter that the Feds had retaken Jacksonville on October 5th—they might well try to rescue their hero, Jerome McKenzie.

So he was quickly moved northward.

Risa was not allowed to see him, though she wondered bitterly what good it would do her if she were. His fury had been apparent in his eyes, his voice, his words. He blamed her, and he was never going to forgive her.

She was no happier with her father, convinced that Angus had set her up, despite his denials. "Daughter," he'd insisted as she burst in upon him at his officer's quarters with dawn breaking, "I knew nothing about it until just moments ago."

"Father, you want him dead! You threatened him often enough, in the press, to me, to others—"

"I was furious, yes, that some fool Rebel captain had taken *my* daughter prisoner. But you've gone off and married the man—you're having his baby! No, girl, I don't want the man dead! But you mark my words, young lady. He'll be better off a prisoner of war than a captain running an ever-tightening blockade! Think about it, Risa, if he remains a prisoner, he may live to see the end of the war!"

Her father didn't understand that Jerome wouldn't stay a prisoner. He would find some way to escape—risking his life in the process. And prisons—North and South—could be just as scary as battlefields. The mortality rate in prisons was chilling—up to nearly twenty-five percent.

"He could starve, or die of disease. You don't know him. If another prisoner is weak or ill, he'll give up his food. He'll fight for others."

"Risa!" Angus had protested, folding her into his fatherly arms. "I didn't bring about his capture, I swear it. I admit, I might have done so had I known that he was in St. Augustine—both because I am a Yankee general and your father—but I didn't know that you were entertaining your husband beneath my very nose! Yet this I can do, my dear. I can make it known that he is my son-in-law, the father of my soon-to-be-grandchild, and that I want him coming out alive."

"Oh, Father! Can you promise to keep him alive?" Risa asked anxiously.

He shook his head. "No man can keep such promises in this war, child. No man. But I will keep a watchful eye on where he is taken. Now, as to you. I must return to Washington—and then back to battle. Naturally, now you will come with me."

"No, Father."

"But, Risa—"

"First, we will see to your foot. Then, when you're healed, you can go back to Washington. I'll join you there soon, I promise," she told him.

He argued with her, and persisted. Which was good. Because while he was intent on arguing her future, she managed to get the officers in charge to realize his situation, and send across the river with a white flag. She *needed* to reach Julian, but wasn't going to try to do it on her own again.

Julian entered the city in safety, with promises that he would be duly returned across the river.

As Angus lay on an operating table, watching Julian examine his foot, he said, "Son, you ought to be wearing Union blue."

Julian smiled. The Florida troops had few actual uniforms left, and Julian was wearing homespun cotton breeches and a soft mustard shirt—neither uniform issue.

"People sometimes think, sir, that Ian and I are twins. But never let him fool you. I'm actually about a half inch taller, which quite drove Ian mad when we were very young men. Now he simply denies it."

Keeping his eyes steadily on the man who so carefully examined his foot, Angus demanded, "Why, son, would you patch up an old Union general like me?"

Julian smiled without looking up. "I'm a doctor, General Magee. I've sworn an oath to heal."

"Can you save my foot?"

"Yes, I think so."

Angus firmly tapped Dr. Cripped, who attended the examination. "Now, see there, sir! This young Reb can save my foot."

Thayer Cripped rolled his eyes to Risa, who shrugged. "I'm afraid he didn't get to be a general through tenderness, tact, and diplomacy," she informed him. "However, Julian's skills are quite remarkable."

Thayer nodded, and addressed Angus. "Sir, I will gladly learn what I can from the Reb."

Despite Angus's protest, Risa helped Thayer Cripped deliver the anesthesia as Julian ordered. Chloroform was soaked into a small sponge, which was set in the narrow end of a cone and brought closer and closer to the patient's face as he breathed, until he fell asleep. Julian worked swiftly, talking to Thayer all the while, giving him advice as to the things he had learned that proved most effective in the treatment of illnesses and wounds.

"Anesthesia has only really been used for about twenty years," Julian commented. "In this war, we are truly testing its use. It's a shame we usually have nothing but whiskey for our patients to drink—and bullets for them to bite. Now, when, soaking up blood, sir, use a new sponge with each soldier, I have found this to work miracles."

"Sometimes, that's not expedient—"

"But it seems to lower the cases of infection dramatically, and I believe my insistence on using fresh sponges and bandages has allowed me to save many limbs—while keeping my patients alive. Many of us have come to the conclusion that fresh air and well-ventilated spaces for recuperation are tremendously important as well. Of course, I've heard from my cousin about conditions on the battlefields at places like Manassas and Sharpsburg, where the doctors work so fast that there isn't time for anything but cutting. Still, I feel that when at all possible, we have to practice our craft with all the care we can."

Thayer Cripped nodded in wonder.

When the surgery was over, while Thayer Cripped looked after Angus, Julian sat briefly with Risa in her little house, enjoying strong-brewed coffee with imported French brandy. "You do stand condemned in Southern eyes, Risa. Did you send for Jerome so that he could be captured?" he demanded.

She flushed, aware that she appeared to be guilty.

"No. I didn't even send for Jerome; I hadn't known that he was near here. *You* must see the truth of it. I was trying to reach you about my father's foot."

"How interesting. A civilian boy came saying that Mrs. McKenzie was summoning the captain. Jerome and I are both captains, but he had just arrived with supplies. We assumed you were aware that Jerome had come in, and that you needed him."

"I swear, I didn't arrange it. The Yankees must have known that he had come down the river, and someone must have been watching for him. Your cousin will never believe it, though."

"Knowing my cousin, it will be difficult. Caging Jerome must be much like caging a wild Florida panther.

He will be all but crawling walls. Where is Jerome now, do you know?"

"No. They wouldn't tell me. They wouldn't let me see him. The Rebs are all convinced I betrayed him, but the Yanks are all equally convinced that I'd be smuggling messages in and out so he could escape if I were to see him."

"Ah," Julian murmured.

"What is that tone of voice? I'm telling you the truth. If you don't believe me, you can just go straight to hell!" Risa declared angrily. "Except," she amended more quietly, "I am grateful to you for saving my father's foot—and possibly his life."

Julian grinned. "I meant no special tone of voice—you are as prickly as my cousin! And you don't need to be grateful. What I said is the truth. I'm a doctor. I'm not in this war to kill, but to heal."

Risa nodded slowly.

He sighed, setting down his cup. "I wish I could stay longer, but I can't. I have always loved this city, and the coffee is much better now with the Yanks in charge—but it is enemy territory to me at this time. I have to go back to our camp."

"Julian, I need one more favor, I need your help."

"Oh?" he inquired warily.

"I swear, I have nothing evil in mind. As I said, I don't think that Jerome will ever forgive me, and I'm furious that he should condemn me so unfairly, but I still want to have my baby at Jerome's family estate. No matter what either of us feels at this moment, that land is our child's heritage, and it's where I want to be."

Julian hesitated. "What about your father?"

"I don't intend to tell my father."

Julian leaned forward. "Risa, it's my understanding that your father ripped into your friend Finn for bringing you down to the south of the state when you went off to search for Alaina. Your father threatened him with prison—"

"Finn is fine, walking around as free as a bird. But naturally, I couldn't ask him to help me again. I was assuming that Jerome's men will be moving his ship?"

Julian sat back, watching her with narrowed eyes. "They will be," he said, admitting the obvious.

"Would they be heading south?" she asked. "Please, I swear you can trust me!"

He rose. "If I can help you, Risa, I'll contact you."

"Thank you!" She kissed him on the cheek, and thanked him again on her father's behalf. Julian left.

And Risa waited. Her father continued to deny knowing how Jerome had been discovered. Both Austin Sage and Finn came to commiserate with her, but neither could tell her what had happened. "Shouldn't have married him," Finn told her cheerfully. "And you shouldn't have lured him here."

"I didn't lure him here!" she snapped. "If you're my friend, you should be finding out what happened!"

"Oh, Risa!" he told her unhappily, setting an arm around her comfortingly. "Now, if only you'd flirted with me when I tried to catch your eye before you sailed off with the Reb, you wouldn't be in this fix with your husband wanting to throttle you, eh?"

"Finn, I feel so much better!" she assured him. But he did make her feel better. He was there if she needed him.

A week later her father, still limping but much the better, returned to Washington with the stern warning that she was to follow soon. She promised to do so, making certain she gave him no exact time as to when she would.

Three days after her father departed, a young messenger in a greatcoat tapped on her door and briefly told her that the *Lady Varina* would be departing for Biscayne Bay the following night. She thanked him and watched him disappear into the night. She shivered and looked around herself, wondering if the night had eyes. But there was no one about.

The fighting continued at a sporadic pace as harsh winter weather swept over the land. Campaigns to be waged into the following spring were set into motion. In the western theater, a general named Grant—who was managing many victories when other Northerners were not—was setting his eyes on Vicksburg, Mississippi.

In the east, the Army of the Potomac began movements against Fredericksburg, Virginia, a healthy, prosperous town between Washington and Richmond.

Jerome had been brought to Old Capitol Prison, right
in the heart of Washington, D.C., where information was
readily available—even during the first weeks, when he
was kept in solitary confinement.

Imprisonment, even in solitary, was not half so hard
as living daily with the feeling of being a complete fool.
His anger against Risa did not abate, but seethed inside
of him, like a foul evil brew bubbling within a cauldron.
Old Capitol was not a pleasant place. It was dilapidated
and rat-infested. But it was in the heart of Washington,
surrounded by not just the politicians, but numerous citizens, good Christian men and women, who would not
allow cruelty toward enemies who were often also
friends and relations.

Eventually, word that he was being held there seeped
out, and the Yanks no longer cared that it was known.
He was not badly treated. He had a cell by himself that
was ten feet by ten feet and contained a bunk with a
rough straw mattress and a rickety old washstand. He
paced his ten feet endlessly, and was grateful that, after
the initial period, he was allowed to mingle with the
other Reb prisoners in a common room for several hours
each day, and his meals were not taken alone. The food
was standard prison fare, but many of the Rebs, though
not disparaging of the Confederacy, commented that it
was actually superior to their army rations. There were
far worse prisons, and he knew it. People talked of a
place in upstate New York where one out of every four
prisoners died; but naturally, the prisoners had no proof
of these rumors, and their guards often knew even less.

He was respected by his fellow prisoners and given a
key place in the decision making among the officers,
though as a captain, he ranked lower than several. He
was surprised to discover that he was not hated by the
Yanks. He received a bucket of aromatic stew from a
guard's wife one night, because, she told him, he had
dealt justly with the men from ships he had taken: living,
even in warfare, with a code of ethics. He had, in the
early days of the war, deposited the wife of the guard's

younger brother on a Bahamian island to be picked up
by a Union ship, and so, the lady was grateful to him.
This attitude surprised him somewhat, since he'd never
figured that the war had given any of them the right
to be murderers. But perhaps, that was what they had
all become.

Most of the guards were decent men, trying to get by,
intent on surviving the war. Some of them were weary
of it, and wished that the North would just recognize the
South and let it go.

There were a few sadists among their numbers, however. Men who would casually kick over a soldier's precious ration of food. Taunt them with rumors regarding
their families, and inform them with pleasure about the
death of a father, son, brother, or friend.

In his first weeks in the prison, Jerome seldom slept.
The sounds of the rats chewing within the walls and
scurrying across the floor drove him crazy. Most of the
time, a few violent motions on his part at least sent the
creatures scampering into their holes. But one especially
enterprising gray fellow would not be turned away even
when he threw his boots or food bowl at it. It grew so
bold as to crawl upon his chest while he slept, and he
came to call the fellow Beauregard, and gave him scraps
of food at night. Anything to endure the tedium, anything to survive.

Days became weeks. He heard about the troop movements across the country, and he studied the prison
walls, the boarded and barred windows, and the yard
where he and his fellow inmates were allowed exercise,
for some means of escape.

Tandy Larson was one of the more sadistic guards.
He wasn't authorized to beat the prisoners, but he found
excuses when men didn't move quickly enough, or when
they were on the wrong side of the yard, to whip them
with the butt of his rifle. Jerome incurred his wrath early
on by gripping him by the collar and breaking his rifle
on a day when he'd started pistol-whipping Lieutenant
Anthony Hawkins of Mississippi.

Guards came rushing from all over, but Jerome hadn't
touched Larson other than to drag him off of Hawkins.
He wasn't a fool, and he wasn't going to get shot—there

was a way out of Old Capitol, and he was going to
find it.

But from that day onward, Larson had it out for him.
Returned to his cell after exercise one day, he found
Beauregard lain out on his bed, a hat pin stuck through
his little rat heart. It wasn't fitting to mourn a rat—not
since the war brought on more dead men daily, and inmates were constantly trying to kill the creatures off to
lower the population. But he'd liked the damned rat—
he hadn't seen so much courage and gumption in many
men. He kept quiet about the incident. He had humiliated Larson in front of his peers, he supposed, and Larson meant to make him pay.

He'd been at Old Capitol nearly a month when Larson
approached him in the mess hall, where he sat with
other prisoners.

"Heard from Mrs. McKenzie, Captain?" Larson
sneered mockingly. "You may be a hero for the South,
sir, but your lady fights a better war than you! First,
she snared you—then she snared your ship!" Laughing,
Larson turned away.

Jerome very nearly killed him then. Moving like the
wind, he was on the man, and Larson was on the floor,
bereft of his rifle again, with Jerome's knee in his throat.

"Talk fast, man. If you're going to talk, say everything
you've got to say."

Larson, bug-eyed and choking, made squeaking noises.
Jerome eased his hold a little.

Hawkins stood near Jerome, warning him. "Rest of
the guards are on their way, guns cocked, McKenzie!"

"Talk!" Jerome ordered Larson.

Larson was beet red. "Your ship was taken—with
your wife aboard, along the Florida coast."

"Where is my wife now?"

"I don't know—I imagine the Yankee officers honored her right off for helping them capture the ship."

"Where's my ship, my crew?"

"Some of the crew members were released, some of
them are headed for Elmira Prison; the ship will be reoutfitted for use. Don't know where they're taking it!"

"Captain—" Hawkins warned, too late. A half dozen
guards had come down, and even those who liked Je-

rome had no recourse now. A rifle butt crashed across his head; he saw stars, then nothing.

He awoke later in his own room, where he was kept in solitary for another week. His head pounded for days. And with the pain came a renewed pulse of fury. First he imagined Risa on a medieval rack, then lashed to a mainmast with him wielding a cat-o'-nine-tails. But curiously, the visions just made him ill, and he knew all that he wanted to do was shake her until her teeth rattled—and lock her away in a tall dark tower, where she could do no more harm. He wondered duly how she had managed such a vicious betrayal. It had been one thing to be played a fool himself. But she had managed to get herself aboard his ship—she was his wife, expecting his child, his men would be quite unsuspecting—and get the sailing information to the Yankee authorities. His crew had been good to her. The men had adored her. Now half of them were rotting in Elmira Prison, famous for its death and disease.

Right before Christmas, he received letters from his family. Sydney had been working on getting him exchanged for her Yank cavalry now colonel, who had now mended completely. His Uncle Jarrett had been appealing to old friends in Washington, and his brother Brent had been harassing officials in Richmond. Ian had tried to see him, and been informed that he might be allowed visitors by February.

He didn't hear a word from his traitorous wife.

During January, while freezing, the men talked—and fought the war within the walls of the prison to keep warm and sane. The big news was about Lincoln's *Emancipation Proclamation*, something he had drafted before Antietam, but held on to until there had been something he could claim as a Northern victory. By January, word of his proclamation had spread everywhere. The document freed all the slaves in the states "rebellious" to the United States government.

"It's darned ridiculous!" Norman Jaye, a captain of artillery from Tennessee, said. "He's freeing Southern slaves—how can he do that? Why ain't he freeing Northern slaves? And how's he gonna free the slaves where he's fightin' a war already?"

Jerome, who had listened carefully when the document had been read in the prison, smiled. "Gentlemen, I'm sorry to say it, but I think that Mr. Lincoln, with this document, let loose his most powerful weapon."

A storm of protest followed his words.

He and the other men sat, stood, or lounged against the few tables in a common courtyard, shivering, but it was a place to be together where the guards left them alone.

"Captain, you should explain yourself," Anthony Hawkins suggested.

"Lincoln is a smart man, and it's a fact that he doesn't believe in any form of human bondage. Many of the Northern states have already abolished slavery on their own, but Lincoln can't risk turning the border states against the United States government, and we all know that places like Maryland have many Confederate sympathizers. He thinks he won a major victory at Antietam, though we argue that. I don't fault Lincoln for being any kind of a hypocrite; he wants to hold the Union together, and he wants to rid his country of the institution of slavery. No—he can't really free the slaves in the South, not at this point. But he's just scored a tremendous moral victory in the North, convinced some folk who might have been tired of the war effort to go on with it—and probably swayed European opinion in his favor."

"But heck, sir!" Granger Oak, a dirt-poor private from Georgia protested, "I don't own no slaves—my pa couldn't afford 'em! I still feel we have the God-given right to make our own decisions—"

"Granger, we're all aware that only rich men can own slaves, and not all rich men do. My grandfather was against slavery, and no McKenzie has owned slaves since. But we'd be lying to say that since our cotton economy is based on slave labor, many of the rights we're fighting for didn't have to do with slavery. Maybe we do have a moral obligation to end slavery; if so, we also have a moral obligation to see to the education and welfare of these hundreds and thousands of people we have enslaved."

"C'mon, Captain, you're talkin' about darkees—"

"Private!" Anthony Hawkins interrupted impatiently, "I can tell you this, I've seen red men, white men, and black men with intelligence and ability, and if you don't see that, you're a fool."

Jerome arched a brow to him, amused, and wondering if that hadn't been for his benefit. "There's going to be more bloodshed before any of this is resolved," he said quietly. "Yet, in my opinion, gentlemen, the South has been dealt a blow. What Lincoln lacked in generals, he's made up in political cunning."

A hail of protest went up—arguments raging. Jerome just sat back and listened. And he wondered dismally if the South could ever win the war.

At the end of February, Larson found good cause to taunt Jerome again. This time he did so more carefully, through the small, barred opening on his cell door. "Hey, there, Rebel redman!" Larson called. "Thought you might want to hear the good news. You know of a Jamie M. McKenzie, there, Captain?"

Jerome held his temper, knowing that he had to do so. His time would come. "My father is James."

"Naw, not your old man. You know a *Jamie* M. McKenzie?"

"No."

"Funny—that's the name of your son, Captain. Born right here in the capital of the good ol' U.S. of A.! A Yank babe, Rebel redman. Your son's born a Yank!"

His raucous laughter shrilling through the halls, Larson walked away.

Jerome slammed his hand in fury against the wall, again, and again, until his palm was ragged and bleeding.

His son. He had a son. Jamie. For his father? What was Risa trying to do? Was she all right?

He clenched his teeth, remembering how ill his mother had been. He reminded himself that his wife was a very young woman, healthy and strong. He tormented himself again with the thought that childbearing was always dangerous. Risa had to be all right. If there had been any bad news to tell regarding her, Larson would have been only too happy to give it to him.

He looked around the walls again. Be damned. He was getting out of here. Going south. And somehow, he was taking his son with him. As to his wife . . .

Well, he had a few plans regarding her as well.

* * *

Angus Magee had never imagined that he could be sorry to have his daughter in Washington. Especially, not when she had just given him his first grandchild.

Not that he could be with her often. His troops were quartered south of the city, and he had to make an effort to get into his town house, where his daughter was living—having been brought to him under guard by one of the naval commanders who had secured the capture of McKenzie's ship. She had been absolutely furious, and when he had demanded to know what she was doing on the Southern ship, she had explained about wanting the baby to be born on her husband's property.

"But, you're back in the North now, Risa. The child is yours as well. I am equally a grandparent with the McKenzies. And you must stay! It's Christmas, and your babe is all but born. Trying to travel could . . . well, frankly, you could harm yourself and kill your babe now."

Risa had good sense. Mostly. Except, apparently, she had lost it when she had become involved with the Confederate naval captain.

"I plan to stay here now, Father, I've no other choice, but—dammit! I can be a good Yank without betraying my husband, and I didn't do it, Father! I had nothing to do with that ship being taken, and they keep toasting me here in Washington for betraying my husband! This is horrible, and I don't know who is causing all this, or what is going on."

Angus hesitated, not wanting to add fuel to fire. "Daughter, this war is plagued with spies! You of all people should know that! You were friendly with that notorious Rose Greenhow, your friend Alaina was a spy . . . Risa, probably someone has been watching you, and knew what you were about. It doesn't matter now. What matters is your baby."

"Yes, I know that."

So she had been sensible, and Christmas had been happy, and then his grandchild had been born.

Oh, and that grandchild! The boy was pure pleasure, healthy, big, screaming, and caterwauling from the very first, determined on his own way, and letting them all know he wasn't happy when he didn't get it. He was born with a thick thatch of dark auburn hair and large, questing blue eyes. His father's eyes, Angus decided, deep, crystal blue, and not touched by aquamarine like Risa's. Babies' eyes changed, Angus knew, but he had a feeling his grandson's coloring was set.

Risa's labor had been remarkably easy. She hadn't screamed, cried, or carried on, but borne it all in a stoic silence, indicative of her mood of late. Since her arrival, after the capture of *Lady Varina* off Florida waters, she had energetically pitched her efforts into petitioning the White House for clemency for the crew members who had been sent to the infamous New York prison. She had written to Julian McKenzie, to Sydney, to Alaina, and to her in-laws, but she had made no effort to see Jerome, aware that a strict ban on visitors had been set upon him. She was aware, Angus felt, that her husband was as convinced as everyone else that she had brought about his capture—and that of his ship. Maybe she didn't push the point because she wasn't eager to see him.

But then, of course, the baby was born.

To Angus, his daughter was more beautiful than ever when blessed with the glow of motherhood. Her cheeks had acquired delicate new hollows, and there was an aura of maturity about her that was compelling. She had always been poised; now she was almost regal. She made her decisions firmly, and carried them out with a speed that would have done any general proud. She learned that Ian was in Washington for new orders, and she sent a messenger to ask him to stand as a godparent to her child—as she had done for his. She next learned that her sister-in-law, Sydney McKenzie, was very near, behind the enemy lines with a prisoner who was about to be exchanged. Sydney couldn't come to Washington—or she didn't want to do so. But she couldn't refuse to be a godmother for her own nephew, and Risa was undaunted. She arranged the passes and paperwork, and made arrangements to have James Magee McKenzie baptized in a little church on the outskirts of Manassas.

Personally, Angus wanted to slap young Miss Sydney McKenzie. Despite his being a Yankee colonel, she could greet her cousin Ian with warm hugs and affection.

Yet she was as cold as ice to Risa throughout the ceremony—although she did seem quite smitten with her
new nephew. Risa made no attempts to exonerate herself with Sydney. She was cordial and polite, and when
young Jamie was duly baptized, they all went their separate ways, Risa, Angus, Ian, and Jamie back to Washington, and Sydney back behind Rebel lines.

It was hell for Angus to see Risa so tormented, no
matter what her facade.

"Daughter, what are your plans now?" he demanded
gruffly, on the day he managed to ride home to celebrate
his grandchild's month-old birthday. "I can request a
pass for you to see your husband—"

"No, thank you, Father. I understand that he has been
able to write to his family. He has not written to me."

"So . . . ?"

"Well, I plan to petition until the men from the *Lady
Varina* are released. I plan to care for my son and to
find work at the hospital. And maybe, since I am continually so accused, I will find work as a Union spy."

"Risa! I forbid you—such work is dangerous—"

"I wasn't serious, Father," she said quickly.

But the sizzle in her aquamarine eyes was frightening,
and he wasn't so certain she was jesting. She was deeply
wounded; and, he feared, she was deeply in love with
the husband who had so wounded her.

He realized that he'd really yet to meet the man himself. Perhaps that was a matter which should be rectified.

Chapter 22

It was a bitterly cold day in March when a young soldier walked Angus Magee along the corridor to one of the prison's holding rooms.

"You're his first visitor, sir, and I imagine they only let you come because you are General Magee. They're mighty afraid of this fellow, though he seems a right fine man to me. I've seen a few occasions when he could have done some real damage to Yanks—then again, he might well have gotten himself shot for it as well. Anyway, sir, he's there, waiting," the young soldier said, indicating a closed door with a small barred opening at eye level.

"Thank you," Angus said.

"We can arrange a guard to be with you—"

"No, thank you. I wish to see the prisoner alone."

The young soldier hesitated. Angus felt a moment's irritation, well aware that the soldier was worried, comparing his age and lesser height and size to that of the prisoner. He wasn't a short man, and by God, he was still a powerful man—not so far from his prime. But he hadn't come for a contest of strength. He had come because of Risa.

The soldier opened the locked door for the general. "As you wish, sir. I will, however, be within shouting distance. And I'm armed."

The door opened and closed. Angus heard the bolt slide as he stared across the empty room at the man who stood with his back to him, staring out the barred window. Broad-shouldered, despite the leanness caused by war and deprivation, Jerome McKenzie was still imposing in the large, worn wool Confederate issue overcoat he wore.

The temperature here was freezing.

Hard on a man accustomed to the year-long heat of the subtropical peninsula of Florida, Angus thought. Then he reflected that he was glad, with only a touch of malice, that McKenzie might be cold.

He deserved the discomfort simply for *being* a stubborn Reb.

McKenzie turned to him impassively, surveying him.

And Angus surveyed his son-in-law in turn.

He was a great deal like Ian; the two were built so similarly that they might be one and the same from a distance. But there was a touch of red to this man's heavy dark hair, and, admittedly, a touch of the "noble savage" to his cheekbones. He was a striking man, the mixtures of blood in his veins giving him a powerful and unique appearance. But it was still a pity Risa couldn't have married Ian before the war—that would have avoided this wretched dilemma for all of them. Ian was on the right side of things. He and Risa had so very much in common. It still boggled Angus's mind. How she had met this man, and conceived a child with him . . .

"You know who I am?" Angus said gruffly.

McKenzie smiled, a rueful, self-mocking smile. "My father-in-law?" he said, stepping into the room to meet Angus.

Angus wasn't sure what happened then. Maybe it had just been McKenzie's tone of voice. Maybe it was the wretched pain Risa had been suffering. Then there was that deep bitterness in the sound of the man's words! Whatever the reason, when McKenzie stepped forward, Angus took a swing at him.

His fist connected with McKenzie's face, though just barely. McKenzie was lightning fast, and caught Angus Magee's wrist, deflecting—but not halting—the blow.

Angus saw the man's eyes. Pure blue fury. He tensed, thinking it might well be time to call on the soldier outside to come shoot the prisoner before McKenzie decided to break his neck in return. But McKenzie merely straightened, a pulse thundering at his throat, that fire of fury still burning so fiercely in his eyes.

"Why didn't you hit me back?" Angus demanded.

"Because you're Risa's father."

"You could have sent me to the floor, son."

"I could have killed you, sir," he said smoothly. "But you're my wife's father. And a Union general. And I intend to live—and get out of here."

"Good reasons," Angus muttered.

"Tell me, sir, how is my son?"

Angus smiled. "Fine. Now, you tell me this—did you ever force yourself on her?"

"Is that what she said?" he inquired bitterly.

Angus shook his head slowly. "No."

"Then, why don't you believe your own daughter?"

He hesitated, surprised, arching a brow. "I'm asking you."

"I never forced your daughter into anything, sir. It pains me to admit that she has thus far been much more apt at maneuvering situations her way," he said flatly. But then he hesitated. "I did force the marriage."

"You forced her to marry you?"

Again, Jerome McKenzie offered Angus his dry, mocking smile. "It seemed the right thing to do—under the circumstances. Especially, after Ian told me he'd taken one in the jaw over the situation—from you— when he'd known damned well he wasn't guilty. Naturally, you may rest assured, General, that he passed on your violent sentiments to me. I wasn't fast enough to block Ian that day—a right to the jaw from him was the last thing I was expecting—so I was duly tendered your paternal opinion of what had happened."

"You deserved it."

"No, sir, not really. The lady had neglected to inform me of the situation; indeed, she had made it quite plain that I did not dress in the proper color to meet her standards. She had stated that she wanted nothing more to do with me. She was seeking a man in blue."

"My daughter didn't betray you, Captain."

McKenzie inclined his head. "That, sir, is your opinion."

"Captain McKenzie, I'm telling you, not even I knew anything about what happened at St. Augustine until after it was over. . . . And as to the other—"

"She deliberately went to my brother to find out the

plans regarding my ship. Amazingly, she was aboard when it was taken, just days later."

"Sir, that doesn't mean——"

"Sir, I beg to differ. Look," McKenzie said impatiently, "you are a Union general, sir. Your daughter is back in the bosom of your love. This is not a matter that should distress you."

"What distresses me is that I think my fool daughter is in love with you."

McKenzie arched a brow. "Well, sir, I think you should set your mind at ease regarding that thought!"

"Young man, you stand there disparaging my daughter——"

"I'm sorry, General. But do consider the fact that I am standing here in prison." He hesitated, and Angus thought he saw at last a flicker of something in the man's eyes. "She is well?"

"Extremely."

He nodded. Angus realized that he was carefully controlling his emotions—and that he was concerned. "Childbirth can be a trying time. I had always imagined—in a different life, before the war, of course—that I'd be present at the birth of my children, with my wife. She managed with no real difficulty? She is honestly well?"

"I'd not lie about my daughter's health, sir."

McKenzie nodded, eyes downcast. "Well, General, I'm not sure why you came, but——" he broke off. "Sir, I must say that, whatever arguments you have against me, I am deeply disappointed that you used them against my family."

"What, sir, are you talking about?"

"Well, I received your letter—that which came through my brother Brent and threatened my life—but before that, I received a communication in Richmond as well, threatening all my family. Soon after, an absurd kidnapping attempt was made against my sister."

Angus drew himself to his full height. "How dare you, sir!"

"General, I'm telling you——"

"Indeed, sir, I do not doubt the veracity of such a happening, but how you could imagine that a soldier of my record and status would bring the war against a young girl—"

"Sir, your own daughter had been involved," McKenzie reminded him.

But Angus shook his head furiously. "My argument was always against you, and no one else."

McKenzie, studying him, obviously accepted that as the truth. "I wonder then . . ."

"You've enemies elsewhere, young man. Despicable, dishonorable enemies, it would seem."

"Indeed, so it would seem."

"I'd not harm a hair on your sister's head unless she were dressed in Southern gray and firing at me from across a battlefield."

"I believe that, General Magee."

"Good."

McKenzie hesitated then, watching him. "Would you tell me about my son?" he asked quietly.

Again, there was a tear in the man's eye, and a yearning sound in his voice.

"You would be proud and delighted, Captain McKenzie. Young Jamie is a strapping fellow—I'd say he already weighs more than ten pounds. He is a beautiful child, lots of dark red hair—and your eyes. I can definitely see it now. He thrives. Perhaps I can manage to bring him—"

"No," McKenzie said harshly. "No—thank you, sir. I do not want my son in this prison."

"As you wish. And as to Risa—"

"I would not see her here, either, sir," he said coldly.

Angus hesitated. "What if . . . what if you remain throughout the war?"

"I will not. It may take several more months, but I will be exchanged. . . . I believe an exchange is being arranged."

"Truthfully, sir, with no malice intended, I pray that your stay here is long. There is no chance for the South to win this war—we are far stronger, and I do believe that God's right is on our side. I offer you no insult, sir. The tragedy of this war is that so many Southern soldiers are so fine, so brilliant with strategy, and so brave! They prolong the inevitable, and add to the death. But I understand that every man has his sense of honor, Captain McKenzie. And so, I pray you remain in prison."

"General Magee," Jerome McKenzie said evenly, "you must bear in mind, sir, that we are fighting different wars. Ours has always been a war of defending our home property. Yours is a war of invasion. If the South had intended to take Washington, we might well have ended this long ago. Sadly, one of our functions is to prolong the pain we all endure—and exhaust the Northern citizens. If the people rise against the politicians, we may both go our separate ways, and find a new peace. Just as the colonies left Britain, sir, the South desires to leave the North."

Magee shook his head. "It won't happen, Captain. I'm an old warhorse, and I can see the future. Lincoln is an unusual man, battling the hail of arrows that come his way. God knows, he is a strange man, but one up to this task! He believes passionately in the Union, and he will prevail."

"That remains to be seen."

"I am afraid so."

McKenzie studied Magee. He offered the older man his hand. "Thank you for coming, sir. It has been a pleasure to meet you, after all this time."

"I wish you were on our side, son."

"In all honor, I cannot be." He smiled suddenly, and his striking face came alight with the charisma that had surely swayed his daughter. "And, yet, if you will allow me, sir, it is an honor to call you father-in-law."

Magee nodded gravely. "There is no one quite as surprised as I at this moment to find it an honor indeed to call you my son-in-law as well." He saluted. "Take care of yourself, Captain. There may yet be an end to this war."

McKenzie saluted in return. "Keep your head down, General. And look after my son until I can do so myself."

"That is a request with which I can gladly comply," Angus agreed. Then he turned to the door, and knocked on it. "Guard!" he called.

He left the cell without looking back.

But when he exited the prison, he went to see an old

friend who was involved with prisoner exchanges. He discovered that his son-in-law was indeed scheduled to be exchanged. "He's a special case, but then, they have one of our real important fellows that's been kept at Libby for some time now."

"I want McKenzie kept in prison," Magee declared.

"Ah—the fellow had the nerve to elope with your daughter, eh, General?"

Angus shook his head. "No. I want the fellow alive to raise my grandson, sir, and that's the way it is."

Jerome had been oddly touched by the visit from his father-in-law. Magee was an old martinet, but he seemed to be a man with tremendous strength of mind and heart.

He longed to hold his son. To see the baby's face. And he was—even if he still believed she belonged locked in a high tower—relieved to know Risa was well. His mother's ordeal after his baby sister's birth had left him shaken.

Soon after Magee's visit, he was startled to be taken back to the room where he had met with the general. He was surprised to see that a bench had been brought into the room—and that his sister Sydney was seated there. With a glad little cry, she jumped up to greet him, and he hugged her fiercely, rocking with her, incredulous that she should be there.

"I don't know what's going on, Jerome!" she told him, pulling away and pouting at the soldier who stood guard within the door, as if he were suspicious of what might take place between the two. "It was all set. I had come just below the battle lines with Jesse—Colonel Halston, you know, the Yank you met at the hospital. He'd been transferred to Libby, and then he was going to be exchanged for you—but then we got here, and everything went wrong! It's been just absurd."

Jerome scowled at the soldier on guard who shrugged unhappily. "Do you mind? She's my sister. I hardly intend to offer her harm!"

"But, sir—"

"Soldier, we've personal family matters to discuss."

"Ma'am, your brother is known to be the Devil himself, so you can rest assured that I'm right outside the door," the soldier said.

"I do not need protection from my own brother!" Sydney said indignantly.

The soldier nodded and slipped outside the door. "Well, not most of the time, anyway," Sydney amended mischievously.

"Sydney!"

"Sorry. It's just that you do always think you're in charge."

"I'm your older brother. But tell me, quickly, before they decide to come in on us—is Halston in Washington already?"

"No . . . no, they won't turn him over until an actual exchange is contracted. But now they're dragging their heels, and saying they won't exchange you, that the Rebs are going to have to agree on another prisoner!"

Jerome sank down onto the bench, running his fingers through his hair and grating his teeth together. "Damn him. Damn her."

"Who?" Sydney asked puzzled.

"Magee. And Risa."

"Jerome, I know that Magee is the Yank to end all Yanks, but I met him, and he's a decent man—"

"Exactly. And he thinks he's being decent, keeping me here. I'll guarantee you, he's gotten to the upper-ups around here and insisted I not be exchanged." He frowned, looking at her. "You met Magee?"

Sydney nodded. "At the baptism. Oh! Jerome, I didn't tell you yet! I was so angry with your wife, I was ready to refuse, but it was your child, you see, so I agreed to be godmother."

"To Jamie?"

"Of course—oh, Jerome! He's adorable. He's the spitting image of you. A little tiny Captain McKenzie with this great cap of hair already! And McKenzie eyes. You could pick those eyes out in any crowd! He's a beautiful baby, Jerome, really. Not in the least wrinkled up. He's strong. He was just a few weeks old at the baptism, already pushing himself up. He's going to have a temper, that one! I hated having to give him back to . . . her."

"Risa was well?"

Sydney hesitated. "Yes, she was just fine. She was . . . aloof. Cool and calm throughout the day, ignoring my rudeness, and I promise you, I was very rude. But she's so tall . . . so slender, and poised! It's easy to see how"— Sydney hesitated and shrugged—"how she manages so much."

"Her father denies her involvement in any of this," Jerome murmured.

"You talked with Magee?"

"Yes. We disagree on which side to be on, that's all," Jerome murmured. He stood, pacing the small room. "Sydney, I have to get out of here."

"Oh, Jerome, I'm trying so hard! Mother has been writing letters, father's family is ready to start another Seminole war. Ian has been arguing himself silly, though he wrote me that he thinks you're better off locked up for the remainder of the war. Except that he knows you'll try to find a way out no matter what—"

"Yes, he's right. Are you going to be able to see me again?"

"I believe they'll let me come again."

"Tomorrow?" he asked anxiously.

Sydney nodded slowly. He was already planning. . . .

Anthony Hawkins, the Mississippian, was the one to come up with the best idea.

They sat together in the mess area, sipping coffee, watching the men move about, eyeing the guards.

"There ain't no way for a man to go shootin' his way out of here," Hawkins noted grimly. "You have to do it like a damned ghost or the like. You're in the heart of the Yank territory. The very damned heart of the place. You threaten the wrong person here, and you'll be gunned down like a dog before you move two feet."

"Well, I admit, getting a rifle and trying to shoot my way out wouldn't work too well. I'd need an arsenal."

"The only way to walk out of here would be—to walk out of here. You know, like the womenfolk who come."

"Mmm."

Jerome suddenly sat straighter. "We got anybody can get a message to my sister?"

Hawkins hesitated, swallowing his coffee. "Ricky

Boyle's old grandmother comes every Tuesday. She could reach Sydney."

"Boyle's old grandmother?" Jerome inquired, smiling. "Is she—the delicate sort?"

"Delicate?" Hawkins snorted. "She's fightin' Irish, all the way. Dragged eleven children and their children out of the potato famine of '49 back in the old country. Delicate? Hell, no, sir, she's the Devil in a dress!"

"Good! Just the woman I need. And surely such a fine old Irish lass will have a few friends?" Jerome suggested. "Have you a mind to escape with me?"

"Captain, I guarantee it!"

"Any others? We must be able to trust them."

"I know all the Mississippians. And there's a Florida boy here. Robert Gray. Rode with Dickison."

"Good. No more than four of us—but that number will do well. You choose the other two, men who are eager to go, and who can take orders. Now, listen closely, here's the way it's going to be done . . ."

Things went amazingly well, all according to plan, except that there was a slight hitch with Sydney.

On the day decided upon for the escape, the Irish Roses Ladies' Choral Group arrived at the prison, intent on bringing the melodic word of God to the poor Rebs. Old Maureen Boyle had outdone herself, arriving with so many ladies, it was quite impossible to keep track of them as they flitted about, warning the guards that they were all subject to the Word of God. Sydney slipped in with the ladies, but she was very nervous, and when she came by Jerome's side she told him, "They're carrying out the exchange! Colonel Halston was returned to the city last night, and they've released a general from up at Elmira in your stead."

"So what's the matter?" he asked her.

"I just wish that—oh, nothing. I wish it would have all gone through as planned, that's all."

"This will work; you'll see."

As Maureen's ladies visited the prisoners, the four who intended to break out received little bits and pieces of costume from them.

They sang hymns. They sang hymns so long that the

guards began to drift: Larson, leaning on his rifle, actually snored.

By the time the ladies left, the guards were delighted to see them go. The women departed arm in arm, still singing to one another boisterously.

Jerome did not make a good woman—he was far too tall. But they had all carefully shaved, and he had been given an excellent wig and hat, and padding that gave him admirable breasts. As he hunched over and departed the prison, he heard Larson comment, "My God, but there were some ugly women among that bunch of God seekers!"

"Ugly, indeed!" muttered Sally O'Reilly, an attractive woman of about forty with wild red hair and beautiful green eyes. "That's why the fellow tried pinching us all afternoon!"

"He didn't!' Maureen Boyle protested, horrified.

"He did! But we must go back, and when we do—when we're not on a mission such as this—I will smack him with my reticule," Sally swore.

"Right now, we had better hurry along, Grandmother, eh?" queried Ricky Boyle, who had opted to escape with them.

"As you say, me boy. Hurry along, lasses, hurry along!" Maureen advised.

They came to Mrs. Boyle's house in the center of town. There, the men cast aside their women's garments, and the good ladies offered them the clothing of their menfolk—most of them dead, Jerome was sorry to hear. The ladies prepared a bountiful meal, meat and kidney pies along with dishes of potatoes and hot apple pie. They had to keep their nerve, and not leave the city until dusk. If they left too early, they'd be spotted in the light. Too late, and a cry would have come up in the city because their absence from prison would be noted. Roll call was taken once in the morning, and a count was taken again at night.

Just at dusk, they were due to slip aboard a wagon load of corpses bound for points south. Such wagons were seldom stopped or inspected by the pickets.

Washington was filled with Southern sympathizers. Jerome wondered if Lincoln ever realized just how many. At dusk, they left the Boyle house, slipping quietly along the streets, into the shadows, one by one. They reached the junction near the bridge that would take them to Virginia. It was then that Jerome realized Sydney had fallen behind.

Sydney had been totally unprepared for what happened. She had been afraid—oh, God, yes, all day she'd been afraid, in absolute terror! She hadn't thought that the Irish matrons could really manage the feat of getting the men out. She had been certain that a guard would take one look at her towering brother, and know he was no lady. But Jerome had walked out and no contingent of guards or soldiers or civilians had come after them. But somehow, while walking down the street in her place among the men, she had found herself swept into the shadows.

She had tried to scream, but a hand came over her mouth and prevented so much as a grunt escaping her. Then she heard a warning voice, "Miss McKenzie, pay me heed. I can cry out an alarm right now, and all but guarantee that every one of those Rebs will be shot down on the spot—your brother included. Or I can keep quiet—and you and I can have a little conversation."

Even before he released her, before she could turn, she knew that Jesse Halston—so recently released!—was her detainer. And she knew she mustn't let out any sound then.

Her brother would come back for her. He would die before he let harm befall her.

When she was free, she spun around, and stared at Jesse, pure fury flashing in her brilliant green eyes. "You bastard! My brother Brent saved your life, I tended you for months on end, you fool, and you're threatening—"

"Shut up, Sydney, and pay attention," he snapped, and his hazel eyes were like a fierce gold fire reflected in the gaslight. "If I wanted to cause harm to Captain McKenzie, I could have done so by now."

"Then—"

"I intend to let him go. He was cheated out of his release—North and South, everyone knows that. In fact,

I intended to tell him his wife is visiting her father, where Magee and his men are camped out near Fredericksburg, getting ready for the spring campaigns."

"Then—?" Sydney persisted.

"You're not going with him."

"What?"

"He's risking his life. Most Yanks wouldn't hurt a woman, but you get caught with him, or get in the midst of fire . . . well, men aren't always responsible for what happens." Jesse Halston, tall and imposing in the shadows, nodded his head, indicating Jerome, who had turned back to find Sydney. "Miss McKenzie, you're going to tell him that you've opted to remain in the city, that you can return South safely with proper military passes at any time. Do you understand? I am armed, with two six-shooting Colts."

Sydney stared at him incredulously. After all that she had done for this man! But . . .

"Sydney!"

She heard her brother's voice, and she rushed out into the street, anxious to meet Jerome before he found her in the shadows with Jesse.

"Jerome, I'm sorry, so sorry, but—I've decided not to go with you."

"What? Sydney, I can't leave you here—" he began with a fierce, determined frown.

"No, wait, you must listen, Jerome, it's only logical! I don't have to escape the city! I'm not a prisoner, I came here to return a Yank. I don't have to use subterfuge to get back, which wouldn't matter, but I'd just slow you down."

Jerome was shaking his head. "Sydney, I can't leave you on the damned streets alone—"

Sydney froze, aware then that Jesse Halston had stepped from the shadows, and come forward to meet her brother. Jerome arched a dark brow, his features impassive, his blue eyes darkening to ebony as they narrowed.

"I would die for her, Captain!" Jesse said determinedly, standing behind Sydney, his hands on her shoulders. "But she risks bullets and other dangers if she runs with you. You know that to be true, Captain McKenzie."

Jerome's eyes remained hard on Jesse; Sydney was surprised that Jesse didn't quail beneath her brother's withering stare. Jerome had the capability of looking as savage as any painted warrior about to take scalps.

But her brother looked at her then. "Sydney, if you want to stay with him, he's right. Running, you risk the dangers we face. And you can, logically, return by a more normal route at will—if this is your choice. Except that, if you had planned on meeting Colonel Halston here, I wish you might have shared that information with me!"

Sydney forced herself to smile, moistening her lips. Naturally, Jerome thought that she had planned on meeting him. And she had to let her brother believe that to be true.

"I'm sorry, Jerome. I didn't think you'd trust him. After all, she said sweetly, "he is the enemy."

"I just told Sydney, Captain McKenzie, that your wife is in Virginia. Magee's troops are camped near Fredericksburg."

Jerome arched a brow, watching Jesse with greater interest. "And my son? Do you know where I might find him?"

"Ah, sir, a nursing mother seldom leaves her infant."

Jerome nodded his acknowledgment. "Thank you. I entrust my sister to your care, as it's her choice, and, admittedly, far safer than her accompanying me. However, Halston, if any ill befalls her—war or no war, it will be in hell itself, I'll find you."

"Have I raised an alarm, Captain?" Jesse queried. "Have I done anything to hinder your escape? I am far too indebted to your family. But you had best be going, before your time runs out!"

"Sydney?" Jerome said, his tone gruff.

She threw her arms around him and hugged him. "Go, please, Jerome, go. Trust me, I'm fine. Please, go!"

He nodded, and released her.

Then he shook hands with Halston. "Keep her safe, sir!"

Jerome's eyes met hers once again. She forced a smile,

slipping her arms through Jesse's and leaning her chin against his chest.

Jerome smiled, nodded slightly, and turned at last. He sprinted into the shadows, and was swallowed by the darkness.

Sydney waited until she was quite certain he was gone.

Then she turned on Halston, tears stinging her eyes. She took a wild swing at him, trying to slap him. "Ingrate! Bastard!" she charged him.

He caught her arm before she could strike him, pulling her close. "I'm damned sorry, Sydney, I just couldn't let you take such a risk."

"Fine, let go of me now."

"No."

"No! What do you mean, no?"

"I mean no!" He shook his head, staring into her eyes. "No, I'm afraid not, and that's it, Miss McKenzie. You're coming with me. I just swore to your brother that I'd keep you safe."

"Oh, don't be ridiculous! How—"

"Shut up, Sydney!" he snapped, and firmly shoulder-butted her in the midsection to throw her over his shoulder. "For your own good, Miss McKenzie, like it or not, you're coming with me."

"I won't; I'll call for help—"

"Scream—and I'll tell your would-be rescuers that your brother and a group of Rebs are escaping across the river. Damn you, Sydney, hold still and shut up!"

Thus warned, teeth gritted, Sydney opted to shut up. For the time.

Chapter 23

Risa hated the quiet of night. She was haunted by dreams in which she lived the events in her life over and over again. Not that she could have changed much. She was a Yankee. She believed that the power of the fledgling United States was in their unity. She believed, equally, that no man had the right to own another. God alone could own a man's soul.

But she had never meant to betray the Confederates—not her husband, or her friends.

Sometimes, in her nightmares, she saw again the moment Jerome was taken. Saw his eyes, the way that he looked at her, when he realized they were surrounded. She relived those terrible seconds when she had feared that he would fight to the death, bringing down a number of Union soldiers, but perishing, too, before her eyes. Sometimes she saw again the way that the men of the *Lady Varina* looked at her when they realized that they were being encircled by Union ships that had to have been told of their location and destination to arrive so opportunely. She had denied any wrongdoing with fierce dignity to Hamlin, Michael, Matt, Dr. Stewart, and others, but she could still remember the quiet way they had surrendered—and the looks they had given her.

As the winter progressed and they moved toward spring, her father was in town much less frequently. And her own campaign was at long last successful. By constantly hounding a number of the right authorities, she'd managed the promise of release to the men of Florida who had been taken to Elmira—once all the proper paperwork was carried out. She'd hired a lawyer to take the case, and he had argued the injustice of imprisoning men who had released their Yankee counterparts time and time again, with no ill done them. Yankee sailors who had received better medical attention from the *Lady Varina*'s doctor than their own wrote at her behest, and so she had managed what she had set out to do.

She was weary of the proper venues afforded to young ladies in the city of Washington as far as the war effort went. She began to feel as if she was losing her mind. There was so little for her to do to ease the torment that continually plagued her, other than stare at the facade of Old Capitol now and then, ache to see Jerome—and wonder in what ways her husband might be plotting revenge. Her father had told her that he did not wish to see her, or the baby.

So she determined to work with the soldiers again, the injured and the sick. Anything to keep her thoughts at bay.

Not that Jamie didn't keep her busy—he did. Sometimes, when she held him, she could feel deep in her heart that nothing else in the world really mattered. She was convinced he was the most miraculous infant who had ever lived. His eyes were so bright, and ever watchful. He never lost a strand of hair—it grew in thick, a lustrous, dark auburn. He wailed more loudly than a bugle call, and smiled at a young age—and, she assured her father, no, it was not gas in the intestines!

At first, Angus was not happy when she arrived at his camp. He was afraid for her and his grandson. They faced an enemy known for its lightning-quick ability to attack, and they were on the enemy's home ground— Virginia. But when she arrived, he didn't have the heart to send her home, and as he yelled at her, he also rationalized to her and himself that his troops were not now on the offensive—he was leading raw young men just recruited to fill in for the thousands who had died. He worked hard with them—relentlessly drilling them to whip them into disciplined forces who would not break under pressure.

As the days went by and Risa proved herself an asset, Angus became pleased that she had joined him. She started up her duties in the field hospital once again, frequently writing letters for homesick young boys plagued by illnesses that dropped them before they

could even face enemy bullets, and reading to young
men who had bandaged heads—or had simply never
learned to read. Through campfire talk, she was aware
that Hooker was planning a heavy cavalry movement
against Lee's army, and she knew as well that her father's men would be moving into action soon.

But she never saw that action.

She had spent the day with Dr. Lemuel Hernandez, a
man determined not only on saving lives, but maintaining the quality of life whenever possible. He had
chosen today to operate with a technique known as re-
section or exsection, in which the damaged part of an
arm or leg was removed and then the limb was re-
connected. It could be a very successful operation, one
that left a man limping with a shortened bone, but walking on his own leg, nonetheless. It was often impossible
to perform in the midst of heavy battle when many men
were seriously wounded and speed was of the essence,
but whenever he could, Dr. Hernandez tried to make
use of the procedure. He was a dedicated, no-nonsense
man in his late fifties, and he found Risa's calm de-
meanor in a field operating tent to be necessary for his
concentration. He was capable of working hours on end,
however, without so much as a sip of water. But he was
always so grateful to her and so many soldiers were
helped, she was glad to work with him. His long, brutal
regime was one that she loved; she didn't get any time
at all to think. If she was going to survive the war with
any sanity left her, this was surely the way to do it.

She returned to her tent after working with him one
long chilly day in early April to find that Reba, a free
woman of color her father had hired to look after them
both, was pacing Risa's tent with a very distraught
Jamie—who was howling away angrily.

"What happened? What's wrong? Did he hurt himself?" she asked anxiously, taking him from Reba's arms.

Reba, a tall, slender, very capable woman, drew herself up and sniffed. "Miss Risa, this boy is hungry, and
you told me you would tend to him, and I am not a wet
nurse, so I'm sorry if he's carryin' on, but that's the way
of it! Did he hurt himself!" she objected. "Not in my
care, no ma'am!"

"Reba! I'm sorry!" Risa laughed, delighted to be holding her son.

"He's a handful that boy, and when he's hungry . . . my, my, he does carry on more than most!"

Risa tugged at the dozen little buttons on her day dress until she could bring her baby to her breast. When he first rooted on to her, she felt the same little thrill of motherhood that rushed through her each and every time, and for long moments she did nothing but adore her son. "I'm sorry, Reba, there were a number of operations today."

"Honey, you don' owe me no apology—you just need to know your boy has got a strong will—and strong lungs, is all. Should I fetch you something to eat? Or you want me to wait a spell, till the boy is sleeping?"

"No, I'm fine—"

"You nursin' a boy like that one, you need your strength. They had some stew tonight—one boy went out and got himself a deer. I'll bring some, and leave you be. Wash water's still warm, and you've got a nightgown there, laid out on the bed."

"Thank you, Reba," Risa said gratefully.

Jamie filled his stomach quickly, burped with a total lack of manners, and fell contentedly to sleep. He'd probably worn himself out, crying for his supper, but Risa was so tired, she was glad. Once he was safely sleeping, she realized that she was ravenous. She ate the stew Reba had left on the top of her trunk.

"Mrs. McKenzie, ma'am!"

The call sounded from right outside her tent. Setting down her bowl, she lifted the canvas flap and stepped outside. Major Alynn, one of her father's officers, stood waiting for her, saluting stiffly.

She saluted in return, wondering why Alynn always greeted her so.

"Ma'am," he said, "there's rumor that Captain McKenzie escaped Old Capitol."

Chills immediately raced through her body. Rumor. Had he, or hadn't he? She prayed that he was alive, yet he was surely risking his life. He would have to cross Union lines to come South. If he was seen, would he be shot down in cold blood?

"Rumor?" she forced herself to say aloud.

Alynn looked at her, then shrugged uncomfortably. "We heard it from a few Rebs who had deserted, so we're not sure. Your father ordered me to make certain you were aware of the situation. He wants you to plan on moving your belongings in with him tomorrow."

"Now, Major—"

"Your father's orders, ma'am. He's worried about you."

"I'm in the middle of a Yankee camp, Major. No man could possibly come to take me from here," she said, yet she felt a strange foreboding. Jerome had come into a Yankee camp once before.

"Your father wants you moved . . ."

"Well, Major, thank you. Please tell my father that we'll discuss it tomorrow."

He saluted her again. "There will be a man on guard at your tent throughout the night."

She saluted him back, even though she wasn't actually in the military. "Thank you, Major. Good night."

"Don't worry, now. You are surrounded by Yankees!"

She stepped back into her tent, shivering in earnest, and sat on her bunk. She had known that Jerome would find some way to escape. She had feared his determination all along.

Now she could only hope that he wouldn't be like a wildcat, running recklessly. He had a long way to go through enemy territory. She was terrified for him. Should she be afraid for herself? Her father, who had seen Jerome, wanted her moved in with him. For her safety. Her own father had seen with what anger her husband condemned her.

She stood, annoyed with herself. She was safe here— in the center of a camp with thousands of soldiers. To-night she had a guard watching her tent. He wouldn't risk coming here; he'd remember he'd been captured in Yankee-held St. Augustine. He wouldn't want to be captured, and sent back to prison.

She couldn't jump at every footfall; she had to have faith in the Yankees guarding her, and pray that Jerome cherished his freedom more than he longed for revenge. She stood, washed in the now-tepid water that sat on the rough wood camp desk in her canvas tent. Despite the fires burning about the camp, the night was chilly, and she quickly shimmied into her flannel nightgown, and settled beneath her blanket.

She still shivered. And despite her exhaustion, she couldn't sleep. Damn him.

She tried counting sheep, but her sheep turned into wolves, and they all had his face.

It was absurd; she had to sleep. She could not.

She must have dozed. And it was natural, after what she had heard, that she should dream.

No, not dreams. Nightmares haunted her. At first she seemed to be swirling in a mist, seeing the faces of the injured, hearing the screams of the men as they lay on the operating tables. She pitched restlessly about, wanting to waken. The mist seemed to clear, and she was at sea again, in Jerome's cabin. She felt the sudden pitch and sway as Hamlin Douglas tried to steer the *Lady Varina* in a course to elude the Yankees on their tail. Rushing deck side, she saw Yankee ships bearing down on them from the north.

Two more ships came swiftly from the east. Two more from the south . . . Hamlin looked straight at her. "Someone knew where we'd be and when, Mrs. McKenzie. If your husband was here, we might outrun these bastards. But he's not here. And I can't risk you and the lads at so dangerous a game."

Dr. Stewart, at Hamlin's side, had set an arm around her. "If there's firing, you could be in real danger. None of us would risk the babe. And . . ." he cleared his throat. "Well, you're a Yank. They'll be delighted to have you, they'll treat you splendidly. And with our surrender, it's likely there will be no deaths . . ."

"You'll surely have friends aboard the Yank ships, won't you, Mrs. McKenzie?" Hamlin asked her pointedly. Not a direct accusation, but . . . How had the Yankees known where they would be? Had someone been watching her all along? She had tried to be so careful.

"Don't choose a course of action because of me!" she had told Hamlin angrily. "Do what you would do if I were not aboard! Gentlemen, I did not do this! I'm telling you—"

"Go back to the cabin, Risa, please. You could risk the babe here—" Dr. Stewart told her.

"I could risk the babe in the cabin just as well. And I told *no* one I was sailing on this ship. I'll stay deck side now, no matter what occurs!"

So she stayed topside. And the first lieutenant who stepped aboard to accept the surrender greeted her like a long-lost relative, even though she'd never seen the man before in her life. As she was taken off the ship, she could feel Jerome's men staring at her, feel the reproach, as if it burned into her back. It had been a terrible feeling—Judas must have felt much the same, but Judas had at least been guilty! Oh, the way they had looked at her! Yet not even their fury could compare to the way Jerome had looked at her that night in St. Augustine! He hadn't given her a chance, he had condemned her without a word. He would never believe her, never forgive her. She would never forgive him, never!—for not trusting her. Yet she couldn't forget the way his eyes had touched her, filled with pain, betrayal, and anger. As he looked at her now . . .

She was dreaming, of course. Of Jerome, bent over her, face darkened with soot, but eyes so blue against the blackness. He was playing Indian in this dream, dressing up in war paint. How strange. It felt as if she had tossed, turned, and awakened. She was groggy, exhausted, and yet . . . God, the dreams were so real. She was in her tent, in the darkness, campfires burning nearby, and he was there. He wore dark, tight breeches, and a black cotton shirt. His dark hair was long, touching his shoulders. His eyes hard, still condemning.

She blinked, wishing to banish him from so familiar a place in her dreams. But he didn't disappear.

She awakened fully, sitting up, a gasp of surprise rising in her throat. God, no, it was impossible, he couldn't be here, he was an arrogant fool, thinking that he could just come to her in the dark! He'd been captured in Yankee territory once before! There was a guard at her tent!

She never uttered a sound. He clamped his hand over her mouth, his touch far more rough than any she had felt from him before. She grasped for his arm, to protest his brutal hold, but he gave her a firm shake.

"Don't move!" he commanded. "And don't make a sound."

Tears of pain stinging her eyes, she nodded. He let her go. The hell if she would stay still! She tried to leap up from the bunk. She barely managed to take a step. He could move like the night wind, with uncanny grace and speed. He tackled her, bringing her down to the canvas-covered ground. He was swiftly atop her, and his eyes burned with true blue ice fire as he stared down at her, a hand once again clamped firmly upon her mouth.

"Not again, my love. You'll not cry out an alarm, weave a web, or set a trap!" His whisper was so harsh and venomous that she forced herself to remain still. Yet all her strength of will could not keep her from trying to writhe free as he stared at her, impaling and condemning her so mercilessly with his eyes. She tried to push his hand away, to strike out at him, scratch his face.

He slammed her arms back and gripped her cheeks with such a hold that tears nearly flooded her eyes again. This time, she went still, and stayed that way.

He was leaner, harder, meaner than before, she determined. Prison had not improved his humor.

"Open your mouth, and you'll never sit again!" he threatened. She couldn't possibly open her mouth. She felt paralyzed. He had escaped. He was real. And he had come straight here. For her, his wife? To have her? No . . .

He had come for revenge. Of that, she was certain.

Wary of his dark anger, she lay quietly, but then could not help but gasp as he rose, wrenching her up and into his arms in a single fluid motion. He moved in silence, carrying her swiftly out the front of the tent.

He was mad, insane. He was an escaped Rebel soldier, surrounded by enemies. But he defied them all, cloaked by the night. And he meant to take her somewhere, for he carried her toward a large black horse that waited, hidden by the darkness, near her tent.

He wouldn't really hurt her—or would he? She had never felt such heat emanating from a human being. His every stride reminded her of his unyielding strength.

And anger. And sense of betrayal. Fear brought a protest to her lips. "No!" she gasped. "Jerome, no!" She kept her voice low. She wanted to escape him; she didn't want him captured again.

She didn't want him shot down.

But neither did she dare face this terrible rage in his heart. "Jerome, please, you can't—I will not allow—"

"Shut up!" he warned fiercely again, eyes burning into her soul. "Not a word, not a whisper. Don't even breathe."

Oh! How could he! She wanted to scream and bring down every Yank within miles! "Don't you tell me what to do. There was a guard on this tent, you fool! How dare you—oh, God, did you kill him? Are you insane? Our child is sleeping—"

He stopped dead, looking down at her.

"Mrs. McKenzie, I would dare the Devil himself at this moment, but I give you fair warning—I will not be captured again. I didn't kill the guard; he is knocked out. Our child is already gone."

She froze, aware of the cobalt malice in his eyes and the steel hard determination in his features as he stared down at her. "Gone—where?" she whispered in breathless panic.

"Home. South. Where he belongs."

She remained motionless, eyes locked with his, afraid now that he would drop her like so much refuse if she protested again.

He had taken their child!

And if she didn't maintain control, she would burst into tears of panic. He could not mean to take his revenge by stealing Jamie, kidnapping her—and deserting her somewhere far from her child. Could he?

Did he think that she wouldn't dare cry out, demand that he be tortured into telling her where their child had been taken—and by whom?

She could! She could cry out!

But she didn't. He might leave her. She didn't want to be left. He had Jamie.

He continued his impatient stride toward the large black phantom horse. He lifted her, all but throwing her atop the animal, before leaping up behind her. The big black reared slightly, then plunged forward to Jerome's urging. And they raced through the camp, dodging tents here and there, leaping over smoldering campfires.

Risa clung to the creature's mane. She felt Jerome at her back, felt the ripple of muscle within his arms and chest, felt the burning heat of his body as he maneuvered the horse out of the camp.

A sleepy picket cried out, "Who goes there?"

But Jerome galloped on, heedless of the demand. They raced like the wind, soaring over a makeshift fence posted along the road.

She heard the sounds of shots being fired, and yet she knew that they were in no danger—they had already traveled beyond the range of the fire. They continued down the road and she nearly screamed aloud as they plunged straight into a canopy of trees, but there was a trail within those trees, and they sped along it.

It seemed that they raced forever.

She kept thinking that surely, soldiers would come in pursuit. But they did not, and she realized that Jerome had moved with such speed in the darkness that they would be all but impossible to follow.

They would not be pursued.

The night wind seemed to soar and buffet around them into eternity. She was blinded by the whipping wind, by her hair, blowing into her face. She could barely breathe, and she feared if she should fall or be thrown, she would be trampled to death beneath the huge black, because the animal couldn't possibly stop. Her heart thundered, and she was certain that their mad dash could only end in sheer disaster. Yet when Jerome at last reined in, her heart was still thundering. She was still afraid, but Jerome ignored her, leaping from the horse and moving into a copse. As he did so, three men stepped from the trees, leading lean dark horses. One of them carried a bundle that squirmed in his arms. Jamie.

Risa cried out, leaping to the ground herself, nearly falling, the animal was so large. She caught her balance and ran in her bare feet and white flannel nightgown toward the stranger, but she stopped short when Jerome took the baby from him, walking a distance away while easing the blanket from around his little face.

"Hello, ma'am," the fellow who had held Jamie said. He stood resolutely between Risa and Jerome. "I'm Anthony Hawkins. How do you do? Sorry to cause such a stir, but Captain McKenzie couldn't wait to see his boy. These fellows here are Robert Gray and Ricky Boyle."

Jerome's companions were handsome young men—as lean and hard-looking as her husband. They were fellow escapees, she thought, and she knew that she was right.

She nodded in wary acknowledgment of the introduction. "You came into my tent and stole my child?" she inquired coldly.

"No, ma'am. Your husband went into your tent, and handed me the baby. We couldn't risk the babe making noise, you understand."

"Oh, yes, I understand," she said, staring at him. He stared right back at her, the other two men flanking him, separating her from Jerome.

"He's a might handsome boy, ma'am," Hawkins said.

"Thank you."

Did his father agree? she wondered. Thankfully, Jamie was sleeping, or else he'd probably be screaming his head off.

But then she heard her son give out a little cooing sound—and she realized irritably that he was perfectly happy to be in his father's arms. Men. None could be trusted.

Jerome turned with the child then, rewrapping him more snugly in the blanket as he walked back toward them. He didn't look at her. Holding the baby, he remounted the large black horse. "Anthony, if you'd be so good as to escort my wife . . . ?" he inquired.

His eyes touched hers, dispassionately. She realized that she was standing barefoot on the cold ground in a thin white flannel gown, and he didn't seem to notice that she wasn't decently clad, or care. And she felt a terrible chill seeping over her as she remembered the last night they had spent together. They'd shared more than passion, she thought. There had been warmth between them, the beginnings of something that might have been very real . . .

She was in love with him, she thought, feeling quite

ill. And he looked at her . . . oh, the way he was looking at her! As if he didn't really want her with them at all.

She swallowed hard, determined not to plea or beg, or make a fool of herself. She lifted her chin. "You should really let me take the baby, Captain," she said quietly.

He stared down at her, holding his son, and the reins of the huge black. "No, my dear, I don't think so. You've had him quite a while now. And I've never seen him before. If you wish to accompany us, Anthony will be glad to assist you."

"And if I don't wish to accompany you?" she inquired.

He shrugged, as if he couldn't care less what decision she made. "If not . . . well, I'm sure a Yankee patrol will be by here come morning."

She would have given anything to hit him. Just once. She longed to walk over and spit at him. But he had Jamie.

She walked to Anthony Hawkins. "Nice horse. Did you get your mounts at Old Capitol?"

"No, ma'am."

"Where did you steal them from?"

"A Yank patrol just this side of the river."

"Ah."

"Now, wait, we didn't exactly steal them," Ricky Boyle protested. He had a barely discernible, old-country lilt to his voice. "This is war—and this is Virginia. So I think that we confiscated them from the enemy."

"And," Anthony Hawkins added dryly, "I think that the Yanks originally confiscated them from us. They have brands on them from a horse farm in Mississippi."

"Guess we got to thank the Yanks, though, for feeding them well," Robert Gray said, and grinned.

The baby—at long last, the little traitor—suddenly started to cry.

Risa instinctively turned away from Hawkins and the horse she had been about to mount, and headed for her child. She set her hands upon Jerome's thigh where he straddled the horse, folding them almost prayer fashion.

"Jerome, he needs me!" she pleaded.

His eyes remained merciless, but he let out an oath

of irritation. He bent down, setting the baby into her arms. When she was holding him securely, he caught hold of her around her waist, and lifted her to sit side-saddle in front of him. A small victory won, she thought. No, a victory won—and lost.

For his arms were around her, warm, strong, and powerful. His body, at her back, was fire. And she ached inside.

But his heart, beating a fierce, staccato rhythm, was nothing but ice.

Chapter 24

That night they stayed at an abandoned plantation which had apparently not yet been discovered by scouts foraging for either North or South. When they arrived, it was painfully evident that the people who had once maintained the beautiful old home had simply left—a teacup remained on a cherrywood table in the formal dining room. Wardrobes and trunks were filled with clothing. The larder was filled with jars of preserves, and even the smokehouse had meat. The slaves had apparently all run off, taking little or nothing with them. All that remained were the spiders, rats, and the cobwebs.

She slept with Jamie in the least dusty of the rooms, having spent hours before lying down in an effort to clean it. She remade the bed with sheets found in a drawer. It was a sad task. While dusting off the mantel, she believed she found the secret to the empty house. She came upon a letter that informed a Mrs. Everett Dolenz—apparently left behind when her husband and son rode off to war in a cavalry company formed in their home county—that both her husband and son had been killed in the battle that had taken place at Sharpsburg, Maryland. It seemed that the woman had just walked away from the house once she had received the letter, as if she had felt in her heart that there was no reason left to keep a home. Photographs on the mantel showed the family—a dignified father, serene mother, handsome young son.

Risa said a little prayer for them all before lying down to sleep at dawn, and in her prayers she asked that they not mind the fact she and her baby made use of their home. She prayed that her father would not be worried sick.

And she prayed the war would end. She wondered if she could bear it if she were ever to lose her husband and child, and she lay awake, miserable, realizing that the war could go on for a very long time, and she could lose everyone she loved.

She slept alone with Jamie. Jerome had apparently wanted no part of her; she hadn't seen him that night since he had helped her down from the horse. He had warned her, however, that if she tried leaving with Jamie, she would come to deeply regret her actions.

Once Jamie had awakened and been fed, Risa set about the task of making him more diapers. She searched through Mrs. Dolenz's trunks for clothing. She was grateful to find that the woman had been about her height and weight, and that it was easy to find undergarments and a simple cotton dress that would wear well with travel. She didn't know where Jerome intended to go, or how long they would be on the road, so despite the wonderful smell of food coming from below, she was determined to be ready to ride at a moment's notice. She packed extra clothing carefully in a carpetbag she found, then sat at Mrs. Dolenz's desk and wrote her a letter telling her who she was, what she had taken, and promising that she would repay her for the things when she was able to find her.

An uneasy feeling filled her as she finished writing, and she turned to find that Jerome stood in her doorway. His hair was damp and his cheeks were freshly shaved, and he seemed to have found fresh clothing among the offerings in the mansion as well; he wore dark breeches, a clean, muted ivory shirt, charcoal waistcoat, and a dark navy greatcoat with frocked shoulders. His eyes were fathomless, his features impassive as he watched her. Seeing Jamie kicking and throwing his little arms about on the bed, he went to his son, sitting at his side. He allowed Jamie to wind his chubby little fingers around his own. His back was to Risa as he asked her, "What are you doing?"

"Writing the lady of the house."

"How do you know there is a lady?"

"I found a letter, informing her that her family had been killed."

He turned to her, arching a brow. "So what have you said to her?"

"I told her that I borrowed some of her things, and that I will repay them as soon as I can."

He looked back to Jamie. "That wasn't necessary. Sometime soon, either Rebel or Yankee troops will find this place, and it will be stripped clean."

"But if they do not," Risa insisted, "she may come home one day. And she should know that not all the world is cruel and vicious."

"But *war* is cruel and vicious, and unfortunately, that's the simple truth," he said, but his words were far more weary than mocking or angry. He rose. "Leave your note if you wish. Gather what you want, and get something to eat. I want to make some real distance by nightfall, and that will entail some long, hard riding."

He left the room. Risa set her letter beneath the clock on the mantel, and began to gather up her things when Anthony Hawkins arrived at her door to give her a hand. He was an expert at carrying a child, tucking Jamie comfortably beneath his arm while warning Risa that she really needed to get something to eat; they wouldn't be stopping for a long while.

"You're good at that," she commented, indicating the way he held Jamie.

He grinned. "I've got a wife and two little ones back in Corinth, Mississippi, Mrs. McKenzie. And I miss them sorely. Holding this boy touches my heart just fine."

Risa nodded. "I hope you get to see your wife and children now."

"That will depend on the Southern war department, once we report back," he said. There was no rancor in his voice. He was a soldier, and he would follow orders. And he was a Southerner, she thought; he would do what was needed for his cause.

She followed him downstairs and into the dining room. Only one plate remained, piled with bacon and grits, a cup of steaming coffee at its side. "Better hurry now," he warned.

She sat down, well aware that she needed to eat. If

Jerome had warned that it would be a long day, it would be so. She needed nourishment herself to nourish Jamie. But as she sat, she looked curiously at Anthony Hawkins, who had chosen to settle upon a boxed window seat with Jamie, and wait for her.

"Ahem," she murmured. "It might have been safer for you all had you just headed straight south."

"The captain hadn't seen his child, Mrs. McKenzie."

She stiffened. "He asked not to. He told my father that he had no desire to see me or the child."

"No man wants to meet his son in prison, ma'am."

"Or his wife?" she inquired curtly, wondering if she was damned by any man who had befriended Jerome.

"This war is a hard thing. A man has to follow his heart, and what's right in his soul. It's tough on a fellow, when he's got to make such a decision, when his wife follows a different path."

She inhaled deeply, taking a sip of coffee, and looking at him. "I was a Unionist long before I ever met the captain, sir."

"No one has accused you of being a traitor, Mrs. McKenzie."

"Ah. I see. I wasn't actually being a traitor when I brought about Captain McKenzie's arrest—because I have been a Unionist all along."

Hawkins seemed puzzled. "Well, I s'pose that would be the way of it."

She wanted to scream.

And then she felt again that strange tremor along her back. She jumped up and turned. And indeed, Jerome was lounging in the doorway, listening to what had surely sounded like a confession.

She stared at him angrily for a long moment. He returned her stare.

"Well, I assume you're ready," she said briskly.

"You assume right."

"Then, let's go," she said, and started past him.

He caught her arm. "I don't want any trouble today, Risa."

"I don't intend to give you any trouble, Captain McKenzie."

"No matter where I take you?" he inquired, his voice suddenly an amused drawl, his brow arched.

"No matter where you take me, Captain. You do have my son."

She walked out. Robert Gray and Ricky Boyle had the horses in front of the mansion already. Robert came forward to help her roll her carpetbag, and attach it to the back of the black's saddle. Jerome mounted and reached down for her. When she was seated before him, Anthony handed her Jamie, and they started south.

They stayed off the major trails, not knowing who was controlling what areas in Northern Virginia. At one point Jerome quizzed her about troop movements here, but she could honestly tell him very little, other than that Hooker was planning a major horse battle.

So they rode, she and Jerome ahead of the company. The miles were long and wearying. After several hours Jamie awoke and grew restless, and when she hesitated in feeding him, Jerome impatiently demanded to know what was wrong.

"He's hungry."

"Which is the main reason you are with us," he told her irritably, which instantly caused a stiffening in her spin. "Well, feed him," Jerome advised her.

"It is awkward, to say the least."

"Is it? Well, it needn't be. The others are far behind, and I promise not to fall into a fit of uncontrollable lust at the sight of your bared breast, my love. I'm far too aware of the danger."

Her back went rigid against his chest. "I didn't cause what happened, McKenzie, and I won't say it again. But since you insist on being such a self-righteous ass, you can bet that I'll be a danger to you in the future!"

He was quiet for a long moment, and she was suddenly sorry that she had spoken in anger. He held the cards right now. If he set her down and left her in the middle of the road, there would be little she could do.

"Well, then," he murmured, "the battle lines are drawn."

Jamie chose that moment to set up a ferocious howl, and Risa knew that she had little choice but to feed him. But as she balanced Jamie and tugged at her buttons,

Jerome reined in and took off his greatcoat, setting it over her shoulder and affording her a certain privacy.

Later, as the day grew dark, she dozed. She awoke in a panic, only to discover that Anthony was carrying the baby, and she had been sleeping against Jerome's chest. They were deep into Virginia.

Jerome had found his way to the picket lines for Lee's troops, and they were being given a military escort into the Confederate camp.

Cheers went up among the men who were at ease and preparing their suppers at various campfires. They lined up to welcome and applaud the men who had escaped Old Capitol—especially since they were being led by the ship's captain who had defied the blockade to provide many of them with shoes, medicine, weapons, and ammunition. They were taken first to the tent of a Colonel Blount, who provided the men with corn whiskey and Risa with chicory coffee. Then, as Jerome and the others departed to meet with the officers in charge, Risa and Jamie were escorted to a tent that had been vacated for her by one of the officers. It had a bunk, washstand, folding chairs, and a small desk.

She sat on the bunk with Jamie, grateful for the consideration shown her, yet nervously aware that she was surrounded by the Army of Northern Virginia. A guard was posted just outside. She wondered if he was supposed to keep her from escaping, or keep some angry Reb from doing her harm.

She had not been there more than thirty minutes when she heard her name being called. "Risa McKenzie? Hello? May I come in?"

Startled, she jumped up, holding Jamie close to her thundering heart. She didn't know why she was so afraid; she didn't know who had called so politely to her. She swallowed hard. "Yes?"

The tent flap opened and a man stepped in. He was unmistakably a McKenzie, green-eyed, dark-haired, very handsome. His features bore the same strong lines that hinted of the Indian blood in both Jerome and Sydney.

"Brent?" she murmured.

He grinned, smiling, reaching out for the baby. "Yes, I'm Brent. And this is my nephew?"

She nodded, hesitated only briefly, and handed the baby over. He sat on the camp bunk, inspecting his nephew. As he had been when meeting his father, Jamie was an angel. Smiling and cooing at his uncle.

"He's a handsome fellow!" Brent declared. His military jacket was threadbare in spots; his boots were heavily worn, she saw. He looked up at her, eyes assessing. He smiled. "So the would-be-perfect bride for my Yank cousin has become the scourge of the South!" he said, but his voice was light, teasing. "I see why. You're a beautiful woman—it's easy to understand the havoc you've caused in my family."

Deeply irritated, she sighed. "I tried to help Alaina McKenzie, and have been in hell ever since!" she told him, speaking evenly in an attempt to control her anger. "As to—"

"You look well," he interrupted. "No problems with the labor?"

He was a physician, she knew. She flushed anyway. "No, everything was fine."

He looked at the baby again, testing Jamie's grip. "I'm glad. My brother was probably sick with worry—no matter what you had done. After my mother—"

"But your mother is well, isn't she?"

"Very, the last I heard. She had such a difficult time with our baby sister Mary. Well, I am delighted to get the chance to meet this little fellow. Naturally, I pray we all survive this war, but my brother is a man who tempts the Devil. It's good to know that my father's line of the McKenzie name will continue now, whatever befalls us."

"Please, don't talk so morbidly—"

"I'm not morbid; I'm realistic," he told her, smiling at the baby, then looking at her again. "Quite frankly, I've heard mixed reports regarding you, Risa McKenzie."

"I'm surprised that they are even mixed," she murmured wearily. "Most of what I've heard simply condemns me."

He smiled, displaying a deep dimple in one cheek. "Soldiers trade across battle lines, and generals, North and South, who went to school together still send one another gifts—before commencing with artillery fire. I've

exchanged injured Yankee soldiers with Union doctors
who claim you are better than a dozen male stewards in
the operating tent, that you are remarkably poised, calm,
and efficient. Which is saying something, when you consider that Mrs. Dorothea Dix, who heads the Union hospitals, is so strict on hiring nurses. Nurses are supposed
to be over thirty, plain as pumpkin pie, and dress like
old Puritan widows. How did you manage to make it to
the field?"

Risa laughed. "I'm a military child. I've been a dozen
places with my father. Trust me, women do get by Dorothea Dix, usually by applying directly to the surgeon
general. Then women have come into service to care for
their relatives, and stayed for other soldiers. It is unusual
for me to have become so experienced on the field. I
thank my father for that. But," she reminded him,
"Alaina has worked frequently with surgeons, and I understand your sister Sydney worked in several of the
Richmond hospitals."

"Confederates quickly discovered we were more desperate," he told her. "So—among other reports on you,
I heard from my cousin Julian. If he thinks you're good,
you're good. Want to assist me?"

She frowned. "Now? In the darkness?"

"Tomorrow morning. I want to do excisms on a few
patients, see if I can save some limbs—before we wind
up in battle again and I find myself cutting people like
a butcher," he added with a touch of bitterness.

She nodded slowly. "Naturally, I'd like to help you. I
mean, if . . ."

"My brother allows it?" he inquired, and she was certain that he baited her.

"If I'm still here," she said.

"Good." He stood, reluctantly returning Jamie to her.
"I look forward to your help. Good night."

He left the tent. Worn from lack of sleep and hard
riding, Risa dozed lying with Jamie at her breast in the
camp bed. She slept restlessly that night. She could hear
the drone of conversation from a nearby tent, and she
was certain she heard her husband's voice, and those of
his brothers. And from somewhere, she heard feminine
laughter as well. Camp followers. They came with the

North and the South. She prayed that her husband wasn't with a whore, and she realized that no matter what battle lines she had drawn, she was deeply hurt by his rejection of her. Despair plagued her, cutting like a knife.

She barely swallowed back a startled scream when she realized there was a tall figure standing in the tent. She managed not to make a sound, and she realized it was Jerome. He stood, head bowed in pensive thought for a long time. She made no move.

After a while he came over to her. She kept her eyes closed, feigning sleep. When she opened them, he was gone.

In the morning it was Brent McKenzie who came for her, accompanied by a heavyset hospital steward and a stout, big-chested woman. "This is Maisie Darden, and she'll watch Jamie for you," Brent told her.

Jamie had eaten and was sleeping, but the smile that lit up Maisie Darden's face when she saw the child assured Risa that she could safely leave her child with the woman. As they went out, Brent asked her, "Sure you're up to this?"

"Do you mean, am I sure that I want to help save the lives of Rebels?" she inquired matter-of-factly.

Brent stopped, looking at her squarely. "Yes."

"Yes, I'm sure," she said.

Soon after they began, she was startled to realize that they had been joined by another assistant. Jerome.

Watching the brothers work in unison, she began to wonder if they needed her at all. Despite the wall of frigid ice that had arisen between the two of them, she discovered that she worked well enough with her husband. She was experienced. Jerome had a great strength, she had dexterity.

As the day went by, she became impressed with her brother-in-law. He described his intentions to everyone assisting, and despite the speed with which it was necessary to operate, he remained calm and courteous throughout, carefully rationing the little anesthesia they had, and clearly indicating the instruments he needed when he needed them. Jerome and Brent's competent steward made the work much easier than what Risa was accustomed to, and she sometimes forgot the amount of help they had. At one point, when a clamp didn't stop the patient's bleeding quickly enough, she swiftly crawled atop the table to use her weight as the necessary pressure until the clamp could be adjusted. They finished working when the light began to fade. Risa was very tired. She sat out on the grass as the sun set, and was startled when her husband came and sat beside her, offering her a silver flask. She looked at him warily. "Brandy," he told her.

"Thanks," she said, taking the flask. "Is this due to the fact that I managed not to kill any Rebs today? How could you trust me in that field hospital?"

She took a sip of the brandy, choked and coughed as it went down. He took the flask back and drank deeply. He recapped the flask and squinted out at the setting sun.

"I knew you wouldn't hurt defenseless men."

"Oh?" she said, her heart hammering with hope.

"There are thousands of Rebs surrounding you here. You wouldn't have had a chance," he said.

She rose, and started to walk away from him, but he was on his feet as well, and before she had taken two steps, he had caught her arm, swinging her back around to face him. She was certain he meant to offer an apology.

He didn't.

"We leave first thing in the morning," he told her.

"Where are we going?"

"Richmond," he said, and he walked away.

Anthony, Ricky, and Robert remained with the army, rejoining their units. Anthony came to say good-bye to her as she was pouring herself coffee from a campfire the next morning, telling her that he'd be given leave after the next engagement to go home for a month. He'd been in the war since the first bitter fighting, and he was due a furlough. She told him that she was glad, and impulsively, she hugged him good-bye before he left, realizing only after he was gone that Jerome was leaned against a tree, chewing a blade of grass, watching her. He didn't say a word, but straightened, and moved away.

Indeed, he had very little to say to her, riding the

large black gelding alone as a wagon brought her the rest of the way into Richmond, where he was apparently scheduled to discuss his position with secretary of the navy, Mallory. But again, as they neared Richmond, she found herself deeply irritated to discover that her husband was a hero—crowds gathered around as he rode, while reporters plied him with questions about Old Capitol, his escape, and his days as a successful blockade-runner. He was a good spokesman, she granted him grudgingly, polite and modest in all his replies, and especially charming to young children.

Once they arrived, Jerome took his leave of her, saying that the soldiers would see to her welfare while he attended to military matters. An older soldier, a man with steel-gray hair and wise brown eyes, was her escort. She had a feeling he was far more than an escort—and that he had been duly warned to guard her carefully. His name was Alfred More, and he took her and Jamie to a handsome boardinghouse near the White House of the Confederacy. Jerome would be busy for quite some time, she was warned. He had garnered a great deal of information during his captivity and ride south.

Risa found herself left alone with a man always posted at her door. She paced restlessly. A meal was brought to her, and later Lieutenant More asked her if she'd like a hip bath brought. The concept of a bath sounded wonderful, and she agreed. She lingered in the water until it grew cold. Though it was late, she was too restless to go to bed.

With her windows open to the spring air, she could hear the sounds of music coming from somewhere. It seemed incongruous at first. Beautiful music playing, when the war was so painful. The lovely waltz ended, followed by a jig. Eventually, "Dixie" was played, and after it, "The Bonnie Blue Flag." She listened to the music, leaning out the window, tapping her feet on the floor. She wondered where it was coming from. Looking down the street, she saw the White House of the Confederacy, and the many carriages that waited outside. She started when she saw her husband, standing outside the open entry door on the porch, engaged in conversation with a short man in civilian clothing, a slightly taller man in uniform—and a woman.

Her first reaction was sheer, unreasoning anger. He was at a party—flirting!—while he'd left her to cool her heels, trapped in this room, alone in the capital city of her enemies.

She hesitated, then quietly opened the door to her room. Lieutenant More was not outside; the young private who had accompanied him earlier was there. He was seated on a chair against the wall, his head leaned back. He dozed.

She carefully closed the door.

She had packed at the plantation for travel, not parties. She had nothing elegant or dressy. Still, one of the gowns had a lace border over the breasts, and by quickly ripping away the high-topped bodice above the lace, she acquired a somewhat daring "after dusk" décolletage. Since she was nursing, her cleavage was admirable, to say the least. She quickly swept up her hair, pinning it loosely so that fiery tendrils escaped to touch her throat and shoulders. Stepping back from the mirror atop the dresser, she pinched her cheeks, and took a long look at her image.

She was lacking a decent petticoat, but they were in the midst of a war—few women would be completely in fashion. Being too fashionable at this point would surely be in poor taste, here in the South. She would do, she determined.

Then she decided she was mad. She was going to walk down to the house, uninvited, to the Rebel's party?

She couldn't . . .

She had to. Jerome seemed to know the brunette hanging on his arm far too well. And she was a general's daughter. Generals' daughters commanded respect from both sides in a war.

Scooping up Jamie, she tiptoed back to the door, opening it quietly, barely breathing for fear her son would awaken. But Jamie seemed to feel the sense of adventure—or stupidity!—that had seized her, and he was silent and angelic as she quickly moved down the stairway, and out the front door.

The house was perhaps two blocks down the street.

She walked the distance quickly, but when she arrived, Jerome was no longer on the porch. As she stood there undecidedly, a tall, buxom, dark-haired woman with flashing eyes and a handsome face approached her from the house. "Hello, my dear, you're looking so woeful and uncertain! Can I help you?"

Risa started to reply, but then her words froze, and she all but panicked. There was no backing out now.

She knew the woman. She knew her well, because Jefferson Davis, now President of the Confederate States of America, had recently been the secretary of war, and her father had often met with him in years gone by.

"Why, Risa!" the woman exclaimed. "Risa Magee! McKenzie, now, isn't it? And, of course, your captain is inside! Come along, let me bring you in!"

"Mrs. Davis, I . . ." she began, ready now to turn and run. She'd been insane. What was she doing here?

"Call me Varina, dear. You used to do so, you know. I must introduce you around. I can't imagine your husband losing you so carelessly—in fact, I can't imagine any man letting you stray too far. Your first little one?" she said, indicating Jamie. She reached for him. "May I?"

"Of course!" Varina adored her own children, and children in general. She and her husband had lost their firstborn, Risa knew, deepening her appreciation for babies. "But I'm so afraid he may . . . er, drool on your beautiful gown."

"Ah, my dear! As if that would disturb me! Now, come—"

Risa hesitated, shaking her head. "I think I've made a mistake. I shouldn't be here. Jerome is very popular, and I believe that we've created a tremendous stir of gossip, first with my father raging against him, and then . . . well, all these accusations that I brought about his imprisonment and saw to it that his ship was captured!"

Varina laughed softly. "Well, your father is an old tyrant, dear. A good man, but an old tyrant. Would that he were with us! But, my dear, this is the truth of it. Some people will always talk, but I have known you only to be honorable. And so if you say that you're innocent . . ."

Varina's dark eyes sparkled.

"Well, I'm not completely innocent."

"Oh?"

"I am a Yankee."

Varina shrugged. "It's better to invite in a known enemy, than trust the friends with daggers at your back. Come. It is my party, dear, and you are invited."

She turned and started into the house, with Jamie in her arms.

Risa had no choice but to follow.

Chapter 25

A small entry with false marble floor led into the main rooms of the house. The musicians were to the right, in the parlor behind the dining area. Furniture had been moved aside for dancing, and the house was filled with people. The ladies might be suffering through the shortages caused by the war, but they were, for the most part, beautifully dressed.

Many were in black.

Risa immediately felt curious stares as she moved through the house with Varina. She was grateful to be with the First Lady; no one would dare accost her under the circumstances, though she could see that many were wondering who she was, while others surely knew. Naturally, as Varina began to introduce her to people, word spread. She could feel the whispers and the gossip rippling through the room.

But they were in Varina's home, and decency would be maintained. She introduced her each time as Mrs. McKenzie, "wife of our death-defying hero!" and showed Jamie off as if he were her own. To cinch the matter of Risa's right to be there, she brought her to the President himself. Tall and gaunt, his cheeks far leaner and his eyes more haunted than Risa had remembered, Jefferson Davis recognized her after the first few seconds of concentrated staring. "Ah!" he said, taking both her hands. "Dear Varina, do you see how she has grown? Well, how is the old bugger, your father? I miss him, that I do. Sorry he's on the wrong side of this war, but then he's a born Yank, and that's that. Came from old New York Irish stock, and that's hard to change. He must still be spitting fire regarding your marriage to a Rebel, my dear."

"Well, he'd have preferred a Yankee, sir, no doubt."

"But he must be proud of his grandson!"

"He's gorgeous, isn't he, dear?" Varina said.

As they spoke, one of the officers in the crowd approached the President. Varina stepped between them, sweetly speaking to the man. "We've the daughter of an old friend with us tonight—and the wife of a true Confederate hero. Excuse my husband for just a few moments to dance with the child, won't you, General?" she inquired. "I do swear, I hear a waltz coming up from those fiddles."

Startled, Risa found herself dancing with the stiff, black-clad President. She smiled. "That was very kind of your wife. Your guests will have to be nice to me now, won't they?"

He grinned, and she knew he had a sense of humor, though his political enemies denied the fact.

"Varina is the jewel of my life. She was not just being kind to you. Everyone knows that the general and I fight at every opportunity. She stepped in to make sure that we don't get into an argument tonight."

It was as she danced with the President that she saw Jerome again. He was still in the company of the very lovely brunette, but now he was staring at her. And for once, he was truly astounded. When she caught his eye, she felt a fierce chill.

He didn't cut in on the dance. He kept watching her, and she saw the blue fire slowly but surely build in his eyes. When the dance ended, Davis bowed to her. When he straightened, Jerome was beside them.

"Sir, I hadn't realized that you knew my wife."

"Since she was a little girl, Captain. So many people do forget my years in Washington, and the pain with which I said good-bye to many friendships there. Ah, well. I shall turn your lady over to you now, sir. And if you're lucky, I suppose, my wife will return your baby before too long. We're blessed with our own family, but Varina will never have enough children around her."

"Thank you, sir," Jerome said.

"No, Captain. My thanks to you. Men such as yourself prove the impossible can be done. Now, if you'll excuse me . . ."

He walked away, and was immediately besieged. Risa felt her cheeks coloring as Jerome stared at her, but she met his eyes squarely.

"What are you doing here?"

"You brought me here, remember?"

"No, I did not bring you here."

"You brought me to Richmond. And I do hate to miss a party," she said sweetly.

"Well, you're going to miss this one," he muttered darkly, his hand on her arm. "Next thing you know, my dear, you'll be bringing about the fall of the entire Confederacy."

"I wish I had that power!" she told him in a low but heated voice. "I wish I had the power to end the bloodshed!" she continued passionately.

He still meant to lead her swiftly out, she was certain. But before he could say any more, there were a number of men at their side, bringing champagne for both of them, and greeting Jerome with affectionate approval. "Here's to you, Captain. And to Mrs. McKenzie!"

Jerome introduced Risa to the soldiers surrounding them. More people came around. The men, then the women. She didn't know what they were thinking; she was polite in return, gracious, admitting that she was a Yankee—but that her husband was a Southerner, and therefore, it seemed, they were moving southward. There was a great deal of laughter. One young, dark-haired lieutenant said cheerfully, "We were wondering when you were going to arrive, considering that this get-together is in honor of your husband's return to the Confederacy. We're anxious for him to return to the seas— and supply us anew."

Startled, she stared at Jerome, fighting another wave of red fury. The party had been given for him.

And he hadn't intended to tell her, and he certainly hadn't intended to bring her.

The musicians started playing again, and the lieutenant asked Jerome for his permission to dance with her. Jerome bowed, mockingly acknowledging the request. She tried to demure, saying that she must retrieve her son, only to discover that Jamie had been taken upstairs to the Davis nursery, and was being cared for there.

She began to dance, and found herself swirling around on the floor again and again. She lost track of Jerome, seeing him occasionally as he flew by, each time with a different lady of Richmond.

Including the very attractive brunette, who eyed Risa with such knowing amusement that she was tempted to stop in the middle of the music and scratch the woman's eyes out.

Naturally, she would never behave so outrageously. She wasn't about to give these people any cause to fault Yankee women.

She did, however, finally get her chance to meet her rival. She stood in the center of the parlor, waiting for a middle-aged major to bring her a glass of punch.

"Ah, Mrs. McKenzie!"

She turned. The brunette was approaching, hand extended regally.

"Yes, how do you do?" Risa murmured, extending her hand in return.

"Divinely, thank you!" the woman drawled. "I've heard so much about you, yet I hadn't expected the pleasure of meeting you this evening. Jerome had said that you weren't attending."

"Well, I was very tired," Risa murmured. "He thought I wanted to rest, but . . . I couldn't stay away. I'm so sorry. I'm at a disadvantage here. You know my name, while I don't know yours."

"Oh, dear! Everyone knows your name. You're quite infamous, you know!" the woman said, and winked, as if her words were not meant at all maliciously.

In truth, they dripped venom.

Risa smiled. "Indeed? But *you* are . . . ?"

"Janine Thompson. My father is Pierce Thompson. Ah, well, you are a Northerner. He's very important in our state's political arena, and did—before the war I'm afraid—export the most cotton in the whole of the state."

Janine Thompson. The woman the newspapers had hinted Jerome intended to marry. His onetime fiancée? He'd never actually explained the situation.

She felt ill. Janine was very pretty with her dark hair and perfect, snowy complexion. She spoke casually, yet there was an underlying streak of bitterness about her that was frightening.

Risa determined she would allow no jealousy to show. "Congratulations," she said lightly.

Janine arched a perfectly shaped brow. "Ah, but you are the one deserving the congratulations. On your marriage. And your child, of course."

"Thank you."

"I admit to assuming that I might be in your place . . . but then . . . how old is your child, and when did your marriage take place?"

Risa arched a brow herself. "Why, Miss Thompson, how very rude."

Janine Thompson smiled, and moved close to her. "The truth is not always pleasant, is it? Society judges harshly, and I do hope your child does not bear your shame."

"How dare you speak so of my child, Miss Thompson—"

Janine Thompson ignored her. "You, apparently, do not know what it's like to lose everyone . . . one by one. We become rude, and truthful, under such circumstances. You misused a Southern hero, and you see, I would have loved him. I wouldn't have betrayed him. I would have lived for him. And now I wish that I'd played your game, and planned a baby, rather than more carefully choosing my times."

Risa determined that she was going to maintain her temper—no matter what this woman said. Because there was an edge to her voice that hinted at a disappointment so deep it was unbearable. She longed to slap Janine Thompson. She was equally tempted to burst into tears and race from the house. She forced herself to realize that Janine was in pain—and striking out at her perceived enemy.

"Miss Thompson, I cannot regret my child, I adore him. If you'll be so good as to excuse me—"

"I can't excuse you. I'd have cherished him each night. So handsome a man. So excellent a figure. So unique a man, down to . . . to that little star-shaped birthmark on his left buttock . . . you'd really no right. No right at all . . ."

Risa was stunned. A young woman of Janine's position, North or South, talking so . . .

About her husband!

Did he have such a birthmark?

"Miss Thompson," she said firmly, "I am sorry, very sorry, for whatever you have suffered. I must go now."

She quickly started through the room. When she turned back, Janine was standing exactly where she had left her—talking to herself. But then a young man came up behind her, and she swirled around, and laughingly accepted his invitation to dance.

Risa found herself trembling, electric with emotion. When had Jerome last been with Miss Thompson? Had he entertained plans for this evening? Was that why he kept Risa away? Should she be angry, or sorry, and could she do anything at all, since she was the enemy?

As she tried to flee the dance floor, she found Varina returning with Jamie. He had spent the evening being entertained by the Davis children, and was now probably very hungry and sleepy. "Lieutenant Clark will be seeing you back to your Richmond facilities," Varina said with her soft drawl. "Your husband still has business; he will be along shortly." She gave Risa a quick hug. "It's good to see you, child. Even under the circumstances."

Risa hugged her fiercely in return, squishing Jamie a little in the process. He mewled a protest, and she and the First Lady both laughed.

Business. Jerome had business. She didn't see him, and she didn't see Janine, and she seethed.

The lieutenant saw her back to the boardinghouse, where More was waiting for her and not his young assistant. He had clearly been told that she had escaped his watch, and he was in trouble—and angry.

She didn't try to speak with him. She quickly entered her room. She fed Jamie, slipped into her nightgown, and began to nervously walk the room. She was alternately glad that she had defied Jerome so boldly—and terrified that she had done so. She was plain furious with Janine Thompson. She practiced what she would say when Jerome arrived.

But the hours went by, and he didn't come. And somewhere along the line, despite the tempest of emotion that burned through her, she lay down. She reminded herself that she was a general's daughter. She was ready for whatever war they might wage.

Then, to her dismay, she found herself crying. She tried to stop the tears. Eventually, she did. At last she fell asleep.

Jerome could not believe her audacity. In Richmond, the very heart of the Confederacy, she had come striding right up to the President's own residence. He had completely forgotten that she most probably knew Davis and his wife, though of course both her father and Davis had long been involved with the military and politics.

In her simple dress, she had outshone them all. She was beautiful. She had moved with grace, walked with pride. She had mocked and defied him at every turn. And he was ready to strangle her . . . yet at the same time, he had to admit that he admired her courage.

He was bone-tired, anxious to sleep, but Davis had asked him to wait until they had a few minutes alone before leaving, since Jerome meant to start out the next morning for the North Carolina coast. He'd been offered a small ship, not up to the standards of the *Lady Varina*, but perhaps a sound enough vessel to help him steal his own ship back.

With the guests gone, Davis closed off the doors to the small room on the ground floor that was his study and his wife's sewing room. "I wanted to let you know, sir, that I do and do not have any information regarding the strange incidents occurring in your life," Davis told him, offering him a glass of port.

"I'm sorry, sir?"

Davis sat, rubbing his temples between his thumb and forefingers. "First off, many of your old crew members will be waiting for you in North Carolina. Your wife hired a Yankee lawyer, and somehow managed to get them released due to the fact that you were reputed to be so merciful in your dealings with the soldiers you captured on Union ships."

"My wife—hired a lawyer?"

"She did."

She hadn't said anything to him about having done

such a thing. Not that he had given her much of a chance.

But did that exonerate her? Perhaps she had wanted his ship taken, but hadn't wanted tragedy to befall his men—as so often happened at Elmira.

People did strange things for strange reasons. He knew that Magee had tried hard to keep him a prisoner, *after* he had forgiven him for abducting Risa. He had wanted to keep him out of the war, keep him alive.

"I'm grateful that my men are free."

"Now, as to that strange happening with the carriage when your sister was here . . ."

"I met my father-in-law, and he absolutely denied anything to do with the threat to my sister."

Davis nodded gravely. "As the war progresses, we discover more and more spies where we would never imagine we might find them. Recently, a soldier confessed to his physician on his deathbed that he had been the one to kill the carriage driver that night—shooting the man when he might have hit your sister. The Reverend Osby, attending the man at his demise, had little idea of what he was talking about, but he kept mentioning the White House of the Confederacy, so Osby made a point of contacting me. The soldier said he'd been paid out of Florida. So, sir, though I can't help you more, it would seem that you have a serious enemy in your own home state. Though it seems reckless to me, you—like Robert Lee—have often managed to carry out the impossible, and we need the impossible, so I support your decision to try to get your ship back. But I beg of you, be wary. It's enough to fear the regular fire of war; however, when there is clandestine danger to be faced as well, it's a scary situation."

Jerome rose, shaking Davis's hand, and then saluting. "I will get my ship back, sir. And justify your faith in me."

Jerome left the White House, walking slowly down the dark, deserted street. For the first time he felt a gnawing at what he had thought was righteous anger.

The Magees had not been part of Sydney's near abduction. Perhaps Risa was not guilty of other crimes?

He shook his head, lips tightening, as he told himself

he could not fall prey so easily to such hope. She'd had
the decency to try to see that his men were freed. His
ship was still gone.

And he'd still spent months imprisoned. He had an
enemy in Florida. That did not mean his enemy was not
his wife. And yet . . .

He returned to their rooms, nodding curtly to the embarrassed young guard on duty who had apparently been
the one to let her escape. He entered the room, and in
the darkness found his way to the bed. Moonlight filtered through the windows, and he looked down at her,
sleeping with her arm carefully curved around Jamie.
She was wearing a thin white nightgown, chaste with its
high buttons, yet in the moonlight it allowed him to
clearly see and appreciate every lush curve of her body.
Instant arousal overtook his senses, and he stepped away
from her as if he had been burned.

Why not? Why not move his sleeping child, slip in
beside the woman who was his wife, and ease the fires
of hell that plagued him? God knew, it had been one
hell of a long time.

Did it matter, in the middle of the night, if she had
betrayed him or not? When all he sought was a moment's solace and hunger's satisfaction. Come morning,
he could walk away.

But he couldn't. There were subtle snares she had tied
around him. She was proud, she was strong, she was
defiant. She didn't falter at the worst of times, and yet
she could move around a dance floor among her enemies
with sheer elegance and grace. She had never pretended
to embrace his cause, and yet her faith and belief in the
Union had been unwavering, while sometimes he
doubted his own wisdom, and the righteousness of the
South. Yes, states had rights, yes Florida had seceded,
and yes, he was a Floridian. And God knew, he loved
his home. Loved it passionately, believed even in the
godforsaken swamp that crept upon his land.

But slavery was wrong. The Yankees weren't so almighty great—they wanted the slaves freed, but they
weren't quite ready to see them educated and given the
same opportunities as the whites. The peculiar institution
of slavery should end . . . just not all at once.

They would pay for this war, he was suddenly certain. For decades, perhaps centuries, to come.

How could he condemn her? He had fallen in love with her, and he had begun to believe that they could create a life, that their love could grow. And yet, while he had been falling in love . . .

She had been planning. And she had brought him down.

But he wanted her. It had been forever since he had seen her, held her. Touched her, made love. His senses cried out in a wild fury, his body burned.

He clenched his hands into fists at his sides.

What difference did it make? he mocked himself. *Have what you want now, for this is Southern territory, and you cannot be betrayed here. There are no soldiers to come in the night, there is no chance of being taken as a fool. Have the night, take the night, seize the bloody moment now, it had been long, so long, so damned long . . .*

He was about to reach for her, in anger.

But Jamie suddenly stirred, kicking out his little legs. She shifted. The baby began to cry softly. She didn't exactly awaken; she shifted again, unbuttoning her gown. Her eyes barely opened before they closed again as she drew Jamie closer, instinctively leading him to her breast. He hungrily began to nurse as she gently cradled him to her.

Jerome stood still. He touched his son's cheek, and delicately traced a blue vein in his wife's breast. She was soundly sleeping again, and didn't move.

He frowned, touching her cheek. It was damp. She had cried herself to sleep.

He turned and walked away, left the room, and went down to the den of the boardinghouse. A fire burned low in the hearth, shadows crept gently around the room. He poured himself a brandy, and stared at the flames for a long time.

Then he determined his course of action.

Chapter 26

To Risa's dismay, she woke to find her husband gone. He had left her a letter, curt and to the point. He was putting to sea as quickly as possible. Lieutenant More was to escort her south by rail through Virginia, North Carolina, South Carolina, Georgia, and into the northern part of Florida, where state troops could meet her. They would bring her to Julian and, as soon as Jerome was able, he would meet her at his cousin's camp.

She was deeply disappointed, and angry, having been ready to confront him after the party. He had been in the room, she knew, because his belongings that had been there were gone. Jerome hadn't told her where he was going, but she was more upset to learn that Pierce Thompson and his daughter had departed Richmond as well. She told herself that Jerome was going off to sea, that he was going back to the war. The fact that the Thompsons had left at the same time meant nothing. Janine was a sad creature, broken by the war.

Yes, but she was a creature familiar with Risa's husband's buttocks. And Risa couldn't help but burn with jealousy at the very thought of the other woman near him. Especially when . . . when he wanted nothing to do with herself.

Varina sent her a basket of food to take on her trip, warning her that decent meals might be hard to come by. The First Lady's letter was slightly distracted; there had been a cavalry clash with a number of wounded, and the capital city was buzzing with soldiers and dispatches, medical personnel, and ambulances. Risa wished her well.

It occurred to Risa that she could possibly escape her

"escort"—since she had done so quite easily once already. But despite her deep-rooted anger—or perhaps, because of it—she was willing to go southward.

One more time. Just once. She would meet him on his terms.

There were soldiers everywhere, guarding the railroad as they traveled. The trains had become the link for people, messages, troops, and goods. The Confederates were desperate to keep their lines of communications open.

The cars were filled with soldiers going from place to place. They were likewise filled with refugees. Displaced mothers, fathers, and children. People who had lost their homes.

Risa talked with one woman from Northern Virginia who did not care who won the war. The woman was gaunt to the point of starvation; her cheeks were pale and pinched, and she did her best to soothe her two- and three-year-old babes. She owned land. Even on her own, she could make a go with some farming. Her husband had been killed when a shell had exploded while he'd been trying to save some of their livestock.

The livestock were all gone, consumed by soldiers, Yank and Reb. Her house had burned down. She was trying to reach her sister in Georgia.

Risa arched a brow to Lieutenant More, who did not mind when Risa gave their food to the woman. The smile on the woman's face, the light in her eyes, when she received the simple gift was worth whatever discomfort they might endure.

Six days into traveling—the trains stopped continually, and they had to get off once or twice to allow for troop movements—they came to Georgia, and it was possible to buy food again. Along the way, Risa had acquired a real liking for Lieutenant More. He reminded her of her father, and she missed her father and prayed for him.

The railroad took them into the northernmost area of Florida, but to come down the western side of the St. Johns to reach the Rebel camp inland, they had to ride. The terrain was rugged, and they could not take a carriage; the best was a poor wagon, and Risa asked if they might just ride.

The horses they found to purchase were sad bony creatures. They had more heart than they showed, for despite the baby and the grueling journey, the Creek man who hired on as their guide managed to move them thirty-five miles the first day, and by the middle of the third day, they reached the Confederate camp. Julian and Tia were there, but Risa was both saddened and angered when they both greeted her coldly. After all, Julian was the one who had made arrangements for her to sail aboard Jerome's ship before it had been seized.

It was late when they arrived. Risa was exhausted and Jamie was cranky, so she did little at first except meet with Julian, Tia, and a Major Vail, who was currently in charge of the forces at the camp. Like everyone else, Major Vail was wary of her, warning her that she was to have no communication whatsoever across the river with the Yanks. As the wife of a true Confederate hero, she was naturally welcome in their camp; but there were rules, and she would adhere to them.

She was brought to Tia's tent. During her time in the camp among the pines, Tia had done much to make her living arrangements pleasant. Her camp beds were nothing more than cots, but she had trunks, a mirror, a desk, and even artwork decorating the small area—pictures done by the injured men, many of them very good. Risa lay on the cot and fed Jamie, and dozed herself.

She awoke to find Tia staring at her with watchful, angry eyes. She sat up, adjusting her gown, and taking care not to disturb Jamie. She glared back at Tia and snapped, "I did not betray Jerome!"

Tia arched a cool brow without replying. "Have you seen my brother Ian?"

"Not in a while. But the last I heard, he was in excellent health."

Tia began pacing the small space.

"There has been another major battle in Virginia. Chancellorsville. A terrible battle. They say that it was Lee's most brilliant victory, and yet the losses . . . thousands dead. Union and Southern."

Risa rose, staring at Tia.

"The Army of the Potomac—"

"And the Army of Northern Virginia. So many dead

and injured. Among them, Stonewall Jackson." She winced. "Shot by his own men! They took him for a Yankee!"

She spat out the last word.

Risa hesitated. Stonewall Jackson, injured. The legendary man. Religious, harder on himself than he could ever be on his own men, adored by them all. Honored by Lee. If he died . . .

The South could not afford to lose him, she thought. Yet it was hard to mourn the injury of a Southern general when her own father might be among the dead.

"Tia, please, if you know anything about my father—"

"They send us lists of the Southern dead, not the Northern," Tia told her coldly, then relented. "We would have heard had your father been injured; he's a well-known man. News travels, North and South."

Risa exhaled on a long breath. Please, God, let it be true!

"Tia?" Julian called from outside the tent.

"Come in, Julian," his sister said.

He entered and stared at Risa. He didn't have to say anything. She clenched her fists behind her back. "Damn you, Julian, I didn't do it. I didn't tell anyone I was boarding that ship. I didn't tell anyone that Jerome was coming to see me—you know that I had sent for you, not him! I am not guilty of all this! Yes, I do want the South to lose the war, and quickly. But I wouldn't have risked the life of the father of my own child—"

"You knew he'd be imprisoned!" Tia said.

She stared at Tia. "He's your cousin—you've known him all his life! How could I know that—his temper and arrogance are such that he'd take on a dozen armed men. To capture him is to risk killing him."

Tia glanced at Julian, maybe, just maybe, believing Risa.

Julian shook his head slowly.

"Someone must have been watching you. "

"Anyone could have been watching me. St. Augustine is a Yankee-held city."

"Yes, but there have been other things . . ."

"Like?"

"A note from your father threatening Jerome . . . and our family," Julian said.

"My father honestly confronted Jerome! He never threatened your family. I never betrayed anyone; I am tired to death of these accusations, and I tell you, someone else is guilty!"

"Too much is known far too easily," Tia murmured. She glanced at her brother.

"I agree," Julian said.

"I'm telling you—" Risa began.

"Don't tell me anything," Julian said. "Just be a good wife to Jerome, Unionist or not, and stay here without contacting any of your Yank friends. Are you willing to do that?"

"Obviously, I'm willing," she said. "My instructions were to come here to meet Jerome. I came."

"By way of army escort," Tia commented.

Risa swung on her. "Do you think that I would be here now—escort or no—if I hadn't made the decision to come?"

"Well, we'll see, won't we?" Julian asked.

He left the tent. Tia followed him.

Risa lay back down with her son. She thanked God that she was so tired. She slept.

Most of Jerome's old crew awaited him in at the harbor in North Carolina. They were like boys, greeting one another. Michael, Matt, Hamlin Douglas, Dr. David Stewart, Jeremiah, and others. Their ship was called the *Bodkin,* and she didn't compare with the *Lady Varina.* They sailed her out of North Carolina at dusk without being pursued by Yankee runners. She was painted blue-gray; even her canvas sails were gray, and her camouflage was her greatest asset. Her draft was nowhere near as shallow as the *Lady Varina*'s, which was a serious detriment to Jerome. But after they first cleared the harbor and took to the open sea, Jerome met with his officers, and they agreed that first action would be to take back the *Lady Varina.*

In the captain's cabin that night, Jerome met with David and Hamlin, and demanded to know what had happened when the ship was captured. He'd been burning to know.

Old Hamlin Douglas hedged. "Captain, looking back, it's hard to tell. We were at sea. Ships came out of the horizon—enough of them so that we couldn't run or fight. Perhaps if you had been with us . . ." He looked away.

"So many Union ships—they *must* have had information about when you were sailing and where."

David cleared his throat. Hamlin looked at Jerome again unhappily. "Yes, the Yanks knew all right."

Jerome sat back, feeling as if a dark cloud enwrapped him. He could almost understand if Risa had wanted him captured. But not his ship. Too many lives might have been at stake. "Where was my wife during the seizure?" he queried.

"On deck. We ordered her below, but she refused to leave the deck," Hamlin said.

"What was her reaction to the Yanks?"

Hamlin shrugged. "She was told to go with them, she did."

"They greeted her warmly," David added quickly, "but she never appeared to be glad of them, and she certainly didn't greet any one of the Yanks as an old friend."

Jerome smiled. "I'm surprised you can defend her. She sent you to Elmira, of all rotten, infested places—"

"She got us out of Elmira as well. Hired a lawyer, and got us out, and I know that to be the truth," Hamlin said. "The Yank lawyer was there when we were released, and he escorted us through the North. He was a fine, decent fellow, and he said that no matter what rights Lincoln might try to suspend in a war, there were still enough good folks around to see that the law was followed. Not that it was really so much a legal matter— the lawyer said he used Mrs. McKenzie's argument that you and the crew of the *Lady Varina* had never caused a moment's undue hardship to men from the ships taken in battle, and that Yank soldiers had even been given the first medical attention when they were hard hit."

"Maybe she just wanted the ship taken, and us let loose," Hamlin said. "Maybe she thought—"

Jerome lifted a hand. "It doesn't matter."

"But it does, doesn't it?" David said.

Jerome looked at him. "She was on board with you when you were surrounded by Yankee ships. Do you have another explanation for that many Yanks ambushing you?"

The men were silent.

Jerome smiled grimly. "Gentlemen, it is time to retake what is ours."

In mid-May, word reached the Rebel camp in the pines that Stonewall Jackson had died on the tenth. He had survived the amputation of his arm, but pneumonia had set in. Despite Robert E. Lee's message to him that although he had lost his left arm, it was as if Lee had lost his right arm without him. The great man answered God's call, and departed the cares of this life. His wife was at his side; his death created a wave of mourning across the whole of the South. His body was taken to be viewed at the capital in Richmond, where those who did and did not know him grieved. Ironically, one of the North's greatest strategical enemies had been slain accidentally by his own men. All losses were tragic; it was said that Lee found this one unendurable.

Though she understood the pain felt for Jackson, and could not help but admire the man, Risa was far more devastated to hear of another loss.

Anthony Hawkins was now listed among the missing, assumed to have been killed in action during some skirmishing that followed Chancellorsville. He had never taken his leave; he had never seen his wife or children again. When she heard the news, she went to the tent she shared with Tia, held Jamie in her arms, and cried.

Tia burst in upon her there, hands clenched into fists at her sides. "How dare you, how dare you cry over a Southern soldier? How can you mock our pain this way?"

Risa stood, staring at her. "If Ian were slain, and you cried, would you be mocking *our* pain?" she demanded tensely.

"Ian is my brother! Anthony Hawkins—"

"Was a friend, and a special man, and I cared about

him. And if you haven't realized that this war has no
clean lines between friends and enemies by this point,
you need to get out of your sheltered little pine forest,
and see what the hell is really going on!"

Tia stepped back, startled. "I know what's going on!"
she protested. "My brother is a Yankee, my father is a
Unionist. My mother cries in secret all the time because
she's afraid we may all be killed. My sister-in-law might
have been hanged, my cousin was hanged, and she only
survived because my brother cut her down. Sydney remains in Washington, and no one understands why—my
uncle will probably get himself killed going after her.
Brent may well be killed when a cannonball hits Rebel
positions, and Jerome is very likely to be blown out of
the water. I understand it all!" she shouted, and she sank
down on her own bunk, burying her face in her hands.

Risa stared at her, feeling helpless, wishing she hadn't
lashed back at Tia with such fury. She hesitantly approached her, wondering if Tia would accept her sympathy—or strike her with a right hook for the offer.

She decided to take a chance.

She sat down on the bunk beside Tia, speaking softly.

"Tia, I'm sorry, really sorry. I didn't mean that. It's
just that we're all caught in this nightmare, and you
should have met Anthony. He was solid, gentle, moral,
courageous, all manner of wonderful things, and it
doesn't matter who he was fighting for. I'm grieving for
his widow, because she must be devastated, and I'm
grieving for his children, because they'll never know
what a wonderful man he was. I swear to you, I'm not
mocking anyone."

To her surprise Tia nodded her bowed head. "I'm
sorry, too, you can't help the fact that your father's a
Yankee general and that you grew up in the North."

"I suppose I can't," Risa murmured lightly.

"It's just that they say Chancellorsville was such a
great victory, one of Lee's most shining moments, but
we lost thousands of men . . . so many people are dying.
And," she added softly, "the state is collapsing, *Florida*
is collapsing, and there's never enough food or medicine.
The world has changed; it will never be the same. It
wasn't long ago at all that everything seemed so wonder-

ful, and I intended to graduate from finishing school and
do a great tour of the Continent . . . and instead, I work
with Julian, watching men die, and watching little boys
and old graybeards try to hold on to the center of the
state . . . and if I think about the past, I feel selfish, but
sometimes, I just want it all to be over."

"Everyone feels that, Tia. And everyone feels the
pain, and the bitterness. And the loss. We've both
helped treat wounded men from both sides, and we
know that they are all someone's brother, father,
lover . . . son. Friend. I mourn my friends, Tia, either
side. And I pray for my father, your brother—and my
husband."

Tia looked up at her, beautiful dark eyes glittering.
"Tell me the truth—did you betray Jerome?"

"Never. I swear it." Risa's gaze was absolutely steady.

Tia stared at her a long moment. Then she hugged
her, and Risa was grateful. At long last someone believed her.

Jamie, whose little leg was caught in the hug, let out
a howl. Risa laughed, and Tia laughed, and Risa set him
down. Then they laughed and cried together, and Julian,
who had been coming to find his sister, paused.

The war had made them all somewhat crazy, he decided. But listening to the two, he hesitated again, and
then walked on by. He realized that he wanted to
believe.

The next day, Risa woke early. She left Jamie with
Tia and Minea, a Creek woman who helped out at the
camp. Minea had little ones of her own, and Jamie
seemed instinctively to love her and love being with her.

Risa noticed a fair amount of activity as she walked
the short distance from the camp to the river outlet
where they bathed, aware that she was discreetly followed by one of Julian McKenzie's medical stewards.
She never went anywhere without being watched, but
neither did she have anything to fear. Whoever was
guarding her followed her just to the narrow outlet, and
waited for her out by the pines.

She bathed quickly, shivering as she emerged and re-
dressed. She had barely buttoned the last of her bodice

when she suddenly heard the massive explosion of cannon fire somewhere ahead in the distance. Instinctively, she fell to the ground. The cannon was followed by gunfire, and she leapt up then, hurrying out to the pine trail where she was certain her steward waited.

But she ran right into Julian, on a slender nag, who nearly plowed over her.

"What's happening?" she demanded. "Where's Amos?"

"Gone on. There's been an engagement on the river, and Dixie boys have joined in with the Reb navy. There's some heavy action ahead. I'm going for our wounded."

"Naval action?"

"Yes, a ship has come into the river. Risa, move out of my way."

"Is it Jerome?"

"I don't know."

"It has to be!"

"Most probably."

"Take me with you; I can help."

Julian stared down at her, teeth clenched. "No."

"Please! Julian, you know that I can help you! Please, God, use some sense! How could I have had contact with the Union troops! Julian, dammit, please, I can help you!"

He hesitated just briefly, but she hadn't been more than an arm's length from him during all the days she'd been at the camp—there was no possible time when she could have communicated with the Yanks across the river.

"Fine," he said, reaching down to help her mount behind him. "Let's go, then."

As soon as she was up, he clipped his heels against the nag. "Come on, horse, don't fail me now!"

The mare had surprising speed. They raced quickly through the pine trails. In a matter of minutes, they heard the sound of gunfire directly in front of them. Julian reined in and leapt down, turning back for her. He helped her down, untied his medical bag from the saddle, and hurried into the pines. "Duck low!" he warned her. She did so, following him and squinting through to the river. She inhaled sharply. The river was bathed in black powder from the cannon fire. Suddenly, in the black fog, there was movement. A phantom ship glided along the water. Risa stared at her and gasped.

The *Lady Varina*. Repainted, renamed, now called *Glory*. But it was Jerome's ship.

Was he aboard her?

Rebel intelligence had known that the *Lady Varina* had been taken to Fernandina to be used against the blockade she'd once run. The matter of taking her had not been easy, but Jerome had been determined. At least the Yankees had once again withdrawn from Jacksonville, so she was, at the moment, a friendly port.

He and his crew had made a successful run to Bermuda for the firepower they badly needed, which the Confederacy could barely spare. They had gone with holds filled with cotton, and returned with British gold and firearms. Running the coast under the cover of darkness had given Jerome the idea he needed to retake her. He couldn't attack in broad daylight; he hadn't the manpower. He'd sacrifice far too many men, and possibly his ship. And though he'd heard that Lincoln, in a moment of anger, had said that he could create more officers but not horses, *he* couldn't afford to lose his men.

Lying awake one night, he'd remembered St. Augustine—and his father's people. His father and other Seminoles had escaped Fort Marion by nearly starving and slipping through bars. Jerome didn't need to starve anyone to take a ship, but the lessons of silence and stealth used by his father's people might serve him well. They first had to find the *Lady Varina* just moving out to sea. Then they had to board her. Not by seizing her in battle, but quietly. Man by man.

Jeremiah Jones, taking a longboat, discovered her whereabouts and movements as a Yank. Jerome hated using Jeremiah, afraid that the boy would be captured as a spy, but Jeremiah had promised, if caught, to surrender—and tell the Yanks that he had changed sides. He promised he'd then sign an oath of allegiance to the United States.

Jeremiah wasn't caught. He returned to Jerome, who waited aboard the *Bodkin*, with the information they needed. "She's just heading out tomorrow night—to look for us, Captain. The Yanks are nervous. They've been told that you're at sea again in a Rebel ship. The *Lady Varina* is being captained by a Commander Perry Ulmstead, who says he'll hang you from the mainmast of your own ship, the moment he sets eyes on you."

"Really?" Jerome murmured, eyes sparkling dangerously.

"Ah, now, Captain, they could damn well hang you, you being an escaped prisoner and all—"

"They'll have to take me first, won't they?" Jerome said.

The following night, with the ship in sight, having moved into open water, they struck.

Indian fashion.

Longboats riding the current brought them to her helm, where man by man, in breeches and face-darkening soot, in silence and secrecy, they used the rigging from the *Lady Varina* herself to crawl aboard. They were armed with nothing but knives—until they took the skeletal guard crew one by one, and were rearmed with Union navy cutlasses. Two Yanks had been killed in the action, and cast down to their watery graves, while the nine men who had surrendered on demand were tied together by the mainmast. Jeremiah and David guarded them, while Jerome, Hamlin, and other crew members approached the captain's cabin. As they did so, they heard the Yanks talking. "We'll make a lesson of him!" someone was saying. "Hang him till he's dead and rotted and bloating and feeding the seabirds, and mark my words, we'll have less of these Rebel sea rodents breaking through our guard!"

Facing Hamlin, Jerome arched a brow, then nodded silently. They burst through the door of the captain's cabin with such speed that not one of the five men around the desk had a chance to move, much less draw a pistol or sword. Ulmstead was immediately recognizable with the insignias on his uniform—and the fact that he sat in the captain's chair, feet up on the desk. He hadn't quite managed to stand when Jerome cane behind him, his knife poised at the man's throat. "What was that? Hang him till he's dead and rotted and bloating . . . ?"

To his credit, Ulmstead didn't sputter out any excuses. He sat dead still. "Captain McKenzie, I assume?"

"You assume correctly."

"If you intend to murder me—"

"I do not. However, you are sitting at my chair at my desk. May I suggest you vacate it?"

Ulmstead rose. He was of medium height and build, wearing steel-gray, fashionable "muttonchops" on his cheeks to match his curly hair.

"Order your men to lay down their weapons," Jerome advised. Ulmstead nodded to his men. They laid down their weapons. "What is your intent now, Captain Mc-Kenzie?" Ulmstead demanded.

"Well, we'll take her out a bit, then you and your men can take the longboats back to shore."

Ulmstead lowered his head, visibly relieved. He cleared his throat. "You can't take her with any speed. There are sandbars and shoals—"

"And I know them all. Mr. Douglas, If you'll take the helm, you know our course, sir!"

The rest of the crew had to be routed from bunks, and there was some resistance, but in the end Jerome and his men had taken the ship with no losses to themselves and only four Yankees dead and wounded. Jerome waited until dawn to set his prisoners free, then sent them back off toward the coast, supplied with water and rations but no weapons.

When the Yankees had been sent back to shore, Hamlin stood quietly at Jerome's side.

"Now, sir?"

"We wait for dusk, and escort the *Bodkin* down the river with her hold filled with supplies."

"What if they are prepared for us?"

"We fight," Jerome said softly, and turned away.

Risa moved swiftly, close behind Julian, keeping low, as he advanced upon another fallen man. The Rebs were scattered, firing from the trees. It seemed that the Yanks had seen the ship coming down the river, and were battling it with whatever craft they had on hand.

The pines were filling with black smoke and powder, and it was growing harder and harder to see.

"Keep low, Risa!" Julian warned, reaching the fallen man they approached. He turned the fellow over.

"Dead," he said softly, and hurried on. Risa followed, swallowing, trying not to look at the soldier. Julian stopped ahead, where another man lay on the ground groaning, gripping his leg. He was an old soldier. Gray-bearded, gray-haired, gray-eyed. Calm and resigned. He glanced at Julian, but offered Risa a smile.

"Well, now, you're a fine sight to be my last, young lady."

"I will not be your last vision!" she assured him, smiling in return.

"Rip bandages; I need a tourniquet!" Julian said tersely.

Risa expertly shredded her petticoat, wrapping the tourniquet around the man's leg the minute Julian had his trousers ripped away enough to show the pulsing wound. Julian applied the proper pressure to stop the bleeding. "How are you doing, soldier?" he demanded of the fallen man.

"I'm old and in pain, how do you think I'm doing?"

Julian grinned at Risa. "I think he's going to make it." He stood, and started toward the man fallen beside another tree in the nearby copse.

Risa squeezed the old soldier's hand. "Sir, you will make it!" She stood, ready to follow Julian. She heard a whinnying and turned. There was a horseman silhouetted in the dying light. She tried to shield her eyes from the sun.

The horse started bearing down on her. "Julian?" she called, unnerved, and instinctively aware she was in danger. "Julian!" she shouted. She turned and ran into the trees.

"Risa?" Julian stood, looking back toward her.

She ran hard, never turning back. But the horseman ran her down easily.

Something cracked hard on her head, and as the world blurred, she was swept up onto the horse and carried away.

Chapter 27

Jerome used his *Lady Varina* to shield the activities of the *Bodkin* as she unloaded her precious cargo farther down the river. But as they returned Federal fire, he knew that he didn't dare tarry long along the river; the Yanks had strengthened their hold upon the water in the long months that he had been gone.

After a barrage of gunfire, things at last grew quiet; the Yanks had expended what they had on hand. It wouldn't be long before more Federal gunboats would be sent after him—or until he found himself trapped.

"Mr. Douglas!"

"Aye, Captain."

"I'm taking a boat, and going in for my wife and son."

"Aye, Captain."

"I'll be coming with you, Captain," David Stewart said, hurrying behind him.

"You're needed here—"

"We've no injuries here, sir. One burned hand from explosives. And it's bandaged."

"Come, then."

Twenty minutes rowing brought them to the west bank of the river. Another thirty minutes of searching carefully through the pines brought them to Julian.

Julian was on the ground, leaned against a tree trunk, bleeding from a head wound. Jerome anxiously hunkered by his cousin as one of his medical stewards bound his temple.

"Jerome," he said, trying to grin. His words were thick; he was in pain. "Knew you were out there. Knew you'd get that ship back."

"Yeah, we got her. But you—"

"I feel like a fool . . ." Julian said, bowing his head.

He looked up at Jerome then and groaned softly. "They got her, they took her."

"What are you talking about?" Jerome said harshly.

Julian winced. "Easy, now," David Stewart warned. "You've got a major bump growing there."

Julian nodded, shook his head, paled, and gritted his teeth. "Risa. Risa was with me. Right behind me. Out of the smoke, there came a man on horseback. She was running to me. Dammit, Jerome, I know that she was running to me for help. The rider slammed her in the head with the butt of his rifle, and swept her up. I went after him."

"Carrying no weapons?" David murmured.

Julian shrugged. "I suppose even we medical McKenzies are a little crazy," he murmured. "I thought I could tackle the rider. I might have. But someone was riding behind him, and I was knocked out before I could reach the man."

"How long ago did this happen?"

"Twenty—thirty minutes at most," Julian said. "I've kind of lost perspective. Oh, God, I'm sorry."

"Dammit, Julian, for what? You didn't cause the war! I'm just glad you weren't hurt worse." Jerome reached for his cousin's shoulder, and squeezed it. "Don't worry; I'll get her back." He stood, looking at Amos, his cousin's steward.

"Don't worry none, Captain. I'll get him back to camp all right. Like as not, he'll be holding his head and working surgery just fine within the hour."

"Thanks, Amos," Jerome said, turning to his own ship's surgeon. "David, can you take one of the stray horses, head back in, and find my son? I'll meet you back at the ship."

"What are you going to do?" David asked warily.

"Find my wife."

"Jerome," he said unhappily, "the Yanks have her."

"They've had her before."

"They're surely taking her across the river. Back to Yankee territory. She'll be safe, Jerome. No Yank in his right mind would hurt Magee's daughter."

"But what if the Yanks aren't all in their right minds? Did you hear Julian?" he queried. "She was hit on the head with a rifle butt, dammit. Besides, there's something not quite right here, though I don't know what it is. My wife may have been a Yank taken by Yanks, but come hell or high water, she's one Yank coming back to a Rebel ship now."

Her head was spinning. She first became aware of damp earth beneath her, the smell of the river, and moss-laden tree branches dipping overhead. She realized that her eyes were open, the world was still spinning, she could hear people talking. She blinked. The moss still dripped above. The earth remained blanketed in black powder.

"Risa?"

Someone was standing by her. The good Yankee doctor, Thayer Cripped, was at her side. A small boat was drawn up along the embankment; nearby there were several more. Yankees who had crossed the river to skirmish in the woods were returning: some limping, some bleeding. Cripped called them to get to the surgery, and shouted orders to his stewards to help the injured into ambulance wagons. Suddenly, he looked down at her, then dropped to her side. "Risa? You all right?"

She wasn't sure. She tried to sit up. She'd been cracked pretty good at the back of the head. She could feel a bump, and it throbbed with pain.

"You were rescued," Thayer told her happily.

She shook her head. "Rescued! That's what you call a rescue? I was ridden down and knocked out! You didn't—"

"No! I didn't knock you out. I thought the Rebs had injured you somehow. Let's see . . ." Cripped carefully ran his fingers over her skull. "I don't think it's as bad as it feels. A few hours rest, some nice cool water . . . tomorrow morning, you'll be right as rain."

"Risa, are you all right?" she heard.

She twisted, coming up on her elbows. Lieutenant Austin Sage knelt down by her then, looking at her anxiously. "Austin," she murmured. "No! I'm not all right. I was hit in the head, brought here by force, and I was only tending to injured men. My son is across the river!"

"Come on—let me get you out of the range of fire.

You are here now, with friends. We hope you'll stay, but if you want to reach your father, we can get you back with him as well."

"Risa!" Her name was cried with pleasure.

She turned to see that Finn McCullough was hurrying to her side, sandy hair covered by a low slouch hat. "Risa! Thank God you're safely back!"

"I'm not back! My baby is over there—"

Austin held her hands. "Try to stand," he suggested.

She tried to stand and stumbled. "What happened? Why was I attacked?" she cried as Austin steadied her.

"I've got you, Risa, you're going to be all right," he told her gently.

"I appreciate your kindness, but you must let me go. I wasn't rescued, I was attacked—"

"By our soldiers?" Austin demanded skeptically. "Not my men."

"Yes, by your men! How do you think I got here—"

"I found you on the shore, left by a cavalryman; I did see that much," Thayer Cripped admitted.

"Whatever happened, my son is over there, can't you understand? Really, I have to go back to the Rebels."

"Risa, we cannot let you do so! Surely, you realize that!" Sage said somberly.

"No, no I don't—"

"Ah, the general's daughter!" snapped a thundering voice. Risa turned to see Major Dawson, an annoying man with the New Hampshire officers who saw only black and white in the war, never shades of gray. "Bring her in, Lieutenant. We'll talk, we'll see what she knows, then she can go home—or even help Cripped in surgery."

Austin swept her up in his arms.

"Major, this is ridiculous—" Risa protested.

"Young woman, I haven't your father's patience. This is war! Any more trouble from you, and I'll have you locked in a cell in Fort Marion tonight, lady or no! Though in my book, madam, ladies do not fraternize with the enemy!"

"Major, how dare you? Someone just attacked me, and might have killed me—"

"What's that?" Cripped demanded suddenly, tensing.

"Where?" Austin Sage asked.

"Speak up, man!" Major Dawson snapped.

"I heard something in the water . . . that way."

Risa pushed against Austin. "Austin, thank you kindly, you are a good man, but I think I can stand. Now—"

"Don't you see that—down there! Something moved in from the black mist on the water . . . one or two hundred feet down. By the horses . . . listen!" Thayer Cripped insisted.

The horses had indeed started whinnying nervously. Finn McCullough moved instinctively to guard their backs. Cripped looked uneasily around them. Dawson reached for his pistol. "Damn the black powder, the smoke in the air!" Dawson swore. "You can't see a bloody thing!"

"There! A horse and rider," Thayer said.

Risa saw them.

Out of the haze . . .

A horse and rider, moving like one. Riding her down again, she thought, panicking. Did someone mean to kill her?

She wasn't going to be struck, not again. She couldn't be killed, she had to live, she had Jamie.

"Let go!" she cried in panic, slamming her fist against Sage's chest. His hold eased as he grunted; she landed on her feet, and she started running. The rider was coming for her, and she ran, terrified, feeling the earth shudder as the rider bore down upon her a second time.

"Bastard!" she heard Dawson shouting; and a gun was fired, but then Dawson was crying out, and threw himself toward the bushes beyond the embankment. Risa shrieked, running harder, aware that the horse was gaining. She could almost feel the creature's breath on her neck.

"Risa!"

She nearly stumbled. *Jerome's* voice. Oh, God! This side of the river, the enemy's side of the river, alone on horseback, riding out of smoke and twilight. For her.

She turned just as he reached her, sweeping her up, throwing her over his mount. They spun on the wet earth; she feared that the horse would pitch over, that they would both be killed. But the animal found its footing; and they raced down the embankment in the other direction. She grasped to the animal for dear life.

He rode the horse hard out into the water. Jerome's men were waiting in a small boat. Yankee soldiers were pounding after them. "Give me Risa!" someone cried, and in a small boat, she saw Michael. She was handed down from the horse to the boat. The boat shot across the river. Still mounted, Jerome turned toward the east shore, firing his Colt pistols. He leapt from the horse, tossing his guns to the boat, hitting the water himself and swimming until he could hike himself on board the longboat. He landed, barefoot, bare-chested, soaked and dripping. Keeping low, he moved to Risa's side. His eyes touched hers with customary blue fire.

She was worn, bruised, bumped, soaked—and still shaking. She tried to sit up, tried to glare back at him. "I did not cause the Yankees to attack you!" she cried angrily as Michael's strong powerful oar strokes sent them ripping through the water and black powder haze. "I . . ."

The blue of his eyes seemed suddenly to cover the landscape and darken. She wanted to fight; she wanted to say more. But everything was going dark. She tried to rise against him, but she couldn't. She pitched forward into his arms.

"We need to get her to the ship, to Doc Stewart, and quickly," Jerome said. Michael nodded, rowed harder still, as Jerome held his wife. They reached the *Lady Varina*. Jerome heaved his wife over his shoulder, and climbed the ladder to the deck. "Is Dr. Stewart back aboard?" he barked.

"Aye, sir!" Hamlin cried.

"Send him to my cabin, now. Then take us out, Mr. Douglas, take us out!"

"Our heading, sir?"

"South, Mr. Douglas. South. Homeward."

Risa did not know how long she was unconscious; when she awoke, she felt rested, and her head didn't pound at all.

She was in familiar surroundings—Jerome's cabin on

board the *Lady Varina*. The Yankees hadn't changed
anything. The desk remained where it had been, along
with the captain's chair.

The only thing different, was the little makeshift crib,
fashioned out of a drawer, with the squawling baby in it.

"Jamie!" she cried out delightedly.

"Easy, easy now, sitting up!" she was warned. She saw
that David Stewart sat in a chair by her side, catching
up on a variety of Northern newspapers left behind by
the Yanks.

She flashed him a smile, reaching for Jamie. "David,
how good to see you. Honest, I'm fine. My head isn't
spinning . . . it doesn't hurt. I can't even feel the ship
moving."

"It's not moving."

"Oh?" She glanced at him worriedly, but then Jamie
occupied her attention again, and she cuddled him to
her chest. He continued to howl hungrily. She discovered
that she was dressed now in a chaste white nightgown,
but most of the tiny buttons had never been done up.
She flushed slightly at David Stewart, but then remembered his vocation in life, and allowed Jamie to nurse.
"I love you so much!" she whispered to her son, cradling
him tenderly before looking back to David. "If we're
not moving—"

"We're between Castle by the Sea, Jerome's home,
and Belamar. A secluded harbor, known to very few.
The men can give the ship a good going over here. Naturally, there's no shipyard, so we'll have to bring her
north soon, but for now, this is a good place to get our
bearings and do what repairs we can."

"Aren't you afraid I'll share that information with my
Yankee friends?" she inquired tartly.

He grinned. "Do you have any idea of where we actually are?"

"No," she admitted. "But then, I did find Belamar
once."

His grin deepened. "Anyone who wants to can find
Castle by the Sea. But the Yankees would have to want
to pretty damned badly. It could mean another Indian
war, attacking the place, with all the men James has
working the property."

"But we're not at Castle by the Sea?"

"Close enough. In fact, I'm to take you there today."

"Are you sure it's safe?" she murmured, looking back to Jamie.

"*I've* been sure for a long time. But then, I'm afraid that I don't count much in this. Finish with Jamie; I'll bring you some coffee. If you're sure you're feeling well enough, we'll take a boat in."

David hadn't just brought Jamie to the ship, she learned, he had brought Minea and her two little toddlers as well. Her husband had been killed by shrapnel, and she had decided to come along and help out with Jamie, and find out what life was like in the deep swamps where so many Seminoles lived. Risa was glad to have her, and glad that her son had been with Minea, tended and loved, when she had been unable to care for him. She'd been so afraid—of dying!—or that she'd be separated from her baby, she couldn't help but be glad now. And excited, too. This was her husband's home.

As the boat took them down the deep dockage that fronted Castle by the Sea, Risa looked around with awe. It was like coming to Eden. The foliage was dense and riotously diverse. They traveled from salt to brackish water, surrounded by low-swaying palms and mangroves. Sea grapes dotted a sandy shoreline, the water was dark blue here, turquoise there. The land was a rich green, rimmed in sandy beaches.

The house suddenly appeared, beautifully sprawling and huge, yet blending in with the environment.

As the longboat pulled to the dock, she was further amazed to see the number of men with rifles who suddenly emerged from the trees. Indians, whites, blacks, men of mixed blood. One stepped forward. "Dr. Stewart!"

"Billy!" Stewart leapt to the dock, then reached down for Risa. "Mrs. McKenzie, Billy Bones—Jamie's distant kin," he said cheerfully.

Billy nodded courteously to Risa, studying her. "Welcome," he said.

"Thank you." Billy *Bones*? How unusual, and yet it was an unusual place.

David turned to help Minea and her little ones, but

Billy had already stepped to the task, offering Minea a broad, pleased smile.

"Come on, I'll take you to the house," David said.

She followed David's warm invitation. As they approached the porch, the door burst open and a woman appeared. She hurried out, smiling.

She was beautiful. Her hair auburn, long, waving down her back. Her eyes were emerald. She was slim and lithe and at a distance, might have been twenty. As they came closer, Risa saw that she was older. "Risa, dear, we're so pleased to see you. I'm Teela, Jerome's mother. Come in, bring my grandson. Better yet, let me have my grandson!"

She swept the baby from Risa, and turned, moving on into the house. "Come on, dear, come in. Oh, David, I'm sorry, it's wonderful to see you, too!" She swirled about again, kissing David on the cheek. "James, dear, she's here!"

Jerome's father walked into the breezeway, grinning, arching a brow as he looked from his wife, to Risa, to David, to the baby. "Welcome," he said, his eyes on her, then falling to Jamie as he took his grandson from his wife. "Dear—your daughter is upstairs screaming for something I'm afraid I can't give her. You'll have time for your grandson later. David! You've brought my daughter-in-law. What do you think?"

"She's very lovely, sir, and I try not to blame her too much for being a Yank."

"Well, we have to take that as it comes," James murmured, winking at Risa. He was a handsome man, and she knew where her husband had gotten his unusual and striking looks—if not his easy charm. "Risa McKenzie, you are welcome here, no matter what your political leanings. As the mother of my first grandchild, I could certainly offer you no less. Have you eaten? Come along, we've ham and biscuits and gravy, and you look as if you could use the nourishment."

Risa smiled. The elder McKenzies were charming, warm, and welcoming. They were Jerome's parents, and she was shamefully fascinated to meet people so close to her husband. And she was famished as well. "Thank you, sir."

The dining room was both comfortable and elegant, and the buffet by the table was laden with silver serving dishes. There was a great deal of food prepared, as if they'd planned for the arrival of their son's ship. Risa sat with David and James to eat while Minea came and took Jamie upstairs with her own little ones to settle in. Then Teela returned with baby Mary, and after Risa had complimented her new little sister-in-law, Mary was taken upstairs with the other children. Conversation was light and warm at first while she told the older McKenzies all she knew about their son, Brent, daughter Sydney, and their cousins Julian, Ian, and Tia.

Teela shivered and crossed herself, looking down as a little sheen of tears touched her eyes. "If we can all just survive it . . ." she murmured. "But our grandson, James! He's beautiful, isn't he? Now, if we can just keep him here."

"Teela!" her husband warned. "That's a decision Risa will have to make with Jerome."

"There's no chance of Jerome staying here," Risa said bitterly. She was pushing food around on her plate now. She looked up, wondering if Jerome had brought her here to leave her. A nice safe place for an unwanted wife and child. She was out of harm's way—and out of the way where she could cause harm. "Where is he?" she inquired quietly.

"Tending to the ship," David supplied.

"He'll come back later," Teela assured her. "Why don't you get settled? Jerome's room is upstairs. We've had a crib brought in, and I took the liberty of bringing a few things to the wardrobe there—"

"A few things!" James interrupted. "Neither Sydney nor my wife ever missed a fashion trend, I assure you." He smiled at his wife. "In the midst of war, *Godey's Lady's Book* manages to make it here—to the swamp!"

"I have never been ruled by fashion!" Teela protested. She smiled. "Well, we can dress, when need be. But it's so very hot . . . cotton is best around the water in any case. Come, let me get you settled."

It was a strange afternoon for Risa. Jerome's room was unique, reflecting his heritage. There were many Seminole artifacts: pipes and headdresses, little dolls, knives, and colorful mats. There were also exceptional prints by Audubon and others. The bookshelves held fiction and nonfiction. His wardrobe and drawers were filled with civilian clothing, casual workclothes, and more elegant attire from a time gone by. He had grown up here. His window overlooked the sea in the distance, and a sandy beach, and she thought that at sunset, the view must be exquisite.

His bed was a large, handsome four-poster, the carving European. The spread upon it was deep maroon knit and matched the draperies. As the sun began to set, she saw the colors of twilight, and how beautiful it was, and she wondered if he would ever forgive her long enough to sleep with her here, or whether she could forgive him.

Suddenly restless, with Jamie fed and sleeping and the household quiet, she felt she had to get out. Downstairs, James, who sat in his den working near a log fire, studied her thoughtfully, then spoke. "You'll find a brackish pool down the path, surrounded by white sand and pines. It belongs to the family, and it's a beautiful place if you choose to swim. You'll not be bothered there."

She followed the trail. The pool was some distance from the house, but when she arrived, she was delighted. The landscape was crimson, gold, and pink. Wading birds played in the shallow water, beautiful white creatures with long elegant necks and skinny legs. The sand stretched out, white and pure, but bathed in the pink of the sunset. She stripped off her stockings and shoes, and put her toes in the water, and it was deliciously warm. After a moment she stripped off her cotton day dress, laying it carefully over a log. In pantalets and blue-ribboned chemise, she walked into the shallows, about to dive and swim.

"That's all? That's all that you're taking off?"

She spun around. She hadn't realized Jerome had been at the cove, leaning so still and silently against a pine. Barefoot, shirtless, his breeches rolled high, he looked at her from across the sand, arms folded over his chest. She trembled inwardly, longing to run to him, but knowing that she couldn't do so, since he had branded her a traitor.

"I'm very, very careful as to where I discard all my

clothing these days," she informed him, crossing her
arms over her chest as well.

He arched a brow. "As you should be."

"And why is that?"

"Because I would tan your hide were you to be
careless."

"Ironic—when it appears your hide is so well-known."

He frowned. "What are you talking about?"

"Never mind."

She turned away, moving along the waterline. She
gasped when he caught up with her, spinning her around.
But she eluded his grasp and backed away from him
angrily. "Quite frankly, I can't believe that you've
brought me here."

"The location of my father's house is not exactly a
military secret," he said dryly.

"So if it were, you would not trust me."

"Should I?" he demanded after a moment's careful
thought.

"If you think not, why am I here?"

"Because I married you."

"You shouldn't have."

"So I've been told."

"Because I betrayed you."

"More than once, it appears."

"Oh! This time, too?" she demanded furiously. "I hit
myself in the head and ran off to the Yanks?"

"Perhaps you asked them to come—and they believed
they were doing you a favor."

"They probably were doing me a favor, but I didn't
have the sense to realize it."

"You fought them?" he inquired skeptically, his eyes
very dark. "That's why I had to run you down on horseback as well? You could have cost us both our lives."

"I didn't know who you were!" she shouted, frustrated. "I'd already been attacked, I—oh, this is a worthless conversation!" she cried angrily, tears stinging her
eyes.

His jaw was locked; he continued to stand rock-hard.
No quarter given. No hint of emotion in his eyes. "The
point is, I am continually betrayed. And each time,
you're near."

"I never betrayed you, but *damn* you! I am sick to
death of this. I am innocent!" she insisted, and she suddenly felt as if she had simply had it—he didn't listen,
didn't give her a chance. "Oh, but I could kill you!"

She had lost her senses, she knew, but it didn't matter.
She went flying across the sand, pitching herself at him
with a furious impetus. He was unprepared, and she
brought them both crashing down into the sand. He
landed hard, and she was glad for a single moment of
victory. But then she panicked because it had been a
long time since they'd been with one another, so close.
And she was so very hurt, angry, emotional, hungry . . .

She was touching him. Her hands were on his bare
chest. Her limbs entwined with his. Her breasts were
crushed against him, and she could feel the heat of the
sun on his flesh, feel it burn from him to her. The fabric
of her pantalets was far too thin where she lay against
his thighs. His eyes touched her in a way that created a
stir of both passion and fury within her, and her instinct
warned her she desperately needed to escape before she
succumbed. "Stop it, let go, let me up—"

"Mrs. McKenzie, I might remind you that you tackled
me, madam!" He looked slightly amused and slightly
dangerous. There was a warning glitter in his eyes. She
tried to rise, but he wrenched her back.

"McKenzie, I said, let me go—"

"And I said that you brought about this situation!"

"Then, I'm sorry! Let go. I mean it, I hate you. And
I'm tired of being blamed for what I didn't do. And you
can just go right to hell and take all your Rebel friends
with you. I will never forgive you. I don't know just who
the hell you think you are, but you're a fool, and you're
going to get yourself killed. And I don't want to be
around when it happens. I didn't put you in prison, but
I should have, and I wish that you were there now, and
I wish that—I wish you'd let me go!"

Again, she tried to rise. He tried to hold on. His fingers curled around the material of her chemise, and as
she moved, the material gave. She jumped back, holding
the torn piece of fabric over her breast. "How dare you,
how dare you touch me! Look what you've done, and
you have the nerve—"

"Look what *I've* done?" he demanded, jumping up as well, and circling her as she tried to back away from him.

She wasn't quick enough. In a split second he'd caught hold of the garment, and ripped it in half.

"Wretched—Rebel!" she exploded. She started to pummel him, but before she could do much harm, he caught her wrists in a vise and she decided to retreat. In her struggle she lost her footing, and fell, crashing into the water. It suddenly seemed an ideal means of escape. She wrenched free and started to swim; he caught hold of the fabric of her pantalets. Gossamer thin, they ripped to his touch. And his hands were on her bare flesh, dragging her back.

She struggled wildly against him, only to discover the fire burning within herself. Her nipples brushed against the crisp hair on his chest, and hardened. Heat seemed to spear through her, rake up her thighs, rest between them. He captured her in his arms, and she felt him moving, walking to the embankment. He laid her on the damp earth, he fell atop her, fingers laced with hers, breathing ragged as he raised his weight above her, staring into her eyes. "Damn you, damn you!" he swore.

"Damn you! I've done nothing!"

"Have you changed sides?" he mocked.

"Have you?"

"Do you care?" he demanded passionately. "Right this minute, right now, do you care, do you give a damn?"

"No!" she whispered, then slammed a fist against him. "Yes!" she choked out. "Yes, I care, because I didn't—"

"You didn't betray me. I know. I—think."

She stared at him, suddenly silent, wary. "What?"

"Maybe you didn't plan on my capture. And maybe you didn't plan on my men or my ship being taken."

She blinked furiously. Tears dampened her cheeks. "You mean that you believe me?"

"Yes."

"But you accused me—"

"You'll admit that you looked very suspicious—especially, since you are an avowed Yankee."

"Yes, but . . ."

"But what?" he demanded.

She couldn't tell him that she'd never hurt him because she loved him. Couldn't risk her heart, pride, and soul. Not yet. "Do you . . . trust me?" she asked him.

"Yes, I do. But someone around you is trying very hard to destroy me."

"Most Yankees probably want you dead—or in Siberia." Someone. Someone other than her. She felt an exhilarating warmth, an explosion of pleasure in her heart. He believed in her, trusted her, wanted her. Not that he'd exactly apologized . . . yet.

He sighed, obviously frustrated. "No, I think it's more than that. I think someone has a personal vendetta against me. Someone close to you."

"Not my father, Jerome! Not my father!"

He rose, walking away from her. She felt the cold breeze wash over her, and she thought that he had forgotten what they were doing. He hadn't.

He shed his breeches.

And that was when she saw it. The birthmark Janine Thompson had described for her.

She was on her feet instantly, heedless now of the fact that her pantalets and chemise had fallen off her in tatters. Naked as a sprite, she reached for a fallen palm branch, holding it as a club as he turned back to her, puzzled.

"Damn you, what now? You're going to take me prisoner again—with that as your weapon?"

"What now?" she cried angrily. "You *do* have a birthmark!"

"Yes, I have always had it. Put that ridiculous thing down!" he ordered, striding toward her.

"No! Get away from me!"

"What is the matter with you now! I try to apologize, confess to you that I may be wrong, and you—"

"Go back to your fiancée!"

"Fiancée?" he repeated, incredulous.

"She told me—she told me about your birthmark. I hadn't even seen it. Oh, I could endure the fact that you were the enemy—I was an idiot and I fell in love with you anyway—and I could even understand that you might suspect me of treachery, but I can't, I won't, endure this, I just can't. If I didn't care, maybe I could, but I do—"

He was walking purposely, menacingly, toward her.

"Don't come near me!" she insisted again, taking a swipe at him with the palm branch.

He'd had enough. He made a leaping dive for her that brought them both tumbling back down. He jerked the branch out of her hand, threw it aside, and pressed her into the earth with his weight, cupping her cheek with his hand.

"No!" she protested weakly. "You are a savage Rebel wretch, taking every advantage, forcing me—!" she cried.

He smiled. "Only when I need to," he assured her, and kissed her.

She struggled beneath him. But his lips formed over hers, his tongue ravaged and plundered, and his body sent a burning flame and fever sweeping into her. She had to think to regain the fight when his mouth lifted from hers.

"Don't! I mean it. I'm telling you—"

"Did you say that you loved me?"

"No."

"Yes, you did. But you're one damned jealous Yank."

"Would you get off of me? I'm going to call your father!"

He laughed, totally amused by that. "I think my father has probably been here in a similar situation. No help there. No, you'd best listen to me. I was never engaged to Janine. I read it in the papers, the same as you did, but you were the enemy. You learn in warfare never to give your enemy the advantage. And as to being with her . . . we weren't married, but it didn't matter. I wasn't with her. Because you ruined the entire concept of other women for me. Dear God, it's a wretched war, and I should have enjoyed the advances of a beautiful woman, but I couldn't. Do you know why?"

"Why?"

"Because you're just so incredibly good."

"Oh!" she gasped, trying to writhe away again. "That may be worse—"

"Why? Because it's as if we were made to be to-

gether? Because, for your information, Madam Union-
Forever, you've done things to me that I can't explain,
made me feel things I'd never felt. Damn you, I'm in
love with you, and you may be the mother of my son—
and my wife!—but I didn't want to love you. You are
the enemy, and I was so afraid of being made a fool by
you that I made a fool of myself instead. You will get
this straight!" he stated, for she still stared up at him
blankly, "I was never with Miss Janine Thompson, but
I damned well intend to be with you now!"

He rose slightly, knifing her limbs apart with his knee,
and shifting his weight. She felt the extent of his arousal
teasing at the lips of her sex before he thrust into her,
and the world seemed to burst into little prisms of
golden light. She cried out, burrowing against his shoulder, nearly delirious with the feel of him inside her once
again, his body sleek, the damp earth beneath them, glo-
rious sky above them, his heat all but unbearable. And
the way he moved, drawing more and more from her
until she writhed and arched and strained against
him . . . and when she thought that she was dying, he
suddenly withdrew. His lips found her breasts, teased
the tenderness of her nipples, boldly explored her midsection. She tried to rise against him, touching, caressing,
kissing . . . she was forced back to the ground, and his
lips touched her here . . . there . . . his most intimate
kiss settled between her, and drove her nearly to distrac-
tion. When she shrieked his name, he came to her at
last, finding her mouth, thrusting into her again with an
impetus that left her gasping . . . clinging to him, rocking
down from the sweet and volatile climax that had
claimed her. She wrapped her arms around him. Drifted
downward. "I love you . . ."

But even as she whispered the words, he was disengag-
ing himself from her hold, standing, staring toward the
southwest.

Instinctively, she rose behind him. "Jerome, what is
it?"

He swung around, staring at her.

"My father's house is on fire!" he grated out, and he
grabbed his pants, stepping into them even as they heard
the sound of a cannon, exploding into the dusk.

Chapter 28

He was gone before she could reach her dress. She slipped into it with shaking fingers, and came racing after him. Yet, when she would have followed the trail back to the house, she was stopped. Two Yankee soldiers suddenly stepped from the brush to bar the path, and she came to a dead halt, gasping, staring at them.

"Who are you? Where did you come from?"

"You can't go to the house, ma'am."

"You'll let me by this instant! Now. My—"

"No, ma'am."

"My child—"

"It's a Rebel stronghold, and it's going down."

"No, you'll let me by—"

"Risa, no!" came a third voice, causing her to swing around as another man hurried along the path. He was in uniform, wearing a major's insignias.

"Good!" said one of the men beside her. "Major McCullough will explain."

Freckled-face, hard-set and dead serious, Finn McCullough had nearly reached her. He smiled at the look on her face, and swept her a deep bow. "I knew I'd surprise you, Risa. Foolish, gullible Finn! Not such a fool, really. I'm with army intelligence, Army of the Potomac. Hooker got us well organized, and we've been fairly effective under Pinkerton for some time now. You've been incredibly helpful, Risa, giving me everything I needed. I knew that I could get your husband to come for you again if I took you from the Rebel side. God, but I've waited for this! You've done the Union a great service—as I have."

"You've attacked my husband's house, you've attacked civilians! My child is in that house. Other children . . ."

"Shouldn't sleep with the enemy, Risa!" he chided her, and she saw something strange in his eyes. He shook his head regretfully. "You know, I was in love with you. But you never wanted me. Then a dangerous, half-breed Rebel kidnaps you . . . and you have his brat."

Finn McCullough with his sandy hair and freckles. Finn, who couldn't have cared less about the war, about any which way the wind blew, as long as he could run his business. Salvage diver. Helping out in the hospital, hanging on the fringes of society, North or South. A friend, she had thought. Someone she had once felt so guilty about using, when she had asked him to bring her to Biscayne Bay to find Alaina.

She was the one who had been used. Had he been with Yankee intelligence all along? she wondered. Or had he decided that he would have revenge against Jerome McKenzie once Jerome had taken them prisoner that long-ago night? What a fool she'd been, trusting him! She *had* caused her husband's capture and that of his ship, even if she'd done so unwittingly. Damn Finn, and damn his men. The house was burning, and her child might be inside, and her husband, and his family, were in danger. She stared at the two soldiers who were apparently under Finn's command. "You touch me, and I promise you that my father will have you hanged in a Yankee court. The United States does not make war on civilians and babies!"

In a fury she pushed by the soldiers, and went racing toward the house. She was vaguely aware of Finn shouting after her. She didn't give a damn.

The left wing of the structure was on fire, shooting flames. She could hear gunfire, and she saw that sailors and Seminoles had banned together to fight against the force of Yankees who had come ashore on longboats. The cannon fire came from the ships, she realized; the Yankees had engaged with the *Lady Varina* in her safe harbor—a place where Risa had led the enemy.

Jerome was surely engaged in the fighting. But what of his family? Oh, God, she had brought this down on his family. And her child and her in-laws might well be perishing within the burning house.

Surely, they had escaped it! But she had to make sure. She stood on the porch, shouting, but there was no reply other than the snap and crackling of the fire. The heat was immense. She could be killed if she rushed in, but she had to do so. What if someone had been injured, what if someone lay shot and bleeding, what if they were all hurt, what if they had fled, and somehow forgotten Jamie, what if . . .

She ignored the soldiers and sailors battling by the water and rushed into the house, quickly searching the ground floor, avoiding the dining room, where the blaze was centered. She raced up the stairs, heedless of the smoke and flames. "Teela, James! Anyone! I'm here, please, where are you?"

There was no reply. She ran into Jerome's bedroom, looking for Jamie, who had been sleeping in his crib when she left. Minea never would have left her child; neither James nor Teela McKenzie would have ever deserted the sleeping babe, she assured herself. They had all gotten out. And still, she was so afraid. As smoke continued to fill the room, she cried out again. "Jamie! Anyone! Help, is anyone in here? Please, please, please, someone, where's my child?"

"Risa!"

She spun around. It was Finn McCullough, managing to look more military every minute. Now he was holding a Sharps issue revolver. She stared at him, knowing that she was nearly backed against a wall.

"Risa, the house is on fire."

"So it is. But my baby—"

"Don't be a fool, they've gotten the children out. Come on. Risa, damn you, I've got a gun on you! Move!"

"Move! Why? Are you going to shoot me in cold blood?"

He stepped forward then, and she wasn't prepared for the blow he dealt her in the jaw. Head spinning, she fell back against the wall. "You're coming with me, Risa!" he insisted.

"You're not going to ignore me anymore. Poor, pathetic Finn, easily twirled around your finger. But I was good, Risa. I nearly captured his sister. He would have known what it was like to be afraid for a woman he loved. A woman in danger. You should have seen his face the night we took him from your house in St. Augustine. You see, I watched you. I watched you all the time. I spied on your conversation with the good young Dr. Julian McKenzie, and I knew when you'd board Jerome McKenzie's ship, and when it could be taken. And I knew that Jerome would come across the river for you, and that I could follow you both here. The fire will die out, Risa. We weren't after the McKenzie house. Just Jerome McKenzie and his ship."

"You know, you could have a dozen guns, and I'd still never go with you, *anywhere*. I love my husband, Finn. This is our home, and my child is here!"

"Risa, you're being foolish! The South will lose the war. He will lose everything!"

"He may lose the war, but he'll have his heart, his soul, his pride, his life, and his love. He'll have me. Always."

"You're coming with me! I haven't the patience for this!" Finn snapped, and he wrenched her to him, placing the muzzle of the gun directly against her head. "Now!"

He was unbalanced, she thought. Maybe the war had driven them all a little crazy. Maybe he had played his furtive, secretive game so long that he had fantasized the ending, and would let it happen no other way.

She heard a sound and looked to the doorway. Jerome stood there, straight, silhouetted by a burst of angry gold flames behind him in the hall. He stepped into the room, unarmed other than the sword in his hand, held to his side. "Let her go, Finn."

"You get out of the way, McKenzie. Or I'll put a bullet in her brain, I swear it. I'm taking your wife."

Jerome moved out of the way of the door, staring at Risa. "We all have to get out of the house. Quickly."

She nodded. Her lips were too dry to speak.

"Move, McKenzie, get out of the way. Risa, tell him to get out of my way. If he doesn't move . . ."

Jerome walked into the room, setting his sword down,

circling around Finn and Risa. Finn watched him uneasily.

"Risa," Jerome said, "you should know, that night I was taken by the Yanks at St. Augustine was beautiful. It was worth the months in prison."

"Shut up, McKenzie," Finn said. "You're a dead man, and she's coming with me. I'll have her out of here faster than you can utter an Indian war cry or a Rebel yell!"

Jerome ignored him. "I love you, too, Risa. War or no war."

"I'm not leaving here without you, Jerome!" Risa protested, shrieking as Finn brutally tightened his hold. "As soon as he's safely out the door, he'll start shooting—"

"McKenzie!" Finn raged, "I can't kill you both, but if you don't stay away, I'll shoot you, or I'll shoot her. One of you will die."

Jerome still appeared calm. "You won't kill her; I'd rip you in half no matter how many bullets you put into me. Your men are retreating," he told Finn. "They can't take this place; they never could. The last thing the United States wants right now is another expensive, time-consuming, full-scale war with the last of the Florida Seminoles."

"Damn you, shut up, McKenzie!" Finn shouted, and drew the gun from Risa's head and started firing. Risa screamed, wrenching at his arm, but too late. Jerome had fallen to the floor.

"Bastard!" Risa shrieked, striking out at Finn, but he slammed the butt of his gun against her head. She staggered, and he pulled her over his shoulder, then turned and fled down the stairs, past the formal dining room, now an inferno.

She struggled not to lose consciousness, determined she would fight to the end, yet dazed and alternating between hope and despair, knowing that if she had lost husband and child, she no longer wanted to live.

At first she had no strength. Everything was spinning, her head pounded ferociously. Tears stung her eyes, and bathed her cheeks. Then she tried to rise up against Finn, to distract him as he ran across the front of the estate. He was hurrying to the docks, where the small boats waited. A few of his men still exchanged gunfire with those fighting from the outbuildings and copses that surrounded the house. But struggling was useless; he threw her into one of the boats, and when she would have risen, he hopped down beside her, pushing off from the dock despite the cry of a soldier who meant to jump in as well.

"Major, wait, I can't swim, they're taking the other boats—"

But Finn had cast off, and was rowing hard, oblivious to all else. Risa managed to sit up, but when she did so, he hit her with an oar, and the world began to waver anew. She swallowed down a rise of nausea.

"Damn you, I'm trying to save your life!" Finn told her.

"Damn *you,* you bastard! You've stolen my life!"

"Past life, Risa, your past life is over! You'll no longer follow the enemy's drummer."

"You shot him, for God's sake! If you've murdered my husband in cold blood, if he is dead or dies in those flames, I will spend every single day of the rest of my life working to see that you are hanged."

"You be careful, Risa—or you'll spend every day of the rest of your life locked away."

"You can't do that. You forget, I'm not a Rebel. I'm a known Unionist, and the daughter of a celebrated, decorated general. The government—"

"The government would never know," he warned, then smiled. She felt a deep chill, and realized that he had been waging his own vendetta. He didn't intend to return her to a Northern port. She was to come with him, his personal prisoner, and God knew where he would take her, or what he would do with her.

She gritted her teeth. She could outswim Finn McCullough—or drown. One or the other. He had learned how to abuse power and rank and might do anything. She had to get off the boat. She had to get back to the house and pray that she could find her husband and that he wasn't—

Dead. Shot down in cold blood. Because she had led the enemy directly to him.

"Tell me—were you working for army intelligence the first time you brought me down here?"

He smiled. "Not exactly. I was trying to get in at that time. I knew the right people, and I'd been told that the naval officers would pay a pretty price for the Mocassin. Then, after I rotted on an island waiting to be picked up after McKenzie seized me . . . well, if I was going to risk such dangers, I wanted fame and fortune as well. Of course, there was also the matter of vengeance. If I had taken Miss Sydney McKenzie, I'd have seen to it that she was returned to the loving arms of her family with far less arrogance! The right company of men can easily improve a woman's disposition."

"Finn, I grant you this—you were good. I believed in your honesty and gentle character. I'd never envisioned that you could be such a monster."

He smiled. "You'll come to like me again, Risa. In time."

"Never. I'll despise you until the day I die."

"We can change the way you feel. We're nearing *my* ship. We'll change the way you feel before tonight's over, I promise."

Never.

She started to make a move to dive from the ship. He lifted the oar to strike her again, but he never managed to do so. Risa saw a pair of hands grip the rim of the small boat. Then she saw Jerome leap out of the bay, like an enraged Neptune. Water sluiced from his body as he caught Finn's hand holding the oar. As Risa started to rise, her hand at her throat, Jerome dragged Finn overboard. They disappeared beneath the surface of the water together.

"Jerome!" she shrieked his name, for no heads bobbed above the water. She waited, and cried out again. Then she dived in, desperate. But dusk had turned to darkness. The water was murky and dark. She brushed something . . . human hair. Hands gripped her, pulling her down. Down . . .

She looked into Finn's face. He was drowning, trying to use her body to force himself back to the surface. He reached for her face, for her hair . . .

He suddenly jerked back, as if he had been catapulted from her. She shot to the surface, gasping for air. "Jerome!"

She screamed when arms slipped around her from the rear. She swung around, and saw her husband's face, blue eyes reflecting the moon's light on the water. "Jerome . . ."

She threw her arms around him. "It's all right, it's all right, my love. It's over."

"Finn . . . is he dead?"

"I don't know. I would have killed him just now . . . but David came by in a small boat . . . and there are so many dead. I didn't want to kill him if I didn't have to. I'm sorry. Maybe I should have finished him off."

She shook her head vehemently. "I was so afraid he'd killed you, shot you in the house—"

"I had to taunt him, make him shoot wild and think he'd killed me. I went down before his bullets could strike me."

"Thank God . . . oh, Jerome. My baby, our baby, Jamie—"

"He's safe," he said softly, and he twisted around, looking for the small boat that drifted just feet away. Come on . . . let's get back to shore."

He helped her into the boat, then crawled in himself. His steady pull on the oars brought them back to the dock.

He sat in the boat, watching as the fire ebbed. She touched his cheek. "Jerome, what about your family?"

"They were out of the house, don't worry." He smiled, not looking at her. "My mother took the children into the woods. I admit, my father is one of the most savage fighters I've ever known. Hopefully, he'll never need wage war again. But as for you .. it was noble of you to go looking for them."

"It wasn't noble; it was my fault Yankees attacked this place."

He shook his head. "No. I heard most of what he said. Finn was an explosion waiting to be triggered. And I can promise you, the Yanks will waste no more ships or men coming here. Hamlin has taken the survivors out to an island to be picked up, but the casualties were heavy. Fifteen dead, ten wounded, a ship lost—and the Seminoles enraged when the government wants no more problems."

"Your father's beautiful home is destroyed."

"He'll built anew. My father is among the 'undefeated.' He'll never surrender, to any man." He stepped up to the deck, reaching back for her. He took her hand, and she leapt to the deck. Together they walked to the front of the house. James and Teela stood before it. Each held a babe, and neither seemed unduly upset that their beautiful home had been destroyed. "We can sleep in a chickee, like in the old days," Teela mused.

"Mmm," James murmured. "But actually, there's a lot that's still sound, and a lot we can save. The dining room is gone."

"I had grown to despise the wallpaper, anyway," Teela said.

"Well, we shall have new paper now!"

James turned, alerted to the fact that he and Teela were no longer alone. The fire had died down. Much of the house stood, though it was blackened by soot.

"I think you must be very worried about someone!" he said, holding Jamie. He set Risa's baby in her arms, and she nearly sobbed with pleasure and relief.

"Thank you, oh, thank you!"

"Everything under control, son?" James asked Jerome.

"Aye, sir, it is."

The four of them stood with the house and land before them, the ocean to their backs. Risa could not help herself. "I am so very sorry—"

"Don't be," her father-in-law said flatly. "Teela and I learned long ago that nothing in life is irreplaceable—except for life itself. Come here, daughter."

He slipped an arm around her. "This is why I love this place so much. It's new. Wild. A place to grow and build. And it's your home now, too, you know. Even if you don't stay, you'll be back. It's your son's heritage." He smiled at her, kissed her forehead, then walked away with his wife and infant. "I think we should build another wing," he said.

Jerome took Jamie from Risa, tucking him under an arm, and grasping her free hand. He started to lead her down the pine trail to the pool.

"James, what about your men, your ship?"

"Hamlin will take charge of the situation."

"Should I apologize to your father's men—"

"They aren't my father's men, they are his people. They fought with him, as he fought with them. By choice. They don't want apologies or thanks."

She fell silent, following him. He sat on the sandy embankment, cradling Jamie, and looking out at the moonlight.

"It is beautiful, isn't it? The moon on the water, the warmth, the sound of the night birds . . . I forget sometimes what it's like to be home."

"Yes, it's beautiful."

He was silent a minute, then said, "Risa, I love you."

"I love you. So much. If anything had happened to you, I knew that I didn't want to go on. Oh, God, what are we going to do? There is still a war on."

"And you're still a Yank. And I'm still a Rebel."

"What do we do?"

"Survive!" he said softly, pulling her close to him.

"But you're going to set sail again—"

"Not until we've helped my father rebuild."

"But then . . ."

"You could stay here."

"I could. But—it's not that I mind being in the far south. I love it here. I do. Maybe that's why you seduced me so easily here . . ."

"I seduced you? I think you were the seducer."

"I was not!"

"You were. You were shocking. I loved every minute."

She smiled, realizing that he had playfully goaded her. "I love the water, the bay breezes, the palm trees, the sand . . . the warmth in winter. I could stay here, easily. But I'm a good nurse. And the war isn't just this giant thing that is about changing the nation—it's about people as well. Individual people. I can save lives, and most of the time, when men are injured or dying, you can't tell whether they're a Yank or a Rebel. When they're afraid of dying, sometimes they don't even care. If you don't want me taking Jamie back to my father's company, I can understand that. But let me return to St.

Augustine, or even join with Julian in the heartland. I can help—"

"Do you think the Rebels can stand any more of your help?"

"Jerome!"

"Just teasing, my love," he said, then sobered. "If you're with the Rebs, I can come see you."

"And if I'm not, you'll see Janine Thompson?"

"I told you the truth—"

"So did I. Always."

He laughed ruefully, pulling her even closer for a moment. Then he eased Jamie down, making a bed out of his blankets on the sandy embankment. He turned back to Risa. "I'm truly sorry. I was so hurt, and too afraid, to give you a chance."

"I'm sorry, too."

"And I do love you. I never imagined I could love so deeply, or need anyone the way I need you, with all my soul."

"Oh, my love!" she murmured, tears glistening in her eyes.

"There's much more tempest ahead . . . but I believe that we'll weather it. I believe in my family, and that no matter what comes between us, we'll be together in the end. And this land will remain our paradise. It will be a place to heal when the anguish is over. And mostly . . ." he hesitated, smiling ruefully. "Risa, I'm sorry, but I'll probably always be a bit arrogant—even if the South does lose the war."

She shrugged. "I'll always speak my mind."

"I'll want to tell you what to do all the time."

"It's most unlikely I'll actually do it."

He laughed. "I've been a fool. I believe in you. And us . . ." He glanced over at the baby, smiling again. "No matter what the war brings, always know that I love you. No matter where we are in time or place, you needn't doubt me, because there's no one else I would ever want to be with."

"Oh, God, I do love you, too. So much."

"Risa."

"Yes?"

"Times like this may be very rare."

"I know."

"And you know something else?"

"What?"

"We may be political enemies, but we really made a beautiful child."

"We did."

"We could take a chance at making another, you know. Seize the moment, ride the wild wind . . ."

"Mmm . . ." she murmured. "Ride the wind . . . a Southern, Rebel wind, my love?"

He didn't answer with words. She was swept down into the sand, and his lips upon hers were a potent reply.

She didn't know what the future would bring.

But tonight meant surrender.

For them both.

Florida Chronology

(and Events Which Influenced Her People)

1492	Christopher Columbus discovers the "New World."
1513	Florida discovered. Juan Ponce de León sights Florida from his ship on March 27, steps on shore near present-day St. Augustine in early April.
1539	Hernando de Soto lands on west coast of the peninsula, near present-day Tampa.
1564	The French arrive and establish Fort Caroline on the St. Johns River. Immediately following the establishment of the French fort, Spain dispatches Pedro de Menéndez to get rid of the French invaders, "pirates and perturbers of the public peace." Menéndez dutifully captures the French stronghold and slays or enslaves the inhabitants.
1565	Pedro de Menéndez founds St. Augustine, the first permanent European settlement in what is now the United States.
1586	Sir Francis Drake attacks St. Augustine, burning and plundering the settlement.
1698	Pensacola is founded.
1740	British General James Oglethorpe invades Florida from Georgia.
1763	At the end of the Seven Years War, or the French and Indian War, both the East and West Florida territories are ceded to Britain.

1763–1783   British Rule in East and West Florida.
1774   The "shot heard 'round the world" is fired in Concord, Massachusetts Colony.
1776   The War of Independence begins; many of British loyalists flee to Florida.
1783   By the Treaty of Paris, Florida is returned to the Spanish.
1812–1815   The War of 1812.
1813–1814   The Creek wars. ("Red-Stick" land is decimated. Numberous Indians seek new lands south with the "Seminoles.")
1814   General Andrew Jackson captures Pensacola.
1815   The Battle of New Orleans.
1817–1818   The First Seminole War (Americans accuse the Spanish of aiding the Indians in their raids across the border. Hungry for more territory, settlers seek to force Spain into ceding the Floridas to the United States by their claims against the Spanish government for its inability to properly handle the situation within the territories).
1819   Don Luis de Onis, Spanish minister to the United States, and secretary of state John Quincy Adams, sign a treaty by which the Floridas will become part of the United States.
1821   The Onis-Adams Treaty is ratified. An act of congress makes the two Floridas one territory. Jackson becomes the military governor, but relinquishes the post after a few months.
1822   The first legislative council meets at Pensacola. Members from St. Augustine travel fifty-nine days by water to attend.
1823   The second legislative council meets at St. Augustine: the western delegates are shipwrecked and barely escape death.
1824   The third session meets at Tallahassee, a halfway selected as a main order of business and approved at the second session. Tallahassee becomes the first territorial capital.

1823	The Treaty of Moultrie Creek is ratified by major Seminole chiefs and the federal government. The ink is barely dry before Indians are complaining that the lands are too small and white settlers are petitioning the government for a policy of Indian removal.
1832	Payne's Landing: Numerous chiefs sign a treaty agreeing to move west to Arkansas as long as seven of their number are able to see and approve the lands. Thee treaty is ratified at Fort Gibson, Arkansas.
	Numerous chiefs also protest the agreement.
1835	Summer: Wiley Thompson claims that Osceola has repeatedly reviled him in his own office with foul language and orders his arrest. Osceola is handcuffed and incarcerated.
	November: Charlie Emathla, after agreeing to removal to the west, is murdered. Most scholars agree Osceola led the party that carried out the execution. Some consider the murder a personal vengeance, others believe it was proscribed by numerous chiefs, since an Indian who would leave his people to aid the whites should forfeit his own life.
	December 28: Major Francis Dade and his troops are massacred as they travel from Fort Brooke to Fort King.
	Also on December 28—Wiley Thompson and a companion are killed outside the walls of Fort King. The sutler Erastus Rogers and his two clerks are also murdered by members of the same raiding party, led by Osceola.
	December 31: The First Battle of the Withlacoochee—Osceola leads the Seminoles.
1836	January: Major General Winfield Scott is ordered by the secretary of war to take command in Florida.

February 4: Dade County established in
South Florida in memory of Francis Lang-
horne Dade.

March 16: The Senate confirmed Richard
Keith Call governor of the Florida
Territory.

June 21: Call, a civilian governor, is given
command of the Florida forces after the
failure of Scott's strategies and the military disputes between Scott and General
Gaines.

Call attempts a "summer campaign," and
is as frustrated in his efforts as his
predecessor.

December 9: Major Sidney Jesup takes
command.

1837   June 2: Osceola and Sam Jones release or
"abduct" nearly 700 Indians awaiting de-
portation to the west from Tampa.

October 27: Osceola is taken under a
white flag of truce; Jesup is denounced by
whites and Indians alike for the action.

November 29: Coacoochee, Cowaya, sixteen warriors and two women escape Fort
Marion

Christmas Day: Jesup has the largest
fighting force assembled in Florida during
the conflict, nearly 9,000 men. Under his
command, Colonel Zachary Taylor leads
the Battle of Okeechobee. The Seminoles
chose to stand their ground and fight, inflicting greater losses to whites despite the
fact they were severely outnumbered.

1838   January 31: Osceola dies at Fort Marion,
South Carolina. (A strange side note to
a sad tale: Dr. Wheedon, presiding white
physician for Osceola, cut off and pre-
served Osceola's head. Wheedon's heirs
reported that the good doctor would hang
the head on the bedstead of one of his
three children should they misbehave. The
head passed to his son-in-law, Dr. Daniel

Whitehurst, who gave it to Dr. Valentine Mott. Dr. Mott had a medical and pathological museum, and it is believed that the head was lost when his museum burned in 1866.)

1838   May: Zachary Taylor takes command when Jesup's plea to be relieved is answered at last on April 29.

The Florida legislature debates statehood.

1839   December: Because of his arguments with federal authorities regarding the Seminole War, Richard Keith Call is removed as governor.

Robert Raymond Reid is appointed in his stead.

1840   April 24: Zachary Taylor is given permission to leave command of what is considered to be the harshest military position in the country.

Walker Keith Armistead takes command.

December 1840–January 1841: John T. MacLaughlin leads a flotilla of men in dugouts across the Everglades from east to west; his party becomes the first white men to do so.

September: William Henry Harrison is elected president of the United States; the Florida war is considered to have cost Martin Van Buren reelection.

John Bell replaces Joel Poinsett as secretary of war. Robert Reid is ousted as territorial governor, and Richard Keith Call is reinstated.

1841   April 4: President William Henry Harrison dies in office: John Tyler becomes president of the U.S.

May 1: Coacoochee determines to turn himself in. He is escorted by a man who will later become extremely well-known— Lieutenant William Tecumseh Sherman. (Sherman writes to his future wife that the Florida war is a good one for a soldier; he will get to know the Indian who may become the "chief enemy" in time.)

May 31: Walker Keith Armistead is relieved. Colonel William Jenkins Worth takes command.

1842   May 10: Winfield Scott is informed that the administration has decided there must be an end to hostilities as soon as possible. August 14: Aware that he cannot end hostilities and send all Indians west, Colonel Worth makes offers to the remaining Indians to leave, or accept boundaries. The war, he declares, is over.

It has cost a fledgling nation thirty to forty million dollars, and the lives of seventy-four commissioned officers. The Seminoles have been reduced from tens of thousands to hundreds scattered about in pockets. The Seminoles (inclusive here, as they were seen during the war, as all Florida Indians) have, however, kept their place in the peninsula; those remianing are the undefeated. The army, too, has learned new tactics, mostly regarding partisan and guerrilla warfare. Men who will soon take part in the greatest conflict to tear apart the nation have practiced the art of battle here: William T. Sherman, Braxton Bragg, George Gordon Meade, Joseph E. Johnston, and more, as well as soon-to-be President Zachary Taylor.

1845   March 3: President John Tyler signs the bill that makes Florida the twenty-seventh state of United States of America.

1855–58   The conflict known as the Third Seminole War takes place with a similiar outcome to the earlier confrontations—money spent, lives lost, and the Indians entrenched more deeply into the Everglades.

1859   Robert E. Lee is sent in to arrest John Brown after his attempt to initiate a slave rebellion with an assault on Harper's

Ferry, Virginia (later West Virginia). The incident escalates ill will between the North and the South. Brown is executed Dec 2.

1860   The first Florida cross-state railroad goes into service.

November 6: Abraham Lincoln is elected to the presidency and many of Southern states begin to call for special legislative sessions. Although there are many passionate Unionists in the state, most Florida politicians are ardent in lobbying for secession. Towns, cities, and counties rush to form or enlarge militia companies. Even before the state is able to meet for its special session, civil and military leaders plan to demand the turnover of federal military installations.

1861   January 10: Florida votes to secede from the Union, the third Southern state to do so.

February: Florida joins the Confederate States of America.

Through late winter and early spring, the Confederacy struggles to form a government and organize the armed forces while the states recruit fighting men. Jefferson Davis is President of the newly formed country. Stephen Mallory, of Florida, becomes C.S.A. secretary of the navy.

April 12–14: Confederate forces fire on Fort Sumter, S.C., and the first blood is shed when an accidental explosion kills Private Hough, who then has the distinction of being the first Federal soldier killed.

Federal forces fear a similiar action at Fort Pickens, Pensacola Bay, Florida. Three forts guarded the bay, McRee and Barrancas on the land side, and Pickens on the tip of forty-mile long Santa Rosa Island. Federal Lieutenant Adam J. Slemmer spiked the guns at Barrancas, blew up the ammunition at McRee, and moved his meager troops to Pickens, where he was eventually reinforced by 500 men. Though Florida troops took the navy yard, retention of the fort by the Federals nullified the usefulness to the Rebs of what was considered the most important navy yard south of Norfolk.

July 18: First Manassas, or the First Battle of Bull Run, Virginia—both sides get their first real taste of battle. Southern troops are drawn from throughout the states, including Florida. Already the state which had been so eager to secede sees her sons being shipped northward to fight, and her coast being left to its own defenses by a government with different priorities.

November: Robert E. Lee inspects coastal defenses as far south as Fernandina and decides the major ports of Charleston, Savannah, and Brunswick are to be defended, adding later that the small force posted at St. Augustine was like an invitation to attack.

1862   February: Florida's Governor Milton publicly states his despair for Florida citizens as more of the state's troops are ordered north after Grant captures two major Confederate strongholds in Tennessee.

February 28: A fleet of twenty-six Federal ships sets sail to occupy Fernandina, Jacksonville, and St. Augustine. March 8: St. Augustine surrenders, and though Jacksonville and other points north and south along the coast will change hands several times during the war, St. Augustine will remain in Union hands. The St. Johns River becomes a ribbon of guerrilla troop movement for both sides. Many Floridians begin to despair of "East Florida," fearing that the fickle populace has all turned Unionist.

March 8: Under the command of Franklin
Buchanan, the *CSS Virginia,* formerly the
scuttled Union ship *Merrimac,* sailed into
Hampton Roads to battle the Union ships
blockading the channel. She devastates
Federal ships until the arrival of the
poorly prepared and leaking Federal entry
into the "ironclad" fray, the *USS Monitor.*
The historic battle of the ironclads ensues.
Neither ship emerged a clear victor: the
long-term advantage went to the Union,
since the Confederacy was then unable to
break the blockade when it had appeared,
at first, that the *Virginia* might have sailed
all the way to devastate Washington, D.C.
April 2: Apalachicola is attacked by a Federal landing force. The town remains a no-
man's-land throughout the war.
April 6–8: Union and Confederate forces
engage in the battle of Shiloh. Both claim
victories. Both suffer horrible losses with
over twenty thousand killed, wounded, or
missing.
April 25: New Orleans falls, and the Federal grip on the South becomes more of a
vise.
Spring: The Federal blockade begins to
tighten and much of the state becomes a
no-man's-land. Despite its rugged terrain,
the length of the peninsula, and the simple
difficulty of logistics, blockade-runners
know that they can dare Florida waterways simply because the Union can't possibly guard the extensive coastline of the
state. Florida's contribution becomes more
and more that of a breadbasket as she
strips herself and provides salt, beef,
smuggled supplies, and manpower to the
Confederacy.
May 9: Pensacola is evacuated by the
Rebs, and occupied by Federal forces.
May 20: Union landing party is success-

fully attacked by Confederates near St. Marks.

May 22: Union flag officer DuPont writes to his superiors with quotes that stated had the Union not abandoned Jacksonville, the state would have split, and East Florida would have entered the war on the Union side.

Into summer: Fierce action continues in Virginia: Battle of Fair Oaks, or Seven Pines, May 31, the Seven Days Battles, May 25 through June 2, the battle of Mechanicsville, June 26, Gaines Mill, or Cold Harbor, June 27. More Florida troops leave the state to replace the men killed in action in these battles, and in other engagements in Alabama, Louisiana, and along the Mississippi.

Salt becomes evermore necessary: Florida has numerous saltworks along the Gulf side of the state. Union ships try to find them, confiscate what they can, and destroy them.

August 30: Second Battle of Manassas, or Bull Run.

September 16 and 17: The Battle of Antietam, or Sharpsburg, takes place in Maryland, where the "single bloodiest day or fighting" occurs.

September 23: The preliminary text of the Emancipation Proclamation is published. It will take effect on January 1, 1863. Lincoln previously drafted the document, but waited for a Union victory to publish it; both sides claimed Antietam, but the Rebels were forced to withdraw back to Virginia.

October 5: Federals recapture Jacksonville.

December 11 through 15: The Battle of Fredericksburg.

December 31: The Battle of Murfreesborough or Stones River, Tennessee.

1863

March 20: A Union landing party at St. Andrew's Bay, Florida, is attacked and most Federals are captured or killed.

March 31: Jacksonville is evacuated by the Union forces again.

May 1 through 4: The Battle of Chancellorsville. Lee soundly beats Hooker, but on the second, General Stonewall Jackson is accidentally shot and mortally wounded by his own men. He dies on the tenth.

The war continues . . .